Scribe Publications
MONA

Dan Sehlberg was born in 1969. He began studying classical piano at the age of eight, and later became part of the rock band Nova, which recorded an album and played at several Swedish music festivals and clubs in the mid-1980s. Dan has also composed and recorded music for film and multimedia projects.

Dan holds an MBA from the Stockholm School of Economics, and currently works as a partner and financial officer in a Swedish real-estate firm. As an entrepreneur, Dan has launched companies ranging from Sweden's first travel-booking website to social-media ventures.

Dan lives with his wife and two daughters in Stockholm, and retreats to the tranquillity of Sörmland, on the south-eastern coast of Sweden, to work on his books.

Mona is his first novel, and will be followed by its sequel, *Sinon*.

M
O
N
A

DAN SEHLBERG

Translated by Rachel Willson-Broyles

SCRIBE
Melbourne • London

Scribe Publications Pty Ltd
18–20 Edward St, Brunswick, Victoria 3056, Australia
50A Kingsway Place, Sans Walk, London, EC1R 0LU, United Kingdom

Originally published in Swedish by Lind & Co. 2013
First published in English by Scribe 2014

This edition published by agreement with Salomonsson Agency

The Quran quotes are taken from the translation by Abdullah Yusuf Ali, 22nd US edition,
published by Tahrike Tarsile Qur'an, Inc., Elmhurst, New York, 2007.

Abraham Sutzkever's poems were translated by Barnett Zumoff in *Laughter Beneath the Forest:
poems from old and recent manuscripts*, KTAV Publishing House, Hoboken, New Jersey, 1996.

Printed and bound in England by CPI Group (UK) Ltd, Croydon, CR0 4YY

National Library of Australia
Cataloguing-in-Publication data

Sehlberg, Dan, author.

Mona/Dan Sehlberg; Rachel Willson-Broyles, translator.

9781922070975 (Australian edition)
9781922247261 (UK edition)
9781925113037 (e-book)

Notes. Translation of: Mona.

1. Swedish fiction–Translations into English.

Other Authors/Contributors: Willson-Broyles, Rachel, translator.

839.78

scribepublications.com.au
scribepublications.co.uk

To Anna, Natasha, and Rebecca

Prologue

Qana, Lebanon

The little girl in the beautiful dress was taking a big risk. It had rained, and the field behind Grandma's house was muddy and slippery. Her ponytail had slipped and released her dark curls. She was sneaking up on a cat, trying not to scare it, stepping in the brown mud with her white canvas shoes. The cat was nosing at a car tyre that was half buried next to the rusty soccer goal. It was a thin cat with pretty stripes. Like a tiger. Maybe it was a tiger. And maybe she was a magic princess who could speak with tigers. Then something scared the cat and it ran off toward the stone bridge and the roaring brown river. The princess found an old can instead. No, of course it wasn't a can — it was the tiger's little cub, abandoned in the mud. She carefully dried it off with her dress. Her mother often, and accurately, called her 'the chameleon'. Given a little time, her clothes would look like the ground where she played. On this particular day, her mother and grandmother had been too busy in the kitchen to notice her running out into the field in her new turquoise dress. Unlike the dress, the can-tiger was now nice and clean, but hungry. Tigers are always hungry. She pressed the can to her chest, slipping and sliding off across the field.

The two women looked in horror at the muddy little girl as she came into the kitchen, out of breath.

'Grandma! I need a bowl of water right away.'

Elif set down a steaming pan of sambousek pastries that was just out of the oven.

'You don't just need a bowl. You need a whole bathtub.'

She laughed and looked at Nadim, anticipating an outburst from her daughter. Mona did the same, suddenly conscious of her muddy condition.

'Mama. Don't be mad. I found a tiger cub! And it's hungry.'

Mona held one hand inside her dress and urgently stretched the other toward Elif, who gave her a sambousek. As the girl fed her charge, her dress slid up and Nadim caught a glimpse of the tiger. The room swayed suddenly. She had to grab the counter to avoid losing her balance.

'My darling, that tiger is very dangerous. It could bite you. Stand perfectly still.'

Mona smiled happily, glad her mother was playing along. Nadim instinctively pushed her mother aside. She, too, had seen what Mona was cradling in her arms, and started to pray.

Nadim slowly moved closer to her daughter.

'May I have the tiger?'

Mona shook her head obstinately.

'She's only calm when I hold her. She gets scared really easily. Her mother abandoned her.'

Nadim couldn't hold back her tears. Mona was the most beautiful being in existence — her beloved daughter, the miracle of Qana. In a shaky voice, she repeated: 'Give Mama the tiger now. Otherwise Mama will be angry. Super angry!'

Mona saw her mother's tears. She looked nervously at her grandmother, and heard her prayers. Then she extended the hand with the tiger cub. That wasn't a tiger cub. That was a can. That wasn't a can. That was a grenade from an Israeli cluster bomb. Nadim held her gaze steady on her daughter's face. Their

2

hands met. It was as though the nerves in her hand — the small, thin hairs on her skin — were reaching for her daughter with a pulsating intensity. She held her breath and placed her hand around the cool grenade.

The tea in his cup had long since grown cold. People came and went. Everything was happening far away. It didn't affect him anymore. He was empty, and cold like the tea. Dead, but still so painfully alive. Left behind. But it was only his discarded shell, with empty eyes and in wrinkled clothes, that sat motionless at one of the window tables in the small teahouse. His hair was uncombed. He was grimy, inside and out.

He didn't know how long the old man in black had been sitting there across from him. He didn't know where he'd come from or why he'd come. The man's friendly eyes lingered on his frigid façade. The old man placed a hand on his own. It was a rough, warm hand.

'Samir Mustaf.' He gave a start at the sound of his name. 'The Quran says, "But verily over you are appointed angels to protect you. They know and understand all that you do. As for the Righteous, they will be in bliss."'

They sat there, the old man and the empty one. He had no idea how long they sat — maybe an hour, maybe a week. The small café was across the street from Hiram Hospital in Tyre. He should have visited the city with her. Shown her the ruins of the Hippodrome and the beautiful triumphal arch. Gone swimming with her at the beach.

There was a sour taste in his mouth. The old man stood up and took his arm. Pulled him up. Samir followed him stiffly out of the teahouse. He didn't see the street, the cars, or the people. Didn't hear the clamour. He just saw the same image over and over again. His daughter had no face. It was gone. They were gone.

3

He arrived at a waiting car. Someone opened the door. The man spoke in a soft voice. 'There is nothing more you can do here. But there is more you can do.'

Samir sank down into the back seat of the car. The old man didn't follow him, instead closing the door after him. The car immediately pulled out into the bustling traffic. A faded picture of the soccer player Ronaldo dangled from the rear-view mirror. He closed his eyes.

PART I
INFECTION

Five years later. Dubai City, Emirate of Dubai

Burj Al Arab, the Tower of the Arabs, had been called the most luxurious hotel in the world. For a long time, it was the symbol of Dubai, rising 321 metres above an artificial island, in the shape of the sail of a *dhow*. The hotel contained only large suites, and over two thousand square metres of it were covered in gold. All the rugs were hand-knotted.

As one of three entrepreneurs responsible for the project, Mohammad al-Rashid had spent a great deal of his waking time at the construction site during the five years it took to build Burj al Arab. His construction company was one of the largest and most respected on the Arabian Peninsula.

Mohammad had spent a great deal of time at the hotel even after construction was completed. He lived in Saudi Arabia, and many of his business negotiations took place in Dubai. It would be hard to beat the exceptional service and the high level of security that the hotel provided.

Right now, however, both security and service seemed distant. He studied the blue-velvet walls of the large suite. His eyes drifted to the custom-made cushions that were nearly two metres in diameter and sewn with golden thread. The strong scent of the lilies on the bar counter and the dining table made his head feel heavy. He wished he could open the balcony door to let in some fresh air. A big-screen TV displayed silent vacation destinations and happy tourists with broad smiles. He lost himself in an advertisement for Disney World.

The thought of family made his stomach turn. Or was it the strong scent of the lilies? He wondered what the children were doing now. Bunyamin was probably watching TV; he should have completed his homework long ago. Little Azra was sleeping.

Mohammad was not a person who cried. Now, as he tasted the salty tears, he tried to remember when it had last happened. Maybe it was when Bunyamin had his operation. He carefully wiped his face with his sweaty hand.

He looked at her again. She wasn't tall; she was under 170 centimetres. Shorter now that she'd taken off her high heels. He studied her small feet, which were slightly shimmery in their thin, grey stockings. Her legs looked strong. Her dark skirt was tight. She had taken off her jacket and unbuttoned three of her blouse buttons. Or was he the one who had unbuttoned them? He saw the black edge of her bra against her dark skin. He swallowed. How could he even think of sex at a time like this?

He nervously moved his gaze to her face. She was beautiful. It wasn't easy to say no to those dark eyes. At the same time, something wasn't quite right. A nick in the well-polished veneer: her nose. A fine nose, to be sure, but it looked crooked. Broken. It gave her soft face a note of hardness, like some sort of odd cross between a boxer and a model. She seemed completely uninterested in him as she sat there, curled up in the large easy chair, nonchalantly paging through *Vanity Fair*. Her fingers were thin, and her nails were beautifully manicured.

For a fifty-five-year-old, Mohammad al-Rashid was in good physical condition. He did strength training daily. His body attracted the attention of women. He knew that this hadn't escaped her. Nothing escaped her. Under these circumstances, it ought to have been easy for him to get up off the bed, smash her to pieces, and then just leave the room. But what was stopping him was that he wasn't tied up. If he had been, he would have fought his way loose and thrown himself over her. But he wasn't confined by tape, rope, or handcuffs. So this tiny woman, who was no more than half a metre away from him, did not see him as a threat.

Mohammad's sense of intuition was good, and the answer to the balance of power was in her gaze. She had told him who she was and had ordered him to sit on the bed. He was still sitting there, two hours later. His throat was dry. His back ached. And he had started to develop a hangover.

She tossed the magazine aside, sighed, and looked at the clock. 'Should we let in some air?' Her Arabic was flawless.

He nodded gratefully. She stood up and walked over to the balcony door in her stockinged feet. A warm breeze swept through the room. The pages of *Vanity Fair* fluttered, and the scent of lilies blended with eucalyptus. As he studied the woman, who was lighting a cigarette on the balcony, he had the urge to laugh. Laugh or cry. What was she waiting for? Her phone lay on the table by the chair, silent. She had checked it several times. Now she seemed just to be standing out there, dreaming. He sneaked a look at the door on the other side of the room. He could be out in a few seconds. But maybe she wasn't alone. Were there guards outside? That would explain why she was so calm.

'Maybe you'll make it, Mohammad. Maybe not.'

He started, and found her crouching at his side. He hadn't heard her coming. She was so close that he could feel the warmth of her breath. The tobacco. She sat still, a cat ready to pounce. When he didn't move, but only lowered his eyes in silence, she returned to the easy chair.

He thought back to that evening's dinner. Earlier in the week he had heard a rumour about a large office-building construction project. The Japanese chamber of commerce was sounding out land allocations for a commercial business centre for Asian companies. He knew that interest in Arab business opportunities was great in Asia. These days, as Arab companies and banks were

9

battling against high mortgages and vanishing liquidity, foreign projects were extra interesting. So he had called around and learned that a consultant, a woman from Abu Dhabi by the name of Sarah al-Yemud, had been commissioned to do the purchasing. It took him ten minutes to find information about her, and after studying her references he asked his assistant to contact her. He assumed she would contact his company anyway, but he didn't want to take any chances. A dinner had been scheduled for the next evening at the tower's panorama restaurant, Al Muntaha, on the twenty-seventh floor.

He looked at her. She seemed to be deep in thought. She was turned toward the TV, but her gaze was far beyond the silent golf competition on the screen. She looked tired. Small. Her hands were clenched so hard that her knuckles were white.

She had been waiting for him when he arrived at the semi-circle-shaped restaurant, two hundred metres above the water. The furnishings were futuristic, and from the table by one of the large windows they could see Jumeirah beach and the artificial islands, Palm and World. They had eaten a tasty dinner and then moved over to the bar and the deep velvet chairs.

Mohammad liked to say that he was a pragmatic Muslim. He was a believer, but he was selective about the rules. One of his concessions was alcohol. His work sometimes made it necessary for him to drink with his clients. This was a concession he could live with. The fact was that he drank quite a bit these days, even when he wasn't with clients. He had offered Sarah his favourite champagne, Louise Roederer's Cristal. She willingly accepted it. She, too, seemed to be a pragmatic Muslim.

The project was extensive, and Sarah was well informed about local building regulations and advanced prospecting. He had been surprised at first that the Asians had chosen a woman to do the purchasing; women were rare in the business world, not to mention the construction industry. But after only one hour with Sarah al-Yemud, he realised that she shouldn't be underestimated. He groaned at the irony.

After almost three bottles of wine — she hadn't drunk as fast as he had — he started to become less interested in Asian construction and more interested in her legs. When she laughed aloud, he took a chance and placed his hand on her thigh. The laughter stopped. She looked at him from under her curly black bangs. Without saying anything, she drained her glass and stood up. For a moment he thought she was planning to leave him. He looked at her in surprise, but she smiled and nodded at the ten gilded elevators. He followed her like an obedient schoolboy. This was far too good to be true.

But as soon as he closed the door to his suite, she became transformed. There was a new, metallic tone to her voice — a sharpness that didn't fit with the gentle, feminine, and almost fragile person he had just eaten dinner with. He soon received an explanation: she claimed to be part of Unit 101. He knew who they were. The Mossad's executioners.

The fact that she had given him this secret information was worrying in itself. That she also knew that his firm had been responsible for the large-scale construction of a bunker in Iran was even more worrying — particularly because this particular bunker amounted to a top-secret future storage area for enriched uranium. But most alarming of all was that she didn't ask him any questions at all. Instead she just sat in the easy chair and started paging through fashion magazines.

Oh, God. How had the Mossad gotten his name? How much did they know about the bunker project? About his other projects? He silently cursed his own greed. He never should have gotten involved in that damn construction project, no matter how lucrative it promised to be. He had no problem with the

Israelis and never had. Politics weren't his thing.

The phone vibrated. Sarah picked it up, listened in silence, and hung up. She sat there with the phone still in her hand, studying him, nibbling on one fingernail. He couldn't sit still any longer. He stood and threw up his hands.

'Let's bring this long evening to an end,' he said.

She remained in the chair, following him with her eyes. Then she resolutely placed her feet in her shoes, pulled on her jacket, and stood up.

'You're right, Mohammad, it's time to end this.'

He hesitated for a second, but then he darted forward. With his temples pounding, he grabbed the vase of lilies, rushed at her, and threw the vase at her head. In a fluid movement, she ducked, pinched him in the side, and slipped away. He staggered forward, lost his balance, and fell headlong onto the easy chair. The spot where she'd pinched him burned. He quickly got back on his feet and spun around. She was sitting on the bed calmly, as though nothing had happened. Surprised, he stopped short. It was as though it had only been horseplay between siblings, and now big sister was tired of it. Or had she given up? Should he run straight for the door, or take her on first?

His left side hurt so much that he had trouble standing. He fought it, but he sank down into the chair. Role reversal. *Now I'm sitting here, and she's there.* Then he caught sight of the knife in her hand. It wasn't a regular knife; it was more like a box-cutter. He groaned, and grabbed his side. His shirt was warm and wet. She had stabbed him with the knife. How serious was it? She seemed to read his mind.

'I've punctured your liver. You're going to die. Unfortunately, it's going to hurt. It didn't have to end up like this, but sometimes one has to improvise. Your liver is releasing large amounts of blood into your abdominal cavity. The liver can't contract after being stabbed, which makes it all the worse. Plus, your liver is the organ that produces the protein that causes blood to clot. If it's punctured, well … in short, that's not so good for you. That wound is not good for me, either, because my orders were to give you a heart attack. It wasn't supposed to look like murder. That'll be hard to avoid, now that you have a hole in your liver.'

The flashes of pain swallowed his thoughts.

'I don't want to die; I have a family,' he groaned weakly.

She stood up.

'I know you have a family. Enjoy the memories you have, and be happy about your gifts from God. Bunyamin and Azra will be okay. If you have been a good Muslim, your soul will be gathered by angels. Isn't that right? And then, if you just give the correct answers to a few simple questions, you'll be written into Jannah, into paradise, by Allah himself. Then all you have to do is make yourself at home. It will hurt for a few hours, but good things come to those who wait … I can't help you anymore. My part in all of this is over.'

She went to the bathroom, and he heard the sound of running water. The pain caused him to fall forward onto the floor. He lay there, watching a large, dark spot grow quickly on the thick carpet. The material smelled like dust and cleaning products. Had he been a good Muslim? He regretted his pragmatic application of Islam. His thoughts spun. His vision was blurry. He had to find a way to stop the blood. Maybe he still had a chance — a pillow, anything to press against the wound, until he could get medical care. The hotel had medical staff. The fucking hotel had everything. Sarah was his only hope. He tried to speak, but his throat was full of fluid. He gurgled and coughed. Her black heels once again showed up in his field of vision. She pulled him up into a sitting position. He vomited. A brownish-red sludge washed over the floor and the legs of the chair.

'I can tell you a lot of secrets.' His voice was rough and weak.

She crouched down beside him, deftly avoiding everything that was leaking from his punctured body.

'You don't need to exert yourself. We already know everything we need to know. We have other sources. My task here was to stop future problems. You won't be helping Tehran with any more construction projects. Hopefully, your successor will be more careful.'

He sobbed.

'The bunker was purely a business deal … and I know … other things. Important things.'

She looked at her watch.

'What kind of important things?'

She sounded bored. He feverishly searched through his disintegrating memory. The dinner with Omar Fathy. There had been a friend of Omar's brother there, someone he hadn't met before. What was his name again? They'd had a conversation about the bunker project. He had mentioned something else. Something very secret.

Once again he had warm fluid in his mouth, nose, and throat. She stood up. He could hear her soft steps on the thick carpet and then the sharp tapping of her heels on the hard floor. He whimpered. She didn't turn around; instead she walked over and closed the balcony door. She was planning to leave him there.

'Arie al-Fattal!'

He spoke the words with his mouth buried in the dusty carpet. His head was roaring. The blurry shoes stopped halfway to the door. They came back.

'What about him?'

A glimmer of hope. He looked up once more at the gentle face with the crooked nose.

'Will you help me?'

She looked at him in silence and considered his question.

'I still have the tablet you were supposed to take. I don't really want to waste it; but if you give me something valuable, maybe you can have it. It will make your heart stop — no pain at all. Otherwise, you have at least an hour left to live, and that is definitely not something to look forward to. It wouldn't be possible to save you even if you were on an operating table. The liver is essentially impossible to suture.'

One tablet. That was all he wanted. To go to sleep. To escape the flames that were burning him up from the inside. She took out her phone and set it to record. Then she threw out her hands like a theatre director. He tried to speak coherently.

'So you know who al-Fattal is. I met him at a dinner. He tried to interest me in financing an attack against Israel.'

He was interrupted by a coughing fit, and thousands of lights exploded with each cough. The roar in his head increased.

'What kind of attack?' she said impatiently.

'Some sort of technical attack. A new weapon. A virus.'

He whispered this last part. His stomach made him twist and turn with cramps, and, as he did, his throat filled with warm, thick liquid. He ended up on his side, panting weakly like a fish out of water. She waited for more, but she could tell by looking at him that he couldn't continue. She opened the mini-bar beside the bed.

'Apparently the tablet should be dissolved in sugary liquid. To work faster.'

She searched through the drinks.

'I assume a Coke is okay? It's cold.'

He followed her with his eyes. She opened the red can. She held up a little white pill the size of an aspirin. Then she gently shook the can so the tablet would dissolve. He was silent, but his body was wound as tightly as a spring. She helped him drink. He swallowed blood, bile, and Coke. She carefully rested his head on the carpet and stood up.

'There, Mohammad. Now this rough evening will soon be over. Isn't it ironic that the national drink of America is what ended up saving you?'

She set the empty can on the counter with a bang. Then she walked to the door without turning around. The Arab magnate lay still on the floor, like an artificial island in the middle of a large, dark red sea, or a fallen miniature version of Burj al-Arab, with lowered sails. His body was no longer tense. It had only taken a minute for his heart to stop beating.

Stockholm, Sweden

There was still about half an hour left. He dozed off as he sat there waiting. The printouts slid from the folder and out onto the grey stone floor of the conference room, where they made a colourful pattern. He let them lie there and tried to find a more comfortable position in the rigid office chair. The most beautiful sounds in the world ran through his soul.

The door opened, revealing a young engineering student with unruly black hair and a face full of freckles. He said something. Eric reluctantly left Tosca, but only partway, leaving one of the iPod's earbuds in place.

'Do you want a cancer Coke or a real Coke?'

Eric rolled his eyes.

'If you mean Diet, then yes, please. And that cancer talk is all crap. As far as I know, no one has died from drinking Coca-Cola.'

The student pretended not to notice the printouts all over the floor.

'Okay, Professor. I'll put it by the lectern.'

Eric nodded. Then he leaned back.

'With ice and lemon, please.'

He put his earbud back in, and the aria went back to stereo.

He thought about his upcoming lecture. The department office had informed him that a hundred people had registered. Today's speech was a basic review of his research, and as such was well-charted waters. He knew how to avoid the dangerous rocks.

Tosca had arrived at the prison and was singing to her doomed artist. *'Amor che seppe a te vita serbare'* — 'Our love has saved your life.'

Eric left thoughts of his lecture behind and turned to last night's encounter. There were deep scratches under his white shirt. They had made love. When Hanna, hot and trembling, mumbled 'no' and tried to push him away, he had resisted and kept going. She had sensed that he was on his way and tried to defend herself. This was their agreement. But he had been drugged by her scent, intoxicated by her sweaty neck. He couldn't, didn't want to, obey. When it was too late, she had held him close to her, receiving him. Later, as he rested with his head buried in her hair, panting, she had cried. It was just a quiet sniffling at first, and then sounded like pure despair.

'You bastard. You goddamn fucking pig.'

She had clawed him.

The freckled student popped up in the doorway. Eric threw a glance at the clock and nodded. He turned off the music in the middle of the final duet, stood up, and followed the unruly hair for the short walk over to room F2. The first thing he saw as he stepped onto the stage by the lectern was that someone — presumably Freckles — had stuck the logo of the Swedish Cancer Society onto his glass of Diet Coke. School humour.

The buzz in the auditorium quieted. He cleared his throat and let his eyes wander through the audience. He didn't recognise anyone, but he hadn't had much contact with students during the past year.

'Good afternoon. My name is Eric Söderqvist, and seventeen years ago I was a student in the four-year civil engineering program, with a concentration in data systems. Since then, I've continued to focus on scientific computing. Five years ago, I got my doctorate in BCI, Brain Computer Interface — that is, the interaction between computers and the brain. For just over a year, I've been in charge of a research project we call Mind Surf. It's an interdisciplinary project that fuses cutting-edge neuro-research with our most advanced IT. We are collaborating with the Karolinska Institute and Kyoto University, and my team has a number of patent applications in the field. Hopefully, you'll all be as sold on the project as I am by the time my forty-five minutes are up.'

The auditorium was silent. Eric picked up the wireless-presentation remote and called up his first image.

'The brain contains over one hundred billion nerve cells. We can't even count the number of synapses, or contact points, where nerve impulses are transferred from one nerve cell to another. These synapses, along with the nerve fibres, form a network with enormous capacity. Dreams, memories, feelings, movement, and impressions are all processed in constant, ongoing syntheses. Despite the fact that the brain is one of the greatest research areas of our time, we still know very little about our biological supercomputer.'

A click and another image.

'Today we live ever-longer and more healthy lives, thanks in large part to our pioneering advances in both medicine and technology. We have more potent drugs. We have advanced equipment like pacemakers, prostheses, and a number of more-

or-less complex aids for the handicapped. During the last decade we have also become better at transplants. We have started to see the possibilities awaiting us in genetic research and stem-cell cultures. But even with all of these advances, there has still been no change for the millions of people who suffer from severe brain injuries and diseases.'

The images depicted famous faces with famous illnesses.

'In the US alone there are more than five million people with permanent brain injuries, two million who are paralysed, one million with Parkinson's, and one million who are blind. There are twenty million deaf people. Beyond that, there are stroke patients and people with other related problems such as depression. Many of these illnesses and injuries stem from the brain's inability to interpret stimuli and to execute muscle and nerve commands. This is manifested in blindness, an inability to communicate, or partial or complete paralysis.'

Eric took a sip of soda and winked at the freckled student, who was in the first row.

'The processor in a computer is in many ways reminiscent of the human brain. They both operate on binary systems, and communicate via impulses. The similarities make it possible to combine these systems. In the convergence between computer and human, we find solutions to a number of the aforementioned problems. This is my calling. I work to create thought-guided computer systems. And computer-guided thought systems.'

He let the words hang in the air for a moment before he called up a picture of brain waves from an EEG recording.

'BCI programs interpret neural activity and translate it into digital commands. Electrodes register thoughts that then — via the computer — control mechanical prostheses or digital communication systems, for example. In this way, we can restore function to patients who suffer from impaired motor activity due to stroke, spinal cord injuries, MS, or ALS. Those who are paralysed can control various types of aids, or move with the help of prostheses. The possibilities are endless.'

Eric started a film clip.

'What you see here is a monkey who has learned to guide a robotic arm in order to receive food. The monkey controls the arm via a joystick. The monkey also has a BCI implant in her brain, and this interprets the electro-physical signals that are created each time she moves the joystick. Now, here, the researchers are disconnecting the joystick. You can see, despite this, that the robot arm is still retrieving food for the monkey. How is this possible?'

The auditorium was silent.

'Well, the monkey doesn't know that the joystick is disconnected, so she continues to guide it with her thoughts. The BCI system reads these thoughts and converts them into digital commands that correspond to those of the joystick. The monkey continues to receive food, but now with only the help of her thoughts.'

A murmur went through the audience.

'This is an early version of BCI. Today we have come much further. Now we can translate both computer commands into thoughts, and thoughts into computer commands. We can play music for a deaf person, and show a movie to a blind person. BCI will provide the severely handicapped with a totally new opportunity for dignity and participation.'

Eric stepped partway into the beam from the projector, and pictures floated over his face like henna tattoos.

'Of course, there are also a number of other areas of application: video games, for example. And even the American military is investing billions of dollars into BCI research. Imagine being able to use thoughts to guide a weapons system.'

He took another sip of soda and looked at the clock. Ten minutes left. He had to speed along.

'We most often measure signals using EEG, outside the head, and ECoG, just under the skull. We also register field potentials from the parenchyma and firing neurons, so-called AP firing.'

Eric called up the logo of KTH Royal Institute of Technology.

'So what are we doing specifically, here in Sweden? We're trying to combine the latest research from neuro-medicine with the most cutting-edge IT. Previously, there have been issues with the interface — the contact — between computer and human. The most effective BCI systems are based on subdural implants. This means that the sensors must be placed within the skull, which requires surgical intervention. That involves a number of risks; for example, the body might reject the foreign object, or there might be infection. The systems that have previously been used externally have registered very weak alpha and beta waves, and have therefore been limited to simple functions. However, we have developed a completely new type of gel for the electrodes.'

An image depicted a fluorescent purple blob of gel.

'We have been performing research in conjunction with Kyoto University in order to develop this completely unique substance. It's a gel based on nanotechnology. It is made up of very small conductive particles that penetrate — are absorbed — through the skull. Each particle retains contact with the next. The absorption can be compared to the way a nicotine patch works, but in this case, as I said, it has conductive capacity. Thus direct contact with the brain is established. Look at it as a power cord that goes through the skin. Another part of our research, which is almost as revolutionary as the gel, is the sensor helmet itself. Sure, it looks like a bathing cap, but it is considerably more sophisticated. The helmet is made up of fifty electrodes, which cover the head in a wave pattern. The tips of the electrodes penetrate nearly two millimetres into the skin.' Eric noticed that several people in the audience had grimaced, so he hastened to add, 'The gel contains a local anaesthetic that somewhat lessens the uncomfortable sensation of the fifty pins. The sensors' penetration and the absorption of the gel allows us very strong contact with the brain without surgery. We are the only ones in the world who have come up with such a solution, and we have applied for a patent.'

He couldn't hold back his pride. Another image.

'In addition, with the help of specially directed electrodes and our nanogel, we have found a method of making contact with the second cranial nerve — better known as the optic nerve. By linking us to the optic chiasm, the point behind the eyes at which the optic nerves cross, we can send three-dimensional images straight into the consciousness. Our vision for this system is to give those who are completely paralysed, and maybe even the blind, a better means of interacting with their surroundings. Finally, we have spent many thousands of hours developing a control program that interprets the collective signals of the brain. The first cutting-edge program, Mind Surf, allows us to surf a three-dimensional internet. An internet that only exists in the mind, but which is simultaneously more colourful and real than anything else. We will be able to control this three-dimensional world with our thoughts, and it's not even going to require any special training to do so. Our goal is for it to be possible to navigate Mind Surf based on pure intuition. Anyone want to sign up to try?'

One hundred hands shot up in the air. Eric smiled and put down the wireless remote.

'What I've shown you here today is not a vision of the future. It's happening here and now, within the best institution in the world: KTH Royal Institute of Technology. Thank you for your time.'

The room exploded into applause, and several cheers could be heard through the racket. Eric took a bow, picked up the glass of Coke, and stepped down from the podium. Back in the conference room, he found his printouts neatly piled on the table next to his briefcase. All thanks to Freckles. He packed up his things and went back out into the hallway. His mobile phone showed three missed calls. Two were from Hanna; one was from Jens Wahlberg. He dealt with the easiest first. Outside, the air was still. The sky was pale blue, and the sun was very warm. He crossed the small square on his way to Lindstedtsväg, searching his pocket for his car keys. Jens answered on the second ring.

'Oh, you're alive!'

Eric unlocked his Volvo XC60 and took note of the parking ticket on the windshield.

'Why wouldn't I be alive? Do you know something I don't?'

Jens's snorting laughter made the little earpiece crackle. 'Well, a little bird — or rather an eagle, a beautiful sea eagle — whispered in my ear.'

Eric groaned and pulled out onto Drottning Kristinas Väg. 'You've been talking to Hanna.'

Jens cleared his throat. 'I have been talking to Hanna. Jesus, Eric. After that conversation, I considered going down to the editor-in-chief and asking them to redo tonight's newsbill. "KTH professor living under threat of death."'

Eric shook his head and grimaced with the pain of the scratches on his back. Valhallavägen was dense with traffic.

'What did she say?'

'I don't tell her all the shit you say, do I? That confidence works both ways. But she was disappointed. She essentially said you're trying to get yourself a kid by force, in order to lock her into a relationship that ought to have ended up down a Porta-Potty ages ago.'

'Did she say Porta-Potty?'

'No. But you get what I mean. What are you up to?'

Eric was angry. What did Jens know about how things were? As his best friend, he ought to support him rather than preach at him. He got enough of that at home. Jens was Hanna's friend, too, but above all he was a man. Men ought to stick together.

Everything was so easy for Jens. He soared high above the battlefield, free to drift on whichever breeze he liked. Seen from that distance, every conflict became small and abstract. But this was about real loyalty, so he should have to pick sides, damn it. He heard Jens's voice from high up in the clouds: 'Are you still there, buddy?'

'Jens, you don't get how difficult this is. You live your bachelor life in the middle of the evening-paper world. Your reference point is always *Aftonbladet*, with its superficial stories and straightforward headlines. But this is about my life. About real feelings, way beyond the top-ten lists of Sweden's biggest silicon tits.'

'Ouch, ouch. That hurt.'

Eric was immediately sorry.

'You know I didn't mean that. I'm just so fucking tired of everything. I've always been sure of where I was heading, but now my compass is just spinning. I'm feeling the pressure at work. I'm losing my grip on Hanna. Somehow we've lost each other. One day, things are great; the next day, it's all-out war. Maybe I've lost myself.'

Jens was quiet for a moment.

'That's why your compass is spinning. You've lost contact with the North Pole. With your magnetic field.'

Eric smiled tiredly.

'Yeah, I suppose she is like the North Pole. A hundred degrees below zero.'

'Eric, you know she can just as easily be as heated as ... as that fiery little pepper.'

'A jalapeño.'

'North Pole or not, she has always been your stabiliser. And now she's just as worn out and confused as you are. Maybe you need a time-out. A little time away from each other. After all, a compass works the same, no matter how far it is from the pole.'

A red light. Eric leaned his head against the steering wheel.

'Maybe that's true. But distance scares me — just the thought of not sleeping beside her, not seeing her every day. Even if we mostly just argue. As long as we're arguing, at least we're engaging. And we still have fantastic times between fights. If we put more distance between us, we might lose what little we have left. We might not fight our way back.'

There was a gulp on the line. Jens was drinking coffee.

'Who knows? But the way it is now, you're just making things worse. I don't think you should look at fighting as a good thing. You're burning bridges. Maybe it's better to put some space between you. Some temporary space.'

Eric stared down at the black rubber mat.

'Jens, can we meet tomorrow? I need someone who can listen.'

'Sure. Of course. We'll have a long lunch.' All of Jens's lunches were long.

'I have a tough meeting with investors tomorrow morning. I don't really know when I'll be done. But after that ...'

'I'll make a reservation. One o'clock at Riche. I'll wait for you there. And, listen, call Hanna.' He hung up. Eric sat there with his forehead against the warm leather steering wheel.

Hanna was his exact opposite. He was Swedish through and through. She was Jewish, with all of Europe running through her veins. He was ordinary; she was beautiful. He was an absent-minded introvert; she was highly organised and an unparalleled social butterfly. She knew everyone and everything. Each of their weekends was booked full of lunches and brunches, always on her initiative and attended by minute planning. The same went for vacations; they were booked and planned from start to finish. Eric mostly just went along without taking any initiative of his own. At least, that was what she usually accused him of when they argued.

They had met at KTH when they were studying their basic programs. Today she was the director of IT at the Swedish office of the TBI, the Trusted Bank of Israel. She was active in the Jewish community, and she was the chairperson of Friends of KTH. Her calendar was always full. Where was she now? Probably at the bank. He didn't want to call her. The car behind him honked angrily. The light had turned green and was already about to go back to red. He hit the accelerator and just made it through. The angry driver was left behind.

'Hi. This is Hanna Schultz Söderqvist at TBI. Leave a nice message and I promise to call back.' He hung up.

Tabriz, Iran

It was just like any other business meeting. There were four men, two on either side of the long, pale-grey conference table. They were formally dressed. The two closest to the window were wearing dark suits and ties. The two closest to the doors were wearing *dishdashas,* long white robes, and *keffiyeh,* traditional Muslim headwear. Before them were various cups of coffee and tea. There were carafes of water and cherry juice, a big bowl of fruit, and two hookahs. Several documents were spread out on the table, and on one of the short ends of the table was a laptop. The scent of aftershave and coffee was in the air. The sun shone brightly through the large windows. El-Goli park stretched out far below them, and in the background — shimmering in the heat — were the roofs and roads of Tabriz. The air conditioning was on full blast, and the room was chilly.

One of the men in a suit was Arie al-Fattal. He spoke like a seasoned salesman, always careful to seek confirmation from Enes al-Twaijri, one of the white-clad men across from him. Al-Fattal was well-read and knowledgeable. His message was energetic and impressive. Enes nodded with interest. It was unusual for this man to be the one doing the listening. As the CEO and principal owner of the oil group Al-Twaijri Petrol Group, he was one of Saudi Arabia's most powerful businessmen. He had condemned the existence of Israel, and, like his friend the president of Iran, was a Holocaust denier. He had told the *New York Times* that he was proud of the attack on the World Trade Center. Nevertheless, the FBI had reported that, despite his fundamentalist views, he did not constitute an immediate threat. He wasn't labelled a terrorist.

The man beside him, Ahmad Waizy, was not known to the FBI. This was despite the fact that he was one of the main players in the Islamic terror network al-Jihad, which many considered to be the governing arm of al-Qaeda. He had studied to be an imam as a young man, and now he was something of a freelancing jihadist. He was sitting quietly, too, studying the men in suits. He was tired of listening to Arie's shrill voice. He already knew all about the project and didn't need to hear the sales presentation. Hezbollah had, for the first time in its nearly thirty-year history, managed to come up with something good — a key recruit. But now they didn't have the financing to do anything about it. Arie had been engaged to find financiers. He was a clown.

Ahmad concentrated instead on the man who was sitting next to Arie. He looked deflated. His suit was too big, and his tie was messily knotted. Ahmad knew all about this person. For him, knowing was always crucial. The skeleton in the wrinkled suit was, at the moment, one of Hezbollah's most dangerous weapons. He looked malnourished. Apparently, he was something of a prodigy. A computer genius. A pacifist, until he'd lost his family. Could he be trusted? That remained to be seen. From experience, Ahmad assumed that he couldn't trust anyone.

He opened the folder and once again read the description of Mona. A computer virus was nothing new on its own; they had existed in various forms for over twenty years. Early viruses had basically been simple programs, often with code of fewer than four hundred bytes. Mona, which was twenty megabytes, was something completely new. It was a powerful hybrid of two categories of infection: a worm and a virus. The worm worked like a carrier of the virus itself. It made its way into networks via security vulnerabilities, and then it replicated itself. In only a few minutes, the worm could create thousands of clones that then crawled on to other servers, where they replicated again. The worm's functionality took up only 3 per cent of the total code. The rest belonged to the Mona virus itself, which waited under the worm's shell like a Trojan horse.

Ahmad closed the folder and looked again at the man in the wrinkled suit. He had a hard time believing that this emaciated Lebanese man had built all of this.

Samir Mustaf met Ahmad's eyes with their snakelike chill. He felt ill at ease. Ahmad was part of al-Qaeda, and despite his calm outward demeanour his whole being radiated aggression. Samir looked back at Arie. It seemed that he had succeeding in capturing Enes's interest. They desperately needed financing if they were to be able to continue the project. For the past few months he had been working around the clock, and the project was what kept him alive. Kept his shell alive.

Arie pushed a brown paper folder over to the Saudi billionaire.

'Everything is described in greater detail in these documents. I ask that you make sure that no one other than yourself and your most trusted colleagues has access to them.'

Enes put the folder aside without opening it. In a deep, calm voice he said: 'Allow me to recap to make sure I haven't missed anything. This brother,' he gestured toward Samir, 'has developed some sort of computer program, a virus he calls Mona. It is the most powerful virus the world has ever seen. Correct?'

Arie nodded encouragingly.

Enes continued. 'The virus will be injected ...' he looked at Samir. 'Is that how you'd describe it?'

Samir nodded.

'The virus will be injected into the Israeli banking and financial system. There it will take large amounts of information hostage. It will also destroy strategic data, and manipulate information about the stock exchange and interest rates. It will cause great injury to the occupying powers. Faith in Israel will be undermined, and foreign capital will be moved to more stable markets. Massive sums will be destroyed, and so will confidence in the Israeli leaders.'

Enes spoke in a voice tinged with theatricality. Samir noticed that he had repeated several of Arie's expressions word for word. He was unsure whether this was because he liked them or he was being sarcastic.

Enes continued. 'Then, when the unrest is at its peak, Hezbollah's spokesmen will step forth and offer an anti-virus — a medicine to release the digital hostages and restore the banking system. In return, they will demand that Israel revert to the 1967 borders. In addition, the Zionists must free many of our brothers who are currently being held without trial. Have I understood this correctly?'

Arie and Samir nodded simultaneously.

'And in order to carry out this grand — and surprising — project,' Enes went on, 'you need financing. How much do you need and what, more precisely, will this money be used for?'

Enes was looking at Samir, but it was Arie who answered.

'We need three million dollars. This capital will be used to procure equipment, food, lodging, and travel, as well as compensation for a number of helping hands. We must also be able to pay bribes to security personnel. In addition, we need a buffer of $500,000 for unforeseen costs. Everything is specified in the documentation.'

He stopped talking and looked at Samir, who nodded weakly. Enes smiled.

'My knowledge of all this technical talk is very limited. And there's no point in trying to educate me. What I do understand, however, are banking and deal-making strategies. If this virus achieves what you say it will, Prime Minister Ben Shavit will have no choice but to go along with our demands in order to get access to the anti-virus. With that in mind …'

He seemed to be savouring what came next.

'… I'm prepared to finance the project. This could crush the corrupt structure of the occupiers and carry us to victory.'

Samir exhaled and looked at Arie, who flew up, went around the table, and embraced the oil tycoon. Enes returned the embrace, but then held up his hands to hold him off.

'I do have one request, however.'

His tone made it clear that this was more than a request.

'The interests I represent, myself included, have great confidence in this man.'

He placed his arm around Ahmad's shoulders.

'He has shown great determination, and is genuinely engaged in our fight. I want him to participate in this honourable project.'

Ahmad didn't release Samir from his gaze. When he spoke, it was in a surprisingly soft and low voice.

'I would first like to thank Enes al-Twaijri for his faith in me. I would also like to praise you, Samir Mustaf, for your knowledge and loyalty. And you, Arie al-Fattal, for your success in recruiting this gifted brother.'

Arie smiled, but there was a hint of nervousness in his eyes.

'Your plan is well formulated. I do not think, however, that this video game you're suggesting is enough, no matter how good it might be.'

He deftly rolled a pen between his fingers. Samir followed the movement of the pen, from the outside of his hand to the inside and back again. The effect was hypnotic, and he found it difficult to look away.

'In order for this fantastic Mona to truly give us the victory we're all striving for, the computer attacks must be combined with a select few *shahids*. Real-world efforts. Efforts that will amplify the destabilisation.'

Arie took a sip of water, cleared his throat, and looked at Ahmad.

'*Shahids* … so, martyrs. What are the targets?'

Ahmad stared at the tabletop before him.

'"For the Rejecters We have prepared Chains, Yokes, and a Blazing Fire." The Quran also says, "He admits whom he will in His mercy; but for the wrongdoers awaits painful punishment."'

Silence descended upon the room. Ahmad closed his eyes, and Samir thought he could see him silently whispering yet another quote from the Quran. His narrow lips were moving. Enes cleared his throat as the silence dragged on. Ahmad opened his eyes again and smiled at them.

'Allah knows the hidden reality of the heavens and the earth. But there is something none of you knows yet. Something that will lead us to victory.'

All three of them looked intently at Ahmad, who confidently leaned forward in his chair.

'Recall how Caesar had Brutus at his side. Trusted him. Listened to him. And recall how Brutus killed him when the time was right.'

His narrow index finger pointed at them one by one.

'Recall how the Greek spy Sinon pretended to be a forgotten slave and convinced the Trojans to bring the great wooden horse with Odysseus's hidden warriors inside their gates.'

He placed his hands on the table, palms up, and lowered his voice.

'Isn't it fitting that computer viruses are often called Trojan horses? In this important attack, we have succeeded in creating our own Sinon with Allah's help. And this time, too, he will help us to bring our poison inside the infidels' walls.'

All three looked at him in a combination of fascination and surprise. Ahmad nodded thoughtfully as though to let his words sink in. He continued: 'An organisation which shall remain nameless has long been investing extensive resources and taking great risks to get a true believer into the highest levels of the Zionist leadership. Today, this person — let us fittingly call him Sinon — is one of Prime Minister Ben Shavit's closest men and part of the government's innermost circle. Shavit listens to him. When the time is right, when the virus and our supplementary military measures strike fear into the country, when our brothers from Hezbollah present their demands in exchange for a cure, then Sinon will convince him to go along with our demands. As one of his most trusted men, he can influence his decision. That will be the beginning of the end of the Zionists' tyranny — an Israel on its knees.'

Samir was excited. So there was a man on the inside, close to the prime minister. A Sinon. He studied Ahmad, who had stood up and was now standing with Enes; they were conversing in low voices. There was something disagreeable about Ahmad. He was going to be part of their group. Until then they had been a small team that lived together around the clock. Would Ahmad help them? Would he control them? He had demanded that they carry out physical attacks in Israel. If he had read Ahmad correctly, the attacks would be aimed at civilians. Samir pushed aside the images that popped up in his mind, and returned to the project. Work was his only escape from the memories that otherwise kept him awake at night. With the financing taken care of, and with Sinon's help, they could truly succeed. Even if Ahmad scared him, there was something persuasive and powerful about him.

Mona wasn't finished yet. This was no average, run-of-the-mill virus. It was a masterpiece, a singular life form created for a single purpose.

To move forward, Samir needed to decide on an appropriate gateway, the port through which the virus would enter the central banking system. He had weighed several alternatives, but at the moment he was leaning toward using TBI, the most international of Israel's banks. They would need information about the bank's firewalls, system specifications, and network structure. Through the bank's network, Mona could access all of Israel's financial systems. Samir had a contact at TBI's offices in Nice, an old friend from his youth, from his years in Toulouse, who was now the director of the local credit division. He was a Muslim, but they couldn't automatically count on his support. Their friendship ought to be a good start, though. They would need to be physically present in Nice, so they would need a place to live undisturbed, but that wasn't his responsibility. Arie would take care of it.

With this, they were entering a more operational phase, and more people would learn of their identities and plans. Samir was going to trespass in a heavily guarded network, which would leave traces and activate alarms. The risks would increase, but he wasn't worried. No matter what happened to him, it would only affect his shell. What he *did* worry about was that something would stop him from completing the project — that there wouldn't be time to place Mona in the Israeli network. He had sworn over her burned body that she would get her revenge. After this, all that was left was the reunion. They were waiting for him in paradise, and when the time was right he would go to them.

He shivered in the chilly air of the conference room. He would be going back to France. A whole life had gone by since he had left that country more than twenty years before. Here, in north-western Iran, France felt infinitely far away. And his journey seemed very precarious.

Stockholm, Sweden

Mats Hagström took an apple from the bowl of fruit, and bit off a large chunk. As he chewed, he studied the apple as though he were a predator. He bit off another piece and chewed loudly. Eric sat silently on the couch across from him. Framed covers of Donald Duck comics hung from floor to ceiling, filling the walls in the large conference room. The covers started with the first issue in September 1948, and continued into modern editions. Mats was known for collecting all kinds of things, and parts of his collections hung in all the rooms.

Another vigorous bite of the apple. Eric guessed that he would have to wait until the apple was gone before they could continue. He didn't like money-begging meetings. He felt worthless and mistrusted. But he couldn't forego them. The limited aid that his team received from the institution didn't go far.

Mats Hagström was done with the apple. 'Check this out, kid,' he said.

He turned in his chair and tossed the core across the room, toward the wastebasket next to the window. It missed, hitting Donald Duck from March 1956 instead. Juice from the apple ran down the glass of the frame, and the core ended up on the floor. Mats turned to Eric.

'Now you see why I gave up my career in basketball.' He looked back at the bowl of fruit, and Eric feared he would start in on another apple.

'I understand that BCI is very promising. There's clearly a demand for it in the international market. Its scalability is high. Scalability is always the first thing I look for in a potential investment.'

He leaned forward and took another apple from the basket.

'I say *potential* investment, because what made me rich was not the investments I made, but the ones I didn't. Do you understand? I have great radar. It helps me avoid losses before they happen. Those who invest in my funds know I have this radar. Do you follow?'

Eric nodded. He wondered to himself how it was possible to get rich off projects you'd declined. Mats continued: 'So your idea is good, and the market is there for it. But this also means that other people have surely seen what your people have seen. So the next thing I think about, second to scalability, is protection from competitors. If I've understood you correctly, the nanogel is what makes your project unique. The nanogel achieves

35

neurological contact as good as that of systems surgically placed in the brain, but without an operation. Is that right?'

Eric nodded again. Mats looked at apple number two in his hand.

'What is there to stop someone else from inventing the same thing two days after I'd invested in your project?'

Eric was prepared for the question. This was becoming routine; it was his thirteenth investor meeting. So far, he hadn't received any capital. These investors all asked the same things and seemed to come to the same conclusion: it was better to invest in Russian stocks or shares in Ericsson. The lack of money meant that work on Mind Surf was more or less at a standstill. For his part, Eric was living off of Hanna's salary. This was not exactly something that improved their relationship. He took out a plastic folder and handed it over to Mats.

'Here are the patent applications we've submitted. Two of them have already become legally valid, but only within the EU. These patents, however, are based on an earlier substance. We have since made some modifications, and the new patents are awaiting approval. As you know, the patenting process is lengthy. We are safeguarding both our nanogel and our sensor helmet. We've also applied for a patent on the software we've developed.'

Mats looked up from the papers.

'Is that Mind Surf — the thing that makes it possible to surf the net with your eyes closed and your arms crossed?'

'Exactly. Mind Surf reads and interprets more information from the brain than any previous system. The result is an intuitive and powerful system of communication between brain and computer. The program isn't quite finished, but we've already applied for a patent on the holistic graphics and the digital converter that translates information between neural and digital formats.'

Mats turned toward the wastebasket again.

'How long will it be before Mind Surf works?'

He didn't take his gaze from the wastebasket. Eric's answer was directed at the back of his head.

'I'm working day and night to finish the first demo version. I estimate that it will be ready within the next few weeks.'

The back of Mats's head nodded.

'Then here's what I suggest. You finish your surfing program ...'

Mats tossed the uneaten apple in an arc across the room. It landed perfectly in the wastebasket, and he raised his hands in the air: 'Yes!' Then he looked back at Eric.

'Do you know what just happened, kid?'

Eric shook his head.

'I believe in fate. Don't go on talking too much about that, because in my world you're toast if you start going on about fate. But sometimes I just get things into my head.'

He snapped his fingers.

'Maybe there's a higher power. Someone or something that knows it all, that has all the answers. Someone who knows where the FTSE 100 will end next week, where the Dow Jones will close next Friday, or what sales H&M will show in its upcoming report. Are you with me? It's probably not the case. But what if it is? And what if this power really does want to help us, but fails because we're too narrow-minded and dense? We'd rather sit and mess with our technical analysis programs, hedge our bets, and try to discount our way to a reasonable net worth. But what if the most important answers are right before our eyes? If they are, it's important to be receptive.'

Mats adjusted the cuffs of his shirt.

'I thought about all of this just before I threw the second apple. I decided that if I missed, I would say no. If it went in, I'd move forward.'

Eric looked at him in bewilderment.

'You let an apple determine your investments?'

Mats sighed. 'No, not usually. I have a bunch of MBA up-and-comers who count it all, up and down. It's so serious that it gets boring. Maybe it was my basketball training that made the apple land in the garbage. Maybe it was a coincidence. Or maybe it was fate. The only way to find out which it was is to say yes to the investment. If it all goes to hell, we can rule out fate.'

Eric ran a hand through his hair.

'So you want to invest in our project?'

'Yes, of course. And it will be in accordance with the disbursement plan we discussed earlier. Twenty million in four blocks, all to be paid out as you reach the goals we set out. But ... and there is a "but". There always is. I'm not going to make the first payment until you have Mind Surf up and running. It's only going to be a few weeks anyway, and then we'll know that the program really works.'

Eric smiled, but regretted having been so optimistic about the timeline. It might just as easily be months before the program was ready. But what the hell, at least it was up to him now. He stood up and extended his hand. Finally, a yes. Funny that it turned out to be at the thirteenth meeting.

'Thanks. I'll make sure to have a working version for you as soon as I possibly can.'

Mats shook his hand. 'Now you've got a damned-good reason to finish. And let's hope that we have fate on our side.'

As always, Riche was full, and Eric crowded his way between tables. He saw Jens standing and gesticulating at a full table with a view out onto Birger Jarlsgatan. Everyone at the table was laughing. Jens knew every single person there, with no exceptions. As one of the crime reporters at *Aftonbladet*, his social skills were a great asset. Eric drew up next to him. 'Hi there. I'm going to go sit at our table.'

Jens nodded and thumped one of the diners on the back. Eric moved on along the crowded row of lunch patrons and arrived at the corner table next to the wall. He sank into the chair and exhaled. He hadn't been able to relax after the meeting, until now. What had they actually agreed on? He had to prove that they could protect themselves from competitors — that the patent was strong enough to keep encroachers at bay. Above all, he had to get Mind Surf working. But it would be a challenge. He had been running into problems during the last few weeks. Mind Surf worked when it was controlled by the keyboard, but it froze up when he used the helmet. He hadn't been able to locate the error. The conversion engine at the heart of Mind Surf was complex, and it interpreted a great deal of neural information. In addition, the three-dimensional interface worked in real time, which made it vulnerable to a number of potential problems. Perhaps the error was somewhere in the interpreting processor. Perhaps the problem was that the contact with the brain was too weak, after all.

Eric looked out the window at the traffic on Birger Jarlsgatan. A bicyclist wobbled past a taxi, which slammed on its brakes and came within a hair's breadth of being hit by a yellow Porsche. Two young women with shopping bags from Gucci ran across the street.

He was going to sell half his company to Hagström Fund Management. Actually, it wasn't solely his company. He owned it along with the KTH innovations fund. But it felt like his company. It was his idea, and his research. The board of directors at KTH were the ones who decided on the worth of the company. Had they priced it too low? Was that why Mats Hagström had accepted? He felt a certain amount of trepidation at the thought of a new constellation of owners. Mats would come up with more demands. Why did Eric feel so uneasy about it? Why did he always have such trouble listening to authority? Why was it so difficult to relinquish control?

A waiter put down a plate of beef Rydberg. Eric shook his head. 'Thanks, but I haven't ordered yet.' The waiter chuckled, took back the plate, and pressed on through the crowd. Riche was the same as always. He really would have preferred a quieter place, like Teatergrillen or Prinsen — a restaurant where you could speak with fewer interruptions. He studied his friend, who was brazenly leaning over the other table and taking a handful of fries from one of the patrons' plates. No one seemed to find this strange; they just laughed, and someone raised a glass of beer. Jens played by his own rules. He was larger than anyone else in the restaurant. He had blond hair and a beard, which wasn't that unusual, but he was wearing blue loafers, green corduroy pants, a white shirt, and a red scarf. Jesus. Hanna would have gone nuts if she had seen him. She liked to use Jens as a 'don't' example when Eric was dressing himself: 'You can't wear that shirt, you'll look like Jens.' But he thought it was liberating.

Eric looked at the other guests in the restaurant: businessmen in dark suits, models in leather jackets, and rich kids with bandanas and back-slicked hair. Here and there, an artist. Maybe they were actors, or drunks with red noses and messy hair. Which pigeonhole did he fit in? The one for dusty academics? Or dreaming entrepreneurs?

'Eric! My very own Professor Calculus!'

Jens hugged him as heartily and roughly as always. His rough beard scratched Eric's cheek. There was a scent of too much aftershave, and a spot of ketchup on his shirt.

'You know I like to eat at noon. Papa's hungry now! I hope the same goes for you.'

Jens opened the menu with delight; he was always happy

when it was time to eat. Eric smiled and looked down at the options. He wasn't particularly hungry. The tension during the meeting with Mats had made him lose his appetite.

'I'm going to have toast *Skagen*.'

Jens's brow furrowed.

'Whoa. Such imagination. And what will you have after that?'

Eric grinned when he saw Jens's disappointment.

'An espresso.'

Jens shook his head.

'We decided on a long lunch. And besides, I waited an extra hour. I'm having prosciutto figs. They're fantastic — two servings, so you can have some, too — and then salt-fried shrimp. And grilled char. What are we drinking?'

There was no compromising with Jens when it came to drinks with a meal. He would never eat without wine.

'You choose. I know I'll be in good hands.'

Jens waved at the bustling waiter, who nodded, left a couple who were in the middle of ordering, and came to their table.

'Jens — always a pleasure to have such a fine guest. What can we do for you today?'

Jens smiled happily. The abandoned couple shot an angry look at them.

'We'll start with the essentials, my dear Pierre. To start, we'll have a bottle of that good Blanc de Blancen, Deutz 1998. And then we'll have La Chablisienne Grand Cru, from Grenouille, 2004. But, for God's sake, make sure it's colder than last time.'

The waiter bowed and disappeared. Jens tucked in his shirt, which had worked its way out of his pants, noticed the ketchup spot, and chuckled. Then he placed his large hand on Eric's.

'Mr. Söderqvist. How are things with you … *really*?'

Yes, how were things, *really*? Inside? Nervous. Uncertain. Wounded. With Jens, he might as well be honest. They had

41

known each other long enough and were close-enough friends.

'I'm scared, Jens — scared I'm losing my grip on things. I think I've been working too much and I've been too cut off. My job is turning into a suit of armour. I put down the visor and go out onto the battlefield. The worse things get with Hanna, the longer I linger. Running away.'

Jens looked at him thoughtfully.

'Why are you wearing armour in the first place?'

'So I can stand it. Above all, at my job. I feel responsible to my co-workers. To my students. To the investors. To the whole project. And not least to Hanna. I have to get my own salary.'

'We've all watched you lose yourself in your job. Or maybe escape into it consciously. It's like you've been obsessed, especially the last few months. To be honest, I was surprised when you called me back yesterday. It's been a long time. If all you do is live up to other people's expectations, you'll lose yourself. You and the armour will become one.'

'Sure. Hanna knows that, and I know it. And, hell, maybe she has a suit of armour, too.'

Jens looked concerned.

'When the battle is over, you'll be alone. Everyone will be gone. Everything you fought for will have been lost.'

The champagne arrived. Jens took the opportunity to order the food.

Eric thought about Hanna. Why was it all so complicated? They had often joked that they were living in a beautiful piece of crystal, separate from everyone else. But the crystal had smashed to pieces. It was as though the two of them had crossed a line during their fights in the past few weeks, and maybe even more so in the silence between times. Jens held up his glass.

'No more battlefields. *Skål* for peace. And farewell to arms.'

Eric sipped the cool wine.

'When we make love, it's like the armour falls away. That makes me happy. That's exactly what makes it all so fucking hard. We fight one night and make love the next.'

'There's no doubt you still love each other. I hear that from Hanna, too. That might be why you should take a break. Hopefully, you'll both realise you don't want to live without each other.'

Beyond Jens's shoulder, Eric could see that the couple at the other table still hadn't been able to order. The man looked like he was about to cry. The woman looked at him with disdain. Relationships were not easy; women were not easy. He drank some more champagne.

'Well, Jens, maybe you're right. I can't always run away from difficult decisions. I'll talk to her.'

He found himself calculating how much more work he would get done if he didn't have to worry about Hanna. He changed the subject.

'I got a nibble today. Mats Hagström wants to invest in Mind Surf.'

Jens looked at him. For a moment, it looked like he wasn't going to let him evade the question of Hanna. But then he lit up.

'Congrats! Mats Hagström — that's really huge. Now things will start moving.'

'Yes, I hope so. But there's still a lot of work to be done. And with things the way they are … I'm going to have to work even more — the pressure's on and the demands are greater. And Hanna's already halfway out the door.'

The waiter placed a large platter of prosciutto-wrapped figs between them. Jens immediately lifted the platter toward Eric.

'My friend, don't look at the problems. Look at the possibilities. At least you've secured the finances, so you can relax. Have a few figs. Dream your way off to the sunny Arabian deserts. There, all of your thoughts are just whispers in the gentle breeze.'

Tel Aviv, Israel

The three men who sat down at the table represented the core of Israeli intelligence. Jacob Nachman, the director of the radio intelligence unit 8200, had called the meeting. Beside him sat David Yassur, director of operations for the Mossad, and across from him was major-general Amos Dagan, director of the military intelligence agency, Aman. They were waiting for the fourth participant, Meir Pardo, senior director of the Mossad. David Yassur seldom saw his boss, and when he did he always got butterflies in his stomach. He found this irritating, but at the same time it was no wonder. Meir was no ordinary man. He had been born on a train in Novosibirsk in 1943. His parents were Holocaust survivors. His family had immigrated to Israel when he was nine years old.

As a young man, Meir joined the military and was quickly accepted into the paratrooper unit. His list of military merits was long, and David probably only knew of half of them. Meir had been in charge of a number of special units and intelligence operations. In 2002, he had been appointed as director of the Mossad by the prime minister. His staff adored him. He was known at the Mossad for working eighteen hours a day, often sleeping at the office. He woke early, took a long, ice-cold shower, ate a yoghurt, and worked without a break late into the night. It was difficult for his colleagues to keep up with his pace. David was experienced enough not to try. He had other good qualities, and he had a family. Meir's only known passions were pipe-smoking and painting. He painted watercolours. The few people who had been allowed to see his paintings said that he was extremely talented.

Meir stepped into the room. His delicate glasses were pushed up onto his forehead, and he supported himself with a cane.

David grimaced. He knew that Meir was scornful of poor health, especially in himself. He had been injured twice and had to use a cane sometimes, when the pain in his leg showed itself. This put him in a bad mood. Meir grunted at the others and sat down next to Jacob, who cleared his throat.

'My friends, I received a report this afternoon, and I want to tell all of you what it says. During the past few months, we've increased our focus on social media. Among other things, we've launched software that reads blogs around the clock. It deciphers almost all of the world's languages, and searches for patterns and connections that might indicate some sort of hostility toward Israel. It's a type of search engine, but unlike Google, for example, it uses an algorithm that …'

Meir raised a hand.

'Jacob, skip the technical details. What have you found?'

Jacob looked offended, but collected himself and continued.

'We've found several leads and patterns that seem to be connected. The sources are a number of blogs, as well as conversations primarily on Facebook. We've spent today working on a more complete analysis, and this is the picture we're getting.'

He handed out red folders.

'Some form of a Lebanese faction, presumably a small cell with links to Hezbollah, is preparing an attack directed at our banks and stock exchange. We don't have any names yet. Nor do we know where in the world this group is. One lead indicates that they are in France, possibly in Nice. We also believe that one of the targets might be TBI. We haven't succeeded in pinning down a time frame, where their finances come from, or even what they might be planning. It could be some sort of digital attack, by way of the internet.'

The men paged through their folders. David searched his memory. Something caused him to react to what Jacob had just said. He had read something a few days ago. After a few moments, Amos chuckled. Meir looked at the major-general with a frown.

'Is something funny?'

Amos closed his folder.

'This is pure teenage nonsense. Facebook? Twitter! Come on, Jacob. Hell, surely this isn't what all your unit's money goes on, is it? It's the banks' responsibility to have good security. What's it called? Firewalls. There have always been hackers. Surely this is hardly a reason to sound the alarm.'

Jacob held up his hand.

'Amos, if you think only teenagers use the internet, you're screwed. We're all screwed. What I've just shown you is the result of a very effective and well-co-ordinated intelligence project. I've been expecting us to see some sort of internet attack on Israel for some time. Such an attack could have very serious consequences for the whole country. Even for you, Amos.'

Meir nodded.

'I agree that we have to take this seriously. Good work, Jacob. But in order to move forward, we need to know more. Who are they, where are they, how are they planning to attack us, and when? Our units must co-operate. The internet is good, but not all the information we need can be found there. Our job, yours and mine, Amos, is to find the information that Jacob's guys miss.'

Jacob nodded, pleased with Meir's support. Amos looked irritated, but chose not to say anything.

Suddenly David realised what it was he had read. He leaned over the table and whispered to Meir, who frowned at first but then nodded. David sat down and opened his laptop. The others looked at him in surprise.

'A few days ago, one of our agents was on a mission in Dubai. This agent interrogated a Saudi building contractor with connections to the nuclear-weapons program in Iran.'

Amos gave a crooked smile.

'I'm pretty sure I read about a murder and robbery at Burj al Arab. The victim was in real estate. Or, to be more precise, he *was* real estate. One of the most powerful contractors on the peninsula.' He continued with marked irony, 'Strange story ... he was stabbed, but he died of a heart attack. Talk about bad luck.'

Meir became irritated.

'Things didn't go as planned. That's how it goes when you roll the dice. You should know that as well as anyone. Continue, David.'

David nodded. The line about rolling the dice was one of Meir's favourite expressions.

'During the interrogation, it came out that a certain Arie al-Fattal is looking for financing for an attack against Israel.'

David looked at the screen, where he had pulled up the report from Dubai.

'Some sort of virus attack, apparently. We didn't get any more information, but we had assumed that meant a biological virus. But maybe it's a computer virus, to be used against our banks.'

Jacob made some notes on the back of his report. He turned to Meir.

'Why haven't we been informed of this?'

Meir sighed.

'Take it easy, Jacob. We're not done with our analyses. Right now, we're looking for this al-Fattal. We've been keeping an eye on him for a long time. He seems to be a bad apple, and it's time to get rid of him. You will all receive a copy of the Dubai report. Thanks, David. Now we have a name, too. And it's time to inform the prime minister.'

David looked out the window behind Amos, at the hills of Judea. The burning sun was melting against the dark mountains.

Far off in that direction was the expanse of Iraq's dry deserts, and beyond that was Iran with its underground nuclear-weapons laboratories and constant promises to destroy the state of Israel. Even farther away were the troubled mountainous regions of Pakistan, controlled by hundreds of lawless tribes. Somewhere in that area, the leader of al-Qaeda was hiding. It was a world of pure threats and enemies. If his fellow Israelis knew about even a fraction of all the threats his organisation warded off every day, they would find it difficult to fall asleep at night.

The first thing they ought to do was debrief Rachel Papo with Unit 101, and find out what had really happened in that hotel room in Dubai.

Stockholm, Sweden

Hanna still hadn't returned home. The sushi was in the fridge, untouched. Eric was anxious. He always was when they weren't speaking after a fight. When he didn't know what she was doing or thinking. Clearly, he had an unhealthy need for control, or security. The uncertainty made him crazy. Was she still angry? Because usually she called — sometimes several times a day. And he had met with Mats Hagström today; she ought to be curious about that.

It was Friday evening, *Shabbat*, when they always ate dinner together, lighting the candles and breaking bread. He had purchased *challah* from a kosher bakery. But she hadn't called. That meant she was angry. Or sad. Maybe both. Was she staying away on purpose?

He drank some coffee and tried to concentrate on his work. He was playing Chopin's *Nocturne in E-minor, opus 72* on iTunes.

The piano scales rolled forth into the small office. There were folders and piles of paper everywhere. In the middle of the room stood a desk that was completely taken up by the large computer screen. Three servers stood in a row along one of the short walls. Cords twisted every which way across the floor. Next to the desk stood a mannequin that he'd named Marilyn, who was wearing the red Mind Surf helmet on her head. Fifty thin wires in every possible colour covered the helmet like futuristic hair. Someone had suggested that he should submit Marilyn to the Spring Salon modern art competition at Liljevalchs.

It was structured chaos. At least, that's what Eric told Hanna. In truth, it was rather more of an unstructured chaos. Maybe it mirrored his own head — full of ideas and a million thoughts all at once. He liked it that way. The rest of the apartment was in perfect order: Hanna's order. But this was his domain, his last outpost. He thought about what Jens had suggested. A time-out. What would she think about something like that? If she said she thought it was a good idea, would that mean she wanted to get away from him? If she didn't like the idea, would that mean she was nervous about being away from each other? Nervous about what she would do? Or what he would do? Which was worse?

He stared at the screen before him. On it were the inner workings of Mind Surf: long lines of code. Somewhere among those millions of symbols, an error was hiding — an error that caused the system to freeze up every time it was put to the test. Maybe the problem wasn't with the program. What could they do to further modify the helmet and the gel? Could they make the sensors penetrate the scalp by another millimetre or two? Could they make the nanogel more conductive?

His mobile phone jumped in his pocket. It was a text: 'Stuck in an emergency meeting.' On a Friday night? 'Probably home in an hour.' He looked at the clock. Twenty past ten. He put the phone on the table with a sigh. Then he picked it up again and scrolled down to the bottom of the message. 'Kisses.' So maybe she wasn't *that* angry. He immediately felt his mood improve. He wrote an email to the Mind Surf group, which was scattered throughout Sweden and Japan, and described his successful meeting with Mats Hagström. Once the email was sent, he closed his eyes and enjoyed the music.

There was a bang from the door, and he squinted at the clock on the computer. It was a quarter past twelve. He must have fallen asleep. He heard Hanna's high heels and the jingling of her keys on the hall table. He sleepily got up and went out into the living room. She looked at him and smiled.

'*Shabbat Shalom*,' he said in a hoarse voice.

'*Shabbat Shalom*. God, you look a mess. You're taking your professorship too seriously. You don't have to look like Einstein to do research.'

He rolled his eyes and ran a hand through his hair. She seemed calm. He relaxed.

'What happened at work?'

'I got some information from Tel Aviv at lunch — a threat to the bank. It's been crazy.'

She gave him a quick kiss, and he held her to him. She smelled good, despite the long day.

'I need a shower. Why don't you get out some wine? And something to eat?'

'It's almost one o'clock.'

'I know. I'm sorry. But let's eat anyway. It must be dinnertime somewhere in the world. And I want to hear how things went at your investor meeting.' She shouted this last bit from the bathroom.

He went to the kitchen and took out the sushi. In the fridge, he found an open Chablis that was still drinkable. He lit the candles and poured the wine. The bread was still lying under a towel. After a while, he heard Frank Sinatra's 'I've Got You Under My Skin' on the stereo. Hanna came in wearing a towel like a turban, with her bathrobe open. When she saw his expression, she pulled her robe around her and tied the belt.

'Oh no you don't. Let's eat. I'm starving.'

She sat down across from him. Though she was trying to be cheerful, he could see that she was tired, maybe more mentally than physically. He could see it in her eyes, in the wrinkles around them. She watched him as he looked at her. He smiled and broke a piece of bread off for her.

'How are you?'

She took the bread and ate it in silence.

'What do you think? I've had a lot of crappy nights, and today was a crappy day. How are you?'

'Something along those lines. But, actually, today was not a crappy day. I got Mats Hagström.'

She lit up.

'Congratulations! That's great for you.'

He frowned.

'What do you mean by "for you"?'

'Just what I said. It's great for you.'

'It *is* great for me. But also for you. We need two incomes.'

She didn't speak for a moment. Then she raised her glass.

'You're right. Cheers to Mind Surf. How is the program itself going?'

'I can't quite get it to work. It works with the keyboard, but when I try to guide it neurally it freezes up.'

She stuck a piece of salmon in her mouth.

'Maybe the program isn't the problem. Maybe it's a hardware issue. With the helmet. Or the gel?'

He nodded.

'It could be. I'm working my way through all conceivable alternatives, and inconceivable ones, too. I'm a stubborn bastard, as you know, so it will probably work itself out.'

She took a large sip of wine and ate another piece of salmon. She always ate sushi with her hands. He used chopsticks.

'What's this threat against the bank? Is it specifically directed at the Stockholm offices? You don't have any cash there, do you?'

She wiped her fingers with the napkin.

'There's a risk we'll be hacked — some sort of virus attack. Tel Aviv believes that a group with links to Hezbollah is planning something. That's all we know. The main office is working to find out more. As the local director of IT, I have to audit our security and upgrade the firewalls. The same thing is happening at each office around the world. My whole gang is still on the job. I could have stayed there all night.'

'I'm glad you came home. The virus can wait. And your co-workers are capable. Let them work so you can come in and take the credit tomorrow morning, fresh and well-rested.'

Hanna ran her finger along the edge of her wine glass.

'What I've told you is extremely confidential. I can't ... I didn't say anything to you. You know nothing. Imagine if it leaked out to our clients? Their trust is our most important asset.'

Eric stood up and walked around the table. He stood behind her and removed the towel she had wrapped around her hair. The wet strands fell down over the back of her neck. She bent her head forward, and he massaged her shoulders.

'Of course. Trust is TBI's most important asset. And it's the same here at home. We have to trust one another. You have to trust me.'

He felt her stiffen.

'What do you mean?'

He kept massaging her.

'I mean that I don't want to lose you. I want to grow with you, develop with you, and grow old with you. Build a long life. Build a family. You don't need to be afraid of the future. I believe in it completely. In us.' He realised that he was doing the exact opposite of what Jens had suggested. That what he was saying was just continuing to move forward without any real change.

She pulled away from him, but remained in her chair.

'You haven't seen me the past few years. You haven't listened to me. You haven't been ... present. And now that I've had enough, you're trying to make up for ten years of zombie love all at once. In bed. In the kitchen. You have to earn me, Eric. For real. I'm tired of pushing our relationship forward. I'm tired of us. Of you.'

He felt angry and hurt at the same time. He remained standing behind her, awkward. His body felt heavy, as though the earth's gravity had increased. Hanna hunched her shoulders. She was going to start crying. He lowered his voice, uncertain of whether he should touch her.

'You're right. I've been out of it —a narcissistic pig. And I've taken you for granted. I'm sorry. If you only knew. I had this idea that I had to be successful. That you thought it was as important as I did.'

He ran his hand through her wet hair.

'But now ... I understand what you mean to me. So much. I just can't lose you. Call it a second chance.'

She stood and picked up her wine glass.

'You've had chance after chance. You have to do something concrete. Your words and your actions have to match. You talk and talk, but nothing happens. Enough with your babbling and your empty promises. I don't know if you can hear what you're saying, but to me it's always about your needs, your ideas. I don't want to be your fucking psychologist! You'll have to work hard if you're going to save this relationship.'

She went to the bedroom, and he followed her. He still felt uncertain. He wanted to take the initiative — say the right things, feel the right feelings. Halfway through the living room, she turned around with tears in her eyes.

'Don't think you can lock me up. And don't think that you'll solve anything by getting me pregnant. Got it?'

She held a finger up in warning.

'I am not ready for a child. And how could you take care of a child when you can't even take care of yourself? Or me?'

He took a step toward her. He didn't want to become angry. He knew that was wrong. But he couldn't help it.

'Oh, give it up. Do you hear me? *Give it up!* I'm tired of all your bullshit about kids. You and I both know what the problem is, don't we? You're afraid. Afraid of taking responsibility. Afraid of becoming ugly. Afraid of pregnancy. Afraid of the delivery. Afraid of being dependent! Afraid of being left. *Afraid!*'

He was shouting, even though she was less than a metre away from him.

'Well, okay, Hanna, but don't spew your fucking anxiety all over me!'

It came out of him all in a long and far-too-loud rush, a roaring torrent of black water that washed over her. She stood there in silence, looking at him, looking deep into his eyes, as though she were searching for something deep inside them. Her cheeks were wet and her arms hung loosely. She was still holding onto her glass. Time stood still. He was so sorry that it hurt. He wanted to take back every word. But instead the words hung between them with a thundering resonance, bouncing back and forth. She was so small, so fragile. He saw her just as she was. He wanted to embrace her. Kiss her.

She silently turned around and went into the bedroom. She

turned off the light and closed the door carefully behind her. He stood alone in the dark. Him and Sinatra.

Jerusalem, Israel

It was Sunday, and the weekly meeting of the cabinet had just ended. The select four had gone straight to Ben Shavit's home, Beit Aghion, in Rehavia. The grey villa was idyllically situated at the intersection of Balfour and Smolenskin, with a view over the old city in Jerusalem. The neighbourhood of Rehavia had been patterned after garden cities in Europe, with parks that flowered in fantastic colour. There was an exclusive tranquillity throughout the whole area. A dog was barking somewhere; otherwise it was quiet. At the hastily called meeting were Mossad director Meir Pardo, minister of finance Yuval Yatom, minister of defence Ehud Peretz, and strategic adviser Akim Katz. Several of the men had been friends since their time in the army with Ben Shavit. They chose to sit in the shadows out on the terrace, where the mood was casual, and niceties had long since been done away with. A tall palm tree stretched its leaves over the terrace floor. A short assistant in a yarmulke was serving fresh mint tea, while Ben sat heavily in one of the rattan chairs, twisting his wedding ring in a sign of impatience. He turned to the minister of finance, who was also the godfather of his fifth child.

'Yuval, what's bullshit and what should we take seriously?'

Yuval stirred his tea thoughtfully. He was the oldest of them, and he was always calm. Nothing seemed to upset him. During his own most impatient moments, Ben found his slow ways annoying. But he knew that there was intense mental activity going on behind that quiet façade.

'Thus far it could all be bullshit, but we can't afford to take any risks. It's been a long time since we kept bars of gold and bundles of money in our bank safes. Today, our safes have been transformed into servers, and our gold to ones and zeros. Everything is digital. Our security is very sophisticated — no doubt the best in the world. But if we're talking about a well-planned, well-financed attack, we have to assume that our current protection isn't enough. Like we've always said, Ben, 'Hope for the best, but plan for the worst.' That's the correct strategy this time, too. If the virus were to knock out our systems, it would hurt us, but it wouldn't be a catastrophe. We would lose some data, but we can deal with that. After we got up and started over, we would be up and running again. But ...'

Yuval took a sip of tea. Ben twisted his ring.

'... if what we encounter instead is a more intellectual, more sophisticated virus, the consequences could be devastating.'

Akim took off his sunglasses and placed them on the table in front of him. He cleared his throat and looked at Yuval, who was stirring his tea again.

'What do you mean by a "sophisticated virus"?'

Everyone looked at Yuval. Everyone but minister of defence Ehud, who, like Amos Dagan in military intelligence, thought that this was all nonsense compared to the threat of a nuclear-capable Iran or the presence of Russian rockets in Gaza. Yuval drained his cup of tea and looked at his colleagues around the low wooden table.

'A sophisticated virus wouldn't shut down our systems. Quite the opposite — it would want to keep them going. It could manipulate and change data. It could make erroneous transfers between accounts, erase loan information, and manipulate rates on the stock exchange. Some people or businesses might suddenly appear to be debt-free, while others might see their accounts weighed down with Israel's fiscal deficit. We are completely dependent on these systems, day and night. So we can't shut them down, even if we know that they've been infected. We also don't know when the virus will enter the system, or if it's already there, which means that it can passively tag along during backups. We don't know what or who will activate it. Our analysts have done simulations of a number of scenarios, each one more hair-raising than the next. A full-scale attack — if it were successful — could undermine our entire stability as a nation. Retirement accounts, loan payments, credit-card systems, stock-exchange transactions, interest rates … everything could crash.'

In the silence that descended around the table, they could hear the dog barking in the distance. A woman across the street called for her child. Ben looked at his strategic adviser.

'What do you have to say about this mess?'

Akim rested his chin on his hands, which were folded as if in prayer.

'I agree that this threat must be taken seriously. We have reliable sources. But we know too little. We don't know why, how, or who.' He nodded at Meir.

'The Mossad has put together a large team to get more information. They're usually successful, so we will surely know more soon. But we don't know how much time we have, so we need to act now. How, I don't really know. Unfortunately, IT is not my strong point.'

Meir stood up with difficulty, walked over to the rail of the terrace, and made eye contact with one of the security guards on the street. He took out his pipe, filled it carefully, and lit it. Then he took a puff and looked at Yuval.

'We've given this the highest priority. We'll find out more information. But I don't think we can wait. We should initiate a backup — protect everything that's possible to protect. We'll just have to take the risk that the virus might sneak in along with the backup. We should also beef up our firewalls. We have to build a new wall — a digital one this time.'

He fell silent for a moment. Then he looked at Ben.

'Another thing I've thought of involves TBI. Our sources indicate that they will be hit first. One way to protect us might be to minimise the contact between TBI's systems and the rest of our networks.'

Yuval shook his head.

'That's not possible, unless we're prepared to send TBI into bankruptcy. They're one of our three largest banks, and they're the foremost creditor in the business world. In addition, they have hundreds of thousands of private clients, maybe even up to a million. If they can't communicate with external banking, stock, and payment systems, they might as well give up. And that is just not an option.'

Meir nodded.

'That may be so. But that would be better than the whole country giving up.'

Ben didn't need to think for long.

'We can't sink TBI based solely on a rumour. What if we were wrong? And by the time it was confirmed, we might already be infected. No, I'm leaning more toward the backup idea. I realise it will be expensive — and we risk raising a lot of questions. But an extra backup copy of sensitive data ought to be started right away, nationally. If nothing else, it will give us a cheat sheet for what everything looks like before it starts to break down.'

Yuval was staring down at the table, and answered without looking up.

'It's going to take a gigantic amount of resources, if it's even possible. Especially since we don't know what has to be copied.

And, like you say, it's going to raise a lot of questions. I think we can all agree that this absolutely shouldn't get out. That would be almost as devastating as the virus itself — the financial system is based on trust. Let's wait a few days before we decide to do the backup. Maybe we'll get a better picture of what we're up against. And then we'll be able to better define our resources.'

Ben stood up.

'Gentlemen, let's get something to eat. We'll continue this discussion inside.'

Of the five men on the terrace, only one of them knew what truly awaited the country. He stood up along with the others. On the way into the house, Ben placed his arm around his shoulders.

'My friend, I'm too old for this internet stuff. I have an iPhone I can't even turn on. I like enemies I can see. Ones I can touch. Not these clever hidden ones and zeroes.'

Sinon nodded.

'I feel the same, Ben. But I think we have to get used to it.'

Nice, France

Pierre Balzac had died instantly. Shot in the head at close range, he had ended up on the stairs. The same neighbour who had first called the *police municipale* had called again about the gunshot. Sergeant Laurent Mutz had never met Pierre Balzac, but he was still upset about his colleague's death. The local police were almost never armed, so Pierre hadn't had a chance.

There were sirens in the distance, and they were almost entirely drowned out by the loudly revving engine. The van veered sharply, and Laurent grabbed the handle on the ceiling. In his other hand he held his SG 551, the lightweight assault rifle that was standard issue for the GIPN, Groupes d'Intervention de la Police Nationale, the French national task force. Today, his SG 551 was loaded with thirty of the new SS190 bullets, controversial ammunition that could penetrate Kevlar and leave an exit wound four inches in diameter. As usual, Laurent — like his colleagues in the van — was dressed in a dark-blue jumpsuit, black gloves and boots, a black bulletproof vest, a black facemask, a headset, and a helmet with a visor. He carried a gas mask at his belt, just behind his FN Five-Seven pistol. Two stun grenades were clipped at his hip.

Laurent had been having bad luck during the past few weeks. The dogs he'd bet on had all lost — exactly the opposite of what the so-called experts had said would happen. He'd borrowed more money to win back what he'd lost, but it had all fallen apart. Michelle didn't know any of this; she thought their savings were still in their family account, but they were all gone … and just in time for her to think up a dream vacation for them. The down payment should have been made already. He tried to shake off his anxiety, and tightened his grip on his weapon. He had to concentrate on the present.

Across from him sat Rafael Monor. He had a big bolt cutter on his belt, and a pump-action shotgun lay across his lap. Rafael looked at him and grinned.

'Do you think he's still there?'

Laurent shrugged.

'No idea. I wouldn't be, if I were him. Who the hell wants to run into us?'

'If he's still there, he'll have to stand damned still when I step through the door.'

The building façades of Nice rushed past outside the barred windows of the van, and they could glimpse the sea between the buildings. Laurent looked at his watch. It was a quarter past three. Nineteen minutes had passed since the call came in. Would they be fast enough? He went back over what he knew. At seven minutes past two, a female tenant at Avenue du Maréchal Foch 3 had called in a disturbance. According to the woman who called, there were new occupants in the apartment across the hall, which was owned by a Greek shipping company. The new tenants — who, according to the woman, appeared to be of Arab descent — never seemed to sleep. The lights were on in the apartment day and night, and they made noise all night long. Today, after lunch, the woman had heard a sharp bang from the apartment, and when she opened her door there was an odour of burning in the stairwell. She became worried and called the police.

Constable Pierre Balzac had had the misfortune of being on patrol nearby. He answered the call and went to the apartment building to see what was going on. He rang at the new neighbours' door after the woman directed him to it, and it was opened after a number of rings. Something had been said, but the woman was unable to repeat it. Then Balzac was shot by the man who opened the door. The woman, who had seen all of this through her peephole, was shocked, but managed to call the police again. This time, the call was forwarded to the GIPN. The area had been cordoned off by the local police, and no one had entered or left the building since the shot was fired. At least that's what they said on the radio.

The van made a sharp turn, and he was thrown against Louis Menard's rock-hard right arm. His colleague caught his automatic rifle, which he'd dropped as he was tossed around. Laurent shook his head and looked out the window. They passed several police cars and an ambulance.

'We're here.'

Everyone straightened up and checked their headsets. The van stopped short, and Louis stood and threw open the door.

They hopped out and arranged themselves on the street just in time to meet the second black van, which braked in a rain of gravel. Major Serge stepped out and approached the waiting GIPN group.

'Okay. The perpetrator, or perpetrators, are presumed to still be inside the apartment. Monor will take the lead and force the door when he gets the go-ahead. Secure the place with tear gas. Monor, Menard, and Mutz will make up the first wave. Martin, Dubois, and Benoit will follow as backup and get into position in the stairwell. Durocher, Leroux, and Thomas will get into position at the sides and front of the building, and make sure that not a single rat gets out.'

All of them nodded, and Laurent followed his two colleagues across the street at a run. A large number of people had gathered around the cordons. He took the safety off his weapon and ducked into the stairwell. Their target was two floors up. They advanced with weapons drawn, in a well-trained pattern. Number one advanced under cover of numbers two and three. One took up a new position, and two and three caught up. Two continued to another position ahead, and they continued to overtake each other. Always forward. Always covered.

As they came to the first floor, they saw blood on the stairs. They cautiously continued on up. From outside they could hear more approaching sirens and the sound of at least one helicopter in the air. The radio crackled, and Major Serge asked for their position. Laurent responded and then quickly stuck his head out into the landing. The first thing he saw was Pierre Balzac. Laurent proceeded toward the body. The shot must have come from a small-calibre pistol — maybe a .22 — that had left a small entry wound just above the left eye. Pierre Balzac had a surprised expression on his face. The stone tiles under his head were covered in blood, and he was clutching a notebook in one hand.

They stepped carefully past the body and got into position around the closed door. Laurent cast a glance toward the other door and wondered if the woman was still standing there, looking through her peephole. It would have been better than TV. He turned his attention back toward their target. On the door was a brass plate that said 'Thessaloniki Marin Transfer.'

Rafael put down his shotgun and inspected the hinges with his hands. He gave a thumbs-up and fished a small electric saw out of the black bag at his hip. After that, he stood next to the door, his stance wide, and looked at the others. Louis pointed at one of his tear-gas canisters with two fingers. The others nodded, sank into crouches, and pulled on their gas masks. Rafael stood up and got ready, placing the saw against the hinge. Laurent nodded and got the door in his sights. The saw started up and cut through the steel with a deafening howl. When the second hinge detached, Rafael grabbed the doorknob and yanked the door loose; it fell heavily to the stairs. At the same time, Louis took a step forward and threw two canisters of tear gas through the opening, one after another. The whitish smoke hissed out into the stairwell as Laurent stepped into the smoky apartment, followed closely by Louis and Rafael. The other team got into position just behind them. The noise from the helicopters filled the apartment.

Laurent walked forward carefully, his automatic rifle raised. He pushed open a door with his foot. The kitchen table was covered in empty cartons of Chinese take-away. On the floor were Coke cans, pizza boxes, and bottles of water. The window was open out to the street. There was a teapot on the stove. He walked slowly through the room. A glass bottle clattered loudly against the stone floor. His headset crackled. It was Rafael.

'Bedroom secured.'

He kept going. He heard Louis's voice.

'Living room secured.'

He pressed the button.

'Kitchen secured.'

When he came out of the kitchen, he ended up in a servants' hallway with flowery pink wallpaper. On the floor lay an issue of *Le Monde*. Rafael stepped out ahead of him. Louis joined him, and they walked toward the closed door at the far end of the long hallway. Laurent stopped and signalled to the others to take off their masks. Not much of the tear gas had reached this part of the apartment, and their masks were unwieldy, limiting their sight. As he took off his mask, he smelled the pungent odour of burned plastic. It lay like a stifling blanket over the hallway, and mixed with the smell of tear gas, dust, and leather. Rafael reached the door first and waited for the others. Behind him he heard the back-up team's calls as they secured the rest of the apartment. Rafael carefully tested the door. It was locked. He gripped his shotgun in both hands and kicked. The lock broke, and the door flew open in a shower of splinters.

Before him he saw a large room — a library. The walls were covered in bookshelves. In the middle of the room was a set of grey furniture. The heavy curtains at the large windows were drawn, which gave the room a dim light.

Laurent thought once again of the dog races. His mistake had been that he was too uncertain. He listened too much to other people, instead of listening to his intuition. He could have sworn that Island Storm would win. There were very good reasons to think so — his fantastic track record, his pedigree, the test runs earlier that day. And then, when Napoleon Victory crossed the finish line, Laurent had just stood there hollowly. Everything was gone.

Louis gave a start: 'Police! Down on the floor!' Only then did Laurent notice a figure sitting at a desk at the far end of the room, like a ghost in the dim light. It was a man, with his back to them, and he was typing at a computer. There was a pistol on the desk beside him. All three raised their weapons while moving toward him. Menard repeated his order: *'Lie down! Now!'* The man ignored them and kept typing. They were no more than three metres away from him when the man picked up the pistol and shot himself in the head. It all happened so fast that none of them had time to react. The man had acted with no hesitation whatsoever. His head was thrown to the side and he fell heavily from his chair.

Laurent, the first one to reach him, placed his foot on the hand that still held the pistol. The man's body was convulsing, but his eyes were already staring blankly down at the floor. Blood flowed rapidly from under his head. The man appeared to be an Arab, about forty years old, of average build, wearing a burgundy shirt and worn jeans. He was barefoot, and his heels were dry. His body stopped shaking. Laurent pressed the button on his radio.

'Major Serge, over.' A brief silence, and then he heard Major Serge's clear voice.

'Serge here. Status?'

'Target down. Apartment secured.'

'Okay. We're coming.'

Laurent kicked the pistol out of the man's hand, in a routine measure. The man was dead, and would never use his pistol again. Laurent exhaled, dazed by what had just happened. He had been unfocused. Though he had worked on the task force for four years, this was the first time he had seen anyone shot at such close range.

He looked at the man on the floor. How could a person be so cold? He must have been sitting there working when Balzac rang at his door. He'd stood up, walked all the way to the front door, opened it, and shot the officer. After that he had returned to his seat and kept working, even when the door was forced open, the canisters of tear gas exploded, and heavily armed police stormed the apartment. And when he was done with his work … he'd shot himself without a second thought. It was so fucking morbid. Laurent looked around the room. On the table by the furniture, the local phone book was open to Chinese restaurants, alongside an unopened chocolate bar and a pack of Marlboro cigarettes. What the hell had the man been up to in here? He looked at the desk, and then at the computer. The white screen had become dotted with red. He leaned closer and caught sight of a small, animated symbol in the lower corner of the screen. A grey garbage can opened its lid and swallowed a file. The garbage can turned red and then grey again. Another file popped up and was swallowed by the garbage can, which turned red again. He realised what was happening — the computer was erasing its information! He tossed the chair aside and dove to the floor next to the dead body, shoving his way in under the desk. The man's hand crunched under his knee. He grimaced and searched for the cord, found the outlet, and tore out the plug.

Louis looked at him in surprise.

'What's the matter with you?'

Laurent crawled out from under the table, knelt, and squinted at the screen. The garbage can was still munching files. Had he pulled out the wrong cord? His eyes swept the desk and caught sight of a laptop with its lid closed. The screen and keyboard were connected to it. It was running on battery power. Just as he was about to lift the computer up to remove the battery, the garbage can turned green, and there was a faint 'ding' from the laptop in his hand. It had finished deleting.

His headset crackled.

'Boys, come over to the bathroom in the hallway.'

He picked up his automatic rifle and slung it across his back, and they turned back the same way they'd come. The door of the bathroom was open. Major Serge was standing outside it, talking on a mobile phone. When he saw them, he nodded at the open door. Laurent stepped into the small, tiled room. The whole bathtub was full of sooty, contorted computer equipment, and there was also something that might have been binders or folders. Only the binder rings and a few spines had survived the fire. A grey sludge covered the bottom of the bathtub, and the walls were scorched and sooty. There had been quite a fire in here — that was the smell which the woman next door had noticed. The technicians would have to work for many hours if they were to salvage anything of use. He backed out into the hallway. Major Serge was standing with his legs planted far apart, his arms crossed, right outside the door.

'I've spoken with Monor. In my opinion, you all handled it by the book. How are you doing?'

'It was pretty damn unpleasant, but I'll get over it. What kind of sick bastard was he?'

Serge looked at Laurent grimly and clapped him on the shoulder.

'I'm going to find out. From what we found in the bedroom, we know that at least two people lived here. Where the other one is, we don't know. We haven't found anything to identify them — no papers or legible documents. The only thing of any value, besides that soup in the bathtub, is an access card from a bank. TBI.'

Laurent frowned.

'Arabic?'

'Israeli, but don't worry about that. Go home and hug Michelle.'

Laurent smiled and nodded. He walked silently through the apartment, which was now full of activity. People were everywhere, taking photos, speaking into their radios, looking through books, and tearing through drawers of clothes. Big metal boxes of analytical tools were rolled in on a grey cart. He pushed his way through, nodded at those he knew, and made his way out into the stairwell again. Pierre Balzac's body was gone. Only the dark-red stain was still there. He saw prints from his own boots in the dried blood. The peephole on the other side was staring at him. It said 'Marie Scribé' on the nameplate.

His front pocket vibrated and he took out his phone. Michelle's number was blinking frantically. He swallowed and answered.

'*Allô?*'

'Is everything okay, Laurent?' His wife's anxious voice sounded distant and canned.

'Everything is fine, *ma chérie.*'

She exhaled in relief.

'I saw it on TV. Are you there?'

'I'm here. But it's over now.'

'Come home!'

'Of course. I just have to go by the station, but then I'll be home.'

'I'll run a bath for you. And Laurent …'

'What?'

'Have you had time to pay for our trip?'

He stared at the peephole, which stared back scornfully.

'No. I didn't have time today. Tomorrow.'

'Okay. *Au revoir.*'

He stood there with his phone in his hand. How the hell would he sort this out? How do you tell your beloved wife that you've bet away your family's whole savings? What a fucking idiot he was. He opened his breast pocket to put his phone back, but dropped it. The phone struck the marble floor hard, and the battery flew off down the stairs.

'*Merde!*'

He bent down to look for the battery, and found it against the edge of third step. As he picked it up, he caught sight of the notebook that also lay on the step — Pierre Balzac's notebook. It must have fallen down there when they picked up the body. How incredibly sloppy of the ambulance crew! He stuck it in his pocket along with the battery, and went down the stairs. What an afternoon. A bath was a hell of a good idea.

Stockholm, Sweden

Was it possible to overdose on caffeine? Eric was convinced it was not. In any case, he'd done his best to test the limits. The Nespresso machine in the kitchen was spitting out black ristrettos at high speed, which he was knocking back one after another. All this, to stay awake when the house was finally quiet and everyone was asleep, including the phones. He had placed two thick terrycloth towels over the machine so it wouldn't wake Hanna. There was a growl under the towels, and another shot was ready. He emptied the small silver cup in one gulp as he looked out of the window at the early-summer morning. There was not a car on the street, except for his Volvo. It was street-cleaning night. He'd completely forgotten — there was probably a ticket for nine hundred kronor on his windshield. He put down the cup and trotted back into his dark cave. It smelled stuffy and sweaty in there. He'd spent too many hours in too little space. As he sat down in front of his computer, his left hand twitched. This was quite natural, considering that his blood had been replaced with pure coffee.

He hadn't slept a wink in the past twenty-four hours. The

day had consisted of one failure and one success. The failure was that it was impossible to lengthen the sensor needles; in fact, the KTH team even wanted to shorten them. The success was that he had received a FedEx package from Kyoto University, which turned out to contain a new shipment of nanogel. The Japanese researchers had managed to increase the potency of the gel — both the absorption capability and the conductive capacity were several times stronger than they had been. Could this compensate for the short sensor needles? If the improved gel and the upgraded version of Mind Surf didn't work, he was out of options.

He looked at the small, white packet with Japanese symbols on it. Nanogel, version 2.0. It was time. There were still a few more steps to take, but the gel needed thirty minutes to be absorbed by the skin. He might as well put it on. He carefully opened the packet and squeezed a blob out into his hand. The liquid was cold and sparkled purple, as if it had its own energy source. The nanogel contained a substance from jellyfish, with a fluorescing glow that was bright in the dark office. Eric pulled back his hair and massaged the odourless gel in. When he was finished, he went back to doing a few final checks of the program. There was a stinging sensation as the substance began to penetrate his skin.

He went over to Marilyn and removed the sensor helmet. Its colourful hair ran in a long braid from the helmet to the computer. He checked that all fifty wires were properly attached to their respective sensor needles, and then he put on the helmet. It clung to his head like a swim cap, and burned as the sensors penetrated like acupuncture needles. He grimaced, sat down at the computer, and turned off all his control and troubleshooting programs. Then he started the program that controlled the contact between computer and brain. His index finger lingered over the Enter key for a moment. Click. His scalp tingled. Ten seconds passed. He held his breath.

CONTACT ESTABLISHED. RECEIVING NEURODATA.
SIGNAL STRENGTH 92%

He sat stock-still, looking at the blinking message. Ninety-two per cent — that was very good reception. Better than it had ever been. Then he went back to the menu and opened a diagram that showed the status of each individual sensor. All fifty sensors registered surprisingly strong signals. He started the program to surf three-dimensionally, and lowered the dark glasses that were attached to the front of the helmet. He could feel the sensors pricking him, and fumbled to find the screws that further tightened the needles. He gave it a few turns, and groaned with the pain. Vision was sensitive, and if something went wrong he could go blind.

His eyelids tingled. Mind Surf had established contact with the optic chiasm. He could no longer see anything, since the glasses were made of black-painted plastic. If everything worked, he wouldn't need eyes to see.

Eric extended his hand and felt his way across the keyboard until he found the Enter key. He swallowed. The sensation could be likened to the seconds before you scratch off a lottery ticket. Maybe you'll win; maybe not. The dream is alive as long as the ticket is hasn't been scraped.

He thought of the long journey to this day, of all the people who had been a part of it. Of Mats Hagström's money. Of Hanna. He saw her before him, standing in the half-darkness with a sad, searching gaze. He saw himself in the chair. What must he look like, sitting there with cords trailing from his head and the dark glasses on his face? He was the vision of a mad scientist. Was he crazy, or was he a genius? The answer was one digital command away. Either it worked and would be a success, or it didn't work and that was the end of the project — two polar-opposite outcomes. No, there was another possibility: he could go blind, or become brain-damaged. He knew there were risks with BCI. A spike in power or another form of unexpected change in voltage could burn up parts of the brain.

The helmet stung, and he felt jabbing pains in his head. There was a bang from the hallway. The morning papers had arrived. Best to get it over with. He took a deep breath.

Tel Aviv, Israel

David Yassur was fascinated by the coded telex that had been sent to the Mossad from the Israeli embassy in Paris. In this high-tech age, he couldn't believe that anyone still communicated via telex. He didn't even know that the Mossad had such a device. He made a mental note to find out where it was. The decoded copies, which were stapled to the original message, were alarming. The police in Nice had raided an apartment because of suspected terrorist activity within it. The suspicion of crime had led to a report being sent to DCRI, Direction Centrale du Renseignement Intérieur, the French internal intelligence authority. A suspected terrorist had been killed in the operation. This person had not yet been identified.

At the Mossad's request, the telex had been supplemented with an email containing a number of documents, including a photograph of the deceased terrorist. David looked at the black-and-white face, which had a small spot just over the right eye — the entry wound. This was no one he recognised. DCRI had determined that it was a case of computer crime, and had informed SCSSI, Service Central de la Sécurité des Systèmes d'Informations, the national IT security unit. An access card from TBI had been found during the operation, so SCSSI had informed the Israeli embassy. Fortunately, the person who received the warning had taken it seriously and had forwarded it to Tel Aviv. By telex.

He read the report again. In the apartment, they had found several burned computers and hard drives that were impossible to salvage. The dead terrorist had had a page from a notebook in his pocket, but there were no identifying documents. David leaned closer and studied the blurry copy of the notebook paper. It looked like hieroglyphs — probably a code. He looked through the list of seized articles, without finding a notebook. But the paper had to come from somewhere. The messy hieroglyphs were important, he was sure. He held the paper up to the light and tried turning it in different directions. Well, this was definitely the same gang that radio intelligence unit 8200 had reported on. He took Jacob Nachman's report from his worn leather briefcase. Nice and TBI were both mentioned. And, with that, Jacob's suspicions were confirmed. In addition to his boss, Meir Pardo, and the cabinet, he should inform Isaac Berns, TBI's director of IT. They had been in contact recently to discuss the bank's security. Now Berns would have to start going through each pixel in his French operation right away. He would have to determine whether anything had been stolen or damaged, and above all whether there was a virus in their system.

How would they identify the dead man? And where had the other person in the apartment gone? David looked at the photograph once again, mulling it over. Right now, it was the most important piece of the puzzle. If they could establish his identity, they could match it in their database, and with any luck link him to a known terror cell. David couldn't hold back a smile when he realised who he ought to call. He picked up his mobile phone and looked up a number he hadn't used in a very long time. It rang twice, and then came a familiar voice: 'Paul Clinton.'

'Shalom, Paul. David Yassur here. How is Evelyn?'

'You old putz. Are you calling after five years of silence to ask about my ex?'

David's smile broadened.

'You know I've always loved Evelyn. You've made a lot of mistakes, Paul — shooting JFK was one of them — but losing Eve was without a doubt the worst.'

Paul snorted into the phone.

'Go fuck yourself. What can the FBI do for an old combatant? Is it about the threat against TBI?'

David shook his head.

'That's supposed to be a state secret. But it sure is. I have some pictures and names I hope you can run through your fantastic databases: CIA, NSA, IRS, Disney World ... the whole lot.'

Paul was silent for a moment, weighing the risks. David held his breath.

'Sure. Every banana republic comes to big brother for help eventually.'

David ignored this comment.

'Does big brother happen to have a telex?'

'A what?'

'Forget it. You'll receive an email in a few minutes.'

Flight ET703, above Algeria

This time, Samir knew that he would never again return to France, the country that had been his homeland in his teens. When he was fifteen, his family had fled the civil war in Lebanon and sought asylum in France. Thanks to his father's resolve, the family had managed to get over the shock of moving to another country and adapt to their new world. His parents had maintained their Shia Muslim identities while simultaneously adapting to French daily life and, as far as possible, to French culture. For Samir's part, the move to France meant something important: unlimited access to computers.

He had always loved computers, but in Beirut his access had been limited and he'd had to sit at his father's law office, tapping at their old IBM. It was the only computer in the office, and his constant use of it annoyed the other lawyers. Sometimes his friends had popped up and invited him along for soccer, wrestling, or dancing. With time, these visits became more sporadic. Several of his friends became engaged or enlisted in the army. He had lived a different life, symbolically framed by the square monitor at the dusty law office. When he came to France, everything changed. The family was placed in a suburb of Toulouse, in a graffiti-covered concrete jungle. Everyday life must have been difficult for the others, but for him integration posed no problem. Quite the opposite. There were more computers in France — at school, at his parents' jobs, even in his friends' homes. Samir's talents developed quickly, and it wasn't long before his teachers noticed his talents. When he turned twenty-one he received a scholarship that allowed him to go to the US and study at MIT, the world's foremost technical school. His father called the law office in Beirut and bellowed that their little freeloader was on his way to becoming the next Bill Gates.

MIT extended his year at the school to a full Master's degree in computer programming. After that, he was offered the opportunity to have his Ph.D. studies paid for if he taught as well. He met Nadim just after that at a wedding in Beirut. They stayed in the U.S. for almost ten years. His doctoral dissertation ended up being about computer viruses, and the more he studied the subject, the more interesting it became. Three years later, he was an expert in the field. But all of this was before the catastrophe.

Samir sleepily looked up at the dark-skinned flight attendant. She had asked him something.

'What?'

'Would you like a glass of champagne?' She smiled and held out a glass. He shook his head and asked instead for an extra blanket. He was always cold on planes.

It was almost empty in business class — just a few passengers reading, watching TV, or having quiet conversations. There was an air of calm in the cabin. France was already many hours behind him. He had been planning to stay considerably longer. The others had left several days ago, but he had stayed, along with Melah as-Dullah, to make the last preparations before Mona was activated. Samir liked to be alone when he worked, and the apartment had been full of activity toward the end. He was sure that Ahmad Waizy had left Melah there more as a guard than as an assistant for him. Samir was now the property of Hezbollah, and couldn't be left alone. They had a great deal invested in him. Melah had been quiet and discreet. But, as with Ahmad, there was something snakelike about him.

The apartment they had rented was a nice one. It was close to the beach, yet still in the middle of the city. They could come and go unnoticed, without attracting attention — at least, that's what they had thought. It turned out that it was sheer luck he wasn't sitting at the police station right now. Or dead. He had been out buying newspapers on Promenade des Anglais when he'd seen the police cars and cordons outside his building. Heart pounding, he had kept walking, and fumbled out a text message to Ahmad.

After his encounter with the police force, he had wandered around on back streets and through alleys, jostling with tourists and tripping over baby carriages, menu boards, and street musicians. Somehow, he had finally found his way to Galeries Lafayette. He needed clothes. All he had were the ones he was wearing: a pair of worn jeans, sandals, and a faded red T-shirt that said *'Nice dans mon coeur.'* — 'Nice in my heart.' He had a credit card and passport on him. Ahmad's orders had been clear: do not go anywhere without your phone, credit card, and passport. But would the credit card work? Was his identity known to the police? Time and time again he had looked at his phone, waiting for an answer from Ahmad. Where would he run? He chose clothes at Lafayette that were as neutral as possible — two pairs of pants and a few pullovers and polo shirts. Were they already circulating pictures of him? Would they be watching the airports? He cursed himself for not having been more careful. He'd left a heap of scrapped computers in the bathtub. The most important thing was that the hard drives couldn't be salvaged; he had made sure of that himself.

The text that arrived as he was on his way out of the department store contained a transfer destination, a time, a flight number, and a final destination. He was going to Somaliland. *Oh, God.* He had never been to Africa. Why there? Wasn't there a civil war there? He needed a fast and stable internet connection. Was there such a thing in Somaliland?

Of course, Ahmad had thought of this. It would all work out. The Israelis already knew about parts of the operation; Sinon kept Ahmad updated on everything that went on in the cabinet and in the Knesset. After the chaos in Nice, they had to split up the group. Caution was the key to success. They had been spread out all over the world, so Samir had no idea where the others were. Maybe the Mossad already had his name. And maybe Melah had been imprisoned in Nice. How much did Melah really know? Would he talk?

Ahmad had booked Samir to Rome on Alitalia, and from there to Ethiopia on Ethiopian Airlines. Once he got to Addis Ababa, he would transfer to a smaller airline and fly east to Berbera in Somaliland. He had no idea what awaited him there — a fast internet connection, with any luck.

The night was dark outside the oval window. *It is he who makes the stars for you, that you may guide yourselves, with their help, through the dark spaces of land and sea.* Allah is wise and does nothing without a purpose. But what was Allah thinking when he took back such a little servant? So suddenly? Samir hadn't had the chance to close her eyes or kiss her cheeks. He struggled to retain the memory of her. He could see her before him, but realised in despair that it was the same image as in the only picture he had left, the black-and-white picture where she was riding a camel. He would have done anything for a better picture of her, in colour. Now he remembered her in black and white — the copy, not the original. A short quote popped into his head: *'Ceci n'est pas une pipe.'* — 'This is not a pipe.' There was no pipe — just Magritte's image, two-dimensional and static. It was the same with Mona. *Ceci n'est pas une fille.* How had she smelled? What had her laugh sounded like? He was losing vital details.

Hezbollah had contacted him shortly after he and Nadim had moved back to Lebanon. They had tried to convince him to create a virus. Samir had said no. He had friends in Israel, and the war was something abstract and unreal to him. Through his work with Banque du Liban, he instead had the opportunity to create stability through the country's own banking system —

something that suited him better. He was no soldier. But that was then; now he was part of them. Above all, he was not part of anything else. *Whatever good you send forth for your souls before you, you shall find it with Allah: for Allah sees well what you do.* Allah knew what Mona looked like. She would get her smile back. But before he went to his women, he would avenge them.

Samir tried to find a reasonably comfortable position in the airplane seat. The thought of revenge gave him no satisfaction. Somewhere inside he knew that it was not what Nadim would have wanted. But he had made a promise to his murdered daughter. What could be more holy? *Qisas*. Revenge. Life for life. By now, the cabin was quiet, except for the rush from the air conditioning and the distant roar of the engines. He browsed through the playlist on his iPod, found Satie, lowered the volume, and let himself be enveloped in *Lent et douloureux*. He missed his little girl terribly.

Stockholm, Sweden

The world exploded around him. Or within him. Fireworks in sparkling colours detonated in the dense darkness, tossing him forward, headlong. Thousands of square meteorites flew around him, through him. He was falling through a gigantic kaleidoscope. There was no sound, no wind. The meteorites had colourful patterns, which seemed somehow familiar. He fought to regain control. He had to slow himself down. He focused on breathing. In and out. In and out. He fell, but more slowly, floating through a sparkling universe. He realised that these weren't meteorites. They were websites. The familiar patterns were graphics on websites. He recognised the start pages of *Aftonbladet*, KTH, MIT, and iTunes. The internet. He floated on through a silent, immense, endless internet. Unchecked laughter filled him, and he happily stretched out his hands to grab the passing sites. His hands fumbled in the air, empty, as he sat there in his office with the hair trailing from the helmet, and his face almost completely hidden by the black glasses. It took some time to understand how to navigate, but gradually he figured it out. He caught sites, popped into sub-pages, minimised banners, and browsed through links — all with the power of his thoughts. He tried to move the finger to the address bar at the top of the hitta.se search engine. The field turned blue. He thought of di.se, the Dagens Industri site, and watched in amazement as the address came up in the active field. The page turned pink, and that day's paper blossomed before him. As usual, Investor was complaining about price-to-book ratios. He laughed and sent the site away in order to dive down into KTH's homepage, which was floating beneath him. He was becoming more nimble, getting better and better at Mind Surfing. A spot of purple gel glowed next to the keyboard in the otherwise dark room.

Berbera, Somaliland

Above ground it was nearly fifty degrees, but where he sat, ten metres underground, it was considerably cooler. Samir was trying to concentrate on Mona's receptivity protection, but he couldn't stop sneaking glances at the scorpion that was slowly walking across the enormous cement floor. The dry, stuffy air brought with it a stench that was nearly unbearable. He needed to get some fresh air. He stood up, stiff after many hours in the same position. The scrape of the chair echoed through the empty room. The ceiling was over seven metres high. He walked through the room and came to a long corridor that was also made entirely of concrete. In one corner lay old beer cans and rags. Here the air was full of exhaust from the old diesel generator that hummed in one of the storage cabinets. It generated enough electricity to illuminate the corridor, the work area, and the smaller room where he slept for a few hours every day. Most importantly, it provided power for the computer.

He approached a steel ladder at the end of the corridor. The sign on the wall was in Russian. He began the climb upward, which he found difficult — it had been a long time since he was in shape. He was thin and gaunt, with matted hair and an unkempt beard, but his shell was unimportant. The ladder led him to ground level. He surfaced into a small concrete structure where the sun shone in through broken windows. He stepped over the shards of glass on the floor, and opened the rusty steel door. The heat and the light were like a punch in the face, and at first he couldn't see anything. He was standing near the middle of a long, straight road. On the other side were several low, concrete buildings, and a narrow track ran along the road. The area was an old Soviet missile base — a footprint from the Cold War. The Soviet navy had kept its missiles here. Now, thirty-five years later, the base was nothing more than a deserted concrete grave. The missiles were gone, just like the Soviet Union. The area was blocked off by a rusty barbed-wire fence. The only thing that might have suggested the place was back in use was a satellite dish on the roof of the radar building. But no one would notice something like that. They had used an old dish that looked like just another worn-out Soviet relic.

Momba Siad Barre drowsily raised a hand at him from the other side of the road. He and the other Somalis were sitting in the shadow beside the small guardhouse. Their job was to keep unwelcome visitors away. The risk of receiving any visitors, however, was small. Momba seemed to be some sort of local bandit, large and muscular, and almost completely toothless. He had explained in poor English that he was one of the pirates who took freighters hostage off the coast of Somalia. The Somalis were all armed with old Russian AK-47s, and wore cartridge belts crossed over their bare, sunken chests. The whole scene gave a theatrical impression.

Samir had never experienced this kind of heat. The temperature here varied between five degrees below Celsius and fifty above. He was tired. The long journey from Nice had been uneventful, save for landing in Berbera, which had been a near-death experience. Momba had been waiting for him in the baggage-claim area, and had silently driven him to the missile base. There he found a new computer, powerful generators, and the satellite dish. All of this conveyed a silent message from Ahmad Waizy: complete your task; finish the virus.

Samir walked along the wall and followed the rails where the missile carriers had once rolled. The ground was dusty and cracked, and there was nothing green in the vicinity. Maybe it hadn't always been like this. The base was near the ocean. Maybe the landscape had once been fertile, but the sun was relentless, burning and parching everything. His clothes still carried the stench from the bunker. He hadn't bathed in several days, so he was surely contributing to the smell himself.

He rounded the farthest buildings and turned back. He could see Momba following him with his eyes, and happened to think of Melah as-Dullah in Nice. The same question arose here as it had there. Was Momba here to protect him or guard him?

Mona's resistance protection was giving him trouble, and Samir couldn't find his notebook from Nice. It contained information he needed.

When he returned to the building that hid the ladder to the cave underneath, he stopped to piss. As he watched his urine splashing against the speckled concrete wall, he thought about his body, surprised that it still worked so well. It was impressive. He had almost completely stopped obeying its needs. It was as though his own body were mocking him by continuing to function. His heart, stubbornly pumping blood through his body, was disloyal. His lungs, expanding and contracting at the same rhythmic pace instead of collapsing, were betraying him. Before, in his old life, he had often worried about how fragile the human body was. As he had lain awake listening to Mona's faint breaths, he had been filled with helpless anxiety over her vulnerability. He had been careful about what she ate, her exercise, her sleep. But now, when he was doing everything he could to break down his biological machinery, it seemed to be unbreakable.

He went back in through the rusty door and climbed down into the dark shaft. On his way back, he went by the corner where he slept and dug out a chocolate bar. Maybe he was hungry, or else he was feeling guilty, after all, about how he had treated his body. Standing before the computer once again, he carefully checked to make sure there were no scorpions under the table, on the chair, or in the vicinity of his work area. The whole complex was crawling with them.

He picked up his iPod and selected Wagner's *The Flying Dutchman*. Why didn't the resistance protection activate? Now that Mona was practically finished, it was difficult to make adjustments. The drivers were encapsulated to make it more difficult for anti-virus software to discover the attack. He scrolled through the endless code, with Wagner's music accompanying the symbols that flowed across the screen in hypnotic patterns. Suddenly, he stopped and zoomed in on a sequence. Then he leaned even closer to the screen and ran his fingers along a series of symbols. There it was! It was a careless mistake, pure and simple. He leaned back, stared up at the ceiling in frustration, and sighed. There was no point in cursing himself. After all, this was good. He had found the error — the needle in the haystack. Sure, it was pure chance that he had found it, but still. He went into the incorrect string of code and switched the final digits around.

Mona was finished. He chewed his chocolate slowly, and reflected upon his work. Many months of toiling were over. Now all that was left was to upload the worm into TBI's network. This would be simple, thanks to the files he had copied in Nice. Once it was inside the bank's system, the worm would replicate and, like a living thing, spread into all the linked networks. Then, when the time was right, he would activate the virus manually via the internet.

He threw the chocolate wrapper on the floor and wiped his fingers on his pants. Then he got on the internet and opened the file server. There were the TBI files with information about the bank's firewalls and current virus protection. It took him ten minutes to break through the firewall and inject the worm. After sending a short message to Ahmad, he shut down the computer. Silence filled the large room as the fan stopped turning.

The stench from the sewer became too much again, and he went back up the ladder. The sun was lower in the sky, and the air was cooler. The gang was still sitting beside the guardhouse. He walked over to them and nodded to Momba.

'*C'est fini* … Finished.'

Momba smiled. 'Good. Good.'

One of the men offered him a Pepsi, but he shook his head.

'I'm going down to the ocean.'

Momba looked hesitant at first, but then smiled his toothless grin.

'I come.'

Samir nodded and started walking toward the fence. Momba followed just behind him. Once they were out on the road, he caught up and together they walked down to the water. The ground was full of holes and cracks. There were plastic bags, plastic bottles, and other trash everywhere. Mopeds, dented cars, and rusty bicycles passed them constantly. The houses along the road were white with red roofs. Colourful clothes were hung out to dry, and he could see clusters of children playing soccer or jumping rope. Dark-brown telephone poles ran down to the water. The slack lines reached all the way to the ground. It was nearly dusk. Scents of the sea, fish, wood fires, grilled meat, and exhaust filled the air.

There was something here in Berbera that spoke to him — something that made its way into his parched soul. He wasn't sure what it was, but somehow this place gave him hope. The hopeless gives the hopeless man hope.

Momba hummed to himself. Passers-by averted their eyes. He was still carrying the AK-47 on his back. The road turned off toward the harbour, and the beach lay before them. The sand was greyish-brown and coarse. Samir took off his sandals and wandered down to the water, which rolled in with a constant rumble. One hundred and fifty metres out in the water, like a stranded whale, was a large tanker — a giant cadaver with a broken back. Momba pointed at the tanker.

'Bombs. In the war.'

Samir nodded. The sand was damp and cool. Darkness was falling fast. Families were lighting fires along the beach. Perhaps Momba sensed that Samir wanted to be alone, because he left him and walked over to some older men who were standing in a group, having a loud conversation. They hugged him warmly. Samir sat down in the sand and looked out across the ocean. His eyes followed the black horizon far beyond the shipwreck.

The port to the Red Sea. It was almost completely dark now. He couldn't see the waves anymore, but he could hear the swell hissing onto the shore, and he could just see the white foam.

The first phase was over, and he had taken another step closer to the end. There were still important tasks to be completed. The group would gather again in anticipation of the next stage. Besides one brief instruction from Ahmad, he hadn't heard anything from them. The next stage would involve martyrs. Suicide bombers.

The night surrounded him with a fantastic sky full of shimmering stars. It was reflected in the black water, and there in the sand he no longer knew which way was up. He was floating through the universe like Laika the dog, a small piece in someone else's puzzle, tumbling through the night toward a lonely end. The dog had orbited its world 2,500 times before the capsule was destroyed by the atmosphere. Samir lay still on his back under — or above — the enormous curtain with its sparkling holes. Tomorrow he would leave Somaliland.

Jerusalem, Israel

Sinon sneaked a glance at his watch. He was in top shape today. If he could keep up this pace, he would break his personal record. He stood up on the bike, worked the gears, and pulled the Bianchi back and forth so he wouldn't lose speed on the steep incline. The carbon-composite bike had been specially built just for him, and it only weighed six-and-a-half kilos. He biked his circuit every day, sometimes twice in one day. The winding Ruba el-Adawiya brought him up to the crown of the Mount of Olives on the outskirts of the holy city. He was halfway through the circuit, which he had measured at fifty kilometres.

The past few days had been eventful. It had begun when Unit 8200 caught the rumour of a potential virus attack. This was clever of Jacob Nachman, but careless of Ahmad Waizy. Then that Mossad bitch Rachel Papo had stumbled across the name Arie al-Fattal in Dubai. She was thought to be a very special agent. Sinon had inquired about her at the bureau to learn more. She had been born in Sderot, and her parents had died young. She became a sniper in the military, and fought in Gaza and Lebanon during the second intifada. There was also a rumour that she had infiltrated al-Qaeda and had been educated at one of their training camps in northern Afghanistan. The director of the Mossad, Meir Pardo, had taken her under his wing, and she had joined Unit 101 several years ago. Rachel Papo was a she-devil — a bitch with the blood of his brothers on her hands. He would have her skin before the Mona operation was over. He would get her, one way or another.

Sinon's muscles protested, whimpering, but he had learned not to give in to the pain. He kept pedalling upward without letting up on the pace. David Yassur had found an important piece of the puzzle when he'd got hold of the name Arie al-Fattal. And then had come the operation in Nice. It was inexcusable. The whole project could have come to nothing. Melah as-Dullah had chosen the death of a martyr. That was lucky. And thanks to Allah's powerful protection, Samir Mustaf had gotten away. Now the group was spread out. If he understood Ahmad's message correctly, Samir had completed his work somewhere in Africa, and the virus had been uploaded to TBI's network — and not a minute too soon, since apparently David had gone to the FBI for help. How he knew that he should look for clues in the US was a mystery. Maybe it was pure chance, but the FBI had managed to identify Melah, and then they'd obtained Samir's profile. It hadn't been too difficult: he was a Muslim expert in computer viruses who had received his doctorate at MIT and had disappeared in Lebanon. The FBI had sent his collected papers and articles over to the Mossad, with pictures, too. Sinon himself had a copy of this folder lying on his desk. Meir's gang had turned the entire Middle East upside down, but so far Samir was still running free. They would never find him. Not as long as he was Ahmad's responsibility.

His mobile phone rang just as he made it, panting, up to the crown of the Mount of Olives. He braked in irritation and climbed off his bike. A faint mist hung over the valley. On one side, he had a view of the old city and the dome of the al-Aqsa mosque. On the other side, he could see as far as Jordan. Sinon flipped open his phone. It was his assistant, Sophia Francke, one of the few people who had his direct number. Sophia told him excitedly that the finance minister had decided to implement a national data backup. Nothing like this had ever happened before, anywhere in the world. Sophia caught her breath. Sinon listened and looked out over the fertile valley. The initiative, which had been named Project Lehagen, Hebrew for 'protection,' would take time. But no one really knew how much time they had. Now the finance minister wanted to meet with the others in the inner circle. Therefore Sinon had to make an appearance in Jerusalem as soon as possible.

He hung up and shook his head. He'd had the same assistant for more than two years, but no matter how many times he told her not to bother him while he was biking, she kept calling. He changed the SIM card and sent a text to Ahmad, wherever in the world he was right now. Then he took a breath full of the scent of pine and rosemary, and pedalled back down the steep hill. The way down was always a reward. All obstacles were the same. First you had to fight — show Allah that you wouldn't fall short, wouldn't give up. He wasn't surprised that Yuval Yatom had decided to back up the system. This measure was as expected as it was futile. They were underestimating Mona. The virus was already in the system. Project Lehagen was a complete waste of effort. But maybe he should still become involved in it. After all, it couldn't hurt if the backup was delayed for a few days. That would give Mona more time to spread.

The wind rushed past his ears. There was nothing he loved more than this. He knew that there was gravel on the road, that he could meet oncoming traffic, and that his chain could snap. At this speed, that would be the end of him. *Insha'Allah.*

The Mona worm had penetrated TBI's system and made its way into hundreds of pre-determined servers. At 16:34 Palestinian time, the same time that the cluster bomb had exploded in Qana five years earlier, the worms opened their digital shells and, like a Trojan horse, released their load: the world's most powerful computer virus. Mona's first algorithm was activated deep inside TBI's nuclear-bomb-proof server hall, twenty metres below ground.

Stockholm, Sweden

Eric felt like a new person. He had gone to the gym for the first time in several weeks, and he must have sat in the sauna for thirty minutes. Afterwards he bought new pants and a new jacket. He had wandered around Östermalmshallen and picked out the evening's dinner. When he got home, he tidied the apartment, aired out his office, and cleaned out the refrigerator. Now Pavarotti was singing at top volume, the table was set, and the candles were lit. He was just placing the scallops into the frying pan when Hanna stepped into the kitchen with a surprised expression on her face.

'What's going on here? *Shabbes* on a Monday?'

He gestured theatrically toward the set table.

'Have a seat. We're celebrating.'

She sat down and kicked off her shoes. He handed her a glass of Riesling.

'What are we celebrating?'

'That you're the world's most beautiful woman. And that Mind Surf works.'

She lit up.

'Then no wonder we're celebrating! You must not have slept at all last night. I got up to pee around three, and you were still in there.'

'I haven't slept. It doesn't matter — I'm not tired, and I'm way too excited to waste time on sleep. I went to the gym today. It was wonderful.'

He placed three scallops on her plate, drizzled truffle oil over them, and topped the dish with a lime.

'Enjoy your appetiser!'

He looked at her and smiled.

'How are you?'

She took a sip of wine.

'Nothing much happened at work. We upgraded our security and put in some routine reinforcements. But I haven't heard any more from Tel Aviv. Maybe the whole thing was just a scare tactic. After work, I swung by the congregation.'

She ate a scallop.

'It's good. Did you marinate it in garlic?'

'It's a top-secret recipe. How's the rabbi-recruiting going?'

'To hell. You should have seen our meeting. It was worse than the worst of Woody Allen.'

Eric nodded. He knew just what she meant. He had been to the meetings a few times. Everyone had an opinion, and then everyone had an opinion about everyone else's opinion.

'I liked that woman from New York. The one we went and listened to at the synagogue.'

Hanna nodded.

'Me, too. But our little congregation has a hard time competing with the big cities. Next week we're going to meet a candidate from Estonia.'

Eric walked over to the oven and pulled out a pan of lobster au gratin. He served it plain, with a slice of lemon, and sat down across from her again. Their eyes met.

'Hanna, it was totally incredible. I can't describe it. I was floating through my own computer. Through the internet. All those colours and images. Pure magic.'

She smiled. 'Mats Hagström really picked the perfect time to come in — just a few days before the breakthrough.'

'Yes, you can say that again. He acts solely on intuition, and I suppose that's why he's been so successful.'

He leaned across the table and refilled her glass.

'Do you know what we're having for dessert?'

Her lips formed a pout.

'Sex?'

'Well … the sex will come later, after coffee. But before coffee, there's dessert. Today's dessert is called Mind Surf.'

She leaned back and bit her lip.

'You want me … I want to, but … You know I don't like that gooey cap.'

'No excuses. The cook has been working on this dish for the last several years. He will be very disappointed if you don't have a taste.'

He placed his hand on hers.

'It's totally fantastic. You'll be the second person in the world to try it. The first woman.'

She ate her lobster in silence. He decided not to pressure her further. He knew that she was far too curious to resist — he just had to wait. She sipped some more wine, ate a little lobster, and sipped again.

'If I can count on you for the treat you promised after coffee, I suppose I can try the dessert.'

'Yes! I'll go get it ready. You have to start with the gel. It has to sit for a while before you can begin.'

She rolled her eyes. He walked to the office, humming along with *The Marriage of Figaro*, grabbed the packet of nanogel, and returned to the kitchen. She had put her hair up in a bun and was sorting the silverware into the dishwasher. He inhaled her perfume. She leaned her head back as he carefully began to massage the sparkling gel into it.

'Oh, that's nice. Can you massage my shoulders, too?'

'Unfortunately not. This is the world's most expensive massage oil. I can't waste it, not even on your lovely shoulders. But I'm sure you'll get a full-body massage anyway. In a bit. First you have to earn it.'

Twenty minutes later, Hanna was sitting in front of the computer with the sensor helmet on her head and the black glasses pulled down. The colourful braid coiled across the floor to the computer. She made a face.

'It hurts like hell. Are you sure you didn't make the sensor tips longer?'

'Not a millimetre. I wanted to, but they didn't let me — and that was lucky. It wasn't necessary. We might even be able to make them a little shorter, now that we have the new gel. Stop whining and lean back. Let's start the show.'

She sat still, full of expectation. He checked the EEG waves: they indicated perfect contact with her brain.

'Here we go.' Click. She gave a start. She opened her mouth and gripped the arms of the chair. He stood still, watching her, like a parent showing off his new baby. In a way, that's exactly what he was doing. She laughed out loud and started waving her arms. She was breathing rapidly. He leaned forward and opened the browser on the computer so he could follow her journey. He watched as the department store NK's site opened, and the latest collection of purses filled the screen. He shook his head. *Good lord, even now she's thinking about shopping.* The pages scrolled by and sub-pages opened. The address bar turned blue, and tbi.se popped up. She was on her way to work.

He left her and got the wine glasses from the kitchen. When he came back, she was still on the TBI website. She opened her email and scrolled through her inbox. Hanna was sitting completely still; her mouth was half-open. He watched as a new email opened on the screen. Then his own email address popped up. The text area was activated, and a message started to appear, as though it were being written by a ghost:

You're a genius. This is the coolest thing I've ever experienced. The coolest! But now I'm ready for the next course. ;-)

He smiled and kissed her on the lips. The EEG waves gave a hop on the screen. He closed the program, and she sat completely still, breathing in small bursts. He unscrewed the glasses and carefully removed the helmet. She closed her eyes. It was as though she wanted to hold on to the experience for a little longer. Then she opened her eyes and looked at him.

'Whoa. What a gadget! Not just for the handicapped. Think

of the gaming industry. Talk about Christmas present of the year.'

He replaced the helmet on Marilyn.

'Oh well, that's not why we created Mind Surf. It's mostly to help the sick and the handicapped. A commercial version is still far off, but who knows what might happen in the future. Here.'

He handed over her glass of wine. She pushed it aside and threw her legs around him. Her hair was gooey and purple. She looked up at him as he stood there in front of the chair.

'Professor, you've read my thoughts, haven't you? I don't want coffee or wine. I just want the treat you promised me. Here and now.'

Le Cannet, France

Sergeant Laurent Mutz was slumped in his chair at the simple kitchen table. It was the middle of the day, so the house was quiet. Everyone was at work, school, or day care. The sun shone in through the windows, making the dust on the floor glow. Cleaning was not one of Michelle's strengths, even if she was a fantastic woman and as beautiful as a movie star. And she had borne him two healthy sons. He loved her more than life itself. They lived on the top floor of a run-down three-storey building, but they could see the ocean from the balcony, and that was the most important thing. He took a sip of his cold coffee. Michelle was at the café down in Cannes, making crepes and mixing walnut cream. He didn't like having a day off. Major Serge had ordered him to rest for a day, but he was too restless to lie around being lazy. He had already done his daily exercise routine and had read every last line in the newspaper. Now he was staring down into his coffee.

In his mind he went over and over how he had squandered the money. He tried to find a rationale that Michelle would understand, but he rejected each one and instead tried to think of a way to get back what he'd lost. Should he borrow more money and play for even higher stakes? Could he sell something? They had nothing of worth. The car wasn't paid off, the apartment was mortgaged, and the TV was rented.

He knew what would happen. She would look at him and nod. Her shoulders would slump. She would say that she understood, that it would all work out. She wouldn't get angry. Shit, he was such an idiot. She had a whole pile of travel magazines beside the bed. He felt sick when he looked at them. He was able to walk into an apartment full of armed terrorists, but he wasn't capable of looking his wife in the eyes and telling her what he'd done.

Laurent stood up and put the coffee cup in the sink, along with the rest of the breakfast dishes. He walked into the hall in frustration and searched his jacket for his mobile phone. There were no missed calls and no messages. Apparently, his colleagues were respecting his day off. Then he caught sight of the small notebook in the outer pocket. He took it with him out to the balcony and sat down on one of the simple plastic chairs. In the tree across the street he could see a squirrel hopping from branch to branch. Carefree little bastard.

Each page in the notebook was full of writing. He didn't recognise the language. It looked more like symbols than words, on page after page of perfect lines of characters and notes. The whole thing seemed to have been written over a long period of time, using different pens. There was a spot of something on one page, and the ink in several of the symbols had run with the humidity.

The squirrel threw a large pinecone at a white Renault that

was parked under the tree.

Why had Constable Pierre Balzac made all of these strange notes? This was hardly a regular old police notepad. There was something that didn't fit. What the hell did the notebook have to do with the terrorists at Maréchal Foch? He went through the series of events. Balzac had answered a disturbance call from … what was her name? Scribé … Marie Scribé. Balzac must have gone to her door first, to find out why she had called. Had he had the notebook with him at that point? Maybe Marie Scribé would remember. He picked up the phone and called *Pages Blanches*, the French phone directory. They quickly found Scribé's number, and forwarded his call. The phone rang eight times before anyone answered.

'*Allô?*'

'*Bonjour,* Madame Scribé. I'm sorry to disturb you. My name is Laurent Mutz and I'm a police officer. I'm calling because …'

'It is really quite appalling!'

'Madame?'

'The Lord gives us clear commands in Exodus, does He not?'

Judging by her voice, she was younger than he'd thought at first — around fifty, he'd guess.

'You're thinking of God's ten commandments to Moses, Madame?'

'Oh no, absolutely not just to Moses. To us all!'

Laurent watched another projectile leave the tree and land on the white Renault.

'You are quite right. The commandments are for all of us. I have a question I would like to ask you, Madame. It's about yesterday, of course.'

'The Lord did not give us 10,000 commandments, did He? If He had, it might have been difficult to keep track of all of them. He gave us ten. Just ten. Why so few? Because that's all that was necessary. And because He knew that His Earthly servants had limited minds. Only ten, so we would remember them. And now … the fifth … The fifth one was violated right in front of my door.'

There was a rustling sound on the line. He thought he heard her lighting a cigarette.

'You're thinking of the fifth commandment, Madame, Thou shalt not kill.'

'But they shot him. One of the Lord's children. Right in front of my door.'

Was that a sob he heard on the line? He cleared his throat.

'Before this occurred, Constable Balzac talked to you. Is that right?'

'He was very polite. Calm and assured. A handsome man who liked his job. An important job. All of you are doing a very good job, I want you to know that. It's not easy to be a police officer these days. Not with all these Arabs, perverted homos, and druggie beggars. And all the corrupt politicians and children with AIDS. You're all doing a good job.'

'Thank you, Madame. When you talked to Constable Balzac, did you happen to notice whether he was taking notes in a notebook?'

'A notebook? No, I didn't see one.'

Laurent was disappointed.

'Are you sure?'

'I'm sure that he didn't have a notebook with him. And he couldn't use the one I gave him, as full of scribbling as it was.'

Laurent stood up from the plastic chair.

'You gave him a notebook?'

'Poor man. He was so handsome. Here in my hallway one second, and dead in the stairwell the next.'

'Madame, I'll repeat my question. Did you give Balzac a notebook?'

'You don't have to sound so harsh. I gave him a notebook.'

'I apologise. May I ask where you got that notebook, Madame? Was it your notebook, perhaps?'

'For heaven's sake, no. I'm no scribbler. That thing belonged to the blackheads. The ones who shot the constable.'

'How do you know that?'

She blew out smoke. The sound was unmistakable.

'Because I found it just after the blackheads left. Someone must have dropped it. I know it wasn't there earlier, and when I took out the trash I found it on the stairwell.'

Incredible. One notebook had been found twice in the same place.

'Thank you kindly, Madame. You have been a great help.'

'Have I? Well, I suppose that's good. Now be careful. Listen to the Lord, and you won't be led astray.'

He hung up and stood still for a moment, staring at the notebook. Its pages fluttered in the wind, full of line after line of incomprehensible symbols. There was page after page after page of it.

Stockholm, Sweden

They were both sleeping deeply. Eric was on his stomach, as always, with his face buried in the pillow. Hanna was on her back, her arms along her side. Her eyelids were twitching, and her fingertips trembled.

She was wandering through a vast landscape. It was golden. The sky was red. She was naked. Her feet sank into the golden sand. It was neither warm nor cold, and there was no breeze. Was she on her way to or from? No trees, no mountains, no contours. Just sand and an even horizon in all directions. She had never been here before. At the same time, the view seemed familiar. There was a story here. Traditions millions of years old. Even though it was all just sand and sky, there was a dignity, a wisdom, about the place. This was where everything began. This was the place of origin. This insight was clear. It was as though someone or something was holding its breath in anticipation.

Her nakedness exhilarated her. Was there a pre-determined path, or were all directions the same? Something flashed in the red sunlight. She put up a hand to shade her eyes, and squinted at the horizon. Nothing. She stood still, waiting. There it was again. Something in the sand up ahead. She walked faster. The sand was as fine as flour under her feet. She tried to keep her eyes on the reflection, afraid of losing her way. It was farther off than she'd thought. The fine sand made it harder and harder to walk. She kept going. Just as she was certain she'd lost her bearings, she caught sight of the object. A clock. An old-fashioned black alarm clock, half-covered in sand. She picked it up and blew off the glittering sand. The clock had stopped. She turned it over and found the key for winding it. Something inside her cried that it was wrong to wind the clock. She hesitated, her hand on the large key. She looked around. Then she began to turn the key. It was as if her hand had a mind of its own. Her hand turned and turned. She watched her fingers as though they no longer belonged to her. Then it stopped. The key couldn't turn any more. She didn't want to let go, but the damage was already done. She could feel something coming to life deep inside the clock. When she turned it back over, the hands began to move, but they were going in the wrong direction. They spun backwards, their speed increasing. Around and around. She couldn't tear her gaze from the spinning hands. They spun faster and faster. She felt sick. This was the thing that wasn't supposed to happen. Now there was no way to undo it.

The glass cracked with a pop. She sank to her knees, holding the clock close, suddenly in despair. She wanted to protect it. She knew that was more important than anything else. Purple liquid ran down over her hands. It was sticky and cold. The hands of the clock were turning back time. Then a dull rumble rolled across the dunes. She turned around. In the distance, the red sky was darkening. The clock had released something — summoned it. She let the clock go and started to run.

The darkness was still far off, but she could feel the place changing. The sand was wetter. It sucked hard at her feet, and she had to yank them free with each step. She ran, stumbled, and kept running. She didn't have to turn around to know that the darkness was catching up. The storm followed her shadow, swallowing it. She knew that the world was dying. Not just in this place, but everywhere else, too. Everything disappeared into the black storm. Her feet sank deeper and deeper into the wet sand. She fell. The clock appeared again, lying in a bubbling pool of the purple liquid. The hands spun relentlessly behind the cracked glass. The roar of the storm was deafening. On hands and knees, she raised her eyes to the sky, conquered. The red sun was gone. Above her roared the dense, eternal darkness. Then the sand under her disappeared, and she fell headlong into the empty nothingness.

Jerusalem, Israel

David Yassur slammed the phone down so hard that it flew off the desk and hit the floor with a bang. *'Lech lehizadayen! Harah!'* Cursing was unusual in Hebrew, but David had a large vocabulary. His assistant looked at him anxiously. David bellowed, 'Get Jacob Nachman in here.'

She stood up quickly, glad to leave the room. David drummed his hands against the desk impatiently. Everything was going to hell. The backup of the banking system had been delayed, and no one could say why. Directives had gone missing, and important institutions hadn't received the necessary programs. But that wasn't the worst thing. There was a knock at the door.

'Come in!'

Jacob opened the door.

'You wanted to see me?'

David looked at him with a grim expression.

'Have a seat.' He indicated one of the visitors' chairs. Jacob chose to remain standing.

'What happened?'

'I just talked to the minister of finance. The virus is already in our systems.'

Stockholm, Sweden

Eric had prepared a simple breakfast. Now he was paging through the arts and culture section of *Dagens Nyheter*. It had been a long time since they did anything cultural together. He could hear Hanna rummaging around in the bathroom. Last night had been fantastic. It was as though she had regained her faith in him. Was that because he was more relaxed, or because he had managed to get Mind Surf working? He pushed aside his cynical thoughts and concentrated on the theatre listings.

'Shit!'

Hanna ran though the apartment.

'Shit, shit!'

'What is it? Calm down.'

She came into the kitchen with jeans unbuttoned and the strap of her bra hanging across her shoulders. She held her phone up.

'Twelve missed calls. Four emergency reports. Eight texts! Something's happened at the bank — I have to get there pronto! I forgot to take it off silent before I went to sleep.'

She disappeared into the bedroom, but called out to him, 'What did you *do* to me last night?'

'For dessert or for your treat?'

He got up and fixed an open sandwich. Then he took out a mug and filled it with coffee. He met her in the hall.

'Here. You have to eat breakfast. The car is right outside. Call and tell me what's going on.'

She kissed him and slammed the door. He went back to the kitchen, cleared the table, and put another capsule into the Nespresso machine. Ristretto again — the strongest. He was tired. He had been woken several times by Hanna, who had slept poorly all night. He took his cup of coffee to the office and logged onto his computer. Mats Hagström had sent an email to ask how things were going. Eric smiled and wrote a triumphant answer. He closed by inviting him to come over and try Mind Surf. Then he wrote a long email to thank Kyoto University for solving the Gordian knot by making the gel stronger. Just as he sent the email, the phone rang. It was Mats.

'Congratulations! To both of us. Now you know that this old man still has his intuition. Damn good luck that that apple landed in the wastebasket.'

'Yes, you can say *that* again. I'm incredibly pleased with the results. What do you say, do you want to try it?'

'Of course I do! As a matter of fact, I was thinking of coming over right away. Are you at KTH?'

'No. I'm working from home. Banérgatan 41.'

'Splendid. I'm on my way. And you'll be happy to hear that I've already instructed my assistant to send over the first payment.'

'Thank you. Now we're starting the next journey. Together.'

Eric hung up and looked around his office. Then he opened the window and let in the fresh scent of rain. It was almost dark out, even though it was nearly ten in the morning. Thunder hung in the air. He took a sip of coffee and thought of Hanna. What could have happened at TBI?

When Hanna got to work, she was met at the entrance by two of her closest co-workers. They were upset and out of breath. According to the main office in Tel Aviv, the bank had been hit hard by a vicious virus, and the IT department had been working on counter-measures for several hours. The first thing Hanna did was close down the online banking service and their public website. These systems were in the demilitarised zone, which was IT jargon for openly accessible networks. It was not an easy decision to make, and most of the management team was against it. But she was the director of IT, so in the end her word was law. They had to ensure at all costs that their clients weren't infected; that would be catastrophic. The phones started ringing six minutes after the online banking was shut down. One hour later, heavy traffic caused the customer service line to crash. It was no longer possible to reach the bank by the net or by phone.

After Hanna ordered the team to shut down the online banking site, she activated the partial firewalls between the internal systems. They acted like bulkheads on a boat, and were part of the extra protection that had been installed in the past few days. But so far there had been no concrete service interruptions, and on the surface everything seemed normal. At first, Hanna thought perhaps it was all just a drill. But then she read the reports coming in from TBI's offices around the world and realised that this was serious. The bank was severing contact with external networks at the cost of loss of business and angry clients. No one could implement a drill like this and keep their job. The threat must be serious, and the normalcy that the bank's system registered had to be an illusion. Whatever it was that was eluding them, it was good at digital camouflage.

'As long as we're sure where we each stand, I guess it's okay.'

Eric frowned as he massaged the gel into Mats Hagström's scalp.

'What do you mean?'

'That we both like girls, I mean.'

Eric laughed.

'Well, I suppose there *is* something special about you.'

Mats gave a start.

'Eh, watch it. I know you're married. I am, too. Several times over, in fact.'

'The gel has to sit for a while. Meanwhile I'll explain how all of this works. You'll see websites floating in empty nothingness, but try to remain calm. If you get too excited, your brain will start producing meta-signals that interfere with the interpretive filter. The system reads a number of different signals in order to interpret your thoughts as effectively as possible. These decoded signals are translated into digital commands. Sometimes there are lags, and then it will feel like you're moving through syrup, but you just have to wait and the system will catch up again. The lags happen because your brain produces an immense amount of information all at once. Look at it as you thinking faster than the computer.'

Mats grimaced.

'It stings. Is that normal?'

'That's supposed to happen. It means that the gel is penetrating your skin. First it will establish contact with your dura mater, the outermost membrane of the brain.'

'Is there more than one membrane?'

'There are three. In order for Mind Surf to work, we have to get through the innermost soft membrane, the pia mater.'

Mats sat silently for a moment as Eric checked all the outgoing sensors on the helmet.

'Why is it called "nanogel"?'

'Nano means "a billionth". In other words, the particles we've produced are extremely small. These particles are absorbed by the skin, but retain their conductive capacity. Look at them as a lot of wires that go through your skin to your brain. The gel has an intermolecular force based on van der Waal's force.'

Mats held up his hands.

'Now you've lost me, but it doesn't matter. When I see all these sites, what do I do?'

Eric carefully placed the helmet on Mats's head.

'Clear all superfluous thoughts from your head. Focus on what you see and what you want to do. The system is very intuitive, so I think you'll do fine. You'll understand once you begin.'

Mats looked nervous. Eric gave him a brotherly pat on the shoulder.

'Don't worry. This is the world's first completely safe drug. Get ready for the trip of your life!'

The apartment was dark when she unlocked the front door, and Eric must have been asleep for a long time. Why didn't he ever leave a light on when he knew she would be late? Always in his own damn bubble, closed off and absent minded. Hanna went to the kitchen and turned on the light. There was a note on the table: he had left a Caesar salad for her in the fridge. A dry cinnamon bun from 7-Eleven was the only thing she'd eaten all day, but she wasn't hungry. Her stomach ached. Ovulation? Her head ached. Stress? She wanted a cigarette, although she hadn't smoked for several years. She went to the dining room and looked through the display case. Then she sneaked into the bedroom and slipped soundlessly into the closet, where she found a wrinkled pack of Marlboros in one of her evening bags. Back in the kitchen, she poured a glass of Rioja and sat down at the dining-room table. The oven clock said it was sixteen minutes past one. She was completely exhausted. She'd had dreams last night. She couldn't remember what they were about, but a strong sense of unease still hung over her. She thought through her day at work. There was still nothing to indicate that there really was a virus in the bank's network. But Tel Aviv was sure it was there.

Hanna took a deep drag of the cigarette and looked down at the note on the table again. What would happen with Eric now? Would the success of Mind Surf bring him out of his solitude? She was tired of always being the one who took all the initiative, and of being the one who brought it up when things weren't going well between them. Why did she have to assume the role of crabby bitch? If he could choose, everything would just get shoved under the rug, day in and day out. She drank a little wine and ran her finger across the letters on the note. He had nice handwriting. And nice hands. She had noticed that the first time they met. Nice hands were sexy.

But it was hopeless trying to talk to him. It always ended in a fight. She was sick of fighting and of his manic nagging about kids. A kid would mean enormous responsibility, and it would tie them to each other forever. Had he really thought about that? Had he really considered how that would feel? She had no intention of becoming a bitter single mum. She put the cigarette out in the wine glass and felt ill. Smoking was crap.

She brushed her teeth and undressed in the bathroom so she wouldn't wake him up. Then she silently went to the bedroom and slid under the warm blanket. She set her alarm for seven o'clock. Five hours of sleep would have to do. She cuddled up to Eric and fell asleep.

She found herself in a large room that smelled stuffy and mouldy. She lay naked, on her stomach, in a layer of dust half a metre thick — or maybe it was ash. She stood up. She was still holding the old clock in one hand. The hands had stopped just after four thirty. No more purple liquid. Now it was just dusty and dead. She looked around. There were some overturned clothes racks and torn boxes. A mannequin with its arm broken off stared at her with empty eyes. She saw escalators behind the mannequin. Everything was silent and deserted. A cash register lay on the floor beside a counter. The drawer was open, releasing bills and coins. Everything was covered in the white ash.

Then she caught sight of a pile of paper bags next to the escalator. She immediately recognised the logo. She was at NK. This realisation made her afraid. Afraid, but maybe mostly sad. She walked over to the register. The floor was full of glass and rubbish. The grooved edges of the escalator hurt her naked feet as she walked down it, careful not to step on any shards of glass. She came to street level. The large skylights were covered with ash, the showcases broken, and the shelves overturned. It looked like hooligans had gone berserk in the store. But they hadn't been out to steal: jewellery, money, and expensive watches lay in the dust. Everything felt colourless and old. She gasped. A police car lay on its roof just inside the entrance. All its windows were broken, and the frame was dented and scratched. Behind the car she could see the large glass doors that opened onto Hamngatan. Shattered. The car must have crashed through the doors. She looked out at the street. She saw several abandoned cars there. All of them had broken windows; their doors were open, and their insides were torn out. The white ash was there, too. The same ghostly stillness. She walked in an arc to the entrance, afraid to get too close to the wrecked car.

'Little tiger. Where are you?'

She gave a start when she heard the other voice, suddenly conscious of her nakedness.

Eric woke up. Hanna was burning up, gripping her pillow with white knuckles. She must be having a nightmare. He caressed her gently. Her eyelids twitched, and her lips moved. She whispered something in her sleep. He kissed her cheek.

'Who's there?' She turned around slowly, her heart pounding. A child's voice? She walked back and looked up at the other floors. Cables hung from landings, and pipes stuck out of concrete like broken bones.

'Hello, is someone there?'

She listened. There, another sound. Fainter this time. A girl's voice. She moved closer to the escalator. 'Where did you go?'

The girl must be down on the lower level. She started to walk down the escalator. It was considerably darker down here. She stood on the last step while her eyes adjusted. It was pitch-black over by the food departments. To her right stood a wrecked bakery counter, and to her left, kitchen utensils were strewn about the floor.

There was something in the darkness, a shadow. Perfectly still. Could it be a mannequin? But it was so small. She walked a bit farther in among the dark shelves.

'Is someone here?' The shadow didn't move. But now she could see that it was a little girl, standing with her back to her. She took a few more steps, swallowed, and raised her voice.

'Hello, sweetie. You don't have to be afraid.'

The girl turned toward her slowly.

'I'm not afraid.'

Despite the darkness, Hanna could see that her face was dirty and that she was wearing a wrinkled, stained dress. Her hair was uncombed.

'Have you seen a little cat?'

Hanna shook her head and crouched down.

'Who are you?'

The girl cocked her head. 'I'm looking for my little tiger.'

'Where is everyone?'

'What everyone?'

'The people who come here to shop. The people who drive cars out on the street and buy bread over there.' She pointed at the wrecked bakery counter by the escalator.

The girl shrugged. 'They're gone. Everyone is gone,' she answered without much interest.

'How can everyone be gone?'

The girl suddenly looked scared. She looked around.

'You can't be here. He could be here any moment.'

'Who?'

The girl didn't answer; she just stood there silently, looking at her. Hanna spoke more sharply: 'Who could be here?'

The girl looked down at the ground, and wrung her hands nervously. 'The man without a face.'

The alarm clock rang shrilly. Hanna fumbled for it and found the off button. She closed her eyes and gathered her strength. Then she tore herself out of sleep and opened her eyes. Bright rays of sun were playing under and around the blinds. She was wet with sweat, and had a headache. She lay there with her head on the pillow, looking at Eric. He was sleeping peacefully, his mouth half open. The alarm clock hadn't disturbed him in the least. She ran her hand through his thick brown hair. He was an unusually sexy professor — tiresome and egocentric, but sexy. She would have been happy to stay in bed until he woke up. But she knew he didn't like to be woken, and he could easily sleep for another several hours. She got up and showered, standing for a long time with the cold water streaming over her face. This was yet another morning when she'd awoken feeling more tired than when she'd gone to bed. Her whole body ached. Her joints felt stiff and sore, and her temples were throbbing. It must be a migraine. She felt sick. Normally, she would have stayed home from work, but this wasn't a normal day. Anything could have happened at the bank during the night.

When Eric woke up, Hanna was long gone. He pulled on his robe and walked through the apartment, which was bathed in sunlight. When he walked into the kitchen he saw the cigarette butt in the wine glass. He sighed. If she'd been smoking, that meant she was worried. Worried about him, or about work? All of a sudden, he felt dejected. He ought to ask her to lunch. They hadn't seen each other in twenty-four hours. He took a vanilla yoghurt out of the fridge and started the coffeemaker. It was just after nine o'clock. It looked like a beautiful day beyond the windows. In the sunlight, he could see that they needed washing.

At three o'clock he had to be at KTH for a meeting with the team. Before that, he would run the analyses of Hanna's and Mats Hagström's test rounds. And then he would write up a more detailed schedule, now that they were finally going into clinical testing. He took his iPod from the charger, went into his office, selected Verdi's *Othello*, and opened his email. He had received an answer from Kyoto University with a series of test results on the new nano solution. The Japanese, too, seemed fascinated by the powerful contact he had succeeded in establishing with the brain. Eric tried to forward the email to the Swedish team, but he couldn't find the group address. He frowned. How could it just be gone? He typed the addresses manually and sent the email. Then he clicked on the Mind Surf icon. The computer was thinking, but the program didn't open.

He nibbled at the yoghurt, his irritation increasing. What the hell was this? The minutes ticked by. He changed position, impatient. The program finally opened, but some of the colours in the interface were different. He put the yoghurt aside and went into the memory module to bring up Mats's and Hanna's sessions. The program stored information from each session: brain waves, processor activity, graphical information, and domain and IP histories. There were three names in the user list — the pioneers:

ERIC SÖDERQVIST	LOG FILE 0001 (05:15)
HANNA SÖDERQVIST	LOG FILE 0002 (22:10)
MATS HAGSTRÖM	LOG FILE 0003 (11:22)

He scrolled down to Hanna's log and clicked. The computer froze again. He leaned toward the screen. It flickered, and a message popped up:

REQUESTED FILE NOT FOUND

He clicked on Mats's log:

REQUESTED FILE NOT FOUND

What had gone wrong? A slow start-up, strange graphics, missing files … was the problem with Mind Surf or with the operating system? He remembered the missing group-email address, so the problem couldn't just be with Mind Surf. Had the computer acquired a virus? He brought up his anti-virus program. He always had the latest update, so the computer ought to be protected. While the program searched for a virus, he went to the kitchen and got himself some coffee. Back at the computer, he picked up his phone and called Hanna. It went straight to voicemail, so he decided to leave a short message: 'Hi. Remember me? If you do, press one. If you want to eat lunch today, press two. If you think I should go to hell, press pound.'

He hung up and looked back at the screen. The anti-virus had finished searching. It hadn't found a virus. He threw his half-eaten yoghurt in the trash. The problem had made him lose his appetite.

Hanna sat down across from Robert Jarnos, the CEO of TBI's Swedish office. The video-conferencing equipment was already running, and the screen showed an empty conference table, not unlike the one she had just sat down at. The difference was that the conference table on the screen was at bank headquarters in Tel Aviv. Isaac Berns, the company's director of IT, had called a global briefing. Robert looked at her.

'Since HQ seems to be late, maybe you can give me an update?'

Hanna nodded.

'We've implemented extensive security reinforcements in the internal and external networks. We've also been searching the system for viruses every six minutes for the past twenty-four hours.'

'And?'

'Nothing.'

Robert gave a tired smile.

'So there's no danger?'

Hanna didn't return the smile.

'Up until today, this all might have been a nightmare. But, unfortunately, we ran into real problems this morning.'

Hanna glanced at the video screen. The conference table in Tel Aviv was still empty.

'It started in Corporate Finance, when several important folders went missing. When we called up the automatic backup, the system froze. Then, when we restarted, the server at Haninge crashed. Also, the internal network is sluggish in general.'

'Which means?'

'Which means that we have malware in the system — a virus.'

'But you said that you're scanning every six minutes.'

'Indeed we are. Our anti-virus programs can't find anything, but that doesn't mean there's nothing to find. It just means we're dealing with a more sophisticated enemy.'

Robert gave Hanna a long look.

'How are you doing? I don't mean any offence, but you don't look well.'

'I've been sleeping badly the last few nights. Otherwise, I'm fine.'

The speakers crackled, and Isaac Berns sat down heavily before the camera in Tel Aviv. He was a short, ruddy man with an intense gaze. In his hand he held a large coffee mug with Mickey Mouse ears.

'Shalom, everyone. I'll skip the pleasantries and get right to the point. As you know, the bank has been threatened by a virus attack. Early this morning, our systems starting acting strangely. Among other things, data disappeared from our servers in Jerusalem and Haifa. We've also noticed a substantial decrease in capacity — our tests indicate that the network has lost as much as 40 per cent.'

He took a sip from Mickey Mouse.

'We're working with several state authorities to find the virus. As I'm sure you know, the conventional search programs haven't been able to find anything. If we can't find the virus, we can't protect ourselves from it. On the bright side, today we tested a new program that will change that.'

One of the other bank offices asked a question they couldn't hear, and Isaac nodded.

'Yes, it's different from all the other ones we've tested. In short, computer viruses most often use some sort of shield, so-called stealth techniques, to avoid detection. The most common forms are active modification, variable encryption, polymorphism, and metamorphism. Traditional viruses are monogamous — they can only choose one of these disguises — so they can be traced with a good anti-virus program. But newer and more sophisticated viruses can create combinations, and we've even heard rumours of variants that can mutate. In these cases, conventional virus protection doesn't work.'

Another sip from Mickey. Hanna noticed that Robert was filling his notebook with squares, hearts, and circles — a clear indication that he was bored.

'The program we developed last night is based on Nobel Prize-winner Manfred Hoff's algorithm, and it uses a new type of holistic pattern analysis. If any of you would like to know more about it, let us know. But for the rest of you who don't give a shit about how it works, just please start using it. We'll start distributing it right after the meeting. We want to get the search results in immediately. Anyone who finds the virus will receive a special protocol to follow.'

Hanna leaned toward the microphone and pressed the 'talk' button.

'Hanna Söderqvist, Sweden, here. So if I've understood you correctly, you've found the virus?'

She looked anxiously at Isaac, who nodded.

'We have. Our new program found the virus in just a minute or two.'

'Hanna again. Have you also developed some form of anti-virus?'

Isaac chuckled.

'Somehow, it was like the virus wanted us to discover it. Once we knocked on the right door, the virus was happy to open it and show itself. So we know it's called Mona. But that's about all we know. I can't say how long it will take to develop an anti-virus. First and foremost, we have to map out how far it has spread.

Therefore, I want all of you to install the new search program immediately, so we can track all potential infections. By the way, we've named the program *Mona Tza'yad*. Loosely translated, it means "Mona Hunter".'

One hour later, Hanna went back into her office and closed the door. She didn't sit down at her computer; rather, she sank into one of the visitors' chairs. Her migraine was worse, and she didn't feel well. She sat still for a long time, her eyes closed. Then she took off her jacket and unbuttoned her blouse. Her back was wet with sweat. She forced herself to go through everything one more time. The team had installed *Mona Tza'yad*, and twelve minutes later they'd found the virus. It seemed that Mona had infiltrated the whole system. Hanna had implemented all the measures that Tel Aviv had set forth in the protocol. The virus had been discovered in every office, and, after a certain amount of anguish, Isaac Berns had asked her to close down the internal network as well. The practical implication of this was that everyone at the bank could go home. There wasn't much they could do without IT support.

Was there anything more she could do? No, at this point, all she could do was wait for Tel Aviv to crack the virus. She thought of Eric, and felt the need to hear his voice. She reached over the desk and picked up her phone, but just sat there holding it. She suddenly went ice-cold. What was the name she was going to look up? She could picture him, but she couldn't connect a name to the image. She scrolled aimlessly through her address book. After a while, she gave up and lowered her trembling hands.

I can't remember my own husband's name.

The defragmentation of the hard drive would take another few minutes. After Eric had returned home from the meeting at

KTH, he had tried to fix the errant computer. It was still running slowly, and several error reports had been generated during the afternoon. He had cleaned up the system as well as he could, and then uninstalled all programs that weren't absolutely necessary. His last measure had been to gather up all the information on the hard disk by defragmenting it.

He paged through *Fokus* magazine and waited. The meeting at KTH had gone well, and everyone was enthusiastic about the next phase of the project. Tomorrow they would get to test Mind Surf for real. Some of them had been working on the system for several years, so for them this would be very special. Some of the group members had started to doubt they'd ever reach their goal; in fact, as he thought back, he realised that he had been one of them himself. But the ability to run tests tomorrow depended upon his fixing the computer. There was a complete Mind Surf system at KTH, too, but he had made a number of modifications in his own program, and didn't trust the school's version.

He looked at his phone, which lay beside the keyboard. There were no missed calls and no messages. He had tried Hanna several times, but without hearing back from her. The defragmentation was finished, and the computer restarted. He was just about to check the cords between the converter and the helmet when the front door banged shut.

'Welcome home, dear!'

No answer. He found her on the sofa in the hall, pale and shrunken. She still had her coat on. He sat down and hugged her hard.

'Rough day?'

She was crying. He stroked her hair gently.

'Forget work. Just let it all fall away.'

She was still, and leaned her head on his chest.

'I just want to go to bed.'

'Have you had anything to eat?'

'I'm not hungry. I don't feel well.'

She pulled away, let her coat fall to the floor, and walked silently into the bathroom. After a moment, he heard the shower. He went to the kitchen and put the kettle on. She was gone for nearly half an hour. He was wondering whether he should refill the teacup with more hot water when she showed up in her bathrobe. He smiled.

'You look better now. So what actually happened today?'

She looked at him for a long time, apparently debating whether to answer. Then she sighed and pulled the robe tighter around herself.

'Tel Aviv created a program, *Tza'yad*, Hunter — a search program that can find viruses which are impossible to find. We installed it in our system, and ran smack dab into a new supervirus called Mona. I had to shut down the whole mess. Kaput. *Finito.*'

He stood up and took a few steps toward her.

'I was actually thinking more about you. How are you feeling?'

She put her hands in her pockets and straightened her back.

'How the fuck do you think I feel? I feel useless, and I have all day. If you really cared, you would have torn yourself away from your hacking to give me a call.'

He threw up his hands.

'I did call. Several times.'

She turned away.

'Sure. Just go back to your dusty office. Don't let me stop you. I just want to sleep.'

She left him in the kitchen and went to the bedroom. He shook his head. They were on totally different wavelengths. He swallowed his pride, cleared the table, and took the cup of tea with him to the bedroom. He hesitated in the doorway. She was already deep asleep. She hadn't even taken off her bathrobe. He turned back to the kitchen in frustration.

'Do you know where we are?' The girl looked at her with large brown eyes. The white ash was all over her hair.

She nodded. 'Yes, I know. We're in a store.'

The girl's eyes narrowed.

'But do you know when we are?'

'When?'

'Do you know when we're in the store?'

Hanna squatted to get closer to the girl; her knees ached, but she didn't want to get up.

'No, I don't. Do you?'

The girl nodded.

'We're later.'

'Later? How much?'

The girl cocked her head, thinking.

'I don't really know. I'm only eight. But I think we're a little bit later.'

Hanna looked around in the darkness. 'So all of this is the future?'

The girl lit up. 'That's what it's called. In the future!'

He sat at the kitchen table, poking absent-mindedly at the saltshaker, tired but too agitated to sleep. Was her anger justified? The hell it was. He had called her several times. She must have tons of missed calls on her phone. He had sensed that something was wrong. She must have had a really rough day; she'd looked completely out of it, sitting there in the hall. She was totally stressed out. Eric pictured her before him as she stood in the doorway in her white robe. *Find a virus that's impossible to find.* The sentence seemed to tickle something in his brain. He tasted a few grains of salt. They smelled like sea. It had been a long time since he'd gone swimming. *A virus that's impossible to find.* He got up and ran into the hall. Hanna's bag was on the floor. He took out her small white laptop and jogged through the apartment to his office. He knew her password, and he searched the programs on her computer while standing at the desk. He quickly found what he was looking for: *Mona Tza'yad*. He inserted a USB drive and copied the program to it. Then he knelt next to the Mind Surf computer and inserted the drive into the port. The icon popped up on the screen right away, and he sat down at the keyboard.

The girl took a hesitant step closer to her. Their faces were nearly touching. A strange scent surrounded the girl. Acrid, like a solvent. Hanna wanted to put out a hand and stroke her cheek, but something held her back. She looked the girl in the eyes.

'I want to ask you something. You said that all the people are gone. Do you know where they went?'

The girl lowered her voice to a whisper.

'They died.'

Hanna wobbled. Her legs had fallen asleep.

'Do you know why they died?'

The girl looked unhappy. She didn't answer.

'You can tell me.'

The girl shook her head slowly.

'You'll be angry. Super angry.'

Hanna overcame her fear, and took the girl's small hands in hers. They were cold as ice.

'I won't be mad.'

The girl looked at her, ashamed.

'They got sick.'

Hanna squeezed her cold hands.

'Dear child … Do you know what made them sick?'

The girl lowered her eyes. The answer came after a long hesitation.

'I infected them.'

Eric double-clicked on the *Mona Tza'yad* icon and went through the installation. The program started its search right away. He leaned back.

SEARCHING FOR INFECTION

Suddenly, he heard something from the living room. Footsteps? Clicks on the parquet. Each apartment has its own unique profile of sounds: the fridge, neighbours, traffic, movements on the floor. After several years, a person can feel the atmosphere in his body. Someone was in the living room. He held his breath.

SEARCHING FOR INFECTION

Something fell with a crash. He flew out of his chair.
'Darling, is that you?'
The computer gave a *ding*. He turned toward the screen.

ALERT
MONA VIRUS FOUND
PROTECTION PROTOCOL INITIATED
SHUTTING DOWN NETWORK CONNECTIONS TO CONTAIN INFECTION
STAND BY

Something moved. A silhouette was reflected in the screen. He spun around and saw Hanna in the doorway, soaked with fever, a pale ghost in the dim light. She looked at him, eyes wide open. Terrified.
'… Oh God … help me …'

PART II
SALAH AD-DIN

Stockholm, Sweden

He took the digital thermometer from her mouth and studied the display. Forty-point-one degrees. She was wet with sweat. Eric pulled up the blanket and stroked her forehead.

'Darling, you have quite a fever.' Hanna's eyes were fixed on the ceiling. She was breathing hard. He got up.

'I think you should take a big drink.' He handed her the glass of water from the nightstand. She took it with a mechanical motion, vacant.

'I'm going to get a damp towel for your forehead.'

In the kitchen, he let the water run until it was cold, and then soaked a towel and folded it carefully. But when he heard a crash from the bedroom, he dropped the towel and ran back. She was sitting up in bed. The glass of water was on the floor, broken. She was shaking and breathing violently.

'What happened?'

She looked up into his face; her eyes were glassy with fever.

'The girl infected me.'

He brushed away the hair that was sticking to her face, and tried to get her to lie down.

'What girl?'

She resisted him.

'Mona! She's going to infect us all.'

'Darling, you're delirious. Try to lie down.'

She gripped his wrist hard; her nails dug into his skin.

'You have to listen! We're going to die!'

She looked crazy. Had her fever gotten higher? He started to worry.

'I'll drive you to the hospital.'

She fell back down on the bed and curled up in a foetal position.

'I ... can't remember my own phone number. I can't remember my middle name. Or when your birthday is.'

She sobbed. 'There's nothing we can do.'

'Come on. I'll help you up.'

He placed a jacket across her shoulders and got her bare feet into a pair of rain boots. Then he helped her out of the apartment and into the elevator. She felt fragile under the thin anorak, and he kept his hand on her back to steady her. When they came to the street, she stopped and threw up. Eric tried to pull back her hair as well as he could. Then they staggered across the street to the car.

There was almost no traffic, but he still drove in the bus lane, keeping his speed above one hundred. She was no longer speaking. She was just mumbling to herself, wet and snuffling. He put out his hand and touched her face. Her forehead was burning up. Birger Jarlsgatan flew by, and he veered into the Roslagstull roundabout. He nearly lost control, but then he straightened the car and floored the accelerator again.

Karolinska Hospital popped up to their left. His thoughts went round and round in his head, and he had to fight to concentrate on driving. The area around the hospital was deserted, and the greenish-white light from the neon signs drew shimmering spots on the wet asphalt. He stopped abruptly in front of the emergency entrance and ran around the car. The evening was warm, with a faint scent of rain. She fell out as he opened the passenger door, and it was sheer luck that he managed to catch her. He didn't bother to close the car door, and he half-carried, half-dragged her into the hospital. When they came in through the sliding doors, he got help from two young ambulance drivers who were on their way out. They shouted something to a nurse and placed Hanna on a stretcher. Then they took off with her, and Eric ran after them. One of the ambulance guys threw a glance over his shoulder.

'What happened to her?'

Eric answered breathlessly.

'I don't know. She got sick yesterday. She got worse a few hours ago.'

They ran through swinging doors, and passed several people on stretchers in a long corridor. They turned a corner and were met by one of the nurses and an older man in a white coat and glasses. The man pointed.

'Twelve.'

The ambulance drivers went a few metres farther and then turned into one of the rooms. The older man turned to Eric.

'Are you her husband?'

Eric nodded.

'Thomas Wethje, attending physician. What seems to be the problem?'

'I don't know. She got sick really fast. High fever, throwing up.'

'Is she generally in good health? Any allergies? Does she take any medications? Has she recently been abroad?'

Eric shook his head. 'She is ... was ... perfectly healthy.' The man nodded.

'Has she eaten anything unusual? Something that might be poisonous?'

'I don't know. I don't think so.'

The doctor adjusted his glasses. 'I'd like you to wait here, if that's okay.' He pointed at two yellow plastic chairs that stood some way down the corridor. Then he followed the nurse into the room where they'd left Hanna. Eric walked off and sat down heavily in one of the chairs. It was too soft, and the back wobbled as he leaned against it. After a while, the ambulance drivers came out. One of them, a short Asian man, patted him on the shoulder as he walked by.

'It'll be okay. She looked like a strong gal.'

He didn't answer, able only to stare vacantly at the wall across from him. There was a work schedule next to a sign that encouraged good hand-hygiene. Someone moaned in one of the rooms farther off. He thought of the question the doctor had asked — about whether she had eaten something poisonous. He had instinctively answered no. But was it possible that she had? He thought back through the previous day. No, it had to be something else. He remembered her panic-stricken words in the bedroom. She had said she'd been infected by a girl. There was no point in speculating. He could only wait. He studied the work schedule on the wall again.

He had to wait for a long time. Several nurses came and went, but there was no sign of the doctor. Eric tried to remain calm, and not to worry. They were at the hospital now, and everything would be fine. Finally, Dr Thomas Wethje stepped into the corridor and closed the door gently behind him. He sat down next to Eric.

'I quit smoking. I put out my last cigarette a week ago. I tell you, it's not easy.'

Eric looked at him without saying anything. The doctor dug in his breast pocket and pulled out a pack of gum.

'Nicotine. Sort of works, I think.'

He popped a piece of gum in his mouth and then met Eric's gaze. 'She's sleeping. Her fever was forty-two degrees when she came in. That's very high, and it can be life-threatening. It's lucky you came in. We've given her an IV and something for the fever.'

'What's wrong with her?'

'It's too early to say. The first tests showed a very high white blood-cell count. Her body is arming itself so it can protect her. Her CRP test, which measures protein in the blood, is under fifty, so it's not a bacterial infection. That would seem to indicate a virus. I've done several tests. We'll have an answer in an hour or two.'

Thomas cleaned his glasses on his white coat.

'To be perfectly honest, I don't like what I'm seeing.'

Eric went cold. 'What do you mean?'

Thomas shook his head. 'Her body is rebelling. Her pulse is too high. Her fever, too. And she's having trouble breathing. If it gets worse, we'll have to put her on a machine.'

'What?'

'A respirator. She might need help breathing.'

Eric leaned forward in his chair and blew the air from his lungs. 'Oh, God.'

The doctor placed a hand on his arm.

'Try not to worry. We'll wait for the test results. To be on the safe side, we'll keep her isolated, in case it turns out to be something infectious.'

They sat in silence for a moment. The moaning down the hall continued. Thomas's pager buzzed, and he stood up.

'I have to go. There's a coffee machine near the entrance. You look like you could use a cup.'

Ahvaz, Iran

Nadim had just woken up, and all she had on was a long baseball T-shirt. Samir drank in her bare legs and the contours under her shirt. Her hair was beautifully tousled. She was standing in the kitchen, making sandwiches for their impatient daughter. The sun shone in through the window and flashed on her wristwatch.

Mona tugged at her shirt.

'I'm hungry, Mama. When will you be done?'

She laughed and shook her head.

'You're just as impatient as your mama. How will Papa manage with two identical women? He'll go crazy.'

Mona giggled in delight and threw a glance at him. He held to this image of her as long as he could, but then it faded and disappeared, like a photograph that's overexposed until all that is left is a meaningless white space.

Samir opened his eyes, feeling disoriented for several seconds. His surroundings were enchanted, as if he were still asleep. He lay naked in an enormous, round bed. At the other end of the room, the tall balcony doors were ajar, and the thin curtains moved gently in the breeze. Yesterday slowly came back to him. He was in Prince Abdullah bin Aziz's palace on the outskirts of Ahvaz. Outside the window, the river Karun flowed, edged by date palms and mimosa trees. The prince was a close friend of Enes al-Twaijri, the Saudi oil tycoon whom Samir had met at the meeting with Arie al-Fattal and Ahmad Waizy in Tabriz, and who was now the financial patron of the project.

They had gathered at Fajr Hotel near the Ahvaz airport. All of them had flown in from different parts of the world, with Ahmad arriving last. They had been picked up by the prince's private chauffeur, and then the prince had treated them to a grand dinner. This place was in complete contrast to Somaliland, but Samir preferred the solitude and simplicity there to all of this excess. The overflowing meze table and the stiffly smiling prostitutes were off-putting. He had lain awake in the large bed until the morning light trickled through the shutters and crept slowly across the floor. He must have finally fallen asleep.

There was a faint knock at the door. He pulled up the blanket and called out, '*Aiwa, tfaddal!* Come in!' A young woman with a

128

green veil and bare feet stepped into the room. She was carrying a large silver chalice.

'*Sabah alkhair*, good morning.'

She crouched next to the bed.

'I brought you some mint tea. *Fotoor* is being served one floor up, on the balcony. Your friends are already there.'

He ran his hands over his face and collected himself. She placed her hand on his bare leg, which was sticking out from under the blanket.

'Can I do anything for you before I go?' Her expression erased all doubt about what her question encompassed. He took the chalice and shook his head.

'Tell the others I'm coming. I'm just going to get dressed.'

She smiled, her hand still on his leg.

'Would you like my help?'

'No. Leave me alone.'

She bowed and backed out of the room, leaving the door ajar. He lay still. It was quiet, except for the bright sound of birdsong from the window. The sun was warm — a drowsy warmth and a surreal backdrop. While he slept, reality would loosen its grip and allow him to remember. But when he woke, reality waited restlessly for him with sharp claws and a wide sneer. During the night, he was part of the family once again. In the morning, he was always alone. The constant goodbyes turned his life into a vicious circle.

The breeze from the windows caressed him gently. The minutes ticked by. He wanted to stay in this in-between place. He longed to fall asleep again, but at last stretched his hand toward the chalice, took a large gulp of tea, and conquered his weariness.

There was a beautiful view of the fertile landscape from the balcony. The grounds of the palace stretched as far as he could see in all directions. There wasn't a cloud in the sky, and it was very warm. Thin white fabric had been put up like a roof to give shade. The others were sitting on pillows, eating breakfast. Samir approached yet another table crammed full of food, and took some *fool*, bean porridge. He wasn't hungry; he never was any more. He walked over to the men in the shade. They nodded, and he sat down on an empty pillow across from Ahmad, who ignored him. Ahmad was absorbed in explaining something to Arie.

'… a lot of it depends on the weather, too. The colder it is, the better.'

Arie dipped a piece of bread in the bean paste in front of him and nodded.

'If it's cold,' Ahmad continued, 'no one will react to a person wearing a large coat. Then we can hide a belt that weighs up to around ten kilos. If it's warmer — like today — we can't hide that much. Maybe two or three kilos.'

The others were silent. Ahmad turned to Samir. 'You're late.'

Samir chewed on a fig. 'I overslept.'

'Eat quickly. The meeting starts in ten minutes. Be on time — I've invited a guest.'

Ahmad stood up and left them. Irfan al Jamal, the prince's head of security, and Arie remained behind. Samir poked at his *fool* absent-mindedly. Down below the roof he heard a lawnmower and, faintly, pop music. Fragments of another world.

After breakfast, Ahmad, Arie, and Samir gathered in one of the many parlours in the palace. It must have been one hundred square metres in size, and it was filled with precious objects. Large paintings hung on the walls, all with horse motifs and all in gold frames. The prince was a horse fanatic; he owned over four hundred horses for breeding and competition. In the middle of the room, twelve easy chairs stood around an oval table, on which was a bowl full of fruit. A fan that appeared to be made of pure gold rotated on the ceiling. Samir hadn't seen the prince himself since the evening before.

Ahmad's guest turned out to be a Western consultant. Samir guessed that he was under thirty years old. He was wearing a tailor-made dark suit, a white shirt, a dark-blue tie, and silver cufflinks. His hair was combed back.

Ahmad made a sweeping gesture with his hand.

"The virus is causing great harm. Israel's financial stability is under threat. Several leading institutions have issued warnings and are advising their clients to wait and see before investing in shekels.'

He turned to Arie and Samir.

'As active investors, naturally, we are all concerned about the situation. To get a better idea of how things stand, I've invited Jonathan Yates from Ernst & Young's New York office. Despite his young age, Yates is a prominent financial analyst. His focus is on macroeconomics and the Middle East. The floor is yours, Mr Yates.'

Samir noted a certain irony in Ahmad's voice. Jonathan smiled and cleared his throat.

'I'd like to thank you for inviting me, and I'm glad to be here. What a place!'

He looked at them with a smile. No one smiled back, so he hurried to hand out a packet of papers.

'I have compiled my analysis into a brief report. If you turn to page two, you'll find a number of diagrams.'

They paged through their packets.

'At the very top you'll see the New York Stock Exchange. As you know, there are many Israeli companies listed there and on NASDAQ. In addition, a lot of American companies have investments and owners with Israeli connections. Thus we can assume that these exchanges will be affected more by the virus than will ones like the London or Tokyo exchanges. You can see a normal curve during the first ten weeks of the measuring period — relatively little volatility, with fluctuations of plus or minus 2 per cent. Now, if you turn to the eleventh week, you'll see that the line representing the Israeli exchange especially starts to take a dive, and then it recovers but at a lower level. This was where the exchange system started to behave strangely. Yet it was still nothing too alarming. What we're looking at is a normal reaction, probably due to a number of speculative articles in the media. The market was more on guard.'

Samir followed the line with his finger. At the end of the eleventh week, it pointed sharply downward.

'Here is where the news of a virus attack against the Israeli banking system broke. Within twenty-four hours, the Dow Jones fell 5 per cent and the NASDAQ 6 per cent. The negative trend has continued. Altogether, in the period leading up to today, the Dow Jones has fallen 15 per cent and the NASDAQ all of 17 per cent.'

Jonathan looked around to see if there were any questions, and then he continued.

'The markets in Europe and Asia follow essentially the same pattern, but with a somewhat muted effect. This is because they are more distant from the epicentre. Israel is different. Look at TASE, the index of the Israeli stock exchange. During the past few days, it's fallen 31 per cent, which is an enormous amount. And it continues to follow here, as well. TASE opened at negative-one-point-four this morning. These numbers are already on a level with so-called Black Monday, 19 October 1987, when the world's markets underwent a severe correction.'

Arie looked up from the report, pen in hand. He had made an X next to TASE.

'As I understand it, the virus hasn't caused any direct material harm yet, correct? But despite this, you say the market is skittish? And market prices are falling?'

Jonathan nodded.

'Absolutely. As you know, all trading is based on faith. You have to be able to trust the system, the numbers. The least bit of uncertainty, and the ecosystem is paralysed. The media has been crying wolf. Even if no one sees the wolf, they're covering their asses.'

The analyst regretted his choice of words and quickly continued.

'If you turn a few pages forward in the packet, you'll find a number of reports from the leading banks in the US and Europe. They are taking all of this very seriously, and are talking about the financial crisis of 2009. There's a lot of talk about the fragility of the underlying IT systems. As you know, a great deal of the market is run by so-called "rapid-trade computers", completely automated trading systems that buy and sell hundreds of shares per second. The stock exchanges in general, and the rapid versions in particular, are sensitive to disruptions.'

Ahmad turned to the consultant.

'What would be the best outcome in this situation?'

'For Israel to come out and say that they've stopped the virus and regained control — that it's business as usual. Faith in the system must be recovered, and quickly.'

Ahmad smiled. 'And what's the worst thing that could happen?'

Jonathan was quiet for a second, and then put down the report and looked down at the table.

'The worst thing would be if the virus started to cause concrete harm — if the markets were to see real effects, like lost or manipulated data. And if it turned out to have spread farther than what was feared earlier.'

Ahmad was silent for a moment and then threw up his hands.

'Is that really your worst-case scenario?'

Jonathan met his gaze.

'Worse things could happen, sure. Those who are behind the virus could stir things up even more with other sorts of attacks. Or one of Israel's neighbours could take military advantage of the situation. Then we would end up with an international meltdown, far worse than September 11 and the latest financial crisis put together. But I'm not saying this as a representative of Ernst & Young. These are completely private speculations.'

He wiped the sweat from his forehead with the outside of his arm. Ahmad applauded. It sounded small and hollow in the large room.

'An excellent presentation, Mr Yates. That was exactly what we needed to hear. Thank you and goodbye.'

At first, Jonathan looked bewildered, surprised by the abrupt dismissal. But then he collected himself, took his briefcase, and hastily left the room. No one said anything; they all seemed to be deep in their own thoughts. Arie stood up and walked over to a sideboard with two teapots of silver. He poured a cup of steaming hot tea.

'The American's answer seemed too good to be true … almost as if it had been scripted.'

He looked searchingly at Ahmad, who smiled coolly and turned to Samir.

'What's going on with Mona?'

'Mona has spread more quickly than I'd hoped. The program has already infected 77 per cent of the systems I'd been shooting for. The Israelis have found the virus, all according to plan. The infections they've discovered make up only a fraction of those actually infected — only 5 per cent of the virus clones have been instructed to put down their defences, so they are the ones being detected. Israel has created a virus-search program they call *Mona Tza'yad* — Mona Hunter.'

Arie snorted and shook his head. Samir went on.

'Because they are now finding infections in a variety of locations, they trust the reliability of the search program. For that reason, they've started to back up all the systems they don't think are infected. Mona comes along in the backups, which is important for the next phase. So far, Mona has mostly been a passive virus. She has focused completely on spreading.'

'She?'

Ahmad looked at him in amusement. Samir lost his train of thought.

'What?'

'You said "she". Do you consider your virus to be a living being with a definite gender?'

Samir considered the question. Ahmad waved his hand.

'Continue. You said the virus is focusing on spreading rather than attacking.'

Samir nodded.

'Mona has slowed down the infected networks, but that's basically it. I want the dispersion to be as great as possible before I let *her* attack.'

Samir looked first at Ahmad and then at Arie; both of them nodded in approval. He continued, 'I'll wait a few more days and try to get up to 90 per cent infection. Once we've reached that, Mona can attack. At that point, the virus will wreck databases, take a great deal of strategic information hostage, and manipulate critical data such as market and exchange transactions, as well as inter-bank transactions.'

Ahmad seemed to be studying his own hands on the table. In a low voice he said, 'And when will this happen?'

'In a few days.'

Ahmad slammed his hands onto the table with a bang.

'So within less than a week, chaos will be reality. Then it will also be time for our honourable martyrs. That will really shake up the enemy. Then Hezbollah will be able to make their demands. With Sinon's help, the Zionists will do as we ask. The anti-virus program will be hard currency.'

He raised his eyes to the ceiling.

'The withdrawal will be the start of our redress. Allah's boundless love and merciless strength is with us.'

Samir studied Ahmad. His arms were thin, and his knobby fingers had long nails. He was wearing white cotton pants and a beige linen shirt. A string of brown beads hung from one pocket — ninety-nine beads, one for each of Allah's names. Samir knew very little about the man who had been in control of his life for months. Ahmad had never talked about himself, and none of the others had asked. Samir had heard him speak English with a British accent, and he guessed he was older than Samir himself.

Ahmad took out a black cloth bag and moved the bowl of fruit that was in front of him. He opened the bag and poured its contents onto the table. Small, angular objects that looked like barbs on a fence, in all different sizes and shapes, fell out. Small bits of iron with sharp points, they might have been scraps from a foundry or from welding.

'Revenge and redress come in many forms. For the occupying dogs, Allah chooses these, by all appearances, harmless objects.' He pressed his finger onto a point until it made a hole, and he held up his bloody index finger.

'On top of their belts, the martyrs will carry bags with thousands of these black diamonds. When the bombs go off, they will guarantee maximum effect.'

Samir gave a start. A dizzy feeling washed over him, and he got a sour taste in his mouth. *Maximum effect*. He knew better than anyone what shrapnel does to a person. The images struck him like blows from a hammer. He had arrived twenty minutes after the explosion. As soon as he had turned onto the main street of Qana, he had seen the smoke and increased his speed. He wasn't sure why — maybe it was intuition. People were running, sitting, and standing around the smoking house. Several were trying to put out the fire. A short policeman was speaking into his radio. Three oblong bundles lay in the gutter — one small one, and two larger ones. Out of each bundle poked a pair of feet. One of the larger bundles had shoes on — nice, high-heeled shoes. The other large bundle had only stockings. The small bundle had white canvas shoes flecked with dried mud. The policeman had tried to stop him as he furiously tore away the rags they had placed over her body.

Maximum effect. He had stared right at it, on his knees in Qana.

He turned his attention to the discussion in the room once again. As soon as Mona started to attack the infected systems, the suicide bombers would trigger their loads — one in Tel Aviv and two in Jerusalem. Arie and Ahmad studied maps, and discussed times and suitable roads into Israel. Ahmad had learned that the Mossad had managed to link Arie to the virus. Arie looked worried, and wanted to know more. Samir, too, seemed to be on the Mossad's list. Maybe he ought to be afraid as well.

Ahmad leaned back. He had the string of beads in his hand.

'I will personally take care of the operational portion of the next phase.'

There was no question that he was looking forward to the attacks.

'The largest load will be in a vehicle filled with liquid explosive and thousands of these.'

Ahmad pointed at the sharp metal objects on the table.

'The target will be the Hebrew University of Jerusalem.'

Samir didn't know if the plan had been developed after he joined the group, or if it had already existed and had just been waiting for the right person. Not that he cared. He had worked on Mona, day in and day out, driven by raging anguish, without sleeping, eating, or crying. First in a dark, dusty carpet warehouse in the Iranian city of Qom; then in the apartment in Nice; and then at the old missile base in Berbera. Now, as he sat in this magnificent room with its grand view of Karun, he no longer felt any desire for revenge. It had been different while he was burying himself in his work. The days flowed into one another, and weeks turned into months, without giving him time to think about it. But now the doors had opened on an involuntary chance for reflection. *Maximum effect*.

He looked at the Koran that lay beside Ahmad. He leaned forward and picked up the worn book. Without interrupting himself — or even taking his eyes from Arie — Ahmad snatched Samir's wrist. His grip was so firm that it felt like his arm was going to break. Samir gasped and let go of the book, which fell to the table with a thud. They sat still, interlaced. Samir looked into Ahmad's black eyes. Then Ahmad let go and smiled.

'*Ana asif*, I'm sorry. Pure reflex. The final testament follows me wherever I go. Here, you're welcome to borrow it.'

Ahmad's sinewy hand pushed the book toward him. Samir hesitated slightly, but then picked it up and nodded weakly, dazed and with his wrist throbbing. Ahmad turned back to Arie, who looked embarrassed. Samir stopped listening, paged through the 114 suras, and lost himself in the familiar words.

Stockholm, Sweden

Eric closed the door behind him with an unnecessarily loud bang. The apartment was empty. No, not empty. Deserted. A big difference. The scent in the hall, her keys on the chest, the hum from the fridge in the kitchen — all of these familiar things seemed strange and forbidding. The tests had confirmed that Hanna was seriously ill, but they didn't indicate a specific diagnosis. The doctors needed to do more tests.

He hadn't faltered as he kissed her forehead. He kept it together as he hurried out to the lonely car to go home and get a change of clothes. But now he was falling apart. He sank onto the sofa and started to cry. He gripped its arms hard and sobbed uncontrollably, just as Hanna had done when she'd come home earlier that same evening. But this time no one came running with sympathy and cold towels. The apartment just sat there — passive, quiet, and empty — waiting. Their everyday routine, with its predictable rhythms, had been unmasked. Nothing was reliable. There was no security. Everything was fragile, brittle. The mechanisms of their lives could become jammed at any moment, or simply stop working.

A police siren sounded somewhere outside. He thought of Hanna's feverish gaze. He wanted to switch places with her. She ought to be sitting here, healthy; he ought to be lying there, sick. His gaze fell on her handbag, tossed on the floor beside the chest of drawers. He took in the scent of leather and perfume, and the simple essentials of her everyday life: talismans, symbols, and products. He loved her world, and yet he knew so little about it. How the hell could everything change so fast? Just a few hours ago he had been happy — or nearly so. Mind Surf was working, and he was going to take on their relationship and the future with renewed energy. Now it had all come crashing down. Hanna was in intensive care. Mind Surf was infected with some sort of jihad virus. He got up and stood before the large mirror in the hall. His eyes were red and his cheeks were moist. His hair was dishevelled. He pressed his forehead against the cool mirror and breathed heavily, his breath fogging the sharpness of the glass. For a long time they stood forehead to forehead, the reproduction and the prototype. The reproduction and the abyss. Oh, God, how could he help Hanna? What could he do?

'SOS Alarm, what is the nature of your call?'

'It's my husband. Oh my God …'

'What's wrong with your husband?'

'He … he's lying in the kitchen. Please, come quickly.' The woman started to cry.

'Has he had an accident?'

'He's lost his memory.'

'Lost his memory? That's not a matter for emergency dispatch. You'll have to visit a clinic tomorrow.'

'Damn it, that's not why I called! He's sick. Really sick. It's all happened so fast.'

'What kind of symptoms does he have?'

'He's been throwing up. All over. And he has a fever. I think it's way too high. And he's delirious.'

'Okay. Do you think you can drive him yourself, or maybe take a taxi, to the nearest hospital? Could he have eaten something that was bad?'

The woman breathed heavily into the mouthpiece.

'You fucking listen, you pimply little shit. My husband is one of the most respected businessmen in the country. He got sick so fast, I'm afraid he might die. Either you send an ambulance, or else I will personally make sure that you're fired.'

The man at the dispatch centre shook his head.

'There's no need to threaten me. We're here to help. I'll send an ambulance. What is your address, and what is your husband's name?'

The woman answered in a dogged voice.

'My address is Elfviksvägen 62 on Lidingö. My husband's name is Mats Hagström.'

Another brown-plastic mug of weak coffee went down the hatch. He needed to drive away the exhaustion that was creeping into his body and causing him to freeze. Once again he was sitting on a rickety plastic chair, this time beside her bed. She had been moved and was now lying in a larger room with three other beds, all empty. The hospital workers were being careful to keep her isolated, since they still didn't know if she was contagious. The lights were dimmed. Hanna was sleeping and breathing calmly. He held her hand, careful not to touch the IV line. Her body jerked now and then, and her hand trembled in his grasp. Dreams? Eric didn't know what to do. He went over and over the last few days in his mind, trying to find an explanation. Dr Thomas Wethje was still responsible for her care, even though she had been moved. He came by at regular intervals, but seemed to be as bewildered as everyone else. Hanna had an infection. That had been confirmed. It wasn't bacterial; it was some sort of virus. Several hours ago, Thomas had brought a whole flock of doctors with him, and they'd stood around Hanna's bed writing in their notebooks. Before they left, Thomas squeezed his shoulder.

'She's stable. We'll figure out what's going on with her. Don't worry.'

But the doctor's eyes had told a different story. At least, that was how he understood it. He stood up and walked over to the window. Far below, he saw a large courtyard. A few silhouettes stood beside a door, smoking. He looked at the clock. It was already 7.30 in the morning. He hadn't slept at all during the night, and remembered he was supposed to meet with Mats Hagström this morning. They were supposed to be at his office at nine. He went into the hall and blinked in the bright neon light. The unit was quiet, and a nurse with short, red hair was preparing a breakfast cart. He pointed at his mobile phone, and looked at her inquiringly. She wrinkled her nose in disapproval.

'You'll have to go over to the elevators. You're not allowed to use that in here.'

He nodded and made his way down the corridor. His body felt like it had been run over by a semi. He dialled Mats's number. There was an answer on the third ring.

'Hello?'

It was a woman's voice. He looked at the screen to make sure he'd dialled correctly.

'Uh … I'm sorry. I'm trying to reach Mats Hagström.'

The woman answered absent-mindedly. 'Unfortunately, he's not available. I'm his wife — would you like me to take a message?'

'My name is Eric Söderqvist, and I had a meeting scheduled with him this morning. I'm afraid I need to cancel it because I'm at Karolinska Hospital. Unfortunately, my wife became sick during the night.'

The woman was silent for a moment, and he had to look at his mobile phone again to make sure the call hadn't dropped out.

'Hello? Are you still there?'

'I'm still here. We're closer than you think. I'm in the emergency room, myself. Mats became ill during the night.'

Eric sat down on the stairs next to the elevators.

'I'm really sorry to hear that. I hope it's nothing serious.'

'No one knows — not a single bastard in this whole hospital.

Can you believe it? Because I sure as hell can't. They've done test after test, but can't figure it out.'

There was a crackle from the phone. She might have been sobbing.

'Isn't this supposed to be a world-class hospital? The best one we have?'

Eric tried to collect his thoughts. What was going on? The doctors couldn't come up with a diagnosis … just like with Hanna. Had they been infected by the same thing? When? How? He stood up and walked back into the unit.

'Just a minute, I'm going to check with our doctor about something.'

'Wait? Please, that's all I'm doing. Wait, wait, wait. And while I do, he's fading away. Fading away!'

He caught sight of the red-headed nurse. When she noticed that he was talking on the phone, she put her hands on her hips and frowned.

'Didn't you understand me? Mobile phones are not allowed on the unit. Either get out of here right now, or hang up.'

He shook his head, walked past her, and continued on toward the office. She started to follow him.

'Come back. What are you doing? You've got some nerve!'

He stuck his head in through the office door. A young woman with a ponytail looked up from a computer.

'Can I help you?'

'I need to talk to Dr Thomas Wethje right away.'

She looked at the clock on the wall.

'He ought to be here in an hour or so. He's down in the emergency room right now. You can wait in …'

'I can't wait. He had a pager. What's the number?'

The red-headed woman stepped between him and the one with the ponytail, panting.

'Out with you. We're trying to do our jobs here, so hang up right now. The signals disrupt our equipment. Do you understand?'

She had her hands on her hips again. He remembered that Mrs Hagström was still on the line, and turned to the red-headed woman. 'I will, as soon as I've gotten hold of Dr Wethje.'

'Oh, no. The doctor has important things to do. You can't go around bothering him with whatever you want.'

Eric lost his patience.

'Shut it, you goddamned carrot top. I'm trying to save lives, too.'

The nurse looked as though she'd been struck by lightning. For a moment, she seemed to waver, but then she clenched her fists.

'I'm getting security!'

As she shoved past him, Eric was met by the sour smell of sweat. The ponytail looked at him questioningly. He took a deep breath.

'I'm tired and stressed out. I haven't slept all night, and my wife is seriously ill. No one seems to know what's wrong with her. I'd really appreciate it if you could give me the doctor's pager number. It's important.'

She hesitated at first, but then nodded. She stood up and gave him a yellow Post-it note.

'Britta is a real witch. Nice that someone put her in her place.'

He looked at the cute girl in front of him and smiled.

'Thanks. It was my pleasure.'

Eric went back into the corridor as he asked Mrs Hagström if he could call her back. Then he dialled the doctor's number and sat down on the stairs by the elevators again to wait for his call. After ten long minutes, the phone rang: it was an unknown number.

'This is Thomas Wethje. You paged me?'

144

'Hi, I'm really sorry to bother you. This is Eric Söderqvist.'

'Hi, Eric. Can this wait? I'm awfully pressed for time.'

The nurse with the ponytail popped up at the doors into the unit. She gestured at him. He spoke more quickly.

'Just give me a minute. Yesterday I met with a colleague. We'd scheduled a meeting for today, but when I tried to reach him, I spoke to his wife. Apparently, he's a patient here, in the emergency room, with symptoms very similar to Hanna's, and …'

'Mats Hagström?'

'Mats Hagström.'

'His wife sure is a tough lady. She's giving us all hell. Hagström is exhibiting symptoms like the ones we've seen in your wife, but there are also some differences.'

Eric caught sight of Nurse Britta through the glass window. A Securitas guard with a shaved head was marching beside her.

'Can you come down to the emergency room?'

'I don't think I have a choice. A nurse is about to throw me out.'

Thomas chuckled.

'I hear you've met Britta Stensson. You'd be smart to hurry down here. If she gets hold of you, no one can save you.'

Tel Aviv, Israel

Rachel Papo crouched and studied all the pastries in the glass case carefully. She dare not pick the wrong one. Anything could cause Tara to become hysterical — the wrong colour, wrong shape, wrong icing. Last time, a green marzipan rose had provoked an attack that lasted nearly twenty minutes. In the end, Rachel had managed to calm her down, but by then she had already overturned the table and dirtied her clothes so much that they had to go home. But it was Rachel's fault: she had ordered from a waiter without first checking what they would give her. She knew reasonably well what made her little sister nervous. She saw a white pastry with brown dots — perfect. She ordered tea for herself, and a Fanta for Tara. She looked carefully at the glass that the cashier gave her. It absolutely must not be dirty, or have any text or logos on it. It appeared to be okay. She took the tray, and returned to the table in the back corner of the café. Tara didn't like to sit near windows — especially not on so lively a street as Dizengoff.

Rachel sat down across from her sister and smiled warmly. Tara was counting the sugar cubes in the bowl on the table. When she finished this, she immediately started over, sighing, and shaking her head. They had the same thick, dark hair, but Tara's was shorter. Tara's body was bloated and swollen with the side effects of her strong medications. But she was still beautiful — more beautiful than any other person on earth. They were different and alike at the same time. Tara's face was more innocent, soft, and perfectly symmetrical. They had the same almond-shaped eyes. But there was something innocent and genuine about Tara that Rachel lacked. And then there was Tara's straight nose, not broken like her own.

Tara was eight years younger, on paper. Emotionally, she was at least twenty years younger — a small, confused child. It hadn't always been this way, but after their departure nothing was the same. She carefully took Tara's hands and moved the sugar bowl aside. Then she gave her the pastry and poured the Fanta. Tara looked at the pastry for a long time. Rachel stopped pouring and prepared herself for a catastrophe. But then Tara lit up, took the spoon, and ate a large bite. Rachel relaxed and watched her sister's movements. There was something peaceful about her when she ate.

146

They had taken the Singapore assignment away from her. Rachel had done all the preparations: read up on the target, planned escape routes, and selected a suitable identity. But someone else had gone in her place, and she was still in Tel Aviv. At first, she'd thought it was because Dubai had gone to hell and she was in the deep freeze until the inquiry. But what was there to investigate? Mohammad al-Rashid had attacked her, and she had reacted instinctively. It was unfortunate, but everyone who worked in the field knew that you couldn't plan everything in advance. The bureau's second-in-command, David Yassur, had called her to ask a bunch of things about Arie al-Fattal and the virus attack. But then Meir Pardo had written to her. She was being promoted. *You are so much more than muscles*. That's what he had said.

She knew that the director of the Mossad liked her. She had never really understood why. The organisation had nearly ten thousand employees, and Meir was at the top, as close to God as you could get. She was at the bottom of the ladder. But despite that, he had often spoken with her, helped her, and he'd always been careful to keep in touch. And now a promotion had come. No more assassinations for Unit 101; now she would work with intelligence tasks instead.

Rachel had already been at a briefing in her new department. She had been placed in the group that was leading the hunt for Samir Mustaf, the creator of the Mona virus. It was a small, hand-picked team made up entirely of men, except for her. Not just men, she corrected herself: good old boys. Did she even want to get away from Unit 101? She had received a thick folder full of hundreds of documents she was expected to read, and a pile of pictures. All of them were of Samir Mustaf, except for one small colour photo of his daughter, Mona. She was cute as a Barbie doll — big brown eyes, curly black hair, a brilliant smile.

Rachel had a hard time imagining the sorrow at losing a child. She had none of her own, and knew that she never would. But Tara, if something were to happen to her … She looked at her sister. She had stopped eating, and was now blowing bubbles in the soda with her straw. Rachel hadn't succeeded in protecting her the night before their departure, but she would not let her down again. Never again. Nowadays, she had different training; different experience. Nowadays, she herself was a weapon. She would devote her life to avenging her.

She drank some tea. Perhaps she already had avenged her. All those people — she had never hesitated, had never been filled with regret over grown people crying and begging for mercy. She did it to protect Israel, to act against the constant threat to Jewish existence. The country needed all types of defence, even Unit 101. But how many times did a person have to kill in order to be free? Tara would never be free. Never. So, could she understand what Samir did? He had lost his child, and his family. Could she sympathise with him? She let the question tumble around her mind, and sipped her lukewarm tea. Tara had returned to the pastry.

The question was irrelevant. The answer was uninteresting. Samir Mustaf constituted a threat — end of story. There were thousands of such heartbreaking motives, but she could never allow them to affect her. It was up to the mourners to spin their thick silk threads over the fallen body: threads that gave it the shape of a martyr and hero. She was not one of the mourners. She came before them. Tara put down her spoon, picked up the sugar bowl, and started to count.

Stockholm, Sweden

He was driving along Sveavägen. The sound of the engine had a soporific effect, and at one point he had to swerve so as not to cross into the wrong lane. An oncoming car honked vehemently. Eric slowed down. He hadn't slept in over twenty-four hours. It felt strange to leave Hanna, but they were going to do more tests, and he would only be in the way. And he needed to get away, collect his thoughts. The fact that Mats Hagström had become ill had changed everything. Eric had been with both of them. He was the link between them. But he felt fine. Could he be carrying the virus without knowing it? According to Thomas Wethje, it was possible, but not likely. He had given samples of urine, blood, and saliva anyway. The doctor was considering moving Hanna to a more isolated part of the hospital, a special unit for patients who were highly infectious. Eric blinked and changed lanes. Beyond a few symptoms, there was nothing else so far to link Hanna and Mats. But something was alive in them. He could feel it. A poisonous snake, evading X-rays and blood tests, was swimming around in Hanna's blood and biding its time.

Eric made a right turn onto Kungsgatan and sped up down toward Vasagatan. He wasn't going to stay long — just have a coffee and talk for half an hour or so to a rational, conscious person. Then he would go back to the hospital. Jens was worried about Hanna, of course. If Eric was a carrier, could he infect Jens? But when would he have become infected? And why hadn't he got sick? He went through everyone he had seen in the last few days. The lecture at KTH? There was a clear risk of contagion there; it was a closed room, with one hundred people in the audience. Or had Mats been the first to be infected? He could have infected Eric at their meeting the other day — the meeting with the famous apple toss. And then Eric could have carried the virus with him and infected Hanna when they saw each other later that evening. But, in that case, Jens should be sick, too. They had met at Riche right after the meeting. No, that couldn't be it, either. Could it have been an exotic virus that came in the package with the new gel? In the package from Kyoto University? Could a virus survive several days in a package?

He passed Vasagatan and continued up toward Kungsbron. The morning traffic was non-existent, and he soon turned onto Västra Järnvägsgatan. He knew too little about viruses. But considering how virologists had to put so much effort into keeping them alive in labs, it hardly seemed likely that a virus could travel around the world and stay alive. And if there had been a virus in the package, he ought to have been sick himself. Jens, too. He shook his head in irritation. There was something bubbling away in his subconscious. Something important. He'd had the same feeling since he'd left the hospital: he was missing something. He tried to grasp the elusive thought, but it was pointless. He was too tired. *Aftonbladet's* yellow logo sat high up on the wall of the square glass colossus that contained the paper's main offices. He pulled into an empty parking spot and turned off the engine. He sat still for a moment, his head against the steering wheel. The last day swept through his head like a crazy play. The answer was there somewhere, but it was lost in the whole.

He stepped out of the car and breathed in the fresh morning air. The area around the station seemed to be one big construction site, full of cranes stretching toward the sky. Stockholm was growing. He locked the car and entered the building. In the elevator, he ran his hand through his messy hair, and tucked his shirt into his jeans. When he stepped out into *Aftonbladet's* sky-lighted atrium, Jens stood up from one of the red sofas in the reception area and rushed toward him. They hugged. Jens leaned back and looked him in the eye, his arms still around his shoulders.

'What the hell is going on? How is she? And how are you doing?'

Eric shook his head and nodded toward the editorial offices.

'Could we sit down somewhere there's peace and quiet? A conference room?'

Jens looked at him for a long moment.

'You need a bedroom.'

'I need caffeine.'

'We've got coffee over there. Come on.'

They walked across the large editorial area. In the far corner stood three large, red coffee machines. Jens put down two mugs and chose regular black coffee, with the comment, 'It all tastes like shit anyway.' Then he went over to a candy machine that stood next to a small sink. He ran his finger along the glass front until he found what he wanted. He waved at Eric.

'Come here. Press them like this.'

Eric placed his fingers on the buttons.

'Keep pressing. Don't stop.'

Then Jens crouched next to the large machine, fished for the cord, and yanked the plug from the outlet. Eric looked at him quizzically. Jens waited a few seconds before he plugged it in again. The machine gave a growl, and the spiral that held Japp bars rotated and shoved the chocolate down into the box. Jens smiled grimly. 'You have to show the machines who's boss.' He gave the Japp to Eric. 'You need energy. Eat.'

Then he took the coffee mugs and started to walk toward a row of small conference rooms along the outer wall.

'Well, then, you can just go to hell!'

Eric turned around just in time to see a young guy with back-slicked hair and a green tie slam the phone down at one of the editorial desks. A woman with curly blond hair looked at him curiously. The guy pointed at her with a pen.

'Can you believe what that little pinko pig said?'

The woman shook her head. Eric turned away from them and followed Jens. Apparently, a lot had changed at this newspaper, which had once been the flagship of the Trade Union Confederation. Jens waited until he had entered one of the rooms, and then pulled the glass door shut behind him. He sat down heavily in one of the steel chairs.

'Let's try again ... how are you feeling?'

Eric sat down next to him and put his face in his hands.

'It doesn't really matter. Okay, I think. Or ... shit, I don't know.'

'And Hanna?'

'She's not well at all. The doctors don't seem to know what she has. The only thing that's for certain is that she's getting worse. Thomas Wethje's latest theory seems to be that it's some sort of contagious variant of meningitis.'

'Thomas Wethje?'

'The doctor at Karolinska.'

'Meningitis? But didn't they think it was some sort of virus?'

'Meningitis is a virus. And the symptoms are very similar to Hanna's — dizziness, vomiting, fever, and joint pain. But I could tell that he didn't believe what he was saying. No, she has something else inside her. Something evil. The truth is, I'm desperate. I don't know what the hell to do.'

Jens placed his large hand on Eric's arm.

'You're doing everything you can. You're a researcher — not a doctor. All you can do is sit with her and trust that this Thomas is earning his pay.'

'He seems good. Unusually sensible, in fact. But he's fumbling in the dark.'

'Surely he can do something?'

'Fucked if I know. Everything's boiling down to the fact that they don't have a diagnosis to work with. Mats Hagström seems to be even worse off than Hanna. Early this morning he had a serious heart attack, and for a while it looked like he wasn't going to make it. Now both of them are in some sort of coma. Unreachable.'

'Dear Hanna. I'll go see her. You have to take it easy for a few hours. Go to bed. You'll be no help to Hanna if you fall down dead. We'll just have to take turns sitting with her.'

Eric took a sip of coffee. He smiled weakly.

'You're right — it really does taste like shit. It's even worse than the swill at the hospital.'

He thought of something he'd missed.

'I have to call Hanna's work. I forgot all about it, in the middle of this mess ... their director of IT could hardly have chosen a worse time to get sick.'

Jens leaned back and gestured toward the editorial offices.

'You're right about that. All our reporters have got their hands full with the virus crisis. The Israeli stock exchange is about to crash. I don't think anyone really gets how fragile our financial systems are. When people can no longer rely on information about stocks, they stop buying things. And when they do that, everything stops. And it's not just Israel that's hit a wall — it's New York, London, Tokyo, Mumbai, too. From what I've seen and heard, Mona has unleashed an avalanche of distrust and panic throughout the global system. The epicentre is in Tel Aviv, of course, but the shock waves are rolling out over the entire world. The Swedish Civil Contingents Agency has called a press conference for today to try to convince us they're doing what they can to protect the Swedish system. No one has officially taken credit for the attack yet, but more and more sources are pointing at Hezbollah. The American secretary of state is on the way to Tel Aviv, and there's one crisis meeting after another at the EU.'

The rest of the world felt far off to Eric. Unreal. But then he remembered his own infected computer.

'Has anyone found an anti-virus?'

Jens shook his head.

'Not yet. I think every IT expert from Tel Aviv to Oslo is working on it, but so far we haven't heard of any solution. The virus is really extraordinary, not something created by some rotten skateboarder kid in Arizona. No, it's very advanced, and something totally new — a well-planned, thoroughly financed, and, above all, well-executed attack. That's probably why everyone is at such a loss. It's just like with that Thomas Wethje, they're all fumbling in the dark. If they don't understand the virus, how can they find a cure?'

Eric's whole body went cold. The thought that had eluded him fell into place like a concrete block. He was petrified. Jens frowned.

'What? What did I say?'

Eric put down his coffee mug and lowered his eyes. His mind was racing. What had Hanna said when she'd dropped the glass in the bedroom? He had thought she was just delirious from the fever: 'The little girl infected me. Mona ...' How could she know? Why had she said that? No! Mona was a computer virus. Hanna was human, flesh and blood. But she had been infected with *something*. Mats, too. They had both used Mind Surf. But how was it all connected? Could they really be related? During her session, Hanna had navigated to TBI's website — a website that was infected with the virus.

Jens sat quietly, studying him with worried eyes.

'Shit, Jens. You're never going to believe this.'

Jens leaned toward him.

'What? Believe what?'

His mind was racing so fast that he was having trouble keeping up. Hanna had been in biological contact with Mind Surf, by way of the nanogel and the sensor helmet. She had gone to

154

an infected website. The computer had been infected. Somehow, the virus had affected her physically. Injured her. Infected her? Not like a virus in a biological sense; that was impossible, but maybe it had altered something in her. But what about Mats?

'What won't I believe?'

'Wait. Just let me think … '

Mats had used Mind Surf after Hanna. After the computer had become infected. That's how he, too, had been infected — no, not infected, affected. That explained why Eric himself wasn't sick. He had used Mind Surf before Hanna visited the infected TBI site. He sat in silence, staring vacantly ahead. Jens squeezed his hand.

'Buddy, what's going on? Talk to me.'

If it were true, it was his fault. He had made Hanna try it out. She had wanted to make love, not be a guinea pig. But he had only been thinking of himself and of taking the chance to impress her. His eyes filled with tears. Despite the absurdity of his logic, he knew he was right. Mona had hurt her. And Mats.

'Eric, it will all work out. Hanna's going to get better. If she's made it for this long, things will turn around soon. The worst is behind us.'

Eric rubbed his hand over his eyes and looked at Jens.

'What I'm about to tell you is going to sound like it's right out of a Stephen King story.'

Jens stared at him.

'Okay …'

'I know what hurt Hanna. And Mats.'

'What?'

'My program — Mind Surf.'

Jens tried to comprehend what Eric had just said. Finally, he said in a low voice, 'What the hell does Stephen King have to do with it?'

'Not a damn thing. Forget about him. When Hanna tested Mind Surf, she went to the TBI site. The site was infected by the virus. Mind Surf was infected, and somehow — don't ask me how — the malicious code has affected her biologically. The same with Mats. No matter how crazy it sounds, Mona ... infected them.'

He grew silent, expecting to be declared an idiot. Jens sat without speaking for a long time, staring at him. His mouth was half open.

'Now I see why you're raving about Stephen King.'

The two of them sat there, deep in thought. The air felt heavy and close. Jens opened the Japp bar and ate one of the pieces, hardly conscious of what he was doing.

'Maybe you're right that the program is what made them sick. But it might not have a damn thing to do with the virus. I've always said it's a crazy idea to hook people and machines together. Maybe that's what the trouble is. Maybe the brain can't cope with all those digital stimuli?'

'That could be the case, but then I'd be sick, too. Remember, I tested it as well. But I'm healthy. It's because I used the program before it got infected.'

'But a computer virus is just a technical name for a piece of programming — a bunch of ones and zeroes. A biological virus is completely different. How could a person be infected by a computer program? I'm neither a computer genius nor a doctor; I studied structural engineering. But even I understand that the transmission of digital program code to flesh and blood is impossible.'

'Jens! I'm a fucking professor of these things. I get what you're saying. And, anyway, I don't think they've been infected by the virus in the sense that the digital code has been transferred to a biological form. But I'm absolutely convinced that the virus has done something to the neurological signals that passed through the converter. Those warped commands made them sick.'

Jens still looked sceptical. Eric pushed the other half of the Japp bar toward him, but he shook his head and pushed it back.

'You should look in the mirror. You need energy.'

'Isn't it extraordinary that Thomas Wethje, a top doctor at Karolinska, thinks that Hanna and Mats have been infected by a virus? But at the same time he can't come up with a solid diagnosis?'

Jens held up his hands.

'I don't know. I just know that Hanna's sick and you're beat. Maybe you'll come up with a more plausible scenario after you've gotten some sleep.'

Eric felt restless. Maybe he could do something for Hanna after all. He was no doctor, but he did understand computers.

'I need to know more about the virus. I need to understand Mona better.'

He looked out the glass windows at the news desks.

'Who here has the most updated news?'

Jens shook his head.

'You're getting worked up over something that doesn't matter. It would be better if you slept on it.'

Eric stood up.

'I want to talk to someone here who knows what's going on with Mona. Who?'

He looked at Jens, his expression pleading. Jens groaned and got up. He handed Eric the chocolate.

'I'm not taking another step until you eat this.'

Eric broke a piece off and made a show of putting it in his mouth. Then he opened the door.

'Come on.'

They walked to the stairs that connected the levels in the large atrium. On the way up, Jens turned around.

'After this, you're going straight home to sleep. That's an order.'

Eric nodded. They walked through the arts and culture department on the first floor, and arrived at a row of workstations, all cluttered with papers, newspapers, and books.

'Here's the hack pool. Feature things, and the more investigative stuff — long special pieces.'

Sitting at one of the desks was a thin man with purple suspenders. Jens snapped one of the suspender straps against the man's back. The man flew up and turned around, his face bright red. But when he saw Jens, the anger drained from his face.

'Jens, you bastard. Why don't you work at a PR firm and do customer magazines instead? Anywhere but here.'

Jens smiled.

'Carl Öberg, always a pleasure to see you. This is Eric Söderqvist. He's a good friend — my best friend, actually — and he has some questions about Mona. Do you have a few minutes?'

Carl sized him up.

'Jens's best friend? What have you done to deserve such a horrible fate?'

'Studied at KTH.'

Jens turned to Eric.

'Calle has really dug deep into the virus affair. He has contact with colleagues and correspondents out in the field, and he runs off to all of TBI's press conferences. He's got an ambitious analysis of the whole Mona story in mind. He's angling for the Swedish Grand Journalist Prize.'

He leaned forward, but didn't lower his voice: 'To be completely honest, no one here understands where he plans to publish it. Calle still hasn't realised that he works for an evening paper that only wants to run short and preferably frivolous stories. This is not *The New Yorker*.'

Carl made a face and pointed at a chair. 'Have a seat, Eric. What do you want to know?'

Eric pulled the chair closer and sat down.

'I want to know if anyone has developed, or is in the process of developing, a remedy. Is there an anti-virus? What's the latest news?'

'Nothing substantial. TBI is co-operating with the Israeli state, and they seem to have backing from all the American authorities, but so far no one has come up with a solution. The latest last night was that Google has offered to lend processor power to those fighting the virus. That would speed up their work substantially. No one else in the world has so much computing power, so that's definitely a good thing.'

Eric tore a few pages from an empty notebook he found on the desk, and borrowed a pen from a well-supplied desk organiser. He made a few short notes.

'What other news is there?'

Carl sat silently for a moment. Then he turned to Jens.

'Can I trust this guy?'

Jens placed a hand on Eric's shoulder.

'As if he were my own brother.'

Carl rolled his eyes. 'Oh, God. Just the thought that you might have a brother gives me the willies.'

He turned to Eric.

'I'm working on digging up something that might turn out to be a world-class scoop.'

There was no mistaking the pride in his voice.

'This has to stay between us. *Expressen* will have to get its own scoop. Okay?'

Eric nodded and stifled a yawn.

'Early on, we learned that the virus attack started in France — specifically, Nice.'

Eric frowned.

'But I thought it came from the Middle East?'

159

'Yes, it does. Without a doubt. But it was uploaded from the TBI offices in Nice. Information is really scarce, though, so I did my own investigation, using my own sources.'

'What kind of sources?'

Carl blinked.

'That's confidential. I've spent quite a bit of time in Nice, and I still have friends there. Among others, a guy who works in a bar at one of the bigger nightclubs.'

Carl sneaked a look at Jens, who snorted.

'This guy dug down into his circle of contacts and got a bite.'

'A bite? Who?'

'One of the policemen with the national task force. He seems to be having a rough time financially, and he wants to earn more money. He's selling information. I haven't got a name, but I've spoken with him on the phone. We're going to talk again tomorrow evening.'

'And has he said anything of interest?'

Carl nodded triumphantly.

'He says that they raided an apartment a few weeks ago. In it, they found burned computer equipment and TBI access cards. Also, one person was killed during the raid. He's been identified as …' Carl dug through his papers, found a page full of scribbled notes, and nodded to himself. '… Melah as-Dullah. And now for the best part: the French security service has — and this is top-secret — linked him to Hezbollah!'

Carl looked at the two of them expectantly. When neither of them said anything, he threw up his hands.

'Don't you get it? None of this has been in any newspaper. Or on TV. None of it! We can be the first in the world to confirm that it really is Hezbollah behind Mona!'

Jens applauded. A woman at one of the other desks shot him a look of disapproval.

'Well done, Carl! For the first time in your far-too-modest career, you're earning your pay. But do we have any proof? Anything we can print? Surely a picture of that as-Dullah wouldn't be too much to ask for?'

Eric discreetly glanced through Carl's notes. He wrote down three telephone numbers and one name, Cedric Antoine. Carl nodded.

'Sure, you're right. The guy promised that I'd receive photographs and more information. I'll remind him when we talk tomorrow evening. I can tell that this is going to be huge.'

Jens nodded in approval.

'Like I said, Grand Journalism Prize. Have you talked to Bjäreman?'

'Only hints. He'll get the masterpiece when it's done.'

Eric looked at Jens.

'Who's Bjäreman?'

'The chief news editor. The boss. *Capo di tutti capi.*'

The phone rang, and Carl answered it. Jens placed his hand on Eric's shoulder.

'Let's get out of here. It's pillow time for you. And I'll go see Hanna.'

He patted Carl on the head, and Carl reached across the keyboard and fished out a business card, which he gave to Eric.

'Hold on ... Eric, it was nice to meet you. Don't go talking to anyone about this. And if you happen to run across anything interesting, you know who to call.'

Eric put the business card and his notes into his wallet. On the way down the stairs, Jens chuckled.

'A guy who works at a bar in a nightclub ... Jesus!'

'What?'

'Calle's gay. He doesn't advertise it, but everyone knows. One can assume that his web of sources in Nice is pretty male-dominated. Just so you know. He's a really clever journalist — maybe the best one we have at the paper. And a damn good person, despite the suspenders. Did you learn anything from talking to him?'

'Not really. But it does feel reassuring that Google is involved in the hunt for an anti-virus.'

They arrived at reception and ended up standing across from each other at the entrance. Jens leaned toward him and gave him a searching look.

'Can you handle driving home, or should I give you a ride?'

'I'll drive. But thanks anyway.'

'My friend, I'm going to Karolinska to sit with Hanna now. And you have to turn out the lights for at least six hours. Call me when you wake up, and I'll give you a report from the hospital. Agreed?'

'Agreed. It's good to know you'll be with her.'

He walked to the elevator. Jens remained standing in reception.

'Eric … We'll figure this out.'

'Good night.'

Eric returned to his car, which had received a parking ticket. He left it where it was and backed out of the parking area. On his way back down Kungsgatan, he fished out the now-wrinkled Post-it note he'd received at the hospital, and dialled Thomas Wethje's pager. He had driven almost all the way home before the doctor called back.

'Eric?'

'Hi, Thomas. How is she?'

'Nothing new. She's stable, but she's still unconscious. She's in a form of temporary coma. My request to move her to a more isolated unit was rejected. Our regular hygienic procedures are considered sufficient. So there's no risk that this is something highly pathogenic. And, like I said, she's stable. But Mats Hagström is worse. His vital signs keep going up and down, and we've had to take several emergency measures.'

Eric felt his stomach clench. He parked on Banérgatan just outside his front door, turned off the engine, and took a deep breath.

'Thomas, I think I know what happened to them.'

'What? What do you mean, "happened to them"?'

'Well, what caused their condition. It's all my fault.'

'What are you saying? Straight talk, please.'

'Do you remember me telling you this morning what I work with? I think they were harmed — infected, if you prefer — because they were hooked up to Mind Surf. My computer has been infected with the new Mona virus. I think the virus somehow then caused neural discord in Hanna. And Mats.'

Perfect silence came from the other end of the line. Eric held his breath. A little girl with a large pink backpack on her back was bicycling unsteadily past his car.

'Eric, if you want me to try to diagnose them based on the hypothesis that they have been infected by a computer virus … What you're saying is absurd. It sounds more like something out of a science-fiction novel.'

'Stephen King.'

'What? Yes, exactly. King. But now we're talking about your own wife. Forget the computer virus. I have two seriously ill patients here. It has nothing to do with vanishing documents, manipulated stock prices, or crashing files.'

'Doesn't it? Are you sure?'

'Eric, I really hope you don't seriously believe this. I don't mean to be unpleasant, but I don't have time for this right now. You ought to be sleeping, not reading horror novels.'

'Yes, I'm going to sleep. I understand that you can't absorb what I'm saying. But let it sit in the back of your mind. I guess we'll see how things unfold.'

'Sure. Sleep well, Eric. We'll talk again when you're more alert.'

The conversation ended, and he stayed in the car. What had he thought would happen? That a doctor at Karolinska Hospital would believe his theory? After all, it was as absurd as everyone said. And yet, although he didn't know why, he was sure he was right.

When he entered the apartment, he was once again struck by a sense of abandonment. The sun shone in through the windows, and it smelled stuffy and stale. He opened a window in the living room and went to the bathroom. There, he turned on the water in the bathtub and poured in some lavender oil he'd bought for Hanna a few months ago. When he'd undressed, he caught sight of a perfume bottle that stood on the bathroom shelf: Viktor & Rolf's Flowerbomb. He sprayed a little of the perfume into the air, and its soft, floral scent filled the bathroom. Suddenly, she was there; not physically, but still fully present. He sat on the edge of the tub and closed his eyes. Her scent aroused strong, vivid images. He saw her naked in the bathroom — her wet hair, her curvy body, her long neck, narrow shoulders, and beautiful breasts, and the birthmark just under her left breast. He sat for a long time, drinking her in. With one hand, he turned off the water. Then he slid backward, without opening his eyes, into the full tub. The warm, oily water embraced him, and he lay there as if in a trance.

The doctors wouldn't find a cure. He knew that already, somewhere deep inside. Hanna would fade away, and he would only be able to sit there and watch. The virus swimming in her blood, the black snake, was something unconquerable and evil. With each passing hour, the chances of saving her got worse. But what could he do for her? He was no virus expert. Nor was he a doctor or a rabbi. Would he dare to follow his theory to its logical conclusion?

What if Hanna and Mats really were infected with Mona? A computer communicates by electrical impulses, in ones and zeros. A brain communicates in essentially the same way. The converter that Eric had developed read digital information and translated it into neural commands. Could the virus have been converted by the sensor helmet? That was science fiction, and now he had to let go of that idea. If Mona had infected them, he had to find an anti-virus — a goal that he shared with the rest of the Western world.

Considering how many people had tried, it seemed that there was only a slim chance that anyone could build an anti-virus. The only person who could kill the snake was the one who had created it — whoever that was. He thought of what Carl Öberg had said. Nice: there was someone there who knew more about the people behind Mona. The creator of the virus, a person who could be anywhere, was the world's most wanted terrorist at the moment. If Eric, against all the odds, could find him, would he be able to persuade him to save Hanna? A Jewish woman? For the terrorist, Hanna's fate would just be an unplanned side effect. Maybe he would give Eric an anti-virus for that very reason. No, that was obviously implausible. Maybe he didn't even have an anti-virus. And if he did, he would never give it away. Not to anyone.

Eric's body was numb. The apartment was perfectly quiet, and he had the sensation of floating in a massive vacuum. Maybe this was exactly how Hanna felt right now; maybe she was floating around in an endless black void. He could still smell her scent in the bathroom. He ducked his head underwater and held it there for a long time. By the time he returned to the surface, he had made a decision. It might be totally crazy, and he might be completely wrong, but, since no one believed him, he was going to have to act on his own. It was that simple. The odds that he would find the creator of Mona were close to zero, and if by some miracle he did succeed in finding him, he couldn't expect any help from him. It was more likely that he would be killed in the attempt. But during the few seconds he had been underwater, he had made up his mind. He had never been so sure of anything in his whole life.

He was going to Nice, and he was going right away. There was not a second to spare. He would find Carl's friend at the nightclub. With his help, he would locate the policeman who was selling information. He had money; sure, it was the money Mats had invested, but all's fair in love and war. He would buy information that would lead him to Mona's creator. Perhaps he would have to contact him via the internet or on the phone, rather than in person. And then he would beseech him to spare Hanna's life — to give him the anti-virus. His plan was so desperate and unrealistic that he couldn't stop to think it through. If he did, reason would catch up with the dream and destroy it. He already knew that he wouldn't be capable of doing even half of what he had set his mind to. For that very reason, he had to move quickly. He could sleep later.

Wet and naked, he walked through the apartment to the hall to get his mobile phone. On hold with Scandinavian Airlines, he walked into the bedroom, dug a black Gucci bag out of the closet, and threw together some chinos, shirts, socks, underwear, and a pullover. Back in the bathroom, he gathered up his toiletries. On the way out, he grabbed the Viktor & Rolf perfume, which went into the vanity bag, along with a toothbrush, deodorant, aftershave, and hair gel. As he spoke with SAS, he took his iPod and phone charger from the table in the office and placed them in his bag. Back in the hall, he added Hanna's computer. Then he

166

pulled on a thin anorak and closed the front door.

His hair was still wet when he got into the car. He was booked on SAS via Frankfurt. The plane would take off at twenty to two, in exactly fifty-five minutes. He sped out onto Valhallavägen. Jens was sitting with Hanna, so she was in good hands. What would he say to him? They had agreed to talk in six or seven hours. He would land in Nice in just over seven hours' time. There was no point in calling him now — Jens would be furious. A conversation with him might even burst Eric's bubble and make him stay. Better to deal with it in France, where he would be beyond return. Dear God, his logic was completely gone. But now he was desperate. And he had to do everything he could, no matter how crazy it was. Doing something was better than lying there, staring at the ceiling.

The traffic was flowing smoothly as he drove past the exit to KTH. His research, the team … it all felt like a distant planet, a planet he neither wanted to nor could reach. Now, all that mattered was the black snake in Hanna's veins, winding and twisting under her skin. So small that no one could see it. So poisonous that no one could stop it. No one but its creator.

Everything seemed to be covered in soot. Or some sort of greyish-white ash. A light breeze swept past, bringing with it a pile of documents. He looked around. He was standing at the edge of a forest. It smelled burned. Farther off he could see a deserted playground. There were papers everywhere — some partially burned, others completely untouched. He started to walk across the grassy slope to the left of the playground, rounded a small grove of trees, and ended up in front of a tall concrete tower. It was Kaknästornet, the TV tower in Stockholm. The entrance ramp was filled with paper and trash. The doors were open, and within them was a dense darkness. He crossed the parking lot, passing several wrecked cars. He came to the forest on the other side and found a narrow bridle path into the trees. The darkness descended around him. Perhaps the scent was getting stronger. Perhaps the ash was growing thicker on the ground. The bridle path turned away across a hill, and he followed it up the slope. He was plodding through the soot; it was like walking in warm snow.

He stopped when he reached the top of the hill. The Gärdet neighborhood spread out in all directions. He wanted to yell, but couldn't make a sound. The doors of hell opened before him. An endless sea of bodies. Chalk white. Pile after pile of corpses. Large bulldozers stood among the dead. Arms and legs hung out of their enormous buckets like worn-out rag dolls. The bulldozers' windows were broken; they had stopped long ago. Fires burned beyond the endless piles. The flames licked at the crimson sky, sending clouds of grey ash into the air.

This was the end. The end of everything. Inevitably and irrevocably.

Mats Hagström's eyelids trembled slightly, and his fingers twitched. She felt the movements of his hand and stroked his head gently.

'There, there, my darling. It's only a dream.'

She lay her head on his chest and felt the thin hospital fabric against her lips.

'*Tu rêves, mon amour. Tu rêves.*'

Nice, France

At nine-thirty, Eric stepped out of the arrivals terminal at the Nice airport with the black bag in his hand. The oppressive air was warm and full of foreignness. He hailed a taxi.

'*Negresco, s'il vous plaît.*'

It would have been hard to find a more unimaginative place to stay, but it was the only one he could think of. As the taxi cruised along Promenade des Anglais, he turned on his phone. There were two missed calls, both from Mind Surf colleagues at KTH. They were supposed to have tested the system, but he hadn't contacted them. The way things had turned out, they ought to be happy they'd missed their trials. He looked out the window. The dark water of the sea met the sky and created a dense, blue-black background a hundred metres offshore. As always, the promenade was full of flaneurs, runners, roller-skaters, and vendors. Over the driver's shoulder he could see Negresco with its pink cupola and turquoise top. What would he say to Jens? He hadn't called him from Frankfurt as planned. He hadn't been able to. He sat with his phone in his hand and his head full of thoughts until he arrived at the hotel. The taxi abruptly swung to the left and stopped before the magnificent entryway.

He was greeted by the doorman, who was decked out in a tall hat and white gloves, and he stepped into the belle époque-decorated lobby. Eleven minutes later, he was sitting in one of the gold rococo chairs in his small hotel room, dialling Jens's number. After five rings, he answered.

'Hello!'

Jens always answered aggressively, but this time it felt extra threatening.

'Jens, it's Eric.'

'There you are! I was getting worried. I thought maybe you were sick, too. Did you sleep well?'

He still hadn't slept. Sleep seemed more and more abstract. He swallowed.

'I'm in France.'

There was a long silence.

'You're ... in France? Well, why not? Are you joking?'

'No. I know you're going to hate me forever, but ... I'm

convinced that Mona is what infected Hanna. I've come to Nice to try to get hold of Carl's source.'

It was quiet again. Eric struggled on.

'No one's going to believe me, much less help me, so I had to take care of this myself. I have no other choice. Just lying in bed and staring at the ceiling, or sitting at Karolinska with a mug of weak coffee, for that matter, won't work. We're going to lose her. I just know it. We have to do something.'

'And what the hell are you going to do about it in Nice?'

Jens was angry.

'I know it's a long shot. But I'm planning to try to buy information that will lead me to the person who designed Mona.'

'And then what?'

'And then I'll convince him to give me an anti-virus.'

'And then what?'

'And then I'll give it to Hanna and Mats Hagström.'

'How will you get it into them? Are they going to drink the computer program out of a little fluoride cup? Or maybe take it with water?'

'No. They'll get it the same way as they got the virus. Via Mind Surf.'

'So you're going to come to Karolinska Hospital and wrestle each of two people who are in comas into a tight plastic cap full of wires?'

Eric didn't answer. Outside the half-open window, accordion music blended with the rushing traffic.

'Eric, listen to me carefully. You are about to completely lose your grip. Your story is completely nuts. Why didn't you call me before you left so I could stop you?'

'That's why.'

'You have to come home. You're sure-as-hell no help to Hanna if you're sitting around munching on *foie gras* on the

Riviera. You need to be here, by her side. Get a grip and come home. Now.'

Eric stood up and walked out onto the balcony.

'You're right. It's all nuts, and I'm crazy. But I'm not coming home. Not until I've tried. I really don't give a shit about being sensible. All I know is that Hanna is dying, and it's my fault. You'll have to take care of her. I won't be gone long. As soon as I get the information, I'll take the first flight home. Then I'll do the rest of the work from Sweden.'

'Does Calle know about this? How did you get hold of the contact info for the guy in Nice?'

'I took them from his notes when he wasn't looking.'

'What? Do you realise you're sabotaging the scoop of the century?'

'I can't help it. If I'm right, he'll have something else to write about. Then we'll be talking about some fucking scoop.'

'Eric, for the last time. Throw a litre of cold water in your face, look in the mirror, box your own ear — do whatever it takes to wake you up. Quit this madness, and come home.'

An airplane with blinking lights came in low over the water on its way to the runway further south. He looked down at the broad street with its steady stream of cars and mopeds.

'Just one day. That's all I need. I promise that, no matter what happens, I'll come home tomorrow night.'

'What if something happens here? With Hanna?'

'That's why you're there. If you weren't with her, I couldn't do what I'm doing. I trust you, more than anyone else in the world. I'll call you tomorrow at lunchtime.'

'Eric, what's wrong with you? Dammit, you have to — '

He ended the call and stood before his reflection in the balcony door. A pale figure stared back, and above the thin body the evening traffic flowed by on Promenade des Anglais. Jens was right — he was crazy. No question about that. He picked up his wallet and unfolded the paper with his notes from the meeting at *Aftonbladet*. Before he called, he hid his number from caller ID. Then he dialled the first number he'd copied.

'*Bienvenue à la police de Nice. Votre cas?*' — 'Welcome to the Nice police. Your case?' Eric hung up, took a deep breath, and went to the next number on the list.

'*Le Trusted Bank of Israel est fermé pour aujourd'hui. Nous serons à nouveau ouvert demain, à dix heures.*' — 'The Trusted Bank of Israel is shut today. We re-open tomorrow at ten o'clock.'

He hung up and stared at the phone. He had called two out of three options on the piece of paper without getting a hit. The telephone numbers were the only thing he had to go on. If the third number was no good, he was screwed. He would have to go home. He looked at the ten digits. Win or lose?

He made a face and dialled the last number. One ring. Two rings. Three rings.

'*Vous êtes sur le répondeur de Cedric. Parlez après le bip sonore.*' — 'You're on Cedric's answering machine. Speak after the beep.'

He thought quickly.

'My name is Eric Söderqvist and I work with Carl Öberg at the newspaper *Aftonbladet*. I'm staying at Hotel Negresco, in room 321. Call me as soon as you get this.'

Now all he could do was wait. He realised he hadn't eaten anything in over a day, and called room service to order a club sandwich. Then he lay sideways across the bed with his clothes on. He was stiff and sore. And tired — incredibly tired. A car honked somewhere outside. He fished the iPod out of his pocket and scrolled to Albinoni. He thought of the time he and Hanna had been in Nice. It had been an unusually warm weekend for October. They'd swum alone at the rocky beach, and eaten mussels at the only open beach café. He remembered the night they'd sat in a dark bar in the old town, drinking absinthe like David and Catherine in Hemingway's *The Garden of Eden*. She was turning thirty-five. *La vie en rose*. Soon he was fast asleep.

Balakot, Pakistan

Sixty kilometres east of the city of Balakot, along the river Kunhar and deep among the inaccessible mountains in the north-western corner of Pakistan, the barren landscape flattened out into a field with a total area of two hectares, surrounded by tall mountains with steep faces. In the south-eastern corner was the Sohrab military training camp, named for the historic Persian warrior. Sixty years before, the camp had been decommissioned by the army, and after the devastating earthquake in 2005 it had been briefly used as a communication centre for relief efforts. Despite this, the CIA's spy satellites had registered activity at the site during the previous five months. The images had been saved in the servers at CIA headquarters in Langley, Virginia, but no action had been taken.

On this damp but warm afternoon, two men had arrived at camp Sohrab. They had come on heavily loaded packhorses, and were dressed like the local mountain-dwellers. A light fog hung over the field. The particular geography of this place often caused fog to form in the area between the mountains — a natural phenomenon that was convenient for the camp, since it obscured the view of the American eyes in space.

Everyone in the camp knew that the visitors were not from the area. Although no one knew who they were, they knew why they had come. And everyone knew that three of the camp's students had been chosen for them. The chosen ones and the new arrivals found themselves in the largest of the barracks. The students — Ali Askani, Syed Nuledi, and Kashif Kareem Muhammad — sat on the floor with crossed legs. They were dressed in white, and were wearing black bands on their heads. They sat close to one another with heads bent. Across from them, the two visitors sat on simple wooden chairs, conversing with Tuan Malik, the highest-ranking leader of camp Sohrab. They spoke in low voices, and sometimes Malik pointed at the three men on the floor. Incense had been lit to mask an underlying smell of sewage, and the air was heavy and sweet.

After a little more than an hour, one of the visitors got up and walked over to the students. He crouched down and looked at each of them for a long time. Nothing was said. Then he gave a barely perceptible nod, got up, and left the building. Tuan Malik and the other visitor immediately stood up and followed. The men on the floor didn't move. Outside the barracks, Ahmad Waizy went over to his horse and mounted it. He looked around. The camp was empty. The students were in their dormitories, studying the Quran. He inhaled the humid air, finally free of the sewage smell and the incense. Out here, the air smelled of grass and wet earth. This place was fertile and nourishing. It was a good place for a school. They were nearly self-sufficient, which minimised the need for deliveries that might raise questions. He waved urgently to the guide, who was still standing along the short wall of the barracks, talking to Tuan Malik. It would soon be dark. Certainly, the guide had promised to lead him back to Balakot even after darkness, but he wanted to get away as soon as possible. Despite the difficult journey, Ahmad was satisfied. He had found his martyrs.

Ahvaz, Iran

No one would ever be able to create an anti-virus for Mona. Perhaps *ever* was too strong a word; maybe in a hundred years, processor speeds and viral analysis would be so much better that even Mona's code could be cracked. But with current technology, it was impossible if you didn't have an answer key. Mona wasn't really one virus, but rather forty different ones whose strings of code had been braided such that they evolved and changed in patterns that were new each time. He had come up with new software that could reprogram itself like this even back at MIT. The technique was more than sufficient to allow Mona to destroy any computer system unimpeded. But he hadn't stopped there. He had spent several months searching for and identifying previously unknown errors and weaknesses in the systems that Mona would attack — errors that the manufacturers themselves didn't know about. This made Mona a 'zero-day virus,' which meant that she exploited unknown weaknesses and flaws in the programs she infected.

Samir had known that she would be effective; but, like Oppenheimer after the first nuclear-bomb detonation, he was still in awe of the destruction that the virus had caused. Mona had shaken up Israel's financial structure to such a degree that no information could be relied upon anymore. Thirty per cent of all critical information had disappeared, taken hostage behind Mona's impenetrable bars. Twenty per cent of Israel's transactions and backup data had been erased. The remaining information already was, or risked becoming, corrupt. The virus had paralysed the Western world. He himself had a hard time surveying the situation. Incredible sums had been obliterated, and new features on the virus were constantly appearing on CNN and al-Jazeera. Mona had also begun to affect other systems.

Hospitals, traffic-control systems, and mobile-phone operators were reporting disruptions in service. This was something he hadn't foreseen. He had opened Pandora's box and released a force that was beyond all control.

The others in the group were preparing the next step of the operation. Ahmad Waizy had gone away to arrange recruits. Arie al-Fattal was working on the delivery of the explosives. According to the original plan, they ought already to have been on site in Gaza, but their journey had been interrupted at the last minute. Sinon had warned Ahmad that the Mossad knew of the address. While awaiting new directions, they remained in Abdullah bin Aziz's palace. Arie had been very upset. To stay in one place for too long was dangerous. He repeated this every morning at breakfast. Sooner or later, one servant or another would let it slip.

'Don't forget that we're the most wanted people in the world. We must always keep moving.'

Samir was doing anything but moving. He spent most of his time in his room, in front of the computer. He was working on the second part of the masterpiece that was Mona: the anti-virus, Mona's first and last enemy. He was as careful with the anti-virus as he had been with the virus. Samir knew that there were powers within Hezbollah who didn't like the fact that he needed to create a true anti-virus. Israel would never be given the cure anyway; it was just an empty lure. But he had made up his mind: if they didn't want to risk the world collapsing, they needed an anti-virus. Maybe total anarchy was what Ahmad wanted, but that wasn't his own goal. The anti-virus would happen. And he needed to work in order to forget.

Since he knew Mona's stealth signature, the code that made her invisible, it would be easy for him to find the infections. Once that was done, he would use a holistic quarantine technique to isolate the virus and then disentangle the various strings. After he was finished with that, he would have to construct individual countermeasures for each variation of the virus.

The problem was that he had to outwit his own mutated creation — a creation that by now might be more sophisticated than his own knowledge. His work had been made even more difficult since he'd lost his notebook. He cursed his carelessness in Nice.

Nice, France

He was suddenly woken by his phone ringing. The light in the small room was dim, and he could smell food. Eric looked around, still half asleep. He was in a hotel room in … Nice. He caught sight of a tray on the round coffee table. How had it gotten there? In the middle of the tray sat a silver dome, and beside it were ketchup, a bottle of Evian, a glass, and a small white vase with a blue flower. They must have delivered the food without waking him. That was a disturbing thought. The phone rang again. Cedric! He flew out of bed and stumbled over to the desk by the balcony door.

'Hello!'

There was a loud crackling noise on the line.

'Allô?'

'This is Eric speaking.'

He held his breath.

'Hi, Eric. This is Cedric Antoine. I got your message. Sorry I'm calling so late, but I just finished work. May I come by the hotel now?'

Eric looked at the clock. It was 4.23 a.m.

'*Bien*. I'll see you in the lobby. How will I recognise you?'

Cedric didn't say anything for a long moment.

'Didn't C. say anything?'

'No. What?'

'You'll understand.'

The call ended. Eric ran a hand through his hair and gathered his thoughts. Then he went to the bathroom to piss. The man in the mirror looked like him, but was at least ten years older. He rinsed his face in cold water for a long time. Hiding under the silver dome was a cold and bland club sandwich. He ate a few of the chips that surrounded the sandwich, and drank the water in five big gulps. Then he smoothed his wrinkled clothes, took his key, and left the room. With any luck, Cedric hadn't called *Aftonbladet* to talk with Carl Öberg. He arrived at the lobby, which was deserted except for the night receptionist behind the desk. The man gave him a sceptical look.

'Can I help you?'

Eric shook his head.

'No, thanks. I'm waiting for someone.'

He sat down on one of the square red sofas in the middle of the lobby. Beside him stood a large white bust with curly hair and an expression of irritation. The sculpture captured the mood at the hotel. There was something inhospitable about this place. He thought about Cedric. Why had he assumed that Carl had given Eric a description? Was there something remarkable about his appearance? He had trouble imagining what it might be.

Yet another receptionist popped up and starting putting out morning papers on the front desk. Eric read several of the headlines; they all seemed to revolve around financial crises and computer viruses. He had a mild headache. After about half an hour, a tall blonde woman walked through the glass doors that opened onto the street. She was heavily made up and was wearing tight leather pants, shoes with very high, pointy heels, and a clingy red top. Her nails were black. The men behind the desk exchanged a look and went to meet her. The woman saw what was about to happen and swept the lobby with her eyes. She caught sight of Eric and gave an inquiring smile.

'Eric?'

It was a man's voice. Eric remained on the sofa, his mouth half-open.

'Eric! *C'est moi,* Cedric!'

The men in their green uniforms and black gloves looked at Eric with a mixture of surprise and disgust. The older one cleared his throat.

'Do you know this … this person?'

Eric stood up and nodded.

'Sure. Of course. This is my date.'

Cedric smiled happily and looked at the uniforms with a resolute look.

They hesitated. The younger one sneaked a look at the older one, who shook his head, turned toward Cedric, and gestured theatrically. *'Bienvenue à Negresco.'* Cedric swept past him with head held high, but Eric caught up with him after just a few steps and pulled him back out the doors. 'I need air. Let's sit by the sea.' Cedric said something in French that Eric didn't understand, but he followed without protest. The sun had already managed to warm up the morning, and the sea glittered invitingly. The promenade was nearly empty, so they walked across the street without waiting for a green light. They found a white bench in front of the low wall that ran along the beach, giving them an excellent view of the bay. Cedric sat down and dug a pack of cigarettes out of a worn, green handbag. He lit one with a simple Bic lighter and took a deep drag.

'How is C.?'

Eric answered, gazing out at the blue-green sea.

'Everything's fine.'

Out of the corner of his eye, he could see Cedric studying him.

'How do you know C.?'

Perhaps there was a hint of jealousy in his voice. He turned his head and met Cedric's eyes. He was quite a bit older than Eric had thought at first. More tired. His hands were wrinkled, with narrow fingers and cracked nails. The nail polish had been painted on carelessly.

'I guess I'm kind of an errand boy. I run around trying to find my place among all the star reporters. Carl sent me here to learn more about the terrorists.'

Cedric took another deep drag.

'I could tell that you weren't prepared for me. Didn't C. say anything — anything about me at all?'

Eric faced forward again. Far off, a man was swimming. His head bobbed in the waves like a buoy.

'He said you were a friend, and someone who could be trusted.'

Cedric considered Eric's words.

'We were together for almost six months. I was different back then. Not like now. Not this desperate.'

He laughed suddenly. His laughter was clear and nervous.

'I still had my dignity.'

The traffic had picked up behind the park bench, and the promenade was starting to fill with motion. Cedric tossed his cigarette butt over the wall.

'You see, I live far from here. Over an hour-and-a-half by bus, up through the mountains.'

Eric nodded, wondering why Cedric was telling him this. He definitely had no intention of asking him to sleep head-to-foot at the hotel.

Cedric lit another cigarette, and Eric took his chance: 'I want to contact your policeman right away. I'll pay big money if he has good material.'

Cedric nodded.

'He really needs money. Poor bastard. Apparently, he bet it all away. His wife has no idea.'

'What kind of information does he have?'

'I don't know. He says he found something during the apartment raid. Something very valuable. But he's terrified that his name will get out. It's evidence, so I understand why he's stressed.'

'I want to meet him as soon as possible.'

Cedric closed the zipper on his bag and stood up.

'I have to go. The bus doesn't go very often. Stay at the hotel and answer when he calls.'

Several passers-by stared at Cedric. Eric placed a hand on his shoulder.

'You have no idea what this means to me. How much do you want for your help?'

Cedric looked offended.

'Say hi to C. from me. And make sure to answer when the phone rings.'

Then he bent forward and gave him a gentle hug.

'Take care of yourself. You look miserable.'

He turned and walked toward the crosswalk, his steps swift despite the high heels. Eric sat heavily on the bench. He followed the large blonde man-woman with his eyes until he was lost among the morning traffic. Eric turned back to the sea. The black head was bobbing, far away. Cedric was right. He was miserable.

When Eric got back to the hotel room, the bed had been made and the tray was gone. It was seven-thirty. He threw the balcony door wide open and pulled the curtains back from the large windows. The air was full of the sea, even up here. He went to the bathroom, took a long shower, and then put on blue chinos and a white polo shirt. He sat barefoot at the desk. His phone was within reach; there was still hope. All he had to do now was wait. Should he call Jens? Out of cowardice or self-preservation, he refrained.

He started Hanna's computer. There were several folders on the desktop, one of which was named 'Pictures.' He slowly clicked through a world of memories, and stopped at a close-up of her taken in Åre. Wearing a pink hat, with her blond hair in a braid, and white ski goggles around her neck, she was looking at the camera resolutely. Her gaze was so alive that he wanted to touch her, but his fingertips touched only the static surface of the screen. She wasn't real, alas. She wasn't in a little mountain cabin in Åre. She was in a coma at Karolinska Hospital. He threw a frustrated glance at the silent phone.

Then he went back to the computer. Perhaps TBI had some new information about Mona. He found the wireless network and connected to the internet, but when he tried to open TBI's internal network, he got an authentication prompt. He frowned. Then he remembered the fob in Hanna's computer bag. While he was up, he also took a bag of chocolate-covered nuts and a beer from the mini-bar. He quickly got into TBI's net using Hanna's authentication, and found several interesting files. There were new versions of *Mona Tza'yad*, but they still only had the ability to find the virus. There was nothing there that could stop it. One name recurred in the documents: Isaac Berns. Eric knew who he was — TBI's international director of IT. Berns seemed to be the one in charge of everything to do with the crisis at the bank. Eric looked at the flickering screen. He opened the beer and took a large gulp. What if he could get into Isaac Berns's computer? That's how he'd probably find out what was really going on.

But the IT director's access level was completely different from Hanna's. He took another sip of the beer. Could he hack his way in? He put down the can and started on the security system.

It took him an hour-and-a-half to find a flaw in the firewall. The clock on the screen said it was quarter past ten. The phone was still silent. Before him he had a mirror of Isaac Berns's computer. He started looking for folders and documents about Mona, but it was slow going. A lot of the material was written in Hebrew, and he had to use a translation program.

Tel Aviv, Israel

At 10.22, the trespass alarm had been activated at TBI. Nine minutes later, the radio intelligence unit 8200 had been brought in. Jacob Nachman had come down from his office and was now sitting beside a young computer tech.

'How's it going?'

'I'm not really finished, so we'll have to hope he doesn't disconnect. I need a few more minutes. But we know it's an individual with level-three security access who's found a way to reclassify himself as level-one. This intruder is now using that access to go through Isaac Berns's personal files.'

Jacob became impatient.

'You've already said that. Give me something new. Can't we see who it is through the log-in identification?'

'Unfortunately, the ID info seems to be corrupt. Now I'm tracing the IP addresses backwards.'

'And?'

The tech looked up.

'The intrusion came from a French network.'

'Where in France?'

'The signal is coming from a provider in Lyon, but that's not where it's pinging from.'

Jacob took out his mobile phone. The young man leaned closer to the screen.

'Nice! The intrusion is coming from Nice.'

'Where in Nice?'

'It seems to be coming from one of the hotels' wireless networks. Or maybe a restaurant. I have to do a match against the national register. Give me a few more minutes.'

Jacob had already begun to compose an email on his phone. Before he was halfway done, the man smacked his hand on the edge of the desk with a bang.

'Yes!'

Jacob looked at him questioningly.

'I've traced the intrusion all the way to the source.'

'And?'

'Hotel Negresco.'

Jacob clapped him on the shoulder.

'Impressive. Well done.'

He erased the email and instead dialled the number to David Yassur at the Mossad. As it started ringing, he saw that the tech was looking at him triumphantly.

'Was there something else?'

The man nodded.

'He's in room 321.'

Jacob looked at him in surprise as the phone rang at David's end.

Nice, France

Eric was downloading a series of documents from Isaac Berns's computer that seemed to be linked to Mona. It was clear that the virus had already caused a great deal of harm, and in an internal memo to the CEO of the bank, Berns said he feared further attacks. Eric also found two emails to Berns from something called Unit 8200. The first one described the evidence that had been found during the raid on the terrorists' apartment. The other named the two terrorists. The one who had been killed in the raid was Melah as-Dullah — a name Eric recognised from Carl Öberg. The other, who had managed to escape, was named Samir Mustaf. Unit 8200 had linked Melah to an organisation called Jihad al-Binna, which was controlled by Hezbollah and was working to rebuild Lebanon. His mobile phone rang. Eric looked at the screen. The lump in his stomach was back.

'Hi, Jens.'

'Eric, tell me you're on your way home.'

'I'm on my way home.'

'Thank God. I haven't slept all night, and could do with a break. Hanna's stable, but I can tell that the doctors are concerned. You have to come back.'

The hotel phone rang. Eric looked desperately at the blinking light on the phone. Jens continued, 'When do you land in Stockholm?'

'I'll have to call you back.'

'No, wait. I …'

Eric hung up and grabbed the receiver of the brown room phone.

'Hello!'

There was silence on the other end. Had he missed the call?

'Hello!'

More silence. Then a low voice.

'Monsieur Söderqvist?'

'Yes. This is Eric Söderqvist.'

'You want to buy information. Correct?'

'That's right. What kind of information is it?'

'A notebook.'

'A what?'

'A notebook that was seized at Maréchal Foch.'

'What is in it?'

'It belonged to the terrorists. The whole thing is full.'

Maybe it contained a phone number, an address, something that could lead him forward.

'Full of what?'

'Code. Very careful notes. Page after page.'

'Anything else?'

'I promised to get photographs. And I did.'

'Photographs of both of them?'

'One that we took of Melah as-Dullah ourselves, and one that we received at the station of the other, Samir Mustaf.'

His mobile phone rang again. It was Jens. Eric made a face and rejected the call.

'How much do you want?'

'Fifty thousand euros.'

Half a million kronor! How the hell could he get so much money? What if the notebook was useless? Sure, he had the Mind Surf money, but that wasn't really his; it was Mats Hagström's. On the other hand, it would be in Mats's best interest for him to get his hands on an anti-virus. But half a million?

'Twenty-five.'

Silence. He could hear his pulse beating in his temples.

'I can go to down to forty thousand, but that's my best offer. Otherwise I'll sell it to a newspaper.'

'I'll give you thirty thousand.'

Click. The man had hung up. Eric stood still with the phone in his hand, shocked. What had he done? He had just lost the most important person in the world. He sat on the bed and stared at the brown telephone. Maybe it was just a negotiating act. Maybe the man would call again soon, with a new offer. After twenty minutes, he realised that the man was gone. What the hell was he going to do? Cedric Antoine! Cedric had to help him. He could hunt the man down and patch up their relationship.

He dialled Cedric's number, but there was no answer. What if he had spoken to Carl? Then he would never help him. But what if Eric told him the truth? How would he find Cedric? All he knew was that he lived several hours away, up in the mountains. But where? Grasse? Vence? What were the French White Pages called? His thoughts were spinning. The room felt oppressive, like a tiny prison cell without air. He had to get out. Eric took his phone and left the room. When he arrived in the hectic lobby, he was reminded of how he had sat waiting for Cedric on that red sofa earlier the same day. How could he have messed things up so completely? He had lost his only reason for being in Nice. He could see one of the receptionists from the morning staring at him without masking his distaste. Fuck it if the whole hotel thought he was a pervert. The only thing that mattered was getting hold of the tipster. All he wanted was a small miracle.

When Eric came to the glass doors, he saw that the receptionist was waving at him. He sighed and walked to the desk. He was not in the mood for a sermon on the ethical guidelines of the hotel.

Without greeting him, the receptionist said, 'Message for you, monsieur.' He held up a white envelope with the golden Negresco logo. Then, with a scornful smile, he added, 'Perhaps it's from the delightful woman you see?'

Eric took the letter without a word and turned back to the red sofa, sitting beside a fat woman who was looking at pictures on a digital camera. He tore open the envelope. Written on Negresco stationery was a short message:

35,000 EUROS. TEXT 04 93 84 42 99 FOR ACCOUNT INSTRUCTIONS.

He read the text once more. Warm relief ran through his body — he was back in the game. Somehow, he knew that this was the turning point. He hadn't pressed the man too hard after all. Instead, he had gotten the price down, and now it was all or nothing. He picked up his phone and send a blank text to the number he'd been given. Then he sat stock still, with the phone before him as though it were the key to heaven. Perhaps that was exactly what it was. The phone vibrated, and a text popped up on the screen:

SWISS ACCOUNT NUMBER 0AI024502601, IBAN CH78 0055 40AI 0245 0260 I. CONFIRMATION CODE BY TEXT ASAP.

He flew up so fast that the fat woman dropped her camera. Taking no note of her German curses, he ran out through the large glass doors. He had obtained travellers' cheques in Nice before, and knew which bank to go to, although it remained to be seen whether they could help him take 35,000 euros out of his Swedish business account and then send them to the account of an unnamed person in Switzerland. He jogged along the beach promenade and turned off at Avenue de Verdun. And what if he was being scammed? He was about to send a fortune to someone he'd never met. What would Jens have said? Or worse — Hanna? But he was desperate, and desperate people do desperate things.

The footpath was packed with people, and he jostled his way

through Japanese people and families with small children. In the midst of all his despair, he also felt a sense of exhilaration. This was the turning point. Money was just money, and the notebook might turn out to be invaluable. The same went for the picture of the surviving terrorist. He went around a woman who was having problems with her motor scooter, and stepped on the black fabric of a street vendor's table. The man, who was on all fours, turned his face up in anger, but Eric was already past him and running along the narrow Rue Paradis.

When he arrived on the busy Rue de la Liberté, he hesitated. Was the bank to the right or the left? He tried to find the green-and-white BNP Paribas sign, but all he saw were ice-cream parlours and clothing boutiques. The street was filled to the brim with tourists. He took a chance and went right, entering the northbound stream. He came to Galeries Lafayette and looked around again. Had he chosen the wrong direction? Just as he was about to turn around, he saw the sign a few hundred metres away in the direction of the sea. He crossed the street and ducked into the air-conditioned bank, panting. One of the two counters was open, and there were three people in a short line. There were no queue numbers. He stood at the end of the line and took out his phone. There were two missed calls — one from Jens and one from *Aftonbladet*. That was probably Carl, who must have talked to Cedric. He considered calling Jens, but to his relief he saw a sign on the wall with a crossed-out mobile phone. Instead, he wrote a short text to say that he'd gotten a lead, and promising to call that afternoon. Once he'd sent the text, though, he felt powerless. The feeling of exhilaration had disappeared. This would never work. He looked around for the exit. Then it was his turn, and an older man with horn-rimmed glasses and a sharp gaze smiled at him coolly.

'*Que puis-je faire pour vous?*' — 'What can I do for you?'

He swallowed and brought up the text message with the Swiss account number.

'I'd like to transfer 35,000 euros from a Swedish bank account to an account in Switzerland. How do I go about that?'

The man looked at him for a moment, a V-shaped wrinkle between his eyes.

'Is the account in Sweden in your name?'

'No.'

'Is the account in Switzerland in your name?'

'No. I don't know the name of the account holder.'

The V deepened. 'You want to transfer 35,000 euros from an account in Sweden that isn't yours, to an account in Switzerland whose owner you don't know?'

Eric maintained his smile and nodded. The man sighed.

'Wait here. I have to talk to my boss.'

Tel Aviv, Israel

Apparently, the Mossad director's leg was better. Meir Pardo had suggested that they take a walk on Shlomo Lahat, along the marina. It was cloudy but warm, and there were large waves on the sea. The boats in the marina were bobbing violently, and there weren't very many people on the promenade. David Yassur walked with his hands in the pockets of his thin sport coat. Meir was paging through the pictures he'd received from him, and he stopped on a black-and-white portrait. He studied the face in the image.

'Tell me about Eric Söderqvist.'

'Thirty-nine years old. Research professor at the KTH Royal Technical Institute in Stockholm, focusing on BCI, Brain

Computer Interface, which involves — '

'I know what it involves. Is he good at it?'

'If the information we've received is correct, he's just secured financing — from an external investment fund.'

'Which country is the fund from?'

'Sweden.'

'And he's married to a Jewish woman?'

'That's right. Hanna Söderqvist, née Schultz. Very active in the congregation. The couple visits Israel several times a year.'

'And she works for TBI?'

'As a director of IT. She's one of the first ones who found Mona.'

'Who is she?'

'She's the same age as Söderqvist. They met at Stockholm University. Her maternal grandparents are from Poland, survivors of Treblinka. Her grandmother, Eva Schultz, died last year at the age of eighty-seven. Her grandfather, Lev Schultz, is eighty-nine and lives in a nursing home in Stockholm. He has dementia. Hanna has a younger sister, Judith Schultz. The sisters grew up in an assimilated environment, but Hanna has recently started using her maiden name and has become more interested in her heritage.'

'And she's out sick, right now?'

'She called in sick two days after Mona was discovered in the Swedish system.'

'And now her husband has popped up in Nice. He uses her log-in code, and hacks into Isaac Berns's computer — Berns, his wife's boss. And he's searching it for information about Mona?'

David nodded and looked out at the large breakwaters, where the water was being flung several metres into the air. He knew it was best to let Meir sort through this information in peace and quiet. David was hungry; he usually ate before he met with his boss. Meir handed back the pictures, took out his pipe, and sucked on it thoughtfully without lighting it. After a moment, he took the pipe from his mouth and shook his head.

'Strange story. It doesn't add up. But that's how it goes sometimes. Life isn't a straight line.'

David said nothing. Meir smiled at a little boy who was running after a brown dog.

'So what do you suggest?'

'That we bring him in. I want to know who he is, what he's doing, and with whom.' Meir nodded and David went on.

'We normally have three people in Paris, but right now they're on an assignment in Hamburg that shouldn't be aborted. I don't believe we should involve the French authorities, because we can't risk any mistakes. The French have already let one man get away in Nice. This is primarily an Israeli matter. Sure, the world is losing money, but for us it's about survival. We must handle this with our own resources. If we inform the security service, they'll just interfere.'

'You're aware that he is a Swedish citizen? And that the only thing he's really done is hack through TBI's firewall?'

'I agree that there could be a number of explanations for the intrusion. But why now? And why is he in Nice, of all places? I'm prepared to take the risk. We'll have to handle the first stage with kid gloves.'

'And what if it turns out that he does have links to Hezbollah?'

'We'll have to put some cracks in the system. A traffic accident or a regular old robbery — nothing that will attract the attention of the Swedish authorities. You can arrange for a red slip from Ben Shavit to sanction taking out Eric Söderqvist. And we'll bring a 101 member onto the team. Isn't Rachel Papo already part of the hunt for Mona?'

Meir chuckled.

'My friend, everyone is part of the hunt for Mona.'

They arrived at Hotel Alexander and the harbour district. Meir nodded to let the bodyguards know they were going to turn back. He looked at David.

'Do you want to bring him here?'

David shook his head.

'I'd prefer that he stay in Nice. Rachel's used to working with what already exists, right? If she's really the right one for the job. We sure don't want another Dubai.'

They walked for a while without saying anything. Meir was thinking about Rachel. David was thinking about food.

'What do you know about her?'

'Not much. I've read the general reports, and heard that she's smart.'

'I'm going to tell you something about Rachel. She ... I care for her as though she were my own daughter. We haven't spent that much time together, but there's something about her that arouses my paternal instincts.'

David was surprised. This was probably the most personal thing his boss had told him. Ever. Meir had no children of his own. What was so special about Rachel? She could certainly have been his daughter, age-wise. But she was an executioner. Meir read his mind.

'She had a hell of an upbringing. Everything that could go wrong, did. She's Sephardic; her family fled Morocco. She grew up in a refugee camp outside Sderot. Her parents died young. She and her sister ended up with their aunt. The man of the family turned out to be a sadistic bastard. I don't want to dwell on it, but it's a wonder she made it through that. Her sister was never the same again. Rachel handled it in her own way, but she was harmed as well. When I heard of her for the first time, she was barely twenty and had already carried out a number of tasks

193

that would have made the most hardened Sayeret Matkal officer turn pale. After that, she continued to pile on combat hours. She stepped right into one hornet's nest after the other. She's one of the few who have managed to infiltrate al-Qaeda and lived to tell about it. She showed up in field reports time and again. I studied her profile and discovered that she also has a gift for languages; among other things, she spoke flawless Arabic. When we started Unit 101, she was one of our first recruits. At first, I kept the unit under my own direction, which gave me quite a bit of time with her, and I'm still following her. She works hard, and her boss is happy with her. But she's difficult — it's hard to crack through her integrity. The psychologist has suggested that the tasks she picks reflect a death wish.'

Meir sighed.

'We've taken her to the emergency room with self-inflicted injuries twice. Once she was unconscious from alcohol poisoning; the other time it was pills. As if that weren't enough, she has disappeared before.'

'Disappeared?'

'Yes. Without a word. Gone. For several weeks, we didn't know where she was.'

David looked at him in surprise.

'*We* didn't know where she was? The *Mossad*?'

'No. But then one morning she was sitting on the hood of my car, with not a word about where she'd been.'

'Sounds like she's dangerous and unstable. How come she was allowed to stay?'

'The answer is simple: she has never failed. Not once in all the time I've known her. That makes her unique even in our organisation. Sure, Dubai wasn't perfect. And sooner or later, her psych problems will mess things up. She's living on borrowed time; but, on the other hand, most of us are.'

David didn't answer. Meir went on, a bit more forced and as though he suddenly wanted to change the subject.

'In any case, I've decided that Rachel should be promoted to more skilled intelligence work. She has a great deal of knowledge and a sharp mind. We'll see if it works. She wasn't very enthusiastic about the change, but I want to try her out in a new role.'

They approached a motorcade of black BMWs outside the Hotel Diplomat, whereupon the bodyguards joined their colleagues around the cars. A woman in a tight, grey suit, wearing dark glasses and with her hair in a bun, was walking toward them. When she reached them, she nodded to David and handed a mobile phone to Meir. He took it, listened with a frown, and muttered '*ken*' now and then.

Then he turned to David, who was leaning against the beach wall.

'That was Ben Shavit. He's having a hell of a time. The Rabbinate is demanding his head. They've never liked his liberal line, and now the entire Orthodox and nationalist movement is threatening him. The virus is God's punishment, and everything is Ben's fault. He should be in the Knesset to keep those fools in check, but instead he has to go to Washington. Poor bastard. And he knows nothing about IT.'

'Can't he send someone else?'

'No. Apparently the invitation is for him specifically. I suppose they want to show how the free world is fighting side by side to solve the crisis.'

'How can we help him?'

Meir gave a faint smile.

'By giving him Samir Mustaf.'

David nodded resolutely.

'We've found a hundred clues that all point in different directions, and we've put all our resources into finding him. We received a very credible tip that his group might be in a closed-down brewery in Gaza City. We waited there, but no one showed up. Either it was yet another false lead, or else someone had warned them.'

Meir stuck his hands into his jacket pockets.

'Ben asked for an updated report on the situation.'

David looked at a man who was flying a kite on the beach. There was a strong wind, and the large kite flew back and forth in short arcs.

'I'll make up a report as soon as I'm back in the office.'

Meir was watching the kite, too. Then he shook his head.

'I don't think we should bring in the Swede yet. There's too much we don't know. It'd be better to see what he's up to, without outside influence. If our suspicions are confirmed, we'll close up the cage.'

'It's up to you. I found one of our former agents at the consulate in Paris. He's on his way to Nice to take over shadowing.'

Meir turned up the collar of his jacket, still facing the sea.

'Bring Rachel into the team. But remember that she's about to be phased out of Unit 101.'

David nodded curtly.

'I'll make sure to brief her this afternoon, after I've written the memo to Ben. What should I say about Eric Söderqvist in the report?'

Meir started to walk toward the motorcade, and the back door of the middle car opened immediately. As he got in, he leaned out and met David's eyes.

'Nothing.'

The door closed, and the car pulled out into traffic, followed closely by three other cars. David stood pensively beside his own car. Then he turned to the chauffeur.

'Stop by McDonald's on the way back.'

The man nodded and closed the door behind him. They rolled smoothly out of the parking spot and drove along the beach toward downtown. David looked at the black-and-white photograph of Professor Söderqvist on the seat next to him. Using one hand, he covered half the portrait and studied the Swede's eyes. *You have just been given one more day of freedom. I hope you use the time well.*

Nice, France

The Musée National Marc Chagall was beautifully framed by cypresses in a shaded neighbourhood not far from downtown. Eric paid for the taxi, looked around, and then walked into the small park full of lavender in front of the cubist complex. As he stepped into the cool entryway with its bare, concrete walls and faint scent of paper, he stopped and looked at the text message again:

CHAGALL. SIÈGES C13.

He still wasn't certain that he'd guessed correctly. The name 'Chagall' could mean any number of different places. He had bet on the museum, but he had no idea what 'sièges C13' meant. He looked around. To the left lay the souvenir shop; to the right was the ticket counter. He purchased a ticket and went in. There was a certain amount of irony in his being in this particular place. Hanna loved the Jewish expressionist, and the museum was one of the main reasons they'd chosen to celebrate her thirty-fifth birthday in Nice.

The romantic and Biblical motifs moved him more now than

they had then. He stood before a large painting that depicted a man trying to hold onto a woman in a red dress who was floating high above his head. He thought of Mind Surf, of the feeling of floating. He was the man on the ground, desperately trying to hold onto his beloved, who was floating farther and farther away. The painting was called *The Promenade*. It depressed him. He walked on and entered a room with a few large pieces. An older man on a bench appeared to be sleeping. A young couple with bags from the souvenir shop stood whispering in a language he didn't recognise. Each painting seemed to attack him. There was no doubt that Chagall was on Hanna's side. The motifs called out his guilt. There was a woman in red who lay motionless on a bed of flames, surrounded by angels. The bed floated high above a glowing red city. There were snakes swimming in her blood, there were despairing couples surrounded by doves and wild animals, and there was a burning ladder up to an orange sky.

Eric ran a hand through his hair and tried again to concentrate on the text message. There were no numbers or letters anywhere in the room. He had sent more than 300,000 kronor to a nameless account, and all he had gotten in return was a message he didn't understand.

At the very end of the row of rooms, he saw a sign and an arrow: 'Auditorium.' He couldn't remember seeing anything like this on his last visit. He walked through two more rooms of paintings without casting even a quick glance at them. When he got to the door marked 'Auditorium' he looked around. He didn't know why, but he felt he was being observed somehow. The feeling was obtrusive, but he couldn't see anyone who seemed to be interested in him.

He pushed open the door and came into a large hall that was designed like an amphitheatre with a hundred seats. The room was bathed in a violet glow from three large windows with fantastic patterns and motifs. At the very front, on a raised stage, was a large grand piano. There was a sacred calm in the room, and he drank in the atmosphere. It was a beautiful place. He couldn't remember having seen it earlier. Then he caught sight of the small brass plates that assigned a letter to each row. A, B, and … C. Each seat had a number: C1, C2. He hurriedly squeezed his way along row C to C11, C12, and C13. The seat was farthest from the stage, the last one on the left side. He studied the seat, but he couldn't see anything different about it. What was he looking for? The faint light created dark black stripes that looked like deep furrows along the fabric. He bent down and felt the front and back of the seat. Nothing. Frustrated, he sat down on the seat.

A man in a grey T-shirt and black pants entered the room. The sound of the door closing behind him echoed through the room. Eric sat still, holding his breath. The man walked slowly down the aisle and stopped at the piano, reading a plaque. Eric felt something by one foot. He sank down and reached toward the floor. There, in the dark, under the seat and off to the side, lay a plastic bag. He carefully wrapped his fingers around the thin plastic and lifted up the bag, keeping his eyes on the man at the piano the whole time. The bag wasn't heavy, and it contained something rectangular. He wanted to leave the auditorium and look inside. But first he wanted the man to leave.

The man walked past the stage and over to the large windows. He didn't seem to be aware that anyone else was in the room, or else he was pretending not to notice. The seat was starting to become uncomfortable. Eric's back ached, and one knee was crammed into the space between his and the next seat. He breathed cautiously.

Suddenly, his phone rang. The man in the T-shirt stared straight at him. Eric stood up and walked quickly to the exit while fumbling his phone out of his pocket. The man remained standing by the stained-glass windows, watching him. As Eric left the room, the bright light of the gallery made him blink. His heart was pounding and he swallowed hard. The phone rang again. He looked at the screen. It was Judith, Hanna's younger sister.

'Hi, Judith.'

'Eric! Where are you?'

'I'm in France.'

He hurried through the art galleries.

'But you're on your way home, right?' She had spoken with Jens.

'Yes, I'm expecting to be in Stockholm tomorrow afternoon.'

There was silence on the line. He came to the lobby. He thought he heard sobbing.

'Judith, are you still there?'

'What the hell is the matter with you, Eric? Why would you run away when Hanna needs you the most? And what the hell are you doing in France?'

'It's a long story. The short version is that I'm here to try to find a way to cure my wife.'

'In France?'

'It sounds strange, I know, but maybe Jens can explain it to you.'

'Jens? He says you've totally flipped out. He's so disappointed in you.'

Eric looked over his shoulder. He couldn't see the man from the auditorium. He went out the main doors and continued down the narrow gravel path between the mimosa trees.

'Where are you?'

'Where you ought to be, you bastard. With Hanna.'

'How is she?'

'Great. In tip-top shape. Except that she's in a coma, and the doctors are totally at a loss. Except that she's being kept alive by a fucking respirator. Except that she seems to be having horrible nightmares that make her twitchy and shaky. Except that ... '

She burst into tears. The phone crackled and scraped. He caught sight of a small café on the far side of the museum park.

'Judith, I know you're angry with me, but I haven't gone crazy. I really believe that I'm doing what's best for Hanna. I would like nothing more than to be there with you now.' He felt guilty, because somehow he wasn't sure that was entirely true. Maybe this was all just an escape, like she said, camouflaged with fantasies of being a hero.

'May I speak with Jens?'

'He's not here. He's at home, sleeping. Do you realise he's been sitting at your wife's bedside for over twenty-four hours?'

He sat down on a black iron chair under a winding grapevine, and placed the bag on the table. It was green, from Carrefour.

'I know. Jens is a good friend.'

'And what about you?'

'I would have done the same for him.'

'I doubt that. The other guy was about to die last night.'

'The other guy?'

'Your boss.'

'My boss? Oh, you mean Mats. How is he?'

'I don't know. I heard it from one of the nurses. I don't give a shit about him. I'm with my big sister. Who's always been healthy and strong. Who's like a ... like a pale angel I can't reach. You ruined her!'

'Judith, you can throw as much shit at me as you want, but I'm glad you're with her. I'll be home tomorrow.'

'About damn time.'

She hung up. He remained seated, clutching the phone.

'*Vous désirez?*' — 'What would you like?'

He looked up at a tall, fat man with dark, dishevelled hair and a bushy moustache.

'A beer, please.'

The man nodded and walked over to a simple bar counter beside a small, blue stall. Eric picked up the plastic bag. So this was what he got for 350,000 kronor. Inside the bag was a newspaper-wrapped package. He looked around before he unfolded the paper on the table. It contained two black-and-white photographs and a black notebook with rings on the top edge — the kind that detectives and reporters always seemed to use in American movies. He looked at the photographs. One was of a man who appeared either to be sleeping or to be dead. Someone had written 'Melah as-Dullah' on the upper edge of the picture in red marker. The man seemed to be about thirty; he was powerfully built and had a thin moustache. The other picture was of a man who was alive and awake. He was older. The red marker read 'Samir Mustaf.' He had a serious expression, but his gaze was intense. Did this man have something to do with Mona? Could this Samir Mustaf lead him to Mona's creator?

Eric put down the pictures and picked up the notebook. Each page was full of writing and symbols. He frowned and looked carefully at one page. There was no doubt that this was programming code of some sort. But he didn't understand it. Frustrated, he turned the notebook in his hands, studying the text from different angles. Was the key to Mona right before his eyes? Certain things had been circled in some places; in others, long strings of code had been crossed out. This notebook had belonged to someone who worked with incredibly advanced systems development, but it was written in a language he didn't understand. The notebook might as well have been empty. He threw it down on the table in irritation, and looked out over the park. Who had written in it? What was hiding behind the incomprehensible code? Who could help him interpret it? He thought of Isaac Berns at TBI in Tel Aviv. Maybe he could help. But how could Eric contact him? He needed to show him the notebook.

Eric caught sight of the man from the auditorium. He was standing at the museum entrance, staring straight at him. His arms were hanging slack at his sides, his posture looking unnatural. Eric's phone vibrated. He released the man from his gaze and looked at the screen. There was another text, from the same number that had given him the bank and Chagall instructions.

YOU ARE BEING FOLLOWED.

He looked up at the museum entrance again. The man was gone. Eric grabbed the pictures and the notebook, stood up, and nearly knocked over the large waiter who was coming with the beer and olives. '*Excusez-moi.*' He stumbled past the iron chairs and out onto the gravel path. He couldn't see the man in the T-shirt anywhere, and reached the street just as a taxi was pulling out from the footpath. He waved his arms, the taxi stopped, and he yanked open the door and ducked into the bac kseat. He didn't exhale until they were back in the heavy traffic in the Old City, when he felt he could turn around and lool out the back window. Nothing seemed suspicious. He tried to gather his thoughts. Could Carl at *Aftonbladet* have hired someone to shadow him? The thought was absurd. Was it the terrorists, then? Maybe they wanted their notebook back. If that were the case, he was really up shit creek. He'd wanted to talk to them, after all, but now the whole venture seemed frightening. He had pursued a childish fantasy that had suddenly become brutally real. But if it wasn't the terrorists, who was it?

The taxi turned off at Negresco. He didn't want to leave the car. He just wanted to stay in the back seat and drive away, without having to worry about pictures of terrorists and a notebook full of strange code. He paid the driver, and quickly ran up the stairs to the entrance. When he stepped into his hotel room, he sat down on the soft bed and stared blankly in front of him. It was a quarter past five in the afternoon. What the hell had he expected? That he would fly down, get a phone number, call Gaza, and order medicine for a computer virus? He was already in danger, even though he'd barely scraped the surface. If he kept going, the pressure on him would increase. He was no superhero or secret agent. He was alone and afraid.

He placed the bag on the desk and stood at the balcony door, looking out at Promenade des Anglais. Down there, everything went on in the same rhythm: motorists and flaneurs with not a care in the world. He breathed deeply for a long time. Then he sat down at the small desk and started up Hanna's computer. Maybe it was fate. Maybe it was intuition. Maybe sheer madness. But, in any case, he didn't end up with a ticket to Stockholm. Instead, he bought a ticket to Tel Aviv. The notebook was his only hope, and maybe Isaac Berns could decipher the notes. He would search him out. Isaac was Hanna's boss; he had to help. Then he would go home.

Just one more day. For Hanna's sake. Everything he did was for Hanna's sake.

Tel Aviv, Israel

Meir Pardo was irritated. David Yassur could tell that right away when he answered the phone. Maybe David's news would put him in a better mood; maybe not. He threw a glance at the paper and got right to the point.

'He's on his way here.'

'Who?'

'The Swede. He's coming here.'

Meir sighed, obviously distressed.

'I thought I made myself clear when I said you should hold off on seizing him.'

'We haven't lifted a finger. He voluntarily got on a Swissair plane this morning. He's flying by way of Zurich, and will be landing at Ben Gurion at two thirty-five.'

There was a long silence. David moved the phone to his other ear and waited. He could hear a faint smacking sound on the other end. The director of the Mossad was smoking his pipe. Finally, he heard Meir's voice again:

'Why is he flying to Israel?'

David looked out the window.

'That's exactly what I'm wondering. Why is he flying to Israel?'

Montefiore. They always stayed at the swank little boutique hotel on Montefiore Street. The building had been constructed in the Twenties, and had started out as a home. The architecture was a combination of Oriental and pre-Bauhaus details. Hanna had loved their breakfasts, and the hotel was close to her cousin's apartment on Rothschild.

The street was bathed in a dry, still heat. Eric had spoken to Jens in the taxi on the way from the airport. He had sounded blunt and distant. Gone was the entertainer; now he was curt and cold. He had asked when Eric was planning on coming home, and suggested guardedly that Eric call Hanna's doctor.

Eric so desperately wanted Jens's blessing — to get him

to believe in the plan, to sanction it, but all he received was judgmental silence. By the end of their conversation, he had tears in his eyes. He wasn't disappointed or angry at Jens. How could he be? The real reason for his tears was his own doubt, his fear that Jens was right — that he really was running away. But what could he do? Go home and acknowledge that he had been fooling himself? No, it was better to keep going for a little longer. He would only stay for one more day, perform one last act. If the curtain fell, it would crush him. But he had made a decision in the bathtub in Stockholm, and another in the hotel room in Nice. Now he was in Tel Aviv, and he wouldn't go home until tomorrow.

He went up the short flight of stairs and stepped into the hotel. There was a great contrast between this and the bright sunlight on the street. Inside it was cool and dim.

'Shalom.'

A young man with straggly hair gave him a friendly greeting from behind the black-lacquered reception desk. The lounge music was loud, and even though it was only a quarter past four in the afternoon, the bar was already full of people. Eric said hello and checked in on the thin touchscreen on the counter.

'How long do you plan on staying?'

'Two nights at the most.'

He handed over his credit card and waited for the hair to make him a key. He remembered the last time they were here; it must have been at Pesach. He looked out through the open doors, and suddenly saw a woman waving her arms wildly. He excused himself and went over to the doors. By the time he got to the footpath, the woman was standing with her hands on her hips, looking down the street dejectedly. Beside her was a small silver suitcase. She was wearing a thin, brown dress and ballet flats, with a beige Gucci bag hanging on one shoulder. She was shorter than

Hanna — maybe 160 centimetres — and her hair was black and curly. A beautiful woman. Eric gathered his courage.

'Excuse me, is there something wrong?'

She sighed without taking her gaze from the street.

'The taxi left. I still had a suitcase in the trunk.'

He studied the shaded street.

'I think it will be okay. People are usually honest.'

She looked at him in surprise.

'You're not from Tel Aviv, that's for sure.'

He swallowed unconsciously and extended his hand.

'It seems we've chosen the same hotel. Eric Söderqvist.'

She brushed a lock of hair away from her forehead and gave him a searching look. Then she took his hand. Her grip was surprisingly strong.

'Rachel Papo.'

Checkpoint Qalandia, Israel

The Israeli military bus rolled slowly through the notorious checkpoint between Jerusalem and Ramallah. A lone officer was driving, and in the back of the bus sat a solder and two Palestinian prisoners. The prisoners were sitting close together. They had clearly been mistreated, and they sat in silence with their heads bent. In the middle of the concrete labyrinth, they were stopped by two Israeli soldiers. The driver joked with them, and one of the soldiers opened the back door and poked at the prisoners with his M16. 'Boom!' The men started, and the driver laughed brightly. The Palestinians looked tired. Tired and scared. The soldiers spoke, and one of them lit a cigarette. Then the oldest of them nodded to the officer and waved his arm — the vehicle could pass. All four passengers exhaled. Ahmad Waizy turned on the emergency lights and set out for the old city of Jerusalem.

Tel Aviv, Israel

The hotel room was large and light. One wall was covered in books, and the ceiling must have been four metres high. A large balcony looked out onto a green courtyard. On a table beside two black easy chairs stood a large bowl of fruit and a bucket of ice holding a bottle of champagne. Eric threw his bag on the bed, took out Hanna's computer, and sat in one of the chairs. The computer quickly found the hotel's network, and he Googled Isaac Berns's name. After scrolling through about ten pages, he found a mobile number. He also wrote down the switchboard number for TBI headquarters. Berns didn't answer his own phone, and the bank's switchboard informed him that he was unavailable. Eric left a short message.

After the call, his initiative left him and he ended up sitting in the chair with his eyes closed. A moped sputtered by down on the street, and the trees outside the half-open balcony door were full of chirping birds. He was tired from his journey, and he had a mild headache. Without opening his eyes, he felt through the pockets on his jacket and found his iPod. He didn't bother to untangle the earbud cord; he just started the music at random, which happened to be Shostakovich's fifth symphony — a piece he must have listened to a hundred times. The familiar harmonies flowed through his aching body, dissipating tension and undoing knots. He lost himself in the moderato; the cinematic strokes, powerful and strained; the stochastic rhythm, followed by the gentle, lyrical melody played by the first violins. He had always loved this ambiguity. Then came the waltz-like part — nervous, perhaps ironic. He thought of the notebook, and tried to remember the long lines of code and the mysterious symbols. He pictured the men in the black-and-white pictures — one dead and one alive. Had the journey to Israel brought him closer to Samir Mustaf?

After a long time, he opened his eyes and stretched. The music had stopped. The light in the room was softer; it was ten minutes past seven. Still half asleep, he took a few grapes from the bowl of fruit and looked at his mobile phone. This was the second time in a short while that he had found himself waiting for a phone call in a hotel room. He turned on the TV, where CNN's top story was the financial crisis that had been brought on by the Mona virus. Stocks were still falling all over the world, and the screen was filled with image after image of concerned analysts and pale-faced bank directors. All the charts and diagrams pointed down — CNN was talking about a financial meltdown. The virus had hit Israel hardest, but Asia, the US, and Europe had big problems, too. The prime minister of Israel, Ben Shavit, was in the US. CNN showed him shaking hands with the American secretary of state. The commentator said that there was no solution in sight, despite the fact that the free world was united in the fight against cyber-terrorism.

The next clip showed a woman announcing that TASE, the Israeli stock exchange, had decided to close, effective the next day — a measure that had never before been taken in its fifty-year history. Suddenly, Isaac Berns popped up on the screen. Eric leaned forward and turned up the volume. Berns was wearing a wrinkled suit, and he was standing next to an older man with severe facial features, identified as Henrik Goldstein, the CEO of TBI. The two men were standing on marble steps outside a large glass complex. Eric recognised the building: it was TBI's headquarters. Goldstein was answering questions from a female reporter. He vowed that all clients who had suffered a loss would be reimbursed as soon as the most pressing problems had been dealt with. Berns, though, said nothing. Eric guessed that the CEO had forced him to come along for support as an expert.

As CNN cut to a fat analyst at the London stock exchange. Eric turned off the TV and reached for a few more grapes. Was that coverage live? If it was, Isaac Berns was at TBI's offices. But it looked sunnier than it was outside his balcony; it must have been taped. His headache pressed against his temples. He wouldn't be able to get hold of Isaac Berns today — not unless he looked up his home address. That would be a desperate measure. But he was desperate. He didn't give a shit if he bothered Berns while he was in his bedtime slippers; he needed his help. But taking such action might annoy Berns. No, it was better to postpone contacting him until tomorrow. His stomach ached. He stuck the black notebook in his inner pocket and left the room.

The hotel restaurant was full, as always. Café Noir next door was full, too. He walked up the street to Restaurant Pronto and sat down at one of the tables on the footpath. It was warm, and smelled like pine and exhaust. He ordered a martini and took out the notebook. Large chunks of writing had been crossed out in the beginning. Farther on, when the author must have felt surer of himself, it was more cogent and without changes. Eric moved his fingers along the rows of text, and tried to imagine the man who had written all of this. Why couldn't Eric crack the man's code? The pages' content seemed familiar in some strange way. It was as though the focus was blurry, and that if he just twisted the lens a little bit it would all become clear. He had studied more than ten programming languages. Secret codes and ciphers had always fascinated him, from the Enigma technique to pig Latin.

The waiter put a bowl of olives on the table, and handed him an orange menu. Suddenly, Eric caught sight of the woman from the hotel. She had changed clothes — she was wearing black high heels and a dark dress — and had put her hair up. She was walking along the footpath, and would soon pass him. He averted his gaze and returned to the menu as her heels clicked between the walls of the buildings. Should he say 'Hi', or pretend to be absorbed in choosing his dinner?

'Shalom.'

He lowered the menu, and found that she was standing near his table.

'Shalom.'

He felt awkward, as though he had been caught red-handed. She smiled.

'The driver came back with my bag. You were right. There are honest people, even in this city.'

'I'm glad to hear it. Now I can admit that I said it mostly to cheer you up.'

She was wearing a beautiful pearl necklace that sat tightly around her neck. From it hung a thin, silver Star of David.

'So you're manipulative?'

'That's what my wife says. I prefer thoughtful, myself.'

'Okay. Then we'll call it thoughtful. I can actually believe you are. You look like that kind of person.'

There was something about her easy-going, slightly teasing manner that gave him the strange sense they had been friends for many years. Did she remind him of Hanna? Maybe — a dark-haired version of her. And yet not. He gestured. 'To prove I'm thoughtful, I'll buy you a drink. We can toast the return of your suitcase.'

She instinctively glanced at her watch.

'I'm supposed to meet some friends up at the Rothschild. But

I have time for one drink.'

He stood up, walked around the table, and pulled the chair out for her. She sat down. There was something graceful in the motion. In all her motions.

'What would you like …?' He searched his memory. '… Rachel?'

She looked impressed.

'I must have made quite an impression. I'll have what you're having.'

'Then it will be a dry martini.'

He held his glass up toward the waiter. She took an olive and looked at him intently. Then she removed the pit and shook her head.

'I can't think of it.'

'Think of what?'

'Your name. It fell right out of my memory. I blame the fact that I was flustered.'

'A good excuse. Eric Söderqvist.'

'That's what it was! It was on the tip of my tongue. Maybe the olive was in the way. And where is Eric Söderqvist from?'

'Sweden.'

'You don't look Scandinavian.'

'How does a Scandinavian look?'

'Thin, blond hair, blue eyes, and at least two metres tall.'

'Then I'm an unusual, brown-haired Swede, but a Swede nonetheless. And you?'

Her drink was placed on the table.

'I live in England these days, but I was born here. In Sderot.'

He raised his glass. 'Cheers to being able to trust people.'

Something flickered in her gaze. She clinked her glass against his.

'L'chaim. To life.'

'To life.'

The waiter gave her a menu. She placed it on the chair without opening it.

'Tell me what you do.'

'Do? What do you mean? Right now, or in general?'

'Both.'

He thought quickly.

'I'm a journalist. I work for an evening paper in Stockholm.'

She reached for her bag without taking her eyes from him.

'And what is a Swedish evening paper doing in Tel Aviv? Could it be the financial crisis? The virus?'

She fished out a pack of cigarettes. He looked around for matches, but she was quicker, and handed him a black lighter. He lit the cigarette, and she turned her head and blew out smoke. He tried to look unconcerned and studied her profile. Something had happened to her nose; it looked broken. He thought about what he should say.

'I'm working on a side story to the big headlines. About how Israel's outstanding IT has become a curse. If Israel hadn't become so digitised, the virus wouldn't have done so much damage. Something along those lines.'

She seemed to be considering what he'd said. She took a drag on her cigarette and nodded.

'It's not the first time we've been too smart for our own good. Our advances have always been annoying to those who haven't come as far, read as carefully, or earned as much. We Jews make up less than 0.2 per cent of the earth's population. Despite that, we've received 50 per cent of all the Nobel Prizes and 60 per cent of all the Pulitzer Prizes. Naturally, some people become jealous.' Her English was soft, slightly singsong. The atmosphere was charged. But what did it matter that she was a woman? That wasn't why he was sitting there, talking to her. She was an intelligent person. Nothing more. He needed a friend. He wondered what Rachel would say if he told her that she was the second person he had really spoken to in over two days. The last one had been a homosexual transvestite in Nice.

Rachel wrote a short text on her phone. Then she leaned toward him and smiled.

'Are you hungry?'

Somewhere inside his body, a flock of butterflies took off.

'Uh … yes, I'm hungry.'

She put out her cigarette.

'Then let's eat. What do you want? I'd like meat. If they had a cow on the menu, I'd take it.'

She laughed. The Star of David bobbed. Eric nodded.

'Then meat it is. But weren't you supposed to meet some friends at the Rothschild?'

'I was. But I rescheduled for tomorrow. I'm here now, and all I want is a cow and a bottle of wine.'

He ordered a *bistecca Fiorentina* to share — not a whole cow, but well over a kilo of meat — and, on the side, a salad and two portions of white asparagus with truffle aioli. There was no point in taking a chance on the wine, so he ordered a Barolo, 2004. And a bottle of San Pellegrino. When the waiter had gone, he leaned back.

'Now it's your turn to tell me. What do you do all day?'

'I work at the Israeli embassy in London.'

'Ah! A spy.'

She smiled broadly.

'James Bond himself. No, no. I'm an interpreter. Maybe not quite as exciting, but challenging enough.'

'Why an interpreter?'

'I love languages. All sorts. I was interested in them even when I was little, and when I discovered that it was easy for me to learn them, my interest grew into a passion.'

'How many languages do you speak?'

'Six. But I understand at least twice that many — mostly Arabic and Romance languages, but I've also studied Slavic and Germanic ones.'

'Impressive. It must be wonderful to be able to move through all those cultures, and understand their languages. It gives you a whole different kind of proximity. Authenticity.'

'It is wonderful. Unfortunately, I don't travel all that much. There are several countries whose languages I speak fluently but that I've never been to.'

The table was filled with plates. The waiter didn't bother to offer Eric a taste of the wine; he just poured them generous glasses, before squeezing the bottle between a platter of asparagus and a bowl of salad. Eric studied the large pieces of meat.

'Have you ever been to Argentina?'

She shook her head.

'They have the best meat in the world.'

She took a sip of wine. She held the glass with her hand cupping the globe. As she drank, her elbow stuck out from her body at a right angle. There was something unpolished about the motion — something rough. It was a strange contrast to her otherwise very graceful mannerisms.

'Did you know that Israel could just as easily have ended up in Argentina?'

He shook his head in surprise.

'Theodor Herzl, the father of Zionism, suggested two potential locations for the Jewish state: Palestine and Argentina. The fact is, he argued for Argentina because he thought the conditions there would be better for settlers.'

Eric looked at her sceptically.

'Did he think you would get all of Argentina?'

'Of course not. He hoped that Argentina would offer us a territory.'

Eric thought about what she'd just said.

'If you'd ended up there, you would have avoided all the conflicts with angry neighbours. And the war with Lebanon. But I suppose you might have ended up at war with Chile or Brazil instead?'

Her eyes narrowed.

'As you know, religion is at the forefront of most conflicts in the world, and the tension in this region is all its own.'

She pointed at her portion of meat with her knife.

'But, in any case, the meat would have been better.'

Eric took a bite of his beef and nodded thoughtfully.

'But this isn't bad.'

Rachel put down her silverware, drank some wine, and looked at the notebook that Eric had left lying on the table.

'Is that your interview book?'

He instinctively placed his hand on the book, as though to shield it from her gaze.

'Well … I guess you could say that.'

He hesitated. His thoughts were running along two parallel tracks. One was prompting him not to show the book to anyone. The other, the more intense one, was focussing on what she'd said: she was an expert at languages — Arabic languages. She cocked her head.

'What do you mean by that?'

He made a decision.

'It's not my interview book. It's actually not even my book. Or, well, now it's mine. I bought it. But I'm not the one who wrote in it.'

She frowned.

'Who did you buy it from?'

'I can't tell you. Confidentiality, protecting sources, and all that. But I think its contents have to do with the virus attack.'

Her head was still tilted, and her eyes locked onto his.

'And what does it say?'

'A lot. But nothing I understand, unfortunately. It seems to be written in some sort of code.'

She straightened up.

'May I see?'

He handed over the book. She put down her glass, wiped her hands on her napkin, and opened it to the first page. He studied her face. Her curly black hair fell across her eyes. She pushed it away and looked up, smiling.

'Well, you must be curious now.'

'Do you mean you know what it says?' He couldn't hide his eagerness.

She calmly cut a bite of meat and chewed it in silence. He extended a hand.

'Come on.'

'The Ottoman Empire arose in Anatolia in the late-13th century, and lasted until the beginning of the 1920s. At its peak, it included large parts of the Middle East, south-eastern Europe, and northern Africa.'

He looked at her in confusion.

'Interesting. But what about the code?'

She took out a pen.

'Ottoman is a form of Turkish that was influenced by Persian and Arabic. Its written form is based on an extended form of the Arabic alphabet.'

'But it doesn't look like Turkish. Or Arabic.'

'Correct. If it had been Ottoman, the similarities would have been clear.'

217

She took a napkin, placed it beside the notebook, and slowly began to write down Hebrew letters.

'This is a military code. The Ottoman army was sophisticated. They used a code in order to transfer sensitive information.'

'And you just happen to know it?'

'Well, as I said, I've always been interested in languages. But this, in particular, was one of my teacher's side interests. He taught me the code just because it was interesting. It's actually really simple once you've learned the key.'

She had already written three lines of text on the napkin.

'I'm rusty. Here's a bit I can't make out. The fact is, I don't understand any of what I've just translated, but maybe you will.'

She turned the napkin around and pushed it over to him. He looked at the text.

'Sorry. I don't know Hebrew.'

At first she looked at him in confusion, but then she laughed.

'Oh, sorry. I just assumed you did. Let me translate it into English.'

She leaned over the napkin and wrote another line parallel to the Hebrew.

'It's not a normal language. There are lots of special characters. Does it mean anything to you?'

He nodded.

'Absolutely. It's a programming language. What you've written so far seems to be log-in information for some sort of database or chat room.'

She nodded curtly and kept writing. He followed each new letter intently.

'Yes. That's definitely log-in information for a database. And what comes after seems to be a memo. Something to do with authentication.'

'Do you want me to keep going?'

'If you can. You don't have to translate everything — the first and second pages, maybe. That will give me something to work with.'

She looked up.

'Work with? What are you going to do? Are you a computer genius now, too?'

He had forgotten that he was a journalist, and not a professor at KTH.

'I've done quite a bit of programming, too, mostly as a hobby.'

She looked at him a bit too long. She'd seen through the lie. He cleared his throat.

'Would you like some coffee?'

She nodded and went back to her writing. The wine was gone. He caught the waiter's attention.

'Two espressos.'

When the waiter returned with the coffee cups, Rachel leaned back and ran her hands across her face.

'I can't do any more right now. Here.'

She handed over three napkins, all full of writing.

'These are the first four pages. I've translated them from a language I understand to one I don't.'

What he wanted most of all was to rush back to his hotel room and throw himself into the cracked code. But she had worked for a long time, and had finally turned the invisible lens and brought everything into focus. He couldn't just run off. And he liked being with her. He raised his coffee cup at her.

'Cheers to your fantastic gift for languages.'

She smiled. 'To the Ottomans.'

Rachel swallowed the bitter coffee. The notebook lay in the middle of the table; he had folded the napkins with the translation and had stuck them between the pages. What she really wanted to do was take the notebook and make sure that Unit 8200 got it for a complete analysis. That might be a breakthrough. But she couldn't just run off. She was surprised that he'd so readily accepted the transparent lie about the language teacher who'd taught her the code. It was so completely implausible. But he was probably so eager to learn what it said in the notebook that he'd forgotten his good sense. In actuality, it had taken them several days to crack the code. They had only had the notes from the raid in Nice to go on, but those notes hadn't given them much. They just contained incomplete code, and revealed nothing about the terrorists or the virus. But this was something totally different. Eric had a whole notebook, and an address to a database. How had he gotten it?

She studied him. Thick, brown hair. Kind, brown eyes. There was something anguished about him. He never looked happy, not even when he was laughing. He had a narrow, pointy nose. Thick eyebrows. Narrow lips. He looked weak. There'd been no physical training for that body. But there was something attractive about him — a naïve and unconscious charm. He felt genuine. Not in the nervous lies he threw out about being a journalist and programming for a hobby, but deep inside. He seemed like the opposite of a terrorist. But she knew they came in all shapes and sizes. The harmless ones were the dangerous ones. There was a red slip out for him — that made him a sanctioned target, but not before he'd been questioned. They needed to understand who he was, because he was a piece of the puzzle that didn't fit with any of the other ones. She looked at his hands. Hands were important — they were the first thing she noticed in a man. He had nice hands. Office hands. And a small silver wedding ring.

Rachel wanted to smoke, but at the same time she didn't want to appear weak or nervous. She would have to wait. But a drink was different. She smiled gently.

'I'd like another martini.'

He interrupted a monologue about Italian wines, and nodded in agreement. There was something uncertain and almost childish about him, as though he were trying to seem sophisticated but was really just lost. She had a sudden urge to kiss him.

There was something in her gaze that made him nervous. It was impossible to read her intentions. She had been drinking, but she didn't seem affected in the least. For his part, he could feel the alcohol, and decided not to drink any more. When the waiter placed two martinis on their table, he took the opportunity to hand him his credit card. Rachel sipped the drink without saying anything. She had cracked the code. It was fantastic — possibly the biggest thing to happen yet. How was this possible? How could he have gotten so lucky? At the same time, it was scary. What if the code didn't lead anywhere? What if the notebook was just a dead end? He wanted to go to his computer and get it over with. But at the same time he wanted to drag it out, to keep the dream alive. He recalled the feeling he'd had before he tested Mind Surf: the desire to leave the lottery ticket unscratched as long as possible. But this time it was totally different. This time everything was at stake.

She ran her finger around the edge of the glass and said, without looking up, 'What are you thinking about?'

'Oh … everything and nothing. How life happens around us. How we're sitting here in Tel Aviv.'

'Does that bother you?'

'No. But it's … unexpected.'

'Will your wife be worried?'

'She has nothing to worry about.'

'If you say so.'

Perhaps she sounded a bit wounded. She swallowed her drink in one gulp. He signed the credit-card slip and met her gaze.

'Shall we go?'

She nodded, picked up her handbag, and stood up.

'Don't forget the notebook.'

The night was warm and sultry; footsteps echoed between the buildings. They were alone on Montefiore Street, and the buildings kept the traffic to a distant hum. They said nothing during the short walk back to the hotel. Rachel was walking a bit ahead of him, and she stopped at the entryway stairs to wait for him. The lobby was full of a large group that was checking in. Rachel nodded at the bar.

'Nightcap? My treat.'

She pushed her way toward the bar. He caught sight of a black corner sofa that seemed to be free, and sat down on it and leaned back. The air was heavy and close; the room was packed with people and some sort of house music. He yearned for Chopin.

'Let's drink to Israel!'

She sat close to him on the sofa and placed two shots before them.

'Sabra.'

He picked up the glass suspiciously and sniffed the brownish liquid.

'What is it?'

'The national liqueur of Israel. Chocolate, with oranges from Jaffa. I prefer whisky, but I didn't want anything too strong.'

'Thanks.'

The drink was thick and cloying. He made a face.

'Not really my thing. I'd rather have chocolate cake and oranges on their own.'

'Me, too. But now you've tried it.'

The sat in silence for a while. Rachel fingered her glass.

'Where's your wife?'

'In Sweden.'

'Didn't she want to come along?'

'She's sick.'

She looked him in the eye.

'Nothing serious, I hope?'

'She got sick just before I left. I don't actually know what's wrong with her. But I'm sure it will be fine.' There was a lump in his stomach. 'And you?'

'What?'

'Do you have anyone?'

She looked over toward the lobby.

'I'm still looking.'

They were quiet again. He took the silence as a signal to leave.

'Thanks so much for your pleasant company. And for helping with the code.'

She smiled faintly and they stood up. She was staying on the second floor; he was on the third. He followed her to her room. When they arrived at the black wooden door, she turned around and pressed up close to him. He felt her breath against his neck, and could smell a faint scent of jasmine from her perfume. He felt the contours of her body. With her lips against his neck, she whispered, 'I know more than Ottoman codes.'

She played teasingly with his shirt buttons. He hesitated, and then she pushed him away.

'I'm sure we'll see each other tomorrow.'

Then she pulled her key card through the reader and slunk in without looking around. He remained standing outside the closed door.

Herzliya, Israel

As one of the highest-ranking statesmen in the country and a personal friend of Ben Shavit's, he had every right to be there. And yet the building made him nervous. Sinon felt vulnerable, as though he were being watched. If there was anywhere his identity might be revealed, it was here, in the very heart of the Mossad, the intelligence unit's centre for strategy and analysis in the small suburb of Herzliya, just outside Tel Aviv, in this enormous complex of black glass and shiny steel. As always, his errand seemed weak and transparent. Everyone he met seemed to see right through him and to know exactly what he was really up to. And yet they let him in, typed his requests into their terminals, and politely followed him past rows of filing cabinets and server halls to retrieve anything he asked for. He must have been here at least ten times in the years he'd worked for Ben Shavit, retrieving important information that he'd smuggled out to the organisation in Palestine.

This evening was special, like the calm before the storm. A lot of things would change tomorrow. There would be another dimension to the virus threat; the damage would move from messing with ones and zeroes to actually killing. Tomorrow, Ahmad Waizy's martyrs would carry out their heroic actions in Jerusalem and Tel Aviv. The men were already in the country, and the equipment would arrive early tomorrow morning. Soon the time would come for him to use his position and trust in earnest to convince Ben Shavit to go along with Hezbollah's demands. After that, his task would be done and he would finally leave the infidels and return to his own people. He would return as a hero, full of knowledge about the inner workings of the enemy. But before he was finished he, too, had a minor task to accomplish — a task that he had added himself, without checking with anyone.

Maybe it was unnecessarily risky, even foolhardy. But deep down he was a soldier, and he wanted to feel that he personally had caused harm. This time, he himself would be an operative, and it was worth the risk. He would avenge his brothers, and kill the Jews' executioner.

He had created a false inquiry into the Dubai assignment. The papers he carried to Herzliya bore the forged signatures of defence minister Ehud Peretz, and stamps from military intelligence. Dubai had gone wrong, and what was meant to look like a natural death had turned into a sensational murder. The investigation would find out where mistakes had been made. He was the only one who knew that the investigation was fake, and he truly hoped he wouldn't run into David Yassur, or, even worse, Meir Pardo. But it was just past eleven at night, and the likelihood that either of them was out and about in Herzliya was small.

It might seem strange that he was the one to come here with this apparently simple inquiry, and so late at night. But, on the other hand, these matters were sensitive, and he could always claim that the high command didn't want to involve any unnecessary officials. It was sink or swim. Ahmad and the others would denounce his actions, but he had to take her out. He was tired of just sitting still and waiting. He might as well use that time to be productive.

Sinon had come past the obligatory security doors and was now waiting for the night security guard to start up his computer. These systems had not been affected at all by the virus; the country's Intelligence network had no links to the financial structures. The woman in front of him was about forty, and her hair was cut short in a style that irritated him. It was a dull style that made her look like a boy. She was also dressed in pants and a jacket, which made her look even more like a man. He looked at her fingers as they typed on the keyboard. Her nails were painted an ugly green. The woman looked up.

'The person you're looking for has the highest security level. I can't release any details without my boss's approval. Please take a seat, and I'll try to reach him.'

He raised his voice.

'But you can see perfectly well who initiated this order. And you know very well who I am. I didn't drive all the way out to this shithole to stand here and wait. Hurry it up. You have five minutes before I get angry.'

The woman pursed her lips and picked up a telephone receiver.

'I'm just doing my job. This won't take long.'

He went back to one of the benches attached to the wall and sat down. He was looking forward to tomorrow morning's bike ride, to fresh air and freedom. All he could smell in here was sadness. Were the papers believable enough? What if they decided to call Ehud Peretz? He was risking the whole project by being here. This was minor compared to the big plans. But he had made up his mind. Now he just had to keep playing.

A door opened at the far end of the hall, and a pale man in his sixties showed up. He looked like Woody Allen, with the same kind of glasses. The man walked to the boy-lady at reception. They spoke for a moment, and Woody studied the papers that Sinon had handed over. Sinon stood up and walked over to them with determined steps.

'Well?'

The man peered at him through his thick glasses.

'I apologise for the inconvenience. I'm sure that given a position like yours, you appreciate that we take security seriously. Especially in these difficult times.' He smiled faintly. 'But everything appears to be in order. Olga will help you retrieve the information you're looking for. It may not leave the building, however, so if there's something you need to remember, I recommend that you write it down. It's an honour to have you here. I hope you find the information you're looking for.'

The man gave a sloppy salute, nodded at the woman, and left them. Sinon turned to Olga.

'Can you retrieve the folder containing general information like her CV, background, and family relationships? In addition, I need the Dubai report. And her current contact information, such as telephone number and street address.'

'I'll see what I can find. Agent 2913 has a very limited profile, and everything is under class-one protection.'

'2913?'

'That's her duty code. We seldom use names here. To us, she's Rachel Papo 2913.'

Tel Aviv, Israel

Eric returned with a mild headache to the room on the third floor. His mind was whirling. He had never been unfaithful, despite the fighting and the sometimes-deep rift between him and Hanna, and despite their long periods of coldness and distance. Not once. He'd had opportunities — a woman with the team, students. But he hadn't been interested.

When he got to his room he sank down on the floor inside the door. He ran his hands through his hair. Nothing had happened. No matter how beautiful and tempting Rachel was, she couldn't measure up to Hanna. No one could.

The room was dark and chilly. The air conditioning hummed steadily from somewhere on the ceiling. He sat on the floor for a long time, his mouth full of Sabra liqueur. Finally, he got up and went over to the desk. He grimaced at his headache, started the computer, and then took a cold Sprite from the minibar and sank down on the desk chair. He stared blankly at the screen with its undulating Windows symbol, and then stood up and opened the balcony door wide. The mild night air swept into the room, and he stood still, taking several deep breaths. Then he went back to the desk, where he laid out the wrinkled napkins with the translated code on them. He opened the web browser, typed in the log-in query, and waited anxiously. A message written in Arabic popped up, but he didn't need to understand what it said to recognise an error message. He switched the order of what he had thought to be the password and username, only to get the same message. He was going to have to write a program that alternated all possible combinations of the information on the napkins. It was possible the information had already been changed, and if that were the case he would never get in. But it was worth a try.

Eric sipped the soda and started writing code. Half an hour later, the program was finished, and he let it loose on the log-in gate. After working on the unknown firewall for seventeen minutes, the program found a way in. Apparently, the username had been changed, but the password was the same as it had been before. The screen changed colour, turning dark green. He took one of the hotel pens from the desk drawer and added the new username to the napkin. An apparently endless amount of unstructured information was now flowing onto a green background. It was written in English, but despite that he couldn't interpret the programming code. It seemed to be an eclectic blend of familiar and unfamiliar programming languages. After some time, he could make out whole strings of recognisable elements, like familiar islands in an otherwise foreign sea. Maybe this was Mona. Maybe he was sitting here and looking at the virus's hitherto-unknown source code — its DNA.

He saw functions that had to do with cloning. Further down in the code, he recognised the command that queried databases, and in another spot something that was probably there to hide algorithms from search programs. This was top-level code, and the person who created it must have had a great deal of knowledge and plenty of resources. Maybe this was a cloud-based setup, a shared file that had been stored on the internet to avoid being detected locally and to make it possible for several people to work on the same code at the same time from different locations. Maybe it was a backup of Mona's primary programming elements.

Eric had the cold sweats, but he was thrilled despite his headache. As he scrolled through hundreds of screenfulls of code, he found a signature that recurred several times: 'Salah ad-Din.' Further down, he also found a web address that seemed to lead to a chat room. Maybe this was where the creators of the virus communicated with one another? He pasted the address into the browser. Outside the balcony, glass bottles fell to the ground, clinking. Someone laughed aloud. A black page with white text popped up on the screen. Lines of Arabic appeared in clusters — they had to be chat entries. The system had supplied the sender's username under each entry. Although the messages were written in Arabic script, the names were written in Latin letters, probably because they were generated from the log-in information. The first entry, a long one, was signed 'Kah.' The next entry, which only contained a few short lines, was signed 'GW.' There was another short entry from Kah, and after that there was a message in English. It was signed 'Zorba':

PHASE 3 RECRUITS WILL BE TRANSFERRED TO ISR STRAIGHT AFTER AGREEMENT.
:ZORBA

'ISR' could mean Israel. It could also mean thousands of other things. But it could mean Israel. Then there was an entry in Arabic that was signed 'Salah ad-Din'. Judging by the date, the entry was about a week old. He copied the block of text from Salah ad-Din, and started Google Translate. The program wasn't the best, but you could usually understand what it came up with. The translation appeared immediately:

M EFFECTIVE TO 96%. PARALLEL TO PHASE 3 CONTINUING MY WORK WITH NADIM. CERTAIN HESITATION ABOUT OPERATIVE SCOPE OF PHASE 3.
:SALAH AD-DIN

A short message in Arabic followed. The signature was 'A'. He turned again to Google Translate:

KEEP TO YOUR PART. PHASE 3 HAS THE EFFECT NEEDED. WORK ON NADIM IS NOT PRIORITY.
:A

This was totally incredible! He was reading archived discussions between the world's most wanted terrorists.

It was more than he'd dared to hope for. Who was Zorba? Who was A? Who was Nadim? Phase three? Maybe he would understand more if he read some earlier messages. He scrolled up through countless entries. After he'd read about ten of them, he became more and more certain that Salah ad-Din was Mona's creator — or at least a person who was closely involved in developing the virus. A seemed to be in command, maybe at the very top. Zorba didn't show up anywhere else, so maybe he wasn't important. There were other signatures: 'Muh', 'Dal', 'Wrath', and 'Sinon'. Eric concentrated on A and Salah ad-Din.

A was responsible for phase three. Eric moved back through the entries, and found one that explained phase three:

S, MILITARY EFFORTS IN PHASE 3 ARE NOT YOUR CONCERN. THE MARTYRS ARE RECRUITED. ACCESSORIES SHIPPED SEPARATELY. YOU HAVE YOURS, I HAVE MINE. THE FIRES THAT WILL BE LIT IN THE DOGS' CITIES SHALL LIGHT UP THE OVERLY LONG NIGHT AND AGAIN SPREAD WARMTH IN THE LOST LAND.
:A

Martyrs. Military efforts. Fires. So the terrorists weren't going to stop at the virus attack. Were they going to bomb cities in Israel with the help of suicide bombers? Salah ad-Din was engaged only in Nadim, and almost all of his entries seemed to be purely questions about programming. He had to find out what Nadim stood for. Was it a code name for Mona? But wasn't Mona itself a code name? He kept scrolling. He thought he had figured out the Arabic symbols for Nadim, and he looked for them in entry after entry. There! It was an entry from A again. He copied the line of text and ran it through the translation program:

NADIM IS NOT NECESSARY SO WHY SO MUCH TIME ON IT? AN AGAINST INFECT WILL NEVER BE GIVEN TO THE INFIDELS.
:A

Eric looked at the sentence for a long time. An 'against infect'? What could 'against infect' mean? His head pounded, and he squinted. Suddenly, he understood. He was petrified, his eyes filling with tears. The word 'against' had been mistranslated from 'anti'. And 'infect' should be a noun, not a verb: 'virus.' An anti-virus. Nadim was Mona's anti-virus. Eric had been right all

231

along in everything he had done, in everything he had hoped. Salah ad-Din was developing an anti-virus.

Herzliya, Israel

They had given him four thick folders, a desk, and a chair. Now he was sitting alone in a cramped room that seemed to be used more as a storeroom than an office. The light was glaringly white, and he could feel the warmth of the light bulb that was hanging right above his head. The only window in the room had been outfitted with bars; outside it was pitch black. Sinon now had the Mossad's complete file on Rachel Papo — at least the reports that had been kept for posterity. He was convinced that she had carried out a number of assignments that had not been and would never be documented. But these files were thick enough.

There were a number of pictures as well — Rachel when she was young, in a uniform, and as a student. There were also pictures of her victims. Some were archival photos that depicted living people; others had been taken in the field. In those, the victims were anything but living. Rachel seemed to have a fondness for knives. He couldn't bring himself to read the details; they only depressed him. He read with great interest about her private life.

He put his finger on her date of birth and did the maths in his head. She was thirty now. Her mother had been a teacher, originally from Morocco. Her father was a blacksmith with Spanish roots. Her parents had fled Morocco during the Six Day War. She had a younger sister, Tara. Their mother had died in childbirth with Tara, when Rachel was eight years old. One year later, their father had died, too; it had likely been a suicide. Then, after some ups and downs, the children ended up on a kibbutz twenty kilometres north of Haifa. When Rachel was eleven she and Tara went to live with their mother's older sister and her Russian partner. Here, someone had circled the text in blue ink. The aunt worked as an auditor, and was often away on business. The man owned a small transport business. After a year or so, the man had started to assault the girls. According to what must have been a statement from Rachel herself, he had raped them on a regular basis, most often when their aunt was away. Tara had it the worst. They had also been beaten. To believe Rachel's story, it had been sheer torture — bicycle tubes and cigarettes, blowtorches, ice-cold water. It seemed the aunt knew nothing of this, or else she didn't care. The couple had no children of their own. At one point, the abuse was so bad that Tara had to go to the emergency room. The aunt was the one who drove her to the hospital. There, she maintained that the girl had broken her arm and hit her head when she fell off her bike.

After her time in the hospital, Tara had closed herself off in some sort of autistic state. One week before Rachel's sixteenth birthday, when the aunt had left for the weekend, Rachel locked their stepfather into his workroom, took Tara, and left the house. The girls went back to the kibbutz in Haifa, which hid them when their aunt came looking for them. Several years later, the kibbutz handed Tara over to a care facility, and Rachel entered the military.

A yellow Post-it note referred to an item in the *Jerusalem Post*. Sinon paged through the documents and found a copy of the article, published two years after Rachel had enlisted. The Russian-born owner of a transport business had been murdered in his home, shot in the head at close range. He had been found by his wife when she returned from a business trip. The police had found neither motive nor suspect. According to the article, the victim had been well liked and respected.

Sinon placed the clip back in the folder, and then started looking for what he'd come for. He found the information on the back of a grey information card: Rachel Papo's temporary home-address in Tel Aviv. He folded the card and put it in the inner pocket of his jacket. He didn't care how angry this made Woody Allen. As he was about to put the folders back, his eyes fell on another document. He picked it up and smiled. It was the address of Tara's care facility.

Tel Aviv, Israel

Even though Eric had been reading entries for over two hours, he had only read a fraction of all the messages. He was concentrating on the most current ones. The terrorists were preparing several attacks in Jerusalem and Tel Aviv. Phase three would be carried out within the next few days. Nadim was Mona's anti-virus, and Salah ad-Din was working on finishing the code. A only seemed interested in phase three, and stressed time and again that they didn't need an anti-virus. There was no information about where A or ad-Din were. Eric sat still, looking at the latest entry, which had been written by ad-Din seventeen hours before. Eric was having a hard time gathering his thoughts; he was too tired. Outside the balcony door, it was quiet, save for the chirping of the crickets. What was his next move? He couldn't sit there hoping that ad-Din's telephone number would pop up on the screen. He had to enter the conversation himself. If he made a mistake, he would scare them off and destroy the only trail that led to Nadim. But what choice did he have? He created his own account under the username 'ES'. Should he use Google Translate and write in Arabic? No, because then he wouldn't have any control over what he was saying. He hesitated for a few seconds, and then sat up straight and typed in a message:

SALAH AD-DIN, MY NAME IS ERIC SÖDERQVIST. I AM A SWEDISH PROFESSOR OF COMPUTER AND SYSTEMS SCIENCE AND I WOULD LIKE TO HELP YOU. I AM VERY IMPRESSED BY THE MONA CODE, BUT I WOULD LIKE TO SUGGEST A FEW MINOR IMPROVEMENTS IN THE STEALTH CAPACITY. CONSIDER MY PRESENCE IN YOUR CODED CHAT TO BE MY RÉSUMÉ. IT TOOK ME TWO HOURS TO FIND IT AND GET IN. I HAVEN'T TOLD ANYONE ELSE. I HOPE FOR YOUR PROMPT ANSWER.
:ES

Eric leaned back in the chair and waited. Maybe someone else was logged in; maybe not. Maybe they had a push function or an RSS feed that notified them when a new message had been posted. He sat still until his body ached, and he started to nod off. There was no point in waiting; it might be ages before someone answered — if anyone even did answer. He stood up stiffly. The room was dim in the glow from the computer. He pulled off his clothes and lay naked on top of the covers. He thought about the planned attacks. He had to warn someone. He wanted to talk to Jens. Most of all, he wanted to talk to Hanna. She had always been his closest ally, his sounding board, and his best critic. Most of all, he wished he could hear her voice. But he was alone — a shadow on a bed in a hotel room in the Middle East. He leaned over the edge of the bed, pulled out his suitcase, and dug out his toiletry bag. The perfume bottle he had tossed in at the last second had leaked, and now everything smelled like Hanna. He fell asleep with the drenched toiletry bag beside his head.

Ding.

It took him a moment to react. He had been deeply asleep, and at first the sound wove its way into his warm dream like an unnatural trespasser. But then he realised that the sound wasn't part of the dream. He was back in the hotel room, naked, on top of the covers. What had woken him? He sat up, suddenly wide awake. He must have heard a new entry. He stumbled out of bed and crouched before the computer. A few short, white words flickered against the black background:

DEFINE *MINOR IMPROVEMENTS*
:SALAH AD-DIN

Eric sat stock-still, as though his movements might scare away the man on the other side of the net — as though Salah ad-Din could see him sitting there, naked at the keyboard. He had established contact. But what should he do now? His thoughts were going in a hundred different directions. Without taking his eyes from the screen, he cautiously got up and sat in the chair. He had to build up trust. Thank God there was some substance to his claim about the code. He had noticed a sequence of code in what he understood to be the virus's stealth capacity, a sequence that reminded him of a problem he'd had himself with Mind Surf. A doctoral student on his team had shown him a new way to write the alternating calls, leading to faster, more stable reading. If the calls he'd seen in Mona's code were as similar to Mind Surf's as he thought they were, he could use the same fix. He went back to the Mona code and scrolled through page after page, searching for the string he'd seen. There — the code sequence was very similar to Mind Surf's call, even if they resulted in two completely different functions. He copied the code into his reply and prepared a suggestion for a more effective call. The reply came after only a minute:

WHY ARE YOU CONTACTING ME?
:SALAH AD-DIN

He answered right away:

I HAVE ANALYSED MONA. I CAN HELP YOU IMPROVE THE CODE.
I SUPPORT YOUR CAUSE.
:ES

KHALIL ALLAH?
:SALAH AD-DIN

Khalil Allah? Eric went to Wikipedia and typed in the name.
Then he went back to the chat.

FRIEND OF GOD. IBRAHIM. TARAKH'S SON. FATHER OF ISMAEL.
MAY PEACE BE UPON HIM. THE FOURTEENTH SURAH.
:ES

It was transparent — too much cut and paste.

WHY MONA?
:SALAH AD-DIN

TO SHOW THE INFIDELS THAT THEY ARE OUTNUMBERED. TO
HONOUR ALLAH, THE ONE TRUE GOD.
:ES

The screen was empty for a long time. There were no
new messages. Eric breathed heavily, his fingers resting on the

keyboard. Had he lost him? Had he said the wrong thing?

Go in peace. Masha Allah.
:Salah ad-Din

Salah ad-Din had asked him to leave the chat. But he couldn't
— not when he was so close! He could not fail. He thought
feverishly, as his eyes fell upon the wrinkled napkins full of
notes. The Ottoman code! He ran over to the hallway, where he
found the notebook on the floor just inside the door. He rushed
back to the computer, opened the notebook to a random page,
and placed it in front of him on the table. Launching Word, he
looked through its special symbols. It took him forty minutes to
put together a series that were somewhat similar to the symbols
written in the notebook. He wanted to write a sentence of his
own in Salah ad-Din's code. It was far-fetched as hell, but what
did that matter? It was sink or swim. He copied the block of text
into the chat, and sent the message. There was another delay.
The morning sun shone in onto his bare legs; outside the balcony
door, a bird was singing loudly and energetically.

Impressive.
:Salah ad-Din

He was back.

Let me help you.
:ES

Wait until tomorrow night. If you are still behind us,
we will talk.
:Salah ad-Din

WHAT'S HAPPENING TOMORROW?
:ES

THE NEXT PHASE. A CLEARER MESSAGE. TISBAH ALA KHEYR WA
AHLAM SAAIDA.
:SALAH AD-DIN

So the attacks were set for the next day. He copied ad-Din's
last sentence into Google Translate. He had said good night to
him; the conversation was over. Eric would have to wait until
after the attacks before he could re-establish contact. He looked
up at the ceiling. Suicide bombers in Israel — within twenty-
four hours. Oh, God. He had to warn someone, but who? If he
called the police, he would reveal himself to Salah ad-Din, and he
might never be able to contact him again. But if he didn't warn
someone, innocent people would die. He sat there for a long
time, staring blankly at the flickering screen. Maybe Salah ad-Din
was sitting and staring back on the other side of the internet.

He stood up, went out to the balcony, and inhaled the early-
morning air redolent of sea and pine. A rustling noise made him
look down at the garden, where a skinny dog was trying to pull a
garbage bag out of an overturned bin. He turned his face to the
warm morning sun. There was a stale taste in his mouth. He had
to talk to someone, otherwise he would go crazy. It was a quarter
past seven. Even though he hadn't slept for more than a few
hours, he pulled on his wrinkled clothes, grabbed his PC, and
went down to breakfast. In the restaurant were an older couple
and, at a window table, a young man with an iPad. Rachel wasn't
there. He put his computer under his arm, gathered breakfast for
two on a tray, and went up to her room on the second floor. He
hesitated for a moment, but then knocked on the door lightly.
Not a sound. He knocked again. He heard her moving, and then

she opened the door. She was wearing the hotel's black robe, and was barefoot, with messy hair. She was shorter than he remembered, and her eyes were swollen. He had woken her up.

She looked at him without saying anything. Suddenly, he felt like crying. Maybe she could tell. Maybe she could see how tired he was, how desperate he felt. She leaned forward and kissed him on the cheek.

'Shalom,' she whispered, carefully closing the door behind him. Her room was smaller than his. With the exception of the unmade bed, there was no sign that anyone was staying there. The bowl of fruit and the champagne were untouched, and he couldn't see any suitcases, books, or clothes. She, too, had opened the balcony door. She sat down cross-legged on the bed and didn't seem to mind that, by doing so, she'd bared a large portion of her legs. She had some sort of tattoo on her ankle, and her toenails were painted dark brown. He set the tray down in front of her, sank down into one of the chairs across from the bed, and then placed his computer on the table beside the bowl of fruit. She looked at him and tilted her head.

'Why are you sad?'

He lowered his eyes.

'It's a long story. Infinitely long.'

'Are we in a hurry?'

'Maybe not. But I'm too tired. I'd be happy to tell you another time. I'm sorry I woke you up like this, but …'

'It's okay. I was happy to see you. I thought about you last night before I fell asleep.'

'What were you thinking about?'

She laughed.

'Oh, no … You shouldn't ask about a woman's thoughts.' Eric smiled weakly.

'I thought about you, too.'

She cocked her head. 'Would it have been a big deal if you'd slept over?'

'Yes. It would have been a big deal to me.'

At first she didn't say anything; she fiddled with the teabags on the tray. Then she lowered her voice.

'Then I guess it was lucky that you left. Or what do you think?'

He sighed.

'I've only known you for a few hours, but you're special. In every way. But I can't. Not now. I just need a friend — to be close to someone.'

She picked up one of the yellow Liptons, tore the paper, and put the teabag in one of the cups. Then she looked at him again.

'Why did you come here, Eric?'

He reached for the computer.

'Last night, I used your translations to get into the database. The code let me right into Mona's development environment.'

'You're joking.'

'No. And that's not all. From there, I got into a chat room that the terrorists use. There were hundreds of entries going back several months.'

She shoved the tray aside and moved closer to him. 'And?'

'And there I made contact with a person who I think designed Mona.'

It was probably crazy of him to tell her all of this, but he had to trust someone. And he had to talk. He had to share the information about the attacks with someone — share the responsibility with someone. Rachel was sitting very close to him now.

'What was his name?'

'Salah ad-Din. But that's just an alias.'

'Salah ad-Din is the Arabic name for Saladin, the highest Muslim leader in the twelfth century — the man who freed Jerusalem from the Christian crusaders. When he broke through the city's defences, he gave the order to slaughter every inhabitant, to take no prisoners. He's an example to many Muslims.'

'Lovely. He's about to do it again.'

'Do what?'

'Slaughter people in Jerusalem.'

Something sharp glittered in her eyes.

'When, where?'

'I don't know everything, but you can read for yourself. Maybe, with your knowledge of languages, you might understand more. They're planning suicide bombings in Jerusalem and Tel Aviv.'

He opened the computer and placed it in front of her on the bed. She ran a hand through her thick hair.

'When?'

'Today, or maybe tomorrow. See what you can get out of it. Look for "phase three".'

She looked down at the screen. He tried to sit upright in the chair, but the exhaustion was pressing him down. He yawned. Maybe he should eat something to regain his strength, but all he wanted to do was sleep.

Rachel reached for her cup of tea as she brought up more messages. After forty-five minutes, she came to the previous night's conversation between Eric and Salah ad-Din. Her eyes narrowed as she read his entries, his praise of the virus, and his offer of co-operation. She looked at the man across from her, who was now deep in slumber. She took her mobile phone from her pocket, dialled a number, and waited for an answer. It came after one ring.

'It's time.'

She hung up without taking her eyes from Eric.

'Shit,' she mumbled, in hardly more than a whisper. Then she leaned forward and gently ran her fingers through his hair.

'You idiot.'

Stockholm, Sweden

Mats Hagström's pulse rate increased sharply, which set off an alarm. His heart rate had changed several times during the night. His state was similar to a coma, but his brain was working intensely. The EEG was registering wild lines and straggling alpha, beta, and delta waves in rapid spikes. Doctor Thomas Wethje took note of the spikes on the readout, which were usually seen in patients undergoing severe epileptic seizures. But Mats didn't have epilepsy, so the EEG chart was quite remarkable. And concerning. He placed his hand on Mats's warm forehead and whispered, 'Whatever you're fighting — don't give up.'

Tel Aviv, Israel

He was on his way across a warm, summery beach. Waves were rolling onto the shore from about fifty metres out. He was wearing Crocs and carrying a large picnic basket. Hanna was walking beside him with a blue blanket under her arm and one hand on her sunhat. She was wearing a white tunic over an orange bikini. The mild breeze was full of the scents of the sea — mussels, seaweed, salt. Then, just as he was about to take her hand, he slipped. He fell headlong to the ground, and threw up his hands to catch himself, to no avail. Pain flashed through his face, chest, and wrists when he hit the sand. There was thundering and rattling around him; his arms were caught high up on his back. Then his consciousness caught up with him, and along with it came panic. There were several men in black, with large boots and thick jackets. Someone was pressing his weight onto Eric's back, and he was shoved hard against what he now knew was the carpet. He couldn't breathe. He heard commands in Hebrew, and something breaking. His lungs burned, and he gasped desperately for air, trying to lift his head. *Rachel*. He had to protect her. What if they hurt her? He tried to twist around, but he was stuck. They fastened sharp bands around his arms and legs. Someone grabbed him by the collar, and he thought they were going to help him up. Instead, he felt a cold object against his neck, just under his jaw. There was a click, and everything went black.

The impromptu meeting had been short and intense, and its upshot was that David Yassur didn't have time to wait for the elevator. He tore open the door to the stairwell, and on the way down the six flights of stairs from the directorate floor to the interrogation floor, he went through it all one more time. The computer and the notebook had been taken to Unit 8200 for immediate analysis. The groups that were going to carry out the operations against the suicide bombers were ready. The local police in Tel Aviv and Jerusalem had been informed, and potential targets had been identified. The checkpoints were on high alert. Dogs trained to recognise the scent of explosives were on their way to Jerusalem. But, so far, they didn't know the details of the attacks — where or when they might occur. They hoped that Unit 8200 would find out from the computer.

He had met Rachel Papo. She had been there at the start of the meeting to give a report. She was more gentle than he had imagined, and gave almost a girlish impression. But he remembered what Meir Pardo had said about her dark background, about her disappearance and her wounded psyche. And about his own paternal feelings. Rachel had done a good job with the Swede — she'd proved that she was more than a sharp knife. In just a few hours, she'd gotten him to confide in her. The material they had to work with now might mean the turning point they'd all hoped for.

The other good news was that Paul Clinton had flown to Israel. With him came access to the world's greatest security organisation. As it stood now, the resources of the FBI, CIA, and NSA were at the Mossad's disposal. And, right now, the Swede was their alpha and omega. Who was he? How did he fit in? They had discussed a number of possibilities, but none of their theories seemed likely. There was too much that didn't add up. David was going to find out what was going on, straight from the source. Meir wanted to inform Ben Shavit, but first they needed more facts.

David reached the first floor and made his way down the long corridor that led to the interrogation rooms. He passed three empty rooms before coming to a fourth, outside which stood two young guards, a red light blinking above the closed door behind them. He went into the small observation room. There, Paul was leaning against the wall, sipping a mug of coffee. He was large, bordering on fat, and was dressed in a grey suit and white shirt, as always. An interrogation clerk was sitting silently in front of a large pane of glass that looked into the interrogation room. Before her was a control panel for the recording equipment. The pane was made of one-way glass, so it could only be looked through from their direction. David stood close to the window and studied the prisoner.

Where no counsel is, the people fall:
But in the multitude of counsellors there is safety.

The only thing that deviated from the colour scheme of the room was the blue banner hanging on the far wall. Under the quote was an embroidered, seven-armed silver menorah. Eric's eyes lost focus, and the menorah seemed to float out onto the wall around it. He closed his eyes and looked again. His focus was back. His body was tense and aching. He had several small white bandages on his right arm. They had done tests on him — or they'd injected him with something. He looked around with difficulty. He was lying on a cot in a completely symmetrical room. The walls were grey, except for one large mirror. The floor was covered in speckled-grey linoleum, and three angry strip lights shone on the ceiling. The cot he was lying on was across from the wall with the mirror, and in it he could see himself with his legs drawn up and his hands between his knees. He looked strange, lifeless. One time he had been in a fire drill at KTH when they'd thrown blankets over a burning mannequin. That's what the man in the mirror looked like — a fire mannequin wearing Eric's own wrinkled clothes.

In the middle of the room was a square table and three chairs. The stark light from the ceiling blinded him, hurting his eyes. What had happened? Where was Rachel? His mouth was dry. There was a bitter taste he hadn't noticed earlier. The room was cold. He looked at the banner again, wondering who had embroidered the menorah.

'Our motto!'

The man who entered the room nodded at the words.

'Our motto and our symbol.'

He sat down on one of the chairs and placed a yellow folder on the table with a bang. Eric got up from the cot with difficulty.

'Our?'

'Oh, did I forget to tell you where you are? Welcome to the Mossad. I'm sorry we didn't have a nicer room to offer you.'

The voice was clearly full of sarcasm. The Mossad? Of all the unimaginably absurd things. But why? The man at the table looked at him coldly. Not threateningly, but not friendly either. There was something else about him, too — something hard and relentless. He was about Eric's age, and short but powerfully built. His tanned face was lined, and his black hair was shot with white. He was wearing a black polo shirt and dark-brown chinos. He wasn't wearing a watch.

'I'm a Swedish citizen,' Eric said in a low voice.

'And I'm Israeli. That's unimportant. My name is David Yassur, and I'm the director of operations here — number two in rank.'

Eric massaged his sore wrists.

'I want to call my embassy.'

'Sure. And I want to lie around at home watching soccer. But we're here now. Come here.'

He pointed at one of the empty chairs. Eric remained on the cot.

'I have rights.'

'That's where you're wrong. You have no rights. You have no passport, no name, and no nationality. You're just a sack of meat and bone. Your only worth is as an informant. Either you play that role well enough to survive, or else you keep your mouth shut. And if you keep your mouth shut, you're completely worthless. If it had been up to me, you would have been stopped in Nice. I hate those who threaten us as much as I love Israel. You had one chance, but you wasted it. Now I have a few questions for you. You can choose to answer here, or else we'll go down to the basement. I won't be the one to ask the questions down there. This is not a fucking playhouse. This is serious. Got it?'

He was shocked by the man's aggression. The words tore him out of his surreal, dissociative state. This was for real. It was not a movie, not an act. This wasn't happening to someone else. But could they really hurt him? After all, this was a state authority

247

in a civilised country. And yet he realised how naïve this line of reasoning sounded. He was a prisoner of the world's most feared intelligence service. His unsteady legs carried him to the chair, and he sat down. The scraping of the chair legs hurt his ears. He placed his hands on the table and tried to calm down. The man smelled like sweat.

'May I ask why I'm here?'

'Because we're curious about you. Because we don't understand how you fit in. Because you have a notebook that belongs to our enemies. Because you have pictures of our enemies. Because you have been talking to our enemies. Because you're helping our enemies. That's why you're here. For starters.'

His thoughts whirled. What pictures? They must have found the pictures he'd bought in Nice. Helping the enemy? They had read his conversation with Salah ad-Din, seen his fawning suggestions for improving the code. What had they done with the notebook? With his computer? With Rachel?'

'Where is Rachel?'

The man was paging through his papers, and answered without looking up.

'Don't worry about her. You have enough problems of your own.'

He left the folder open and looked at him.

'Eric Hugo Söderqvist. What the hell are you up to?'

There was no point in lying or bullshitting about being a journalist with *Aftonbladet*. Rachel was one thing, but this was the Mossad. But how could he tell them the truth? His story was completely improbable. On the other hand, what choice did he have? He swallowed, and met David Yassur's stern gaze.

'I'm trying to save my wife's life.'

'What's wrong with your wife?'

'She has a virus.'

248

David Yassur didn't bat an eye. Eric kept going.

'She's infected with Mona.'

'Mona, as in the computer virus?'

'That's right.'

'Your wife is infected with a computer virus?' David Yassur shifted position. 'Explain.'

'I'm a researcher, and my area is something called BCI — Brain Computer Interface.'

'I know what that is.'

'Okay. My specific research is on the development of a new method of communication between the human brain and a computer. Or, more precisely, a method for creating better conditions for this communication. By applying a special gel to the head, we can establish very good contact with the brain, without surgical intervention. In addition to this, my team and I have developed software called Mind Surf that makes it possible to surf the internet with the power of thought.'

'Great, but what does this have to do with your wife?'

'She was one of the first ones to test out the system. She is the director of IT at TBI's Stockholm office. When she was hooked up to Mind Surf, she visited the bank's website, which was infected with Mona. The virus was transmitted to the system, and somehow — I don't know how — it affected her health.'

'Affected her health?'

'She became ill shortly thereafter. She's currently being treated at a hospital.'

'Which hospital?'

He didn't want to expose her. But, once again, it would only take them ten minutes to figure it out.

'Karolinska Hospital in Stockholm.'

'Continue.'

'The doctors at the hospital can't cure her. They can only

verify that she's getting worse and worse.'

'But how do you know she's not suffering from something else?'

'She said it herself. And shortly thereafter my main investor, Mats Hagström, got sick as well. His symptoms and the progression of disease were identical to my wife's. He had tried Mind Surf, too.'

'After the computer had been infected?'

'After the computer had been infected.'

David Yassur looked at him sceptically.

'No one believed me. I realised she was going to die if nothing drastic was done. I decided to assume that she really was infected with Mona, no matter how crazy it sounded. If there was a virus, there also ought to be an anti-virus — and the person with the anti-virus ought to be the same person who created the virus. I visited a good friend at an evening paper to throw around some ideas. Then, by chance, I learned that there was a source in Nice who wanted to sell information about the terrorists.'

'How had the evening paper gotten hold of the source?'

'By actively going through their contacts.'

'Who was the source?'

What could he say? Should he expose Cedric Antoine? He wasn't the actual source.

'It was a police officer with the task force who wanted to earn some extra money. I don't have his name.'

'We'll get to the name later. What happened after that?'

'I went to Nice, and bought the information from the police officer.'

'You met him?'

'Not personally. I transferred the money to an account number, and received a bag of information. The bag was hidden at the Marc Chagall museum.'

'Do you still have the account number?'

He nodded.

'What was in the bag?'

'The notebook and the pictures.'

'And you also hacked into TBI's network?'

How could they know that? That must be how they had found him. How could he have been so careless? He had left fingerprints everywhere, whether they were analogue or digital. TBI had traced his trespassing in IT director Isaac Berns's computer, and had tipped off the Mossad. That was why David Yassur had said that he could have been stopped back in Nice. They must have followed him to Tel Aviv. But how did they know when to strike? How did they know he had established contact? How did they know what he and Salah ad-Din had talked about? Then he thought of the lost suitcase, the powerful handshake, the thin dress, the unlikely knowledge of Ottoman code, the tattoos. He sighed heavily.

'Rachel works for you?'

David Yassur didn't answer. Eric's stomach felt hollow. He felt embarrassed and betrayed. He was a pathetic idiot. What had he been thinking?

'Why did you come to Tel Aviv?'

'I couldn't interpret the code in the notebook. I was planning to try to get hold of Isaac Berns, to see if he could help me.'

'Why would he listen to you?'

'No idea. Maybe because he's a good person. Maybe because one of his employees is dying.'

'How do you know Samir Mustaf?'

'I'm guessing he's the creator of Mona. I would like to meet him, but I've never spoken with him.'

'Sure you have.'

'I don't understand what you mean.'

'Salah ad-Din is Samir Mustaf's alias.'

'How do you know that?'

'It doesn't matter. I'll repeat the question: how do you know him?'

'When Rachel cracked the code, it gave me information that helped me find a virtual-development environment. There, I found log-in information for a chat room. In the chat room, I made contact with the terrorists.'

'You call them terrorists. Aren't they freedom fighters? Holy soldiers, fighting for a good thing?'

'No, they're terrorists. Plain old bandits.'

'And Salah ad-Din?'

'I passed myself off as a supporter. A clever hacker who wanted to join up. All to make contact, come closer, build up trust. I had to — have to — meet them, meet him. All to get hold of the anti-virus.'

'How did you even know there was an anti-virus?'

'I didn't, but based on what I read in the chat room, I'm sure there is. It goes by the name Nadim.'

'And why would Mustaf give you the anti-virus?'

'No idea. Faith, hope, and charity? Presumably, he wouldn't give me anything other than a bullet to the neck. But I'll take the chance. I have nothing to lose.'

'Who is helping you?'

'No one. I'm alone.'

Eric felt how true that was. He was truly alone, now more than ever. The man across from him was silent, and a long time went by. Here they sat, two men at a small table — alike, and yet so immensely different. Then David Yassur stood up, took the folder, and left. The grey door closed with a click. Eric just sat there.

When David Yassur returned to the observation room, Paul Clinton was sitting on a chair beside the clerk. The room was stuffy and stale. Through the window, they could see Eric sitting with his head in his hands. Paul was leaning back in his chair, dangerously close to tipping over.

'That was the fishiest story I've ever heard. And I'm telling you, I've heard a lot of fishy stories.'

David nodded. 'Yes, it sure is strange. The question is, how can I present this to Meir?'

Dan Hertzog from Unit 8200 yanked open the door. David looked at him in anticipation.

'Are you finished with the analyses?'

'No. We're not done with the notebook. We haven't even started on the code from the virtual database. It's going to take days, maybe weeks. We chose to prioritise the chat.'

'And?'

'Rachel was right. They're planning three detonations — two in Jerusalem and one in Tel Aviv.'

Paul met David's eyes. Dan went on, 'We found an entry where they discussed dates, places, and times. It was from user "Sinon" to user "A". We still don't know who's behind these aliases. Sinon suggested that all three attacks occur simultaneously in order to show that the sender is one and the same, an organised enemy.'

David stood up and walked over to Dan.

'Where will it be?'

'In Jerusalem, at Hebrew University, and at the bus station near Mahane Yehuda market. In Tel Aviv, at the central station, Savidor Merkaz.'

'Oh, God. When?'

Dan looked first at David and then at Paul.

'Today, at fourteen hundred and fifteen hundred.'

Paul gasped.

'That's in less than two hours!'

David was already on his way out the door. Paul and Dan jogged after him through the long corridor.

'What will we do with the Swede?'

'Forget about him. He's not going anywhere.'

David threw a glance at Dan.

'Do you have any more information? Anything that can help the team?'

'We know it's going to be a delivery truck at the university.'

'And the other two?'

'Suicide belts. We're not totally sure, but that's our best guess.'

They reached the elevators, but as always David kept going into the stairwell, followed closely by Paul and Dan. He took two steps at a time, and Paul was out of breath after the first flight.

'Can we cordon off the areas?' he panted.

'Sure we can, but then there's a risk that they'll detonate somewhere else, anywhere. It'd be best to catch them in the act. It might be possible with surveillance, dogs, and explosive detectors. But it's dangerous, a long shot. It should be easier with the delivery truck.'

They emerged into a hectic office scene. David hurried through the room and on into another corridor. Dan and Paul did their best to keep up with him.

'We're going to the command centre. I have to make sure they've organised the team. Dan, I'm assuming you've already informed them about the place and time?'

'Twelve minutes ago. The police are leading the operation, with support from us. We'll take care of the task itself.'

He stopped talking.

'I'm guessing you don't need me anymore. I have to go back to the unit.'

'Thanks, Dan. Good work.'

David and Paul walked down the hall to a white, windowless

door. David entered a six-digit code into the keypad on the wall and opened the door. On the other side there were about ten men and women in a large room full of screens, maps, and rows of desks.

'We normally lead international operations from this room. Today, it will have to do as a communications centre for local operations as well.'

David went up to a large man with a ponytail who was standing and looking at an iPad.

'Frank, what's your status?'

The man looked up and nodded.

'We've effectively got a green light — just a few minor details left. The police have to get all the cameras at the central station working; they've been down for a few days for maintenance. But our team is ready and synched up with the police. Support, Search, and Analysis are already on their way to the target.'

David seemed to relax a bit. He placed his hand on Frank Harel's shoulder.

'You've got this, right?'

The man went back to his iPad.

'*B'ezrat Hashem*. With God's help.'

Paul had grabbed two coffee mugs, and handed one to David. They were standing in the middle of the room, looking at the large map of Tel Aviv. A diode was blinking near the central station. Paul turned to David.

'What if he's telling the truth? What if he really did trick Hezbollah? That would be fucking amazing.'

David snorted.

'You're saying that he managed to trace them and actually establish contact, all by himself and with no training whatsoever?'

Paul nodded.

'Exactly. Maybe for the very reason that he isn't one of us. His Google profile, his real name, his track record — everything checks out. Add the fact that he knew the Ottoman code, that he found the chat room, and, above all, that he was able to give advice about extremely advanced programming ... it's an unlikely combination. But maybe he really did manage to pique Samir Mustaf's interest. If it's true, he would be useful. We could use him to find them.'

'But do you realise what you're saying? This would mean that the rest of his story is true — that his wife was infected with a computer virus. A computer virus!'

Paul sipped his coffee.

'I don't believe that, but maybe he believes it. That would be enough. I'm sure his wife just has the flu, but he'd got it in his head that she was infected with Mona, and that was enough for him to get involved with this circus. Remember, he showed the chat to Rachel. And he told her about the attacks. We also know he tried to call Isaac Berns.'

David shook his head.

'I think he's lying, but we'll have to find out about that later. Right now, we have three suicide bombers to deal with.'

It was twenty-five minutes past one.

Eric had lain down on the cot again. The conversation with David Yassur had shaken him up. The gravity of the situation had washed over him like ice-cold water, and with it came all the catastrophic consequences he could imagine. He had been so close: he had established contact with Samir Mustaf, and there really was an anti-virus. But now he had missed his chance. There was no way he could contact Salah ad-Din, so Hanna would not receive the anti-virus. Maybe it had never been possible, but he had clung to hope. Really, the whole idea was absurd. Even if

Hanna and Mats Hagström had become ill because of Mona, the chance that a digital anti-virus would cure them was non-existent. And here he was, in a small cell without his phone, passport, watch, or wallet. He was a prisoner, as closed off from the world as Hanna was in her bed at Karolinska. Would they sentence him for crimes of terror and lock him up for good? He felt a nearly desperate need to talk to Jens or Thomas Wethje — someone normal in Sweden, who could give him his sense of reality back. Why the hell had he thought he could play the hero? He held his breath for a long time, looking at the ceiling. How could Rachel have lied so effortlessly? But who was he to judge? He had totally lost himself in a mess of lies and dreams. Now it had all gone to hell. Completely to hell.

Jerusalem, Israel

The earpiece crackled, and Larry Lavon waited tensely for Micha Begin's voice.

'It was negative. Repeat, negative.'

Shit. They had picked up two different people, but neither was the right one. He had been sure of this last one. He thought he had seen the bomb-sniffing dog react. The suspect had been wearing a jacket that was much too thick, and he had seemed nervous. Larry swept the crowd once more with his eyes. Most of the people were standing and waiting for the bus, looking more and more impatient. It was already fifteen minutes late. It was common for suicide bombers to wait for the bus to enter the station, or to climb on board before they detonated their payload. For that reason, Larry's team had decided keep the bus away. Mahane Yehuda was right by the market, and it was full of people.

Larry cast another frustrated glance at his watch. It was three minutes past two — just twelve minutes left. He saw several of the plainclothes police, two of them with dogs, moving among the people in line. A redheaded plainclothes officer was walking around with a scanner, which looked like a short bicycle pump, that reacted to explosives. He wondered how it was going for the other two teams. Had they captured their targets? If a truck full of explosives blew up at the university, they would hear it from here. There'd been no explosion so far.

His earpiece crackled again.

'Come in, Larry. Contact at three o'clock.'

He squinted at the outer edge of the bus stop and caught sight of Micha, along with one of the local police officers and a dog. They were standing behind a short, dark-skinned man wearing a red athletic jacket. Larry quickly started moving in their direction.

'Evidence?'

'The dog is stiff with excitement. Should we call the scanner over, or chance it and take him?' Larry thought quickly. The man was standing amidst a large number of passengers. If this was the wrong person, his team's actions would alert the true bomber. If they were right, but if they gave the bomber time to hit the trigger, there would be many victims.

'Wait. I'll be right there.'

He moved quickly and approached the target diagonally, from the front. The man was standing still with his hands in his pockets and his eyes on the ground. Larry clocked the blue jeans and the white tennis shoes. The shoes looked new — too new. He probably had the trigger in his hand. They often taped it to their palm so they wouldn't drop it if they were knocked over.

At that instant, Larry made up his mind; there was no time to lose. He took a small injector from its holster and, just as he walked by, bumped into the man, pressed the tip of the injector against his carotid artery, and triggered it. A faint click, and the man's legs gave way. Larry quickly extended his arm and caught the body. The neurotoxin had knocked him out in less than a second, and he was heavy and limp. The anaesthetic would last for about an hour. The dog let out an eager bark, and the officer yanked on its leash.

Larry lay the body on the ground, taking no heed of the group of people surrounding them. Sometimes they connected an extra detonator to the zipper of the jacket. But he had to know if it was the right man. He gritted his teeth and pulled down the zipper. The first things he saw were the large green plastic bags that hung over the man's stomach. He tore open the first one, and a stream of sharp steel spikes ran out over his hand. He shoved the bags aside, and exposed the light-brown bomb belt. Then he carefully pulled up the man's right arm. Taped to his palm was a black switch. Larry looked at his watch. It was seven past two.

The large truck was hard to manoeuvre, and Ali Aksani had to fight to turn the sluggish steering wheel at every curve. The stick shift was heavy, too, and it popped out of gear several times, causing the motor to rev furiously. The driver's cab smelled like cigarette smoke and sweat. He would be there soon. He had memorised the directions hundreds of times, and even though he didn't know a word of Hebrew, he recognised the symbols on every sign. There was a lot of traffic. The footpaths were packed, and at every stoplight the people streamed out onto the street like swarming rats. He had a nasty cough that ripped and tore through his chest. It had crept up on him in Balakot. It was cold and damp in the school at night, and there weren't enough blankets to go around. He had coughed and coughed, so much that the other students had started to beat him. They had sneaked up to his bed in the dark and hit him in the face with their shoes.

Last night it had been worse than ever, maybe because of the suspense. But soon he would once again be strong and healthy. Soon he would find peace and be met with boundless love.

The truck popped out of gear, and the diesel motor roared. Ali stomped on the large clutch pedal and managed to push the stick back into gear. Hebrew University was now only a few blocks away. The black detonator-switch hung loosely just under the stereo; if he let go of the gear stick, he could reach it easily. He had practised the motion several times in the garage. He thought of his father. If only he could see Ali now. He was no longer the little boy who fell off his bike and scraped his hands, or the crying little brat who shamefully pissed his pants in the mosque. Now he was the one swinging the sword that they all worshipped.

He came to yet another crosswalk filled with rats, large and small, and gripped the gear stick hard, taking care to keep the motor purring smoothly. He caught sight of a group of Muslim men and women, all of them old. The men were wearing white *dishdashas*, and the women black *abayas* with matching *hijabs*. There was something so dignified about the faithful. In among all these dirty dogs, they moved gracefully, as though they were of another world. Even though they were old and their steps were heavy, there was pride there, and purity. They stopped at the crosswalk. Ali wanted to soften the noise of the angry diesel motor and silence all the other cars. He was sweating. One of the women stepped out into the street before the others. She looked around and then helped one of the older ones. As they came closer, he could see that the helpful woman was younger than the others. Her beauty amazed him — her large brown eyes and her gentle face, framed by her *hijab*. She took them by the arm one at a time to help them across the street. *Hurry up before it turns red.* As she was leading the last one across, their eyes met. It was the most powerful moment of his life. She was an angel sent directly from Jannah. She was a sign from Allah — a sign to him that he was expected and that he was loved. The woman smiled warmly; it was as though he were already inside the gates of paradise. Something was odd about the angel's nose, though. A car behind him honked, but he wanted to linger in the moment.

He was so caught up in the angel's eyes that he didn't notice when she pulled a black TAR-21 out from under her *abaya*. He was squinting to see it when everything exploded in a sparkling light. Without taking notice of the screaming people around her, Rachel Papo stood erect with her arm extended toward the driver's seat of the truck, which was only two-and-a-half metres away. It only took a few seconds to empty the twenty-five bullets from the clip. She stood there with her arm out, studying the driver's seat. There was no movement. The motor was revving loudly; it must have popped out of gear. Finally, she dropped the empty weapon on the ground and looked around. The pedestrians looked at her in terror. The old Muslims she had helped across the street pulled off their *dishdashas* to reveal their police uniforms. As they kept people at bay, Rachel walked up to the truck, leaned in, and turned off the engine. She looked at the body. Even though he was badly mangled, she thought she could see a smile on his lips. She stood there thinking for a moment. Then she turned back to the police, who had put up a makeshift cordon. She could hear sirens in the distance. She ducked under the cordon and disappeared into the sea of people. It was twelve minutes past two.

Kashif Kareem Muhammad was sitting at a café in the Azrieli Centre Mall in central Tel Aviv. He was people-watching and drinking a Coke. He had always loved the soda, and could still remember tasting it for the first time. It was his big brother

Rahim who had ceremoniously poured a few drops into a white plastic cup. They had been sitting on the low stone wall down by the road. Rahim had received the bottle from the shepherd as thanks for the day's work. He had been fascinated by the beautiful bottle with its narrow waist. 'Like a woman,' Rahim had whispered. 'Just as slender and just as sweet.' They had laughed and toasted each other with the black water. Kashif's eyes roamed the boutiques, which were packed with colourful wares: tennis shoes, flowers, newspapers, sweets, and stereos. People streamed around him with bags and packages. How could they shop so much? What were they going to do with all those things? He listened to the music — pop. He liked the rhythm and the English voices. He happened to think of Libya, and of his brother, half paralysed after his fall from scaffolding. What was he doing now? He hadn't seen him in over a year. There was so much he would have liked to say to him. Hopefully, he would receive the letter he'd sent. He tried to imagine his brother's reaction when he read about his great achievement.

His eyes fell upon a woman with two small children, a boy and a girl. She reminded him of his first love, somehow, but her hair was different. And she was thinner. The children had identical jackets. It was strange that Jewish girls and boys dressed alike. They disappeared into the restroom. He put down his bottle of Coke. He was uncomfortable, and was boiling in his heavy clothes. He could see hundreds of album covers in a display window, but the only one he recognised was Madonna's.

He was tired, terribly tired. But not afraid. He had always maintained a distance from the task, a surreal sort of feeling in the face of his big moment. It was as though it would never happen. Not for real. Not to him. When they trained at the school, when they received their instructions, when they put the belt on him, all along it had felt as though the scene would be interrupted, as

262

though something would happen before the moment arrived.

The woman who looked like his first girlfriend returned with her children. She was talking on a mobile phone. Her little girl pulled at the brother's arm; they were arguing about something. He thought about his two friends who were now performing their holy duties. Were they already in Jannah?

Why had they moved him from the central station? The order had come at the last second. He had been so set on the station; he'd studied the drawings, memorised the stairs and doors. He knew nothing about Azrieli. But surely they knew best. The mall was at least as good a place — it had more people. He cast one last glance at the woman with the children. They would soon pass him. He realised, without any real concern, that this time nothing would break the scene. Nothing would happen to stop him. He took a deep breath, looked down at the table, and pressed the little button in his left hand. The digital clock above the sports store had just changed. It was two-fifteen.

Stockholm, Sweden

Mats Hagström woke up in a vast room with no windows. Everything was white. He couldn't remember how he'd gotten there. The last thing he remembered was kneeling in the warm ash, near the enormous funeral pyres. The man without a face had stood in front of him. He had shown up out of nowhere, and when Mats bellowed in despair, the man had placed cool hands over his eyes. He had banished the heat and the burning bodies, protecting him from the gates of hell. Now everything had changed. Here he lay, instead, on a cool, steel bed. White straps ran across his chest and thighs, holding him down. The man was wearing a white coat, white shoes, and white gloves. In his hand he held a cone-shaped wand that was about thirty centimetres long. It was a beautiful wand, sparklingly clean and perfectly shaped. The man's face had no features and no hollows or wrinkles. It was just smooth skin, with no mouth, no nose, no eyes. His head was bald. The man placed his left hand on Mats's chest. He felt the slight pressure of his palm, and could feel his heart beating under the white glove. Mats tried to relax, to breathe slowly. He wanted to show the man that he was not afraid, that he trusted him. The man increased the pressure on his chest. Mats tried to twist away so he could breathe, but it was impossible. It felt like his chest would explode. Then the man struck him with the wand. It shattered his ribcage, smashed his heart, and hit the steel bed under him with a bang. Mats let out a short gasp. The man studied the body, which was now jerking in short spasms. Behind him stood the little girl. She looked at the blood running onto the white floor from the shiny silver bed. The thick liquid made strange patterns as it found its way to the drain. The man turned to her. She tugged nervously at the hem of her white dress. She didn't want to tell, but what choice did she have? Maybe he already knew. She swallowed and looked at the empty head. 'There's another one. I met her.'

Tel Aviv, Israel

They had moved him to a cell that couldn't be larger than seven square metres. In the room was a cot, identical to the one in the interrogation room, as well as a toilet made of brushed steel with no lid. There was nothing more — no windows, no table. It smelled like disinfectant. Eric half-lay on the cot, leaning against the light-grey wall. His clothes had started to smell, and they stuck to his body and itched. He had no sense of time, but it must have been many hours since they'd left him alone. He was thirsty and hungry, and nauseated. It was a strange sensation to feel hungry and as though he were about to vomit at the same time. Could the nausea be caused by hunger? He had thought thousands of thoughts — turned over and over in his head everything that had happened and everything that might happen. He had tried to work out clever answers to potential questions, objections to those answers, and then answers to those objections. He had run back and forth along every mental dead-end, hoping each time to find a way out, a chink he'd overlooked. In the end, hopelessness won out, and he had resorted to staring at the wall across from him. He was drowsy, despite the bright light, and spent his time moving his eyes from the wall to the door to the toilet, and back again.

The door opened, startling him. With some effort, he lifted himself on his elbows, and when he saw the person who was standing before him, he had to swallow to avoid throwing up. She was wearing black boots, black military pants, and a black polo shirt. Her hair was in a bun. The door behind her was still open, but no one came in after her. She crouched down so that her face was level with his. He felt ashamed when he saw her — ashamed that she had tricked him so thoroughly, ashamed that he had fallen for her act so easily. She looked him in the eyes; he had to look away.

'How are you?'

He looked at the lidless toilet.

'So-so. How are you?'

'Look at me, Eric.'

He turned back to her. Her voice was gentle and low.

'I know you're furious with me. You have every right to be.'

'I'm not furious with you. I'm furious with myself. But not you.'

'I had a really nice time with you. You're an interesting man.'

He managed to force out a weak smile.

'Interesting?'

'Yes. And attractive. I was serious when I invited you to my room. I hadn't been instructed to; it wasn't part of my assignment. Rather, the opposite.'

'What are you going to do with me?'

She stood up and stretched her legs. Then she nodded at the cot and he moved over a bit. She sat down, close to him.

'There are differing opinions on what to do. Your story was surprising, to say the least.'

'I told you it was a long story back when we were in your room.'

'It's surprising and very hard to believe. Do you understand that?'

'I understand. Believe me when I say I wish I had a simpler explanation. But it's the truth.'

Now it was Rachel's turn to look at the toilet.

'We know which parts of your story are true. We know about your research; we know what patents you've applied for and who you work with. We know your wife is sick and that your colleague is, too. We know you have friends at a daily paper in Stockholm. You were in Nice, and you transferred money to an account in Switzerland.'

'Do you know whose account it is?'

She nodded. 'A police officer from the national task force. We know you bought the notebook and the pictures. And we know you established contact with Samir Mustaf. Or Salah ad-Din.'

Eric was too tired to say anything.

'What we don't know is why. We don't know if you are who you say you are, or if you're just another Hezbollah volunteer.'

'So what are you going to do? Torture me? Put me through a lie detector? Pump me full of truth serum? Kill me?'

266

'You've watched too many movies. But we are fighting about what to do.'

His eyes were back on the wall. He wondered how they could leave the door open. Weren't they afraid he would escape?

'The information you gave us saved many lives today.'

He turned to her.

'You managed to stop the attacks?'

'Two out of three. Unfortunately, they'd moved the third one, the one in Tel Aviv. We were at the train station, but the bomber was at a mall.'

'How many?'

'Twelve — four of them children. About fifty injured.'

She said it as though she were testing his reaction. To eliminate any doubt, he looked her in the eyes.

'I am truly sorry.'

She didn't say anything.

'Has anyone taken responsibility for the attack?'

'No. If it weren't for the chat, we wouldn't have known that the bombs had any connection to Mona.'

He didn't answer. She changed position, leaning forward with her elbows on her knees, and lowered her voice.

'Eric, listen carefully. I believe your story. Or I believe enough of your story. I also believe that you can help yourself and us at the same time. I actually think you can play a crucial role. There are others who share my opinion.'

'What do you mean?'

'You've done something unique — you've made contact with Samir Mustaf. Not only that, but you seem to be well on your way to winning his trust.'

'Not after you stopped two of his attacks.'

'That doesn't have to mean anything. We might have other sources. If you can get into their cell, become one of them, then maybe we can get what we're looking for.'

'Which is what?'

'Nadim. The anti-virus.'

'How would I manage that? I'm just a plain old IT professor from Stockholm. And also a prisoner of the Mossad.'

'You've managed so far. Doesn't that say something about what you're capable of?'

'Managed? I've ruined everything.'

'No, you haven't. Far from it. The FBI is here. They want to know more about the virus that infected your wife. They've asked us to hand you over so they can fly you to Stockholm.'

'Why do they need me?'

'They want to move your wife to one of their own hospitals.'

He felt the rage flare up.

'What? Where do they want to take her?'

'Calm down. To a NATO base in Oslo. But they can hardly just go in and take a Swedish citizen from a public hospital without some form of authorisation. Apparently, the ministry of foreign affairs in Stockholm is demanding consent, preferably from her husband. That's why they need you in Sweden. Your wife is very sick, so they want to act fast. When the papers are all in order, the FBI assumes you'll come to Oslo, too. Of course, we'll …'

'Hanna will never be some fucking guinea pig! Do you hear me?'

She placed a hand on his shoulder.

'Calm down, remember. You have to let me finish.'

He ran his hand through his hair and then gave a short nod.

'We will agree to hand you over. They'll take you to Ben Gurion airport to transfer you to Stockholm — they have their own plane. But at the airport, you'll run away.'

He looked at her dubiously.

'I'll do what?'

'Run away.'

'Run away? From the FBI?'

'From the FBI.'

'And how will I do that?'

'You'll be given an opportunity. I'm going to help you.'

'And what if I get shot?'

'You won't. Then you will contact Salah ad-Din again and make sure you meet him. Then, if you can manage to get hold of Nadim, you'll be a hero — to Israel, and to your sick friends in Sweden.'

'And what if I can't persuade him to give me the anti-virus?'

'Then you contact us. We'll work together to try to convince him.'

'And what if they kill me?'

'They won't — not if you continue to be as trustworthy as you've been up to now.'

'How will I contact you?'

'You'll call us.'

'Call you? From what?'

'Your mobile phone. I'll work it out so you get back your belongings before we hand you over to the Americans.'

He tried to collect his thoughts. This assignment seemed vague and unmanageable. Rachel read his mind.

'It sounds more complex than it is. I'm sure my boss would have laid it all out more elegantly, more pedagogically. I'm not very good at giving explanations. It's not really that difficult, is it? I'll get you out. You persuade Mustaf to give you the anti-virus.'

'What if I can't contact him again?'

She considered this. 'Then we'll improvise.'

'I don't have a passport. I don't have any money or credit cards.'

'As I said, I'll make sure you get your belongings back. We've even paid the hotel bill for you, so you'll come out ahead. The passport might be difficult, but I'll do what I can. We don't want the FBI to suspect anything.

'Why don't you co-operate with them? Wouldn't that be more natural?'

Rachel shook her head.

'Let's just say that we have slightly different priorities right now. For us, the crucial thing is to trace the terrorist group and get hold of the anti-virus. The FBI seems more concerned about a potential biological threat.'

Eric sighed.

'Tell me more about Samir Mustaf.'

'He was born in Beirut. One younger sister. Shia Muslim family. Lawyer dad; nurse mum. They fled to France when Samir Mustaf was fifteen, and settled in Toulouse. His mathematical knowledge led to a scholarship at MIT. He stayed there for sixteen years, got a Ph.D., and taught.'

'In what area?'

'Computer viruses. He quickly became an expert. He helped the Pentagon, among others, several times.'

'Children?'

'One daughter. He met his wife at a wedding in Lebanon. Then they lived in the US for almost ten years. After that, they moved back to Beirut. Samir Mustaf got a job as head of IT at a Lebanese bank. She worked for Siemens. One day the family was going to get together for a birthday party at his mother-in-law's home in Qana. There was an explosion at the house. We don't know exactly what happened, but the police report mentions a cluster grenade. Shortly after the accident, Samir Mustaf disappeared.'

'Disappeared?'

'He was at the hospital to identify the bodies. Since then, no one has seen him. Our theory is that he was recruited by Hezbollah and that they've kept him hidden since.'

He sat in silence, thinking about Samir's fate. Rachel gave him a small colour photograph. It depicted an angelic girl with big, brown eyes, a doll-like mouth, and thick, curly hair. He looked at Rachel.

'His daughter?'

'Do you know what her name was?'

'Let me guess ... Mona?'

'Mona Mustaf.'

'And who was Nadim?'

'His wife.'

Eric's stomach growled. Rachel smiled faintly.

'Haven't we given you anything to eat?'

'No. The room service at the Hilton Mossad has certain shortcomings.'

She stood up.

'I'll take care of it. And to show you we're serious, I'll get your things. Everything but the computer — we have to keep that. Meanwhile, I suggest you think about my idea. Are you prepared to run from the FBI, make your way into Hezbollah's network, establish contact with Samir Mustaf, and get hold of the anti-virus? If you are, you'll be out of here within twenty-four hours.' She stood up.

'Rachel, who are you?'

She was startled, and it took a second for her to answer.

'A *katsa*.'

'*Katsa*?'

'A jack of all trades.'

'So, not an interpreter in London?' He couldn't mask his anger.

For a moment, she looked tired. Or perhaps sad.

'I hope we'll have a chance to get to know each other better. A second time — you as a professor at KTH, and me as a *katsa*.'

The door closed with a click. He looked at the girl in the picture, Mona Mustaf. His stomach let out another muffled protest. He put the photograph in his pocket.

The wall, the door, the toilet. The wall, the door, the toilet. Waiting made him feel anxious. She had been gone for more than an hour now. He had considered her offer, if you could call it that. Some part of him just wanted to stay in the quiet cell and sleep, to avoid making any decisions — avoid taking responsibility. But, at the same time, he wanted to contact Jens. He had to find out how Hanna was. He needed to hear that she was still strong, still fighting. And now, at least, there was hope. Nadim was real, after all, and Rachel's plan was the only way forward. If nothing else, it would put an end to his being a prisoner. But he knew he would be a quarry on the run.

The door opened, and Rachel returned with a tray of food and a white plastic bag.

'Role-reversal. Now I'm the one bringing food to you.'

She placed the tray in front of him. He took a baguette with cheese, and bit off a large chunk. She watched him, standing there with arms crossed.

'Normally, I don't work on this sort of assignment.' When he didn't answer, she went on, 'I asked to be the one in contact with you.' He could tell that she was fumbling for words, that she was searching for some sort of sign that he wasn't angry. She smiled.

'I think they let me because we get along so well.'

He took a sip of coffee and nodded.

'I'll do it — if you can promise me I won't be shot by the FBI.'

'I'll do my best. I'm sure it's the right decision, for you and for us.'

She emptied the bag onto the bed. There were his keys, wallet, iPod, and mobile phone.

'Unfortunately, I didn't manage to get your passport, but the bag with your toiletries and clothes is on its way. I've spoken with the FBI, and you're going out to Ben Gurion early tomorrow morning.'

After he'd eaten a yoghurt and drunk more coffee, he felt somewhat better. She stuck her hand into one of the front pockets of her pants.

'I wasn't allowed to take the notebook, but I grabbed these.'

She gave him the wrinkled napkins from the restaurant. The translations were still fully legible.

'You'll need this information to get back into the chat room.'

'But what if I don't have a computer?'

'You'll have to go to an internet café — they're all over the city. But be careful. The FBI's going to require us to use all our resources to find you. I can slow them down, but I can't stop them. They'll be hunting for you.' She saw his expression and added, 'It's good for the alibi you'll give Samir Mustaf. If he finds out that the FBI is hunting for you, your story will be more believable.'

Eric forced a smile.

'This is all such a nightmare, so unrealistic, that I just can't absorb any more shit. Maybe I've become immune.'

'I think that's good. Only God knows how much more awaits you. But at least now you're following a plan that might lead to something positive.'

'Sure. If I succeed.'

He picked up his mobile phone, and saw that there was a missed text from Jens. He felt a knot in his stomach as he opened the text. The words that flickered on the small screen made the walls collapse around him with a deafening roar:

MATS HAGSTRÖM IS DEAD.

PART III
TCHAIKOVSKY'S SEVENTH SYMPHONY

Sheikh Zuwayid, Egypt

It was quiet in the car. There was no radio reception, and Nesril Mansour hadn't brought any CDs. A cautious driver, he was driving slowly even though they were on a four-lane highway and there was almost no other traffic. The sun was frying the roof of the small van, which had no air conditioning. They were all wet with sweat; they'd been sitting in the van for six hours, and still had several hours left to go.

Ahmad Waizy was furious. He punched the thin metal roof several times. Something had gone wrong in Israel: the police had stopped two of the three attacks. This could only mean that someone had tipped them off, but how was that possible? Only a few people knew the exact targets. The only one in the country who knew the details was Sinon, but he was a professional and would never let the cat out of the bag. And, besides, it was thanks to him that the attack in Tel Aviv had still succeeded. Sinon had warned him that something was up with the police, so he'd switched the target from the Savidor Merkaz train station to the Azrieli mall at the last minute. He hadn't given Enes al-Twaijri, the project's financier, any specific details, so it couldn't be him. Prince Abdullah bin Aziz hadn't known anything about the martyrs, either.

Everyone who'd known the details was here in the van. He looked at his fellow passengers. Nesril was a simple soldier; he had no access to confidential information. Arie al-Fattal and Samir Mustaf, however, had full knowledge of the attacks. So did the new administrator, Mohammad Murid. One of these three men must have leaked it. On purpose, or out of carelessness?

Who was it? Samir never said a word unless it was necessary; he was always silent and distant. Ahmad wasn't even sure he'd understood the details of the attacks.

He looked at Samir, who was staring out the window with a blank expression. As always, he had his earbuds in. Ahmad didn't understand the skinny Lebanese man. He had worked hard, and delivered what he'd promised. But he always kept to himself, and was taciturn and evasive. Ahmad knew that Samir spent a lot of time brooding — about his task, his beliefs, the family he'd lost. However difficult he was, it was unlikely he was the one who'd leaked information about the attacks.

Ahmad concentrated instead on Mohammad and Arie. Both of them had had contact with the world outside in the course of their work. Mohammad was the one who had arranged the destination for today's journey — their new base. This was an alarming thought. If he'd spilled the beans, their new base in Gaza might be known, too. Would an Israeli commando be waiting for them when they arrived? He looked at Mohammad's narrow face, with its ugly birthmark on the left cheek. He always sat so that his birthmark faced away from the others. Mohammad dressed simply. He had worked for Hezbollah for many years, and Ahmad had done a thorough background check before he was chosen as an administrator. Mohammad was careful and loyal, and a devoted Muslim. Ahmad looked at Arie. He remembered seeing him for the first time at the meeting in Tabriz. He was a swaggering salesman hired by Hezbollah, self-impressed and pedantic. He might have won over Enes, but he had never made a great impression on Ahmad. There were many things about Arie that irritated him. The far-too-expensive watch on his fat wrist — a Rolex? — for a start. The colourful clothes he dressed in. His poor physical condition — Arie huffed and puffed after walking for only a few minutes. His obesity was more proof that he lacked character. How important was he to Hezbollah, really? Surely not at all, now that the financing was secured and the project was nearly finished. Arie met his gaze and smiled. Ahmad didn't smile back.

Samir looked out the window without really seeing. The scenery outside had remained unchanged for several hours — endless desert, with an occasional road sign. They seldom encountered any traffic. He was listening to Chopin, even though he was tired of the piano variations he had stored. He ought to download more music, but he no longer had a credit card, and his iTunes account had been shut down long ago. He had to be satisfied with pirating programs, and the selection of classical music was limited. The van was horribly hot, and each breath was an effort.

Hezbollah had sent their demands to Israel. With this, the project had entered its final phase. He doubted that Prime Minister Ben Shavit would go along with the demands, but it was possible that Mona had done such damage to the country that he had no other choice. Perhaps, as his close adviser, Sinon could convince Shavit to give up; perhaps not.

Nadim, the anti-virus, was essentially ready. Samir had managed to solve the problem of the mutating Mona strings; Nadim could now read and mirror Mona's DNA, no matter how they had evolved in the infected systems. The function was relatively simple, but the application of it was an act of genius. But, as usual, there was no audience to applaud him. He was alone with his creation.

His thoughts moved to Eric Söderqvist, the stranger who had somehow gotten into the group chat room. What could he have found there? For one thing, all the conversations about Mona, Nadim, and the attacks. Was that why the attacks had failed? He had a hard time believing it, but the risk was there. He hadn't told anyone about his conversation with Söderqvist, and he'd deleted all the entries the next day. Was it dangerous for him to be in contact with someone outside the group? Of course it was, but he hadn't revealed anything. Naturally, he should tell Ahmad, but he'd already waited too long. Now it would come back to bite him. And, somehow, he wanted to keep the secret of Eric Söderqvist to himself. It was the first real contact he'd had with the outside world in almost four years. Who was Eric Söderqvist? Where was he?

Arie leaned forward and said something to Nesril. The van slowed down and stopped at the side of the road so they could take a piss break. The silence was overwhelming, except for the hot motor that made popping noises. Arie climbed past Mohammad. Samir remained seated. He didn't need to piss, and he was wet through with sweat and had no desire to stand unprotected in the sun. Nesril, too, climbed out onto the asphalt and stood beside Arie. The streams of their urine could be heard all the way in the back seat of the van. Ahmad leaned over Samir's lap and dug through a bag that had slid around the floor on the journey. He took out a black pistol and, without saying a word, climbed out of the car and walked up to the two men at the side of the road. Things seemed to happen in slow motion as Samir watched Ahmad extend his arm holding the pistol and aim at the back of Arie's head. There was a sharp pop, like a firecracker, and Arie fell forward in the sand. Nesril jumped sideways and fell to his knees. He shouted something incoherent in a shrill voice, and appeared to tug at Ahmad's pant leg. Ahmad ignored him, leaning forward to look at Arie's body. Then he kicked him hard in the head. There was a dull thud. When he returned to the van, he smelled like gunpowder. Nesril came back, sniffling, and shut the door. Samir thought he could see red flecks on his cheek and collar. The engine started. Mohammad looked down at the floor.

None of the four men said anything. The car bumped along the edge of the road for a bit before steering onto the asphalt and going down the endlessly straight road through the Sinai desert.

Jerusalem, Israel

Prime Minister Ben Shavit had built his government as a team. Even though their mandate was weak, and their power was based on a fragile coalition, he had managed to bring together a group of individuals who, at least on a personal level, made an effort to work together. But there would always be times when he had to stand alone. When arguments pro and con were already screwed in so tightly that they couldn't be given another twist. When everyone else backed away to give him space for the final decision — a decision that could be made by only one man, even if there were one hundred and twenty members of the Knesset, and his government was the largest in Israeli history, with thirty ministers.

Twelve of those ministers were now sitting silently before him. The office was too small for so many people. It was stuffy; the dust glittered in the sunlight. He caught Meir Pardo's eye, looking for support. Meir smiled, but gave no hint of his opinion of the upcoming decision. Ben's gaze wandered to Yuval Yatom. The minister of finance nodded almost imperceptibly — he might have imagined it — and then looked away. Ben looked at the minister of defence, Ehud Peretz, who was much more obvious: he shook his head. This was not too surprising; Ehud had never compromised in his whole life. Ben turned to Akim Katz, his strategic adviser and close friend. Akim looked him in the eyes for a long moment and nodded slightly. This was a discreet but clear recommendation. To accept. To take a seat at the bargaining table. To give in, no matter how humiliating it might be.

Akim was an active right-winger, an uncompromising negotiator, and a thick-skinned supporter of the national coalition. For both Yuval and Akim to recommend that he negotiate was a powerful sign. But it was so wrong. Everything he had fought for — indeed, all his convictions — began with the idea that good would always triumph over evil in the end. If you could just hold out long enough, the enemy would break down. But this threat was too abstract in nature. How could they fight against it? *Where* could they fight it? And who would they be fighting? The battle was no longer with people of flesh and blood. This time, the threat was a computer program — they were dealing with science fiction. He looked past the grim men and out the window. It was all wrong; the blue sky and the bright sun were a paradox. The sky ought to be dark and dreary when the country's stock exchange was being slaughtered, and while twenty victims of the Azrieli-mall massacre were still fighting for their lives at Ichilov Hospital. But maybe the sun didn't care.

Ben despised his own indecisiveness. Why couldn't one of their many technicians crack the code? The virus wasn't just Israel's problem. It had spread without respecting national borders or tariff restrictions. It was wreaking havoc in the entire Western world, and it wasn't just financial systems that were affected. By now, the threat had reached hospitals, air traffic, power supplies … The modern world was completely controlled by IT systems. Without them, they were back in the Stone Age. But despite the collective threat, he was the individual who had to make the decision for all of them. Israel was the one that would be sacrificed. He thought about Abba Eban's quote from the Six-Day War, about how the world was divided into two camps: those who want to destroy Israel, and those who do nothing to stop it. The suicide attacks had further increased the pressure. The opposition were like bloodhounds — in the Knesset, in the media, and in the rabbinate, too. Everyone was taking the opportunity to piggyback on the catastrophe; no one offered any suggestions or support. But then, those were the rules of the game. He needed a cigarette. The fact that his doctors had told him not to smoke just made it worse. He cleared his throat.

'I realise this is an extraordinary situation that demands extraordinary measures. We have always said that we do not negotiate with terrorists. But …'

He looked at Akim.

'I *am* prepared to negotiate in order to put an end to this. This time, we were taken by surprise. Next time, we'll be more prepared. I will negotiate, but not with Hezbollah's leader, Hassan Musawi. That will never happen. I will demand a mediating party. It could well be the UN, Sweden, or Norway, but I will not sit at the same table as a murderer.'

Ben lowered his gaze and studied the letter on the desk for the hundredth time.

'And I have a number of opinions about their demands.'

Everyone in the room was silent. This was an unimaginable defeat, and no one wanted to look anyone else in the eye. Ben crumpled the letter and tossed it into the wastebasket.

Tel Aviv, Israel

It would never work. In a movie, maybe, but never in reality. Eric had assumed that Rachel would give him careful instructions — details of a reliable and brilliant escape plan. Instead, all she had done was whisper 'good luck' as she and a guard handed him over to the two men from the FBI. One, a man in a grey suit and a white, unbuttoned shirt, sullenly introduced himself as Paul Clinton. The other, in black pants and a grey sweatshirt, didn't say anything. He had a superior attitude, and hardly looked at Eric. For a time, it seemed that they were going to handcuff him, but when Rachel explained that it wasn't necessary, that Eric actually wanted to go to Sweden and see his wife, Paul seemed to relax. Eric clutched his bag in his hand and kept his eyes on the floor. He didn't dare look at the Americans, afraid that they would see how anxious he was. The handover to the FBI had taken place in the cool entrance of what must have been the Mossad's headquarters, on the ground floor, several floors above his cell. He had sneaked looks at Rachel over and over, hoping for a signal, a hint, or a furtively passed note. But she just shook hands with the men and left them. Had she changed her mind? Was he going to have to fly to Stockholm?

In one way, he longed for home, but returning there would also mean the end. It would signal his absolute failure. All night, he had been prepared to run, to re-establish contact with Salah ad-Din and to continue the hunt for Nadim. Now, he was sitting in the back seat of a big black car with the superior-seeming man beside him. Paul and a short driver sat in the front seat. The car smelled of leather and oil, the windows were tinted, and the doors were locked. They drove at high speeds along Highway 1. He thought of Mats Hagström. Mats was dead. No one had been able to save him. Mona had won, and now he was gone. Eric had felt it all along. He had known that the doctors at Karolinska wouldn't be able to stop the virus, but now it was a fact. Mats was dead, and Hanna was dying. He remembered his conversation with Mats's wife. What was she doing now? She had lost her beloved. Was he on his way to the same fate? If he didn't find Nadim, it was over. For Hanna. For him.

The car cruised through the morning traffic at high speeds, and he could tell from the road signs that they were approaching the airport. He fantasised about cars forcing them off the road and rescuing him, or about a beautiful woman standing by the road and making the driver stop, and of him somehow getting out of the car and fleeing across the field. None of this happened, and they arrived a few minutes later. Even though the car's air conditioning was on full blast, he was sweaty. He had showered, but he already stank of stress. The superior man opened the door for him and brusquely helped him out of the car.

By the time they walked into the busy departures hall, his fantasies of fleeing had subsided, and Eric bitterly prepared to spend the next few hours in the air. The two men remained on either side of him as they pushed through loud and colourful lines. The airport was in total chaos; nothing seemed to be working. The large screens that usually displayed departure times were just flashing incomprehensible combinations of letters, and airline personnel at the check-in desks were trying to calm angry passengers. A teary-eyed woman beside him was speaking into a cell phone.

'I don't know, dammit,' she was saying. 'Everything's crashed because of that fucking computer virus. They're doing the check-ins manually. We don't know when we'll be able to leave — if we even can leave.' For a brief moment, hope was awakened in Eric once more. Would the virus keep them grounded? Would Mona end up rescuing him? That would be ironic. He sneaked a look at Paul, who didn't seem in the least concerned. He just kept moving forward with resolve, brutally shoving his way past all the confused people with overloaded luggage carts and crying small children.

Eric hurried after him. At the far end of the large hall was a shorter line, which was markedly calmer than the others.

They stood behind a black man in a light-grey suit with a small Louis Vuitton bag at his side. The sign at the check-in counter said 'Private and corporate jet check-in'. His hope that the virus would save him died away. Here, everything seemed to be functioning despite the computer problems. A woman and a man were doing manual check-ins, and their unconcerned smiles indicated that they had the situation under control. So the FBI had their own plane. But it was strange that they had to wait in line. Why didn't they just drive up to the plane? Paul read his mind.

'High security. We have to go in through the door back there, and then we can go straight out to the plane.' He nodded at two large white doors directly behind the counter. A young man with two children was just taking their passports from the counter and going through the doors. When they opened, Eric caught a glimpse of a security line and an X-ray scanner. If he went through those, he could give up all hope of fleeing. Should he just turn around and run? But where would he go? They would catch him in a few seconds — they were surely in better shape than he was. Paul showed his FBI badge and his passport. When Eric saw his own passport with its Swedish emblem, he wanted to cry. Sweden was another world — an orderly, structured, safe place, far off on the edge of the world. Their home was there. Jens and Hanna were there. His passport was a painful reminder of freedom, of normalcy.

The woman at the counter returned the documents and smiled at them as they passed. Eric felt like he was going to his own execution. He felt the adrenaline that had built up during the car trip subsiding, leaving behind an empty exhaustion. Two security guards were waiting on the other side of the doors. He put his bag on the narrow conveyor belt, while Paul walked ahead of him through the detector. It didn't go off. That meant he was unarmed. In the movies, all the FBI agents carried large pistols, but apparently they didn't in reality. Then Eric walked through. Nothing. Just as he was going to take his bag from the X-ray machine, it stopped and backed up. His bag went back into the machine. Paul became restless, and sighed audibly. The guard at the monitor said something to his colleague. The bag came back out of the X-ray machine, and the guard lifted it up.

'Is this yours?'

Eric nodded as he tried to think of what had caused them to react — he wasn't carrying a computer, or any liquids, or sharp objects. The guard opened the door to a small, cube-shaped holding area that was slightly larger than a dressing room.

'Come with me. I need to take a closer look at your bag.'

Paul made a move to come along with Eric, but he was stopped by the guard.

'Wait here. This won't take long.'

The room within the white plaster walls was only a few cubic metres in total, with a small table in the middle. On the wall was a poster of things that couldn't be brought on board, and in one corner was a green box of latex gloves. The guard placed the bag on the table and rapped on a side door. Another guard immediately crowded into the already-cramped space. Eric was still trying to think of what could be wrong with his bag when he caught sight of the newly arrived guard's face, and recoiled. The guard had an open wound just above his temple, and his eye was swollen and dark blue. The guards spoke together in Hebrew. Then the injured one turned to him and handed him his bag.

'Listen carefully. On my signal, you yank open the door and run straight across the hall. The Americans are unarmed, but you have to be quick. On the other side there's an emergency exit. It's usually locked, but today it's open. Four floors down you'll find an exit that will take you to the tarmac. There's a blue motorcycle there. Take it and drive straight across the runway. Don't get too close to the big gates. The personnel out there haven't been informed. We've secured most of the people involved, but we couldn't risk briefing the main thoroughfare — too many people. If they get suspicious, they'll stop you. They're armed. You have to go to the south-western part of the field, where there's a smaller gate — a boom and two guards. The boom is open, and the guards are busy with other things. Drive through, and then you're free. From there, you're on your own.'

Eric felt dazed and terrified. He had changed his mind. He didn't want to run now. The guard leaned toward him with a resolute expression.

'There's a helmet hanging from the handlebars. Don't forget to put it on. You have to wear a helmet in Israel — otherwise the police will get you right away.' A rational question popped up in the midst of his whirling thoughts.

'My passport?'

'Unfortunately, I can't help you there.'

Blood had started to run from the wound down onto the guard's cheek.

'What happened to your face?'

The guard smiled stiffly.

'You hit me.'

'What?'

Before he had time to think, the guard punched the plaster wall with a bang and gave him a hard shove toward the door. He tumbled back out into the hall and fell on top of Paul's colleague. Before anyone could react, he heard the guard yell.

'Stop him!'

He flew onto his feet, nearly losing his balance, then shoved his hand into the FBI officer's face and set off, away from the security line. *Emergency exit. Where the fuck is the emergency exit?*

He caught sight of a green sign at the far end of the hall, turned, and came close to slipping, but regained his balance. If he fell, it was all over. Those he passed looked at him in fear. A fat woman made an attempt to stop him, but he was already gone. He didn't dare look over his shoulder. Then he reached the emergency exit, and tore open the door. He stumbled out into a stairwell with a grooved steel staircase, and started down it three steps at a time. Behind him he heard the door fly open with a bang, and several people filled the space above him. He kept going, his pulse roaring in his temples, sure that he would soon be captured.

The stairs ended at the ground floor. He managed to get a steel door open, and found himself on the windy tarmac. He ran toward the corner of the building and saw a motorcycle leaning against the wall. It must have been at least twenty years since he'd driven one. The motorcycle was old and shabby — some sort of off-road type. He threw his leg across the frame and grabbed the handlebars. Panic-stricken, he realised he didn't know how to start it. There was no kick-start, and no button on the handlebars. He heard agitated voices; they were already out on the tarmac on the other side of the building. He caught sight of a key sticking out of the frame, just under the petrol cap. When he turned it, the engine started with a loud rattle. He turned around and wobbled off across the grey concrete. The helmet was still dangling from the handlebars — he'd have to put it on later. Thirty metres ahead, just to the right, was a small white jet with the Stars and Stripes on the tail — the FBI's plane. He passed just in front of its nose, and could see two faces behind the windscreen. The wind was howling, and he had a hard time keeping his eyes open. A strong odour of diesel pierced the air. A Lufthansa plane with engines roaring, looking like a thundering monster larger than anything he'd ever seen — a lethal dinosaur that could squash him like a fly — turned off a nearby taxiway.

At first, it looked like he was going to drive straight into one of its enormous wheels, but the plane turned majestically, and they ended up running parallel instead. The wingtip stuck out several metres above his head, and the sound of the engines cut through his head like a power saw.

He tried to orient himself; he kept an eye on the fence, and saw the large gate a few hundred metres to his left. The wind made his eyes tear up as he tried to see whether the guards had seen him as well. Something flashed in the sunlight, blinding him. He turned his eyes away and concentrated on keeping his speed equal to the plane's. Maybe it was to his advantage to run alongside the large machine; it ought to make it harder to see him. He passed the checkpoint at a distance of a hundred metres, and couldn't make out any activity there. The Lufthansa plane slowed down and turned its nose toward the terminal building. He was once again alone with the rattling engine. He clamped his bag between his legs. The tyres were low. He felt every bump in the concrete, and the handlebars were vibrating hysterically. He tried to remember what the guard had said. The south-western part. *From which direction?* He followed the fence with his eyes, and steered closer so he wouldn't miss anything. He drove past three white helicopters parked in a row. Then he saw the boom. It was a few hundred metres ahead, the fence opened at a little outpost — a white boom, a signal light, and a blue guardhouse. He was approaching fast, and couldn't see any people about. The boom was open, as planned. Then he saw someone sitting in the guardhouse. He held his breath, and drove through the opening without slowing down.

As he flew forward on the straight stretch of concrete, away from the sentry, he expected a bullet in the back. His whole spine tensed; he could feel the point at which the bullet would hit him, just between his shoulders. It would throw him forward, and he would be dead before he hit the gravelly concrete. But nothing happened. He soon came to a wider road, which joined a busier entrance ramp after about a kilometre of warehouses and car-rental lots. He slowed down and stopped at the side of the road, put on his helmet with trembling hands, looked over his shoulder, and then accelerated up the ramp and out onto the highway. A blue road sign told him that it was eleven kilometres to Tel Aviv. He relaxed a bit and began to breathe again. Rachel had done it. He had done it. He had pulled off a completely impossible escape. No one flees Israel's largest airport on a motorcycle — but with the help of the Mossad, the impossible had become possible. He was still conscious of the point just below the last vertebrae in his neck.

After a shaky fifteen minutes, he was back in Tel Aviv. The traffic was thick on Levinsky Street. He drove between two wide lines of cars, hoping that no one would open a car door or change lanes. He wasn't the only one driving a motorcycle. There were around twenty mopeds, Vespas, and motorcycles ahead of and behind him, all of them zig-zagging through the traffic in a death-defying manner. The buildings along the street were two and three storeys high, and their façades were dingy and cracked. Many of the windows had red-and-blue shutters; most of them were closed. On one balcony, someone had hung a large Italian flag. At ground level, there were electronics stores, bakeries, groceries, and bars — but no internet cafés. He passed a newspaper stand. The headlines surprised him, and he nearly lost his balance: 'IT-TERRORISTS OFFER ANTI-VIRUS.' So it was official. Nadim had become a useful bargaining chip in the conflict.

The light turned red, and he stopped. With a sense of vertigo, he realised he was next to a blue-and-white police car. He had been too absorbed in the headlines, and hadn't noticed the cars in line. Thank God he had remembered to put on his helmet.

But he was still wearing the same clothes and riding the same motorcycle. They must have put out an alarm, including a description of him. One man and one woman sat in the police car. They were talking to each other, and so far they had only been looking ahead. He tried to play it cool and turn his head to the side as naturally as possible. His stomach hurt, and it felt like an eternity until the light turned green. He gave the motorcycle full throttle, and nearly fell off as it accelerated. At the T-intersection with Ha'Aliya, he turned right toward Derek Shlomo.

He slowed down and stopped just past a bus stop. A row of motorcycles was already standing there, so he climbed off, hung the helmet back on the handlebars, took his bag, and left the motorcycle with the key in. It wasn't until now that he noticed the heat. The sky was a clear blue, and the air between the asphalt and the building façades was still. The footpath was full of people trudging heavily on. No one was in a rush. It was too warm; they were all like ants under a magnifying glass. The sun was relentless. A few men in military pants were walking around with bare chests; one was wearing his automatic weapon on his back, and the other was carrying his, along with a green bag. Eric passed a pizzeria and a perfume shop. There was a large grey plastic garbage bin outside the store, which was so full that the lid couldn't close. The sickly stench of rotting food was in sharp contrast to the perfume advertisements in the shop window.

Further on, he saw a music store, and walked faster. *Music attracts teenagers ... teenagers know where there's internet access.* He went into the store, which was both cooler and darker than the footpath outside. *I'm a cyberjunkie desperately hunting for a hit. If I don't get on the net I'll die.* Ordinarily, the thought would have been funny, but now it felt all too close to the truth. He was soon back on the street, with an improvised map in his hand. The

X didn't stand for an internet café, but rather for a library that 'might have internet.'

It took him ten minutes to find the building, which turned out to be some sort of cultural centre. The building was shabby, with an ugly dark-brown façade full of cracks and chipped plaster. In the dirty windows were a number of signs giving times of exhibitions and concerts. The door was open, revealing a narrow staircase, and on the way in he met a group of women dressed in leotards and toe shoes. On the first floor, he found two locked doors with Hebrew signs on them. Someone, somewhere, was playing the piano — Chopin. He kept going, to the next floor. There were three doors, with symbols on two of them of a girl and a boy. Bathrooms. The third was a glass door with a simple, handwritten note taped to the glass in Hebrew. Maybe it said 'Library'. He opened the thin door and entered a dim, stuffy room full of books that lay in great piles on the floor and filled all four walls. It smelled like paper and mould. There didn't seem to be any sort of system for the books; it looked like they had been tossed randomly onto the floor or shoved onto the shelves. An older woman sat at a cluttered desk with her back to him. He cleared his throat, startling her. She turned around and studied him over the rims of her glasses. She was wearing a pale-grey shawl and a thick, beige cardigan.

'What are you doing here?'

The question was so unexpected and the place so messy that he was unsure if he was in the right place. Had he just burst into her home?

'I'm looking for the library.'

The woman turned around and adjusted a green reading lamp. Her white hair was in a tight bun. A few strands had wriggled their way out and were hanging loosely down her neck and onto the old cardigan.

'Most people who come here are looking for a specific book. A whole library is ambitious.'

She spoke English with a strong accent. He remained standing near the door, still unsure if he was intruding.

She went on. 'So what are you looking for — a book or a library?'

He cleared his throat.

'Neither, really.'

'Interesting. So what is it, then?'

'An internet connection.'

The words felt wrong. They were superficial and unintellectual. They were misplaced — like a McDonald's sign at the Great Pyramid. He was an academic; he loved books. But right now he needed a computer. The woman stood up and walked over to one of the bookcases beside a small oval window. It was the only one in the room.

'Can you read Yiddish?'

'Unfortunately, I can't.'

She moved a few large books with worn red covers and took out a yellow book with black text. She looked at it for a moment and then went back to him. She was short; her glasses were fastened with a long, silver chain, and one of the earpieces had been repaired with red tape. She handed him the book.

'You're asking for a way out. That's all very well and good, but this is a way in. Maybe it's not as exciting, or even much of anything else. Judge for yourself.'

He looked at the book. *Laughter Beneath the Forest: poems from old and recent manuscripts* by Abraham Sutzkever. The black-and-white illustration on the front cover depicted large trees bending in a strong wind. The woman nodded at the book.

'It's for you. As a memory. Memories are important, and nothing preserves them as well as a book. And anyway, it's just a translation that doesn't fit in here. I don't even know how it got here — maybe some student left it behind. You'll be doing me a favour if you take it with you.'

The woman went back to her place at the desk. He took a deep breath.

'Thank you. But I must insist upon help with the way out, too — the internet connection.'

Without looking at him, she pointed sideways, toward a door that was ajar between the bookcases. He hadn't seen the door at first in the dim light. He walked through the room carefully. Inside, there were more books — stacked in towers, tossed in great piles, or shoved into the bookshelves that covered the walls from floor to ceiling. Under a small, square window was a narrow table with a simple kitchen chair in flaking, green paint. On the table was an old PC. A black-and-white photograph of an old man hung on the wall, right above the computer.

Eric put his bag on the floor, placed the yellow book beside the keyboard, and cautiously sat down on the rickety chair. The computer started with an ominous whine. After what felt like an eternity, the screen came to life, and the Windows symbol popped up. It was the old version, which meant that the operating system hadn't been upgraded in many years. He opened the bag and dug out the flimsy napkins with the log-in information for Mona's development environment. On them was the new username he had scribbled down in the hotel room. He entered the address with rising anxiety, made worse by the computer doing nothing for a long time before it loaded. Then, once again, he was sitting eye-to-eye with the Mona virus. He changed position in the chair and called up the chat. He held his breath and stared at the computer as though hypnotised. The screen went black, and was filled with white text. He was back. But would Salah ad-Din still be there? Would he trust him after the attacks had been revealed? Had he seen through his lies?

He scrolled through the hundreds of entries, page after page of symbols and characters he couldn't read. Then he realised that his own conversation with Salah ad-Din was gone. Salah ad-Din must have deleted it. But why? Did he want to keep their contact secret? Hadn't he told the others on the team about him? He sat still for a long time, pondering what could have happened. The Mossad had gotten in, too, and read the chat. Were they the ones who had deleted the conversation? Could they even do that? No, that would be idiotic. It could only have been Salah ad-Din himself. He wrote a short message:

SALAH AD-DIN, IF YOU ARE INTERESTED MY KNOWLEDGE IS STILL AT YOUR DISPOSAL.
:ES

Now all he could do was wait, knowing that the chance of him receiving an answer was negligible. Last time it had taken several hours for Salah ad-Din to answer. Was it a mistake to put up another entry after the old ones had been removed? What choice did he have? His message floated in the midst of the Arabic script like a white fishing float in a black sea. He leaned back on the creaky chair and caught sight once again of the yellow book: *Laughter Beneath the Forest* by Abraham Sutzkever. He opened it.

The sun returns to my dark countenance
and belief grasps my arm strong and firm
if a worm does not surrender when cut in two,
are you then less than a worm?

He tried to grasp the meaning of the poem. *Are you then less than a worm?*

'When Abraham Sutzkever was digging a ditch as a prisoner, he happened to cut a worm in half with his shovel. He was fascinated that a living organism could become two by way of violence. Instead of dying, it became twice as alive.'

The old woman was standing in the doorway. In her hand, she held two large cups of tea. He smiled.

'Why was he imprisoned?'

She studied him before she spoke, as though she were evaluating whether he was truly interested.

'Fate saw to it that Abraham Sutzkever, who had been a soul full of *joie de vivre* from the start, ended up as the voice of sorrow, but also that of hope and freedom. He saw the suffering in the ghetto in Vilnius and all the death in Ponar.'

'What happened in Ponar?'

'The same thing that happened everywhere else. One of the most vibrant Jewish cultures was decimated in two years. Vilnius was the Jerusalem of the Baltic, and maybe even all of Europe. For many years, it was one of the most important centres of Jewish culture — a great deal of literature in Hebrew and Yiddish was created there. Zionism was born there, as well as the Jewish labour movement.'

'And Abraham Sutzkever was there? In Ponar?'

'Yes and no. He was there in his heart and soul, but never physically. He was close, though, in the Vilna ghetto. He met the thousands who were taken away, and he spoke with the few who returned.'

She entered the room. He stood up and pointed at the chair.

'Please sit.'

She nodded and sat down with difficulty. Then she handed him one of the cups of steaming herbal tea.

'I'm afraid my body is starting to betray me.' He took the cup, and cautiously sipped at the tea so he wouldn't burn himself.

'But you work?'

'Oh, yes. I have to. It's all I have. And it's my promise.'

'Your promise? To whom?'

'To myself. And to him.' She nodded at the photograph above the computer. Eric studied the picture: it portrayed a serious man with a sparse moustache and sad eyes. He sat down on a pile of books alongside the computer, and carefully placed the cup beside the keyboard.

'Abraham Sutzkever? So you knew him?'

'The Vilnius ghetto was dreadful. But it was also brave, productive, and alive. Culture didn't die when it was imprisoned — it just changed shape. Poetry had a particularly important role during our oppression. Abraham Sutzkever's readings were packed. I didn't miss a single one.'

'How old were you?'

'Fourteen. I fell in love straightaway — with his writing, his thoughts, his voice.'

'Your first love?'

'I think it's hard to understand. We lived in a black-and-white world, and here came this splash of colour. It was as though God had placed him with us for comfort, as proof that He was still with us. For me, he became a symbol of everything that was alive — everything beautiful.'

The books were about to topple under Eric's weight, and he had to change position. He threw a glance at the computer screen. There were no new entries.

'And your promise?'

'Abraham Sutzkever was a member of the paper brigade, a group of scholars who risked their lives to smuggle out hundreds, even thousands, of rare, unique books and manuscripts. I helped him collect donations from families in the area. For many people, these books were the nicest things they owned, and being separated from them was a great sacrifice. But with Abraham Sutzkever's name as a guarantee, most of them agreed to donate what they had anyway. The last time we saw each other, he came to my father's shoemaker shop. He said he'd had a vision, a feeling.'

She smiled faintly.

'"You will live". That's what he said. He had caught a glimpse of the future, and I was going to survive. He asked me to take the treasures to the Holy Land, to guard and care for them. We moved in here in 1972.'

'We?'

'The books and I.'

Eric swept his eyes over the hundreds of books.

'And you've been guarding the treasure ever since?'

'Every day, seven days a week, all year round. My family was left behind in the mud outside Vilna. This is my family now.'

The room was really too small for the conference table. Or perhaps it was the other way around. If you wanted to sit on one of the eight wooden chairs, you had to squeeze between the table and the wall. On the table was a plate of biscuits, a thermos, and a cone of white paper cups. A whiteboard covered one wall. On the other walls were framed pictures of El Al planes. Paul Clinton was stuck in his chair, and couldn't lean back in it as he normally did. He had already had time to drink two mugs of coffee and eat three biscuits. He regretted the last one. On the other hand, he lost his focus and became irritated when his blood sugar levels went down. He heard steps and then the door opened. Rachel Papo stepped in, along with a young woman in a dark-grey suit. She nodded at him and then looked at the woman.

'This is Natalie Goldman. She is responsible for security at the airport.'

Rachel pulled out a chair and slid smoothly into it as though it were the most natural thing in the world. He immediately felt fatter. The woman in the suit was still standing at the short end of the table. She looked shaken. Rachel filled a mug with coffee from the thermos. Then she looked at the woman.

'Okay, Natalie. Please begin.'

'First and foremost. I would like to point out that we have been having major problems all day, because of the computer virus. A number of systems are affected, and it's quite chaotic in the terminals. I'm not trying to make excuses, but it might have impacted on the situation.' She gave them a pleading look. When no one answered, she quickly continued.

'Eric Söderqvist took the guards at security by surprise, and left the terminal via emergency exit sixty-seven. This exit is meant to be locked at all times, but for some reason it was open. We're investigating how this could have happened. The exit leads to the tarmac on the south-western side of the terminal. There, Söderqvist managed to steal a motorcycle. He drove 950 metres to the north-western exit at Neve Monosson.'

She looked down at the table, apparently gathering strength. 'There he left the airport via security checkpoint A12. Although the checkpoint was manned, none of the guards managed to stop him. This in itself is inconceivable. Two traffic cameras captured him; one on the 412 at Hal Tamar, and one on the entrance ramp to Highway 1 at Shapirim.'

Paul met Rachel's gaze before he asked with concern, 'Going in which direction?'

'Toward Tel Aviv.'

'Have you informed the police?'

'The police have put out a description to see if he can be traced by camera. Their systems have been infected as well. There's a certain amount of confusion regarding the downtown cameras, but hopefully they'll find him.'

Rachel sipped her coffee and asked, without looking up, 'But no concrete clues?'

Natalie gave a resigned shake of her head. After a moment of silence, she added, 'It shouldn't be possible. It's like … Normally … I mean, we have procedures that …'

Rachel interrupted her.

'Thanks, Natalie. We understand. You must give us a formal report. Do it as quickly as possible before you forget the details. You know where to go?'

The woman nodded and left them. Rachel leaned across the table and pulled the door shut after her. Paul took a biscuit from the plate and chewed it in silence. Then he turned to her.

'The signal?'

'It's strong. He's sitting on Herzl Street in what seems to be a small cultural centre. We can't get altitude, so we don't know what floor it's on. There's a small library in the building that has internet access.'

Paul smiled.

'Smart boy. Then all we can do is wait and hope he gets an answer.'

She nodded.

'What actually happened at the security line?'

'Michael injured a finger. A sprain, I think. But otherwise it went well. We ran after him onto the tarmac, but when we saw him taking off on the motorcycle there was no point.'

'Michael didn't suspect anything?'

'No. But I feel a little bit guilty. He's a good guy. It wouldn't be dangerous to let him in on it, but to be on the safe side … Like everyone else, he's convinced that we lost him.'

Rachel studied the mug of coffee in her hand.

'How long will we give him to make contact?'

Paul answered quickly, 'A day at the most. The problem is really the local police, right? Sooner or later, they'll find him. He's not an experienced criminal who knows how to stay out of sight. Moving around in Tel Aviv is a big risk.'

'So it is. But we had to do it this way. The police leak like a sieve, and now we can take advantage of that. I don't know what kind of resources Samir Mustaf's group has, but if they have contacts on the street they'll soon hear that Eric Söderqvist is on the run. That will make the story credible, and his situation more urgent. We'll just have to hope that he's interesting enough for them to help him.'

Paul took another biscuit. Fuck his spare tire — he was restless.

'What do you think about the letter from Hezbollah?'

Rachel shrugged.

'I'm just a low-paid government employee. I don't hear much of what gets said in the fancy rooms. But there wasn't any news in the letter, was there? We knew that Hezbollah was behind the virus and the attacks.'

'And the demands for the anti-virus?'

'Unacceptable. Ben Shavit will never go along with them. He doesn't negotiate with terrorists.' Paul gave a faint smile.

'That's not what I heard. Nothing official, but if it's true, he's about to give up. The whole world has been dragged along into this crisis, and the prime minister is under enormous pressure.'

'All I know is that he's tough. He can withstand a great deal.'

Paul thought about Eric Söderqvist.

'That guy is going to be important. The question is whether he himself understands how valuable he is. How good is the transmitter?'

'The *transmitters*. There are three of them. He has one in his arm, one in his phone, and one in the fabric of his pants.'

'He has a transmitter in his arm?'

'Yes. We injected a passive GPS chip under his skin.'

'Won't he notice it?'

'It's not visible, but if he happened to rub his skin right there, he would feel a small bump. The phone transmitter is the strongest of the three, and it's the only one that's active — that is, it receives power. But it's not dependent on the phone battery — it has its own energy source. Incidentally, we made a mistake there.'

'What?'

'Some idiot forgot to charge the phone during the night. At the most, it has 20 per cent battery left.'

Paul made a face.

'That was dumb. But he'll probably notice and use it sparingly.'

They sat in silence for a moment. Rachel squeezed the empty cup until it split. She tossed it into the wastebasket under the whiteboard.

'What do you really think about Eric's story?'

Paul shook his head.

'It's screwed up. David Yassur is convinced he's full of shit. It's almost too implausible to be made up. Maybe parts of it are true.'

She cocked her head.

'Like what?'

'I don't know. Maybe he really is after an anti-virus.'

'To save his sick wife?'

'It could be. It could also be for purely commercial reasons. The anti-virus is priceless. He could sell it to Israel. To TBI. Or to one of the other banks that's been hit.'

'If that's true, why would he cook up a science-fiction story about his wife being infected with a computer virus? It doesn't make sense. We know Hanna Söderqvist is sick, and we know the hospital hasn't been able to come up with a diagnosis. We also know that the other man … what's his name again?'

'Hagström.'

'Mats Hagström … he died after exhibiting the same symptoms as Hanna Söderqvist.'

'Why did he die, and not Hanna Söderqvist?'

'Maybe she's stronger and younger. He might have had a weaker heart. I'm sure there are hundreds of possible factors.'

Paul didn't say anything. After a moment he nodded, as though to affirm something he'd been thinking. Rachel looked at him.

'What?'

'You're right that his wife's illness is odd. On the one hand, that would mean he's correct; on the other hand, it's frightening. What if she really does have a virus that's somehow connected to the terrorists? That could mean some sort of biological weapon, right? Maybe Eric Söderqvist is in collusion with Samir Mustaf after all. Maybe he developed a virus, and then — either on purpose or by accident — he infected his wife. We need to find out more about the virus. I'd venture to say it's top priority. We really should move Hanna Söderqvist to the base in Norway. Sweden doesn't have anywhere near the same resources, and, more importantly, our work is being blocked by a hell of a lot of laws. We need a free rein to perform the measures and tests that need to be done, without worrying about any idiotic ethical guidelines.'

Now it was Rachel's turn to be silent. For Paul, Hanna Söderqvist was an object, a thing. Above all, she was a threat. The tests he was referring to would hardly hold up under scrutiny. And they would hardly increase Hanna's chances of survival. But she wasn't a thing. She was Eric's wife, a woman he seemed prepared to risk everything for. And she was Jewish. Paul interrupted her thoughts.

'I think I'll go to Stockholm after all while you keep an eye on

Eric Söderqvist. I'll fly there and talk to the Swedish authorities. Who knows, maybe I'll even be allowed to visit Mrs Söderqvist.'

Rachel stood up.

'Are you going right away?'

'I might as well. And you?'

'I haven't slept since that night at Montefiore. I'm taking tonight off. Eric is on the radar, and we have a good team who will track him if he moves.'

Paul took the last biscuit from the plate. Rachel opened the door and cast one last look at him.

'You shouldn't eat so many sweets.'

Jerusalem, Israel

Sinon was enjoying the mint tea. Sure, it had had gotten cold, but it tasted fresh and a bit sour. He had chosen to have his afternoon tea in one of the deep easy chairs, and not at his desk like he usually did. He sat near the large windows that looked out onto a leafy garden and a large birdbath made of white marble. His office was just two doors down from Ben Shavit's, and it was several square metres larger. Ben was seldom there, and he didn't feel that he needed a more spacious room. But there had been too many people at the meeting today, and Sinon's office had worked better. He had decorated the walls with university diplomas, pictures of himself shaking hands with several of the world's leading politicians, pictures of himself standing beside his beloved bicycle, and the obligatory family photo. He had chosen the furnishings himself: a large desk in dark oak, and a tall office chair of black leather with large armrests and a flexible headrest; a wastebasket made of an actual elephant's foot, a gift from the ambassador of South Africa; and a dark-red carpet and three deep easy chairs of dark-brown leather. Just inside the door was a tripod that held a flipchart, because he liked to sketch when he was explaining things. But today the paper was blank. He couldn't show the true strategy. It wasn't necessary. It was all already in his head.

One by one, the puzzle pieces were falling into place. Ben had decided to negotiate. Although two out of the three attacks had been prevented, the explosion in the shopping centre had provoked a clamour for action from the opposition and the media. Everyone knew that Hezbollah had offered an anti-virus and armistice. What could Ben do, besides go along with their demands? Sinon had seen his anguish, and felt his anger. And he had recommended that he go along with Hezbollah's demands, that he put aside his own feelings, his own pride, and instead do what was best for Israel — no, not just Israel, for the whole world. Nothing was more important than getting access to the anti-virus. Everyone would consider him a hero; no one would think he was weak or a coward. No one except, possibly, for himself. Ben had listened, and now they were just waiting to set up a meeting with a neutral mediating party. And Sinon would stand at his friend's side and make sure that he signed the agreement.

It would be a historic defeat for Israel. A historic victory for all the world's true believers. And for himself.

His thoughts went back to the attacks. How could the police have learned about them? Ahmad Waizy was furious. To him, everyone was a suspect. He'd already shot Arie al-Fattal. Sinon didn't know if he really had been the one to spill the beans. No matter who it was, though, it was right to shoot al-Fattal. Sinon had never liked him. But Hezbollah's section leader had been upset — Ahmad wasn't one of them, and he couldn't shoot one of their brothers at random. Sinon had dealt with it, but it wasn't

Ahmad's suspicions or Arie's death that was bothering him; it was the uncertainty. Even with all of his power and all of his contacts, he hadn't been able to find out who had tipped off the police. Neither Meir Pardo nor David Yassur had said anything. He doubted that even Ben knew. Ahmad was demanding that he quickly find out who the leaker was, but it was hard for him to ask around too much. It could raise suspicions.

The tea was gone, and he chewed the wet mint leaves. His thoughts wandered to his private project: killing Rachel Papo. He was finally finished with his preparations. Everything had been arranged, even though it hadn't been easy. He had worked only with his own contacts, so that no one on the team knew — not Ahmad, and not anyone in Hezbollah. This would be a surprise for them. That murderer Papo would soon be gone, and it would be dramatic: no anonymous robbery/homicide in a dirty alley; no silent heart attack. No, everyone would know that she had been punished for what she'd done, that the wrath of Allah had finally caught up with her. Her dramatic death would be a clear warning to everyone who was a threat to Islam. It would show them that no one — not even their best agents — was safe. Not anywhere. Not even in their own homes. He looked at the clock. It was almost time to go home and change for his evening bike ride.

Tel Aviv, Israel

'Who's after you?' He put the teacup down on the desk again and kept his eyes on it, studying its chipped rim and the scrolling red floral pattern on the greyish-white porcelain. Her question was inevitable. He was too stressed — too out of place in this environment, this culture, this city. She had seen so much fear in her life that his didn't go unnoticed. There were many reasons for her question. Who *was* after him? Or, rather, what was he running away from? The superficial answer was that he was running away from the Israeli police and the FBI. But the real answer lay deeper: maybe he had been running the whole time. He took his eyes from the teacup. He didn't want to answer. Then he caught sight of the computer, and his heart skipped a beat. A new entry was flickering in the chat room. She could see that he had lost his concentration. Maybe she could also sense that he didn't want to, or couldn't, answer the question.

'All right, I know you have better things to do than sit and dwell on things with me.'

He immediately shook his head, but she held up her hand and stood up.

'I'm going home. Something tells me you have nowhere to go. If you want to, you may stay here. There's nowhere to sleep, but if you're tired you can sleep anywhere. Believe me, I know. I'll be back first thing tomorrow morning.'

Eric gave a resigned smile.

'You're right, I have nowhere to go. I'd love to stay here tonight. I'll watch over your treasures.'

She nodded.

'And they'll watch over you.'

He leaned forward and gave her a hug. It happened quickly and spontaneously; it was just something he had to do. She stayed in his embrace without moving away. Then she took her teacup and left him. He stood by the desk until he heard the glass door click. Then he sat down in front of the keyboard and stared at the message.

WHERE ARE YOU?
:SALAH AD-DIN

Was it dangerous to give his address? What did he have to lose?

ON THE RUN FROM THE POLICE. HERZL STREET 44 IN TEL AVIV. :ES

He leaned back and looked up at Abraham Sutzkever. The man stared back at him; perhaps there was something calming about his gaze.

Near Khan Younis, Gaza

He had been forced to tell Ahmad Waizy. His curiosity about the man who had showed up out of nowhere was too great; his thirst for an intellectual sparring partner was too strong. For the first time since Qana, he had felt interested in another person. Why it should be Eric Söderqvist in particular, he couldn't say. Maybe it was his timing. Samir knew that he would never be able to meet Söderqvist if it wasn't first approved and then arranged by Ahmad. If he were to believe what Söderqvist wrote, he was in Tel Aviv, of all places. And the police were looking for him. That complicated things and made it riskier. Was he genuine, or was he a fraud? Ahmad could check whether there really was a description of him out; all he had to do was give Sinon a call. Ahmad had been surprisingly calm, almost uninterested, as he was told about Söderqvist. Samir had doctored his story a bit. He had only said that there had been one entry in the secret chat room — from a Swedish IT professor who wanted to join their mission. He had shown Ahmad the Google hits he'd gotten on Söderqvist's background. The hits verified that he was a reputable professor at the technical institute in Stockholm.

Ahmad had asked several indifferent check questions: 'How did he find the chat?' *I don't know. I assume he hacked his way in.* 'Would he add to the group? Aren't you in the final phase of your work?' *A great deal. The anti-virus is almost finished, but it needs to be tested and packaged.* 'What have you told him?' *Nothing. I wanted to check with you first.* 'Where is he?' *Tel Aviv.*

They sat on their respective white plastic chairs, with a small white plastic table between them. The dirty pieces of furniture, which stood near the ruins of an old farm, were the only signs of life above ground — waste products of the use-and-toss society in the middle of a tightly packed world of sand displaying the occasional purple thistle. In the east, the otherwise dark night reflected the light from distant Israeli cities.

Ahmad felt relaxed. No one had said anything about Arie al-Fattal, who was rotting in a ditch six hundred kilometres away. Their new hideout — or maybe the right word for it was 'home' — was part of a deserted smuggling tunnel. Gaza was full of them, as though gigantic chipmunks had been given free rein under the oblong strip of land between Israel and the sea.

In reality, the chipmunks were an established contracting company that built tunnels on commission for professional smugglers. The section of tunnel outside Khan Younis had been bombed several times, and the walls had collapsed in a number of places. The tunnel was two metres in diameter, and it was three-and-a-half metres below ground. The walls were reinforced with concrete, and light bulbs hung from the ceiling. Side rooms and storage areas had been dug out in several places. Hamas ruled the tunnels, and Mohammad Murid had somehow managed to arrange access to them. Samir suspected that Ahmad was planning more attacks, and that was why he wanted to be close to Israel. These days he was quiet and never talked about his plans. They lived like rats, but Samir liked it better here than in the prince's palace. Ahmad placed a hand on his arm.

'I want you to do two things. First, delete all the information from the chat room. I thought it was secure, but apparently I was wrong. Remove all the entries.'

Samir nodded.

'Then I want you to write and tell the professor that we're coming to get him. I'll take care of the practical matters.'

'But shouldn't we check first to see if he's really running from the police? To see if his story checks out?'

Ahmad smiled.

'Of course we'll check to see if he's telling the truth. But no matter what we learn, we'll go get him. If he's lying, he can keep Arie company.'

Tel Aviv, Israel

Traffic was at a complete standstill on Sderot Ben Gurion. The radio had said something about problems with the traffic lights in Tel Aviv. The computer virus continued to eat its way into the country's infrastructure. Although Rachel Papo didn't want to admit it at first, she kept thinking about the Swede, Eric Söderqvist. She had been to the home to visit Tara, and now, stuck in traffic, she thought about him. He probably wouldn't make contact with Samir Mustaf and the terrorist group again. It was a far-fetched plan. But what if, somehow, he was successful? Then he would be in danger. He had no training, and Hezbollah's military cells were brutal and paranoid. David Yassur was fully prepared to sacrifice him. Eric was bait, and all he had to do was wriggle on the hook for as long as possible.

She thought of his face — soft, almost childish, with grey hairs in his stubble. His hands were nice — thin, but strong. She thought about his absent-minded and muddled manner, of his interested expression when she spoke. She had a mental image of him on the cot in his cell, when they'd sat close together, looking at a photograph of Mona. The whole time, there had been something subdued and distant about him. A weight lay upon him. His sick wife? He would never think of choosing her, Rachel, over that beautiful woman. And why should he? What was she good for? She couldn't cook, couldn't take care of children, couldn't fold laundry. And she had too much baggage. But she wished they had stolen a night together. She wanted him to take her, just for a few hours.

The traffic let up a bit, and Rachel changed lanes without using her blinker. The car behind her honked angrily. She didn't want to be alone tonight, so who could she call? She looked at the clock on the dashboard. It was a quarter past ten. That meant her options were limited.

Captain Dan Lichtman's leave was over. As usual, the three days had gone by far too quickly. He hadn't had time to do even half of what he'd planned. But he'd had his priorities straight; he'd partied with his little brother. The tequila hung across his forehead like a doughy blanket. He was worn out, but happy. Benjamin had appreciated having a night with his big brother. When Dan left he was sitting on the sofa, hung over, staring apathetically at reruns on TV. Dan tightened the straps on his saddlebag and buttoned his leather jacket. The motorcycle was his second-biggest passion. The first was his F-16 Fighting Falcon. Sure, she belonged to Heyl Ha'Avir, the Israeli air force, but when he sat in the cockpit she was his. It was one hundred and ten kilometres from Benjamin's apartment in Haifa to the base, Tel Nof, so he would make it in time. He climbed onto his Harley Davidson, and was just about to start the engine when his phone vibrated in the pocket of his jeans. He pulled off his glove and fished out the phone.

COME AND GET ME. RP

Dan smiled and put the phone back. The engine started with a roar, and he took a short cut across the parking lot and accelerated onto the street. There would hardly be any assignments overnight, so he could afford to be a few hours late to base. He hadn't heard from her in a long time. The last time they'd seen each other, he'd been sore for several days afterward.

Despite encountering a traffic jam on the highway into Tel Aviv, he navigated smoothly between the cars and managed to maintain an average speed of one hundred and thirty kilometres per hour. Forty-five minutes later, he put down the kickstand outside the white two-storey building on Shlomo Ben Yosef. The neighbourhood was dark, and the streetlights didn't seem to be working. He went up the stairs and stopped outside the door. There was no nameplate. He could hear faint music, and he knocked. After a moment, the door opened, but only barely. Rachel Papo looked at him through the opening as he crossed his arms and waited. She opened the door. Her thick hair was down, and the black curls fell over her bare chest. She was wearing only a pair of blue jogging pants, she was barefoot, and she had a cigarette in her hand. He took a deep breath. She was short and thin, all muscle. She had several ugly scars on her body, and on her left upper arm there was a tattoo of an olive tree, the symbol of the Golani Brigade. On one wrist she had a tattoo of a symbol that he didn't recognise; it might have been a hieroglyph. He knew nothing about her work, but she was without a doubt military. And maybe an elite athlete.

Without saying anything, she went back into the apartment. He followed her and closed the door. It smelled like cigarettes and incense. Arabic lounge music was playing on the stereo. Dan threw his jacket on the floor beside his boots, given that there were no hooks and no closet in the hall. When he entered the living room, she was waiting for him with a bottle of whisky dangling nonchalantly from one hand. She still hadn't said anything.

'Wow, aren't you talkative.'

He took the bottle and drank two sips. Then he set it against her lips and tipped it. She took a big gulp. Whisky ran down her neck. He pulled her to him and kissed her shoulders. He stroked her breasts. She pressed against him and got her hands under his shirt. Barely audibly, she whispered, 'Take me if you want me.'

He buried his face in her thick hair.

'I think you can feel that I want you.'

Her hand grabbed his crotch firmly.

'Mm. So what are you waiting for?'

He pushed her away.

'I'm not going to take you to Arab music. Change it, and you'll see.'

She laughed, took back the bottle, and walked over to the stereo.

'All the blood seems to have collected in one place, cowboy. I think you should go lie down.'

He watched as she theatrically leaned toward the stereo. He wanted her so much it hurt. He started to unbutton his pants as he walked into the bedroom. His shirt, jeans, and socks landed in a pile on the floor. Like the rest of the apartment, the room was hardly furnished. There were no paintings or photographs, no books, and no flowers — just a bed in the middle of the room. She probably wasn't here very often. The music changed to

George Michael.

'Perfect!'

He threw himself onto the bed.

The explosion was so powerful that it blew out the wall in the bedroom and tore a three-metre-wide hole in the floor. The house started to burn, and thick, black smoke rose over the roof and blocked out the dark sky. All the car alarms in the neighbourhood went off like a herd of crazy dogs. After a few minutes, several police sirens joined the out-of-tune choir.

It was about an hour after midnight. Even though a simple breakfast was the only thing Eric had eaten all day, he wasn't hungry. He was far too nervous; he had far too much to think about. He hadn't received any new messages from Salah ad-Din. The library was quiet, except for sporadic noise from the street. Far off, he heard a thunderclap and distant car-alarms; closer by, a passing moped with no muffler, and an ambulance siren. He hadn't spoken with Jens in several days; he hadn't even answered the text about Mats Hagström's death. For some reason, he was avoiding making contact with Sweden. He didn't know what the main reason was: his fear that Hanna might be worse, or his shame over deceiving Jens. His weakness disgusted him. In the yellow glow of the ceiling light he could see his own face on the computer screen. Something clattered suddenly on the street as he took his phone from his black bag. A warning message on the screen said that the battery was nearly dead. He didn't have a charger with him. That was that. He couldn't call — he couldn't risk the phone dying. It was his only link to the outside world, to the Mossad, to Rachel. He started a new text to Jens. After hesitating for a moment, he added Doctor Thomas Wethje to the list of recipients:

STILL IN TEL AVIV. PHONE ALMOST DEAD. I'M ON THE TRAIL
OF THE ANTI-VIRUS. TAKE CARE OF HANNA. I LOVE HER MORE
THAN ANYTHING. THANKS FOR EVERYTHING YOU'RE DOING.
/ /ERIC

It was a shit message that would probably just make everything worse, but what could he have written to make it better? He wasn't on his way home. He was in a strange library in Tel Aviv. He was a tiny piece of bait in the Mossad's hunt for terrorists. Where in the world were they? What would he do if they actually wanted to meet him? What would they do with him? These were people at war. People who had planned and carried out fatal attacks against civilians. People who were fighting a battle in which individual lives had no worth. The chance that he would come out of a meeting with them alive was non-existent. That he would also obtain the anti-virus was an impossibility. Suddenly, a new message popped up on the screen:

SEND YOUR MOBILE PHONE NUMBER AND BE PREPARED FOR
TRANSPORT AT 0700.
:SALAH AD-DIN

Jesus Christ. Not only had they taken the bait, but they had fallen hook, line, and sinker for it. *Or maybe not.* Maybe it was a trap. They wanted to stop the leak. Should he contact Rachel? No, that's not what her orders said. He would go along with the transport, and hope that it led him to Samir Mustaf. Only then would he contact the Mossad. After a moment's hesitation, he sent the phone number. They knew that he wouldn't miss the meeting. He knew it, too — whether it was a trap or not. Eric looked at the clock. There were almost five hours to go. He ought to try to sleep. He looked around among the books. *If you're tired, you can sleep anywhere.* That's what she'd said before she left, and it was surely true. Who was he to question her? He went to the door and turned off the light. The room went dark, with only the light from the computer screen remaining, and he fumbled his way back to the desk. He moved the chair and lay on the floor near the computer. He rooted through his bag in the dark, found his iPod, and started the music without bothering to change the track. It was Schubert. His bag made a fine pillow. He turned the ringer volume on his phone up as high as it would go, and placed the phone near his head. He tried to relax, and immediately thought about Hanna. Was she as alone as he was, lying there in the hospital? Maybe Jens was with her. He changed position on the hard parquetry. And Rachel, what was she doing right now?

A car honked out on the street. Eric was still lying down, with his head now on the floor. He must have slid off the bag while he was sleeping. His body ached as he slowly stretched out his legs and grimaced. His neck was stiff, and his lower back was throbbing. Sleeping on the floor came with a price. He picked up his phone to make sure no one had called. There was 10 per cent battery power left, but at least he could tell the time: it was ten past six. He got up and gathered his things, placed the yellow book carefully into his bag, and then turned off the computer and went out through the narrow door.

He remembered that there was a bathroom out in the hallway. The sun was shining brightly through the window in the larger room, and the disorder no longer felt messy. He had started to feel at home with the smells, the sounds, and the books here. This was a peaceful and pleasant place — a place where time was guided by memories, and each book had its own history, its own life. He went out the glass door and into the small bathroom. There, he washed for a long time with ice-cold water, and then stood eye to eye with himself. In less than half an hour, everything would change. If he died in a ditch outside Tel Aviv, would anyone let Sweden know? Would Hanna understand that he'd done it all for her? That he was trying to put things right? He was afraid. In fact, he was terrified. The panic crept through his body, cold and damp. He was having trouble breathing, and there was a sour taste in his mouth. His mind was racing as he tried to think of a way to get out of the meeting. *I have to get home to Sweden, to Hanna. I'll never get to meet Samir Mustaf anyway. Even if I did get hold of the anti-virus, it would never work to save her. Never. Never.* He whispered the word to himself, again and again, as he stared into the red, begging eyes in the mirror. Yesterday it had all felt so far away, but now it was far too close — and far too dangerous. The library was the safest place on earth, with its scent of paper and dust. Time stood still here. No, that was an illusion. Time wasn't standing still. Just while he had been in the bathroom, ten precious minutes had gone by.

He straightened up, ran a hand through his hair, and returned to the library. The large room, filled with books, felt empty without its proprietor. He hoped that she would show up before he had to leave. He sat in her desk chair and tried to relax, but he was far too nervous for that. On the desk was a black-and-white photography book that seemed to be about the river Volga. He paged through it distractedly, without really looking at the pictures. Suddenly, his phone rang. Never had a ringing phone frightened him so much. He picked it up as though it were a scorpion dripping with poison. The screen said the call was coming from an unknown number. He answered. The voice on the other end sounded young, and its owner spoke halting English with a thick accent that he couldn't place.

'I'm outside. A blue-and-white taxi.'

The call ended. It was five minutes to seven. The voice had stolen five minutes of the time he had left. He squeezed his eyes shut, trying to gather his thoughts and emotions. There was nothing more to ponder, nothing more to do. Now all he could do was finish what he'd started — no matter where it led him.

Eric stood up and went out through the rattling glass door and down the stairs. He came to the grey door with its dirty windows that faced the street. Everything that those two square frames contained seemed threatening and frightening: farthest off, the buildings across the street, with their drawn blinds and dirty façades; in the middle, the cars, buses, and motorcycles of all shapes and colours; closest to him, all the bodies that flickered by in a steady stream. He grasped the handle of the door and pulled it open, and the warmth, smells, and sound washed over him. As he stood on the street, which seemed to vibrate with heat and traffic and the strong sunlight, despite the early hour, he squinted and looked for the blue-and-white taxi. He caught sight of it a few cars away, parked in a loading zone with its hazard lights on — a shabby Skoda Octavia, with the number 103 in red tape on the rear window and a grey baggage rack on the roof. The motor was running, and from it came the characteristic knocking noise of a diesel engine. He opened the car door, tossed his bag in the back seat, and got in beside it. The car stank of cigarette smoke and sweet-smelling aftershave. On the floor was an issue of *The Jerusalem Post*. The man behind the wheel looked at him in the rear-view mirror, but didn't turn around. He was fat, his head was shaved, and he had centimetre-thick rolls of skin on the back of his neck. He was wearing a white shirt and black pants that were too tight on his broad thighs, which seemed to run out over the edge of the seat. His pale, sausage-like fingers grasped the gear stick and put it into first.

They made their way into the line of traffic, provoking angry honks. The man yelled something in Hebrew through the half-open window, revved the engine, and finally managed to squeeze between a large delivery truck and a yellow Ford with a faded bumper sticker depicting a German shepherd. Eric studied each movement that the fat man made. He looked at the altogether-too-feminine plastic watch that cut into the fat on his left wrist and sometimes disappeared beneath swollen skin; at the wedding ring on one of the sausages that drummed against the wheel; at his broad back; and at the sweat that moistened his head, like a shiny, transparent *kippa*. Was this the man who would kill him? How would it happen? Where would it take place?

He looked out the window: they were passing a crowded playground. Parents — exclusively women — were standing nearby or sitting on benches, and talking to each other or on phones. Children, happy and colourful, were climbing on jungle gyms, swinging on swings, digging in sandboxes, and running around and around the playground. A redheaded woman in black athletic clothes and jogging shoes, holding a water bottle in one hand, was crouching down and hugging a small boy who seemed to have hurt himself. The boy's hair was the same shade of red as his mother's. Eric wished that he, too, could rest in her arms. He wanted to have a good cry, feel the warmth of her breasts, and, above all, be absolved of responsibility. He wanted to stop being an adult.

'Radio?'

At first, he didn't realise that this was a question and that it was aimed at him. The voice was dull and rough. He straightened up and met the driver's eyes in the mirror.

'Excuse me?'

'Radio?'

'Uh … sure.'

The question bewildered him. Such unexpected banality.

The radio — a concept so integrated into the normal world that it didn't fit in here. But at least he had asked. That indicated something important about their relationship to each other. He wasn't a prisoner, and couldn't be treated any way they wished. Or maybe he *was* a prisoner, but the driver still wanted his permission to turn on the radio. This small detail caused him to relax a little bit. And if the question had been unexpected, that went double for the music that jangled out of the long-since-busted speakers. It was a message from another planet, or at least a different time: Michael Jackson's 'Man in the Mirror'. The sausages drummed against the steering wheel and the gear stick. The traffic became more and more sparse, and the car's speed increased. The playground disappeared and was replaced by grocery stores, bus stations, hotels, and schools. Downtown became suburbs. Michael Jackson's high voice begged for solidarity.

The taxi accelerated up an entrance ramp to a wide highway — Highway 4. Apartment buildings rushed by, so ugly that they made Sweden's Million Program buildings seem luxurious by comparison. The tall, dilapidated once-white concrete buildings with their small windows in long, even rows might as well have been prisons. Maybe that's just what they were. Here, as in every other slum that clung to the outskirts of a city, they were as inevitable as unwanted outgrowth from the urban flora. The highway, with its five wide lanes in each direction, wound slowly inland as the surroundings changed again. Here the houses were lower and farther apart. They drove past a large power plant, fields, palms, and goats, as the city turned into country. Michael Jackson was gone, too. The new song was one Eric didn't recognise: Jewish hard rock. The newspaper at his feet rustled, and he bent forward to pick it up. The entire front page, which was about the Mona virus and the prospects of finding an anti-virus, featured a large picture of Hassan Musawi, Hezbollah's top leader. Hezbollah had claimed responsibility for both the virus and the bombing in Tel Aviv.

It felt surreal to read this. Eric paged through the article, which ran across six pages. Hezbollah had demanded the release of a number of prisoners, as well as an armistice and a list of all imprisoned Palestinians. The demand that *The Jerusalem Post* found to be the most sensational was the recognition of the so-called green line, the border from 1967. Had there been any response from Israel's government? No. They had chosen not to comment. Eric himself was in the middle of this whole mess — in the middle of an enormous international conflict. He looked at the clock: it was twenty to eight. He leaned forward.

'Excuse me. Where are we going?'

The fat man turned his head and glanced at him briefly. He looked irritated, and answered in muddled, poor English.

'I drive taxi sixteen years. I find. You not worry.'

Eric tried again.

'You're driving very well, but I don't know where *I'm* going. Where are we headed!?'

As he spoke, the driver kept nodding as if to show that he understood, that he was listening. Then he laughed suddenly — a short and rasping sound that was the result of having inhaled thousands of cigarettes.

'You to Erez. Not worry. We there in time.'

Erez? He had never heard of the place. *In time*? So there was a specific time to make. Someone, whoever had ordered the taxi, maybe Samir Mustaf, had instructed the driver — who probably wasn't a murderer, but a completely ordinary taxi driver — to pick him up and drive him to Erez. Surely that was somewhere in Israel. Otherwise, a local Tel Aviv taxi probably wouldn't drive him there, right? What awaited him there? Surely Samir Mustaf couldn't be in Israel, could he? It wasn't impossible, but it was unlikely.

'What time are we supposed to be there?'

The man nodded. Then he fumbled around on the passenger seat without taking his eyes from the road. He rooted among empty chip bags, coffee cups, and old issues of *The Jerusalem Post* and *Haaretz*. Finally, he found a small notebook, glanced at it, and returned his eyes to the road.

'Erez eight o'clock.'

Eight. That was in less than twenty minutes' time. His fear returned. It had never truly disappeared, but during the conversation it had softened, dulled. Eric leaned back in the seat. Outside, the fields were empty, aside from occasional brick houses and farms that seemed deserted. Deserted and old. Dire Straits were playing a crackly 'The Sultans of Swing'. The man looked at him in the rear-view mirror.

'You meet someone or go over?'

Eric looked at him, bewildered.

'What?'

'You never know if they block off or not. If you can go or not.'

When he didn't answer, the driver quickly added, 'I sure it will be fine.' *What will be fine? Go over?* He felt like an idiot; he didn't understand a thing.

'What is Erez?' A red semi suddenly changed lanes, and the driver had to brake; he roared in Hebrew and honked furiously. They passed a sign for Ashdod. The man looked at him in the mirror again.

'Erez crossing. Gateway to Gaza.'

The world swung around him. His stomach burned. *Gaza. Oh, God.* He didn't know anything about Gaza, except what he'd seen on TV. That was enough. He looked around the back seat, as if he were searching for a way out. *What the fuck am I going to*

323

do? Call Rachel! He ignored the fact that he wasn't expected to call until he had made contact. They had to protect him. The Mossad had to take responsibility — they had put him into this trap. He tore open his bag and found his phone, fumbling with the buttons for a long time before he realised the unthinkable. He pressed the power button again and again. Finally, he sank down, powerless. His mobile phone was dead. It was no more useful than a rock or a stick. He wouldn't be able to call for help. No one would save him.

The driver looked at him in the mirror and nodded.

'Not worry. Almost there.' Eric sat totally still with his eyes fastened on the headrest of the passenger seat. Almost there.

They were careful to keep their distance from the Skoda with 103 taped on the back. There was no reason to get too close; the receiver in Larry Lavon's lap showed a strong signal, and on the digital map they could easily follow the blue dot as it slowly moved along Highway 4. Larry looked at Micha Begin, who kept his eyes on the taxi a hundred metres ahead of them.

'They are definitely on the way to Erez. Are they going into Gaza? But the crossing is closed to civilians, right?'

Micha nodded and slowed down so he wouldn't get too close.

'It's closed. Maybe they're just going to meet someone in Erez.'

Larry didn't say anything as he studied the dot blinking on the screen.

'They're going to Gaza. I'll contact Central and ask for permission to go in if that turns out to be necessary. Not that I understand how it would happen — the border is closed.'

Micha didn't answer. They passed a warning sign. It was time to slow down; the soldiers at the blockade did not appreciate fast-moving vehicles. The Skoda slowed down, too, and the distance between them decreased. Rusty cars stood abandoned along the road, and several people were on foot — illegal workers who were hoping to cross the border to get home. Large signs in Hebrew, English, and Arabic stated that the crossing was closed to all civilian traffic. The Skoda turned into the large parking lot before the first guard post. An Israeli tank stood at the entrance, and about thirty cars were parked in the lot. All of them had Gaza licence plates — cars that hadn't had time to make it over when the border was closed, and that now sat in the heat, waiting for a different future.

They stopped at the edge of the parking lot and turned off the engine. Along the road, up by the border, concrete barricades lay in uneven rows like giant Lego blocks. At the end of the road, an enormous door of blue steel rose up. This was the gateway to Gaza. Both sides of the steel structure were edged by concrete and barbed wire, and a grey watchtower rose out of the tangle of fences like a stripped tree trunk emerging out of brushy weeds. The Skoda stopped not far from a white van at the far end of the parking lot. Micha leaned forward over the steering wheel, and squinted at the taxi.

'What are they doing?'

Larry put the receiver down on the floor. The blue dot was now standing still on the screen. He straightened up and followed Micha's gaze over the shimmering asphalt. Two men got out of the car. One was fat, and the other, thin — the driver and Eric Söderqvist. The fat man walked over to the van while Söderqvist stayed by the car with a black bag in his hand. Micha repeated his question.

'What are they doing?'

There was a faint odour of burned rubber in the air. The reddish-brown sand puffed up as dust as soon as he moved, and there was a slight breeze. Eric looked over at the white van where his driver stood talking to someone he couldn't see. Then he let his eyes wander along the tall fence, the tightly wound barbed wire, and the black girders that reinforced the structure every three metres. The next row of barbed wire and girders began a few metres inside the gate. The customs station itself looked more like a large bunker of heavy concrete, and it had small, barred window openings. He looked at the enormous blue-steel gate; it must have been five metres high and eight metres wide. Hopefully, he wasn't going into Gaza; it didn't even seem like a possibility. Maybe he would get to stay in Israel after all. His throat was dry and his stomach was empty. A jarring screech cut through the heat of the sun, and a door at the lower edge of the gate opened. Two Israeli soldiers came out and closed the door behind them with a dull bang. About twenty people in greyish-brown rags, many of them barefoot, sat a few metres to the right. One of them held up a sign, but he couldn't see what it said.

'Hey, mister!' The fat driver waved.

Eric started to walk over to him. Things crunched at his feet, and an empty beer can clinked when he kicked it with his foot. A man stood beside the van, putting a large white sign on it. It said 'Press' in black letters. All of the windows were tinted so it was impossible to look in. As Eric approached the taxi driver, a man leaned out through the window on the driver's side of the van. He had curly, brown hair, and was wearing small, round glasses and a white T-shirt.

'Söderqvist?'

'That's me.'

'*Multo bene.*'

The man extended a hand.

'Gino Lugio.'

Eric shook the man's hand and then just stood there, unsure of what he should do. The man who had fastened the sign to the van pulled open the side door and climbed in. Gino nodded at Eric.

'*Dai*, you hop in, too. We have to get going.'

Eric grabbed the handle above the door and climbed in. It must have been fifty degrees in there. There were three casually dressed Europeans in the van: one woman and two men. In the back was a stack of silver-steel cases, and coils of black cable were crammed in between the cases and the wall. The woman was writing in a notebook, and the men were reading together out of a wrinkled issue of *Corriere della Serra*. Before Eric had time to sit down, the engine started, and the door closed behind him. He sank down onto a seat beside the woman.

Instead of driving off, Gino stood up and came over to him. He crouched, swaying a bit until he got his balance. He smelled like smoke and coffee. His brown curls fell across his face, making him look younger than he must have been. He spoke English well, but with an unmistakeable Italian accent.

'Mr Söderqvist, we know you're a Swedish doctor who wants to help in Gaza. We think that's great. There are a lot of people suffering over there. But the Israeli authorities won't let any civilians cross the border, no matter how noble their mission might be. So you can come with us, but you have to do some acting. *Capice?*'

Eric tried to collect his thoughts. His mind was going in too many directions at once. They were Italian. It said 'Press' on the van. The boxes and cables in the back suggested a TV team. *Doctor* Söderqvist? Sure, he was a doctor, but not a medical doctor. Were these people working with the terrorists? He looked at the woman beside him; she had stopped writing, and looked back at him. She seemed worn out — like a person who had seen and experienced too much. Maybe the TV thing was just a cover. But they didn't seem like extremists; they seemed like journalists. Like Jens. He looked at Gino, who was crouched in front of him, swaying.

'Who are you?'

The man smiled and threw his hands out theatrically.

'We are the eyes of Italy. The Rai Uno action team.'

He laughed, but the others remained silent. The men didn't even look up from the paper they were reading. There was a bag of purple sweets between them on the seat, which they kept dipping into.

The woman explained. 'The news on Italy's biggest TV channel.'

Gino went on: 'We've got the opportunity to do a much-coveted interview in Gaza City. And therefore we have promised some ... friends ... to bring you into the country. They're going to meet up with you about ten kilometres from the border. But first we have to make it through the border station. Erez closed completely a few weeks ago. In the past few days, since the attack in Tel Aviv, practically no one has gotten in. We have special permission and good contacts in the local police, but nothing is certain.'

'And what do I have to do?'

'Nothing. With any luck, you won't have to talk. You're a sound technician. We had to leave the real technician at home in order to bring you, because our visa is only good for the exact number of members as named. We'll have to hope that the border guards don't speak Italian. Just sit there and don't speak, and try to look like you're from Milan.'

He handed over a red passport with gold text: *Unione Europea Repubblica Italiana. Passaporto*. Eric took it and studied the photograph. It was of a man with coarse features — a flat forehead, bushy eyebrows, and a wide nose. His name was Enrique Vettese, and he didn't bear much resemblance to Eric. It

seemed totally unrealistic that he was meant to pass as the man in the picture. Impossible. He gave Gino a sceptical look.

'Will they really fall for this? We're talking about the Israeli border police here.'

'Maybe not. In that case, we're all out of luck. We'll have to pray to the Madonna that everything goes well. Maybe the guard is tired, or in love, or about to get sick.'

He gave a quick smile and climbed back into the driver's seat. Then he called out, without turning around, 'Don't forget to give back the passport when you leave us. Enrique won't be happy if you keep it. He's already mad that he didn't get to come along to Gaza.'

He put the van into first gear with a pop, and it gave a lurch and started rolling. They turned around and left the parking lot in the direction of the blue-steel gate. The woman beside him had returned to her notebook. One of the men across from him commented on something in the newspaper, and the other laughed. So he was going to Gaza — the worst possible outcome. Either that, or they would get stuck at customs. He realised that he was hoping to be found out, hoping that the guards would see through the lies, discover his fake passport, and stop them. There would be a lot of bureaucracy, and then they would be refused entry — and be saved.

The van stopped. Now they were just outside the gate, which rose many metres above them. It didn't look like it could be opened, not even if someone really wanted to. It was too heavy, too large, too absolute. A young Israeli guard with a bored expression came up to Gino, and they spoke in English with low voices. When Eric looked at the blue-painted steel that filled the windshield, he saw the remains of some graffiti. He tried to follow the faint lines, but he soon lost them. Someone had graffitied the gate, and the soldiers had scrubbed it clean. But what did it matter if there was graffiti here? On this manifestation of complete failure? Spray paint on a gigantic block of iron that only kept people out or in, that closed off all hope? And who had decided that the gate should be blue? Was it less threatening that way? A more natural part of the scenery? Could an eight-metre-wide steel wall be a natural part of anything?

He became conscious of a discussion going on between Gino and the soldier. There was something about their voices that made him look up.

'Stay here.'

The soldier left them and walked quickly over to the customs station forty metres away. He went by the motley group with their signs. Gino turned around and looked at Eric.

'There's some problem. They weren't informed that we were coming. We have our visa, but he still doesn't want to let us in.'

'What do we do now?'

'Wait.'

His clothes were sticking to his body, and the bus smelled like sweat, perfume, and old, mouldy fabric. Eric tried to find the most comfortable position possible on the hard seat. He sneaked a look at the woman. She was wearing jeans, a burgundy blouse, and tennis shoes. She was thin — too thin. Her ankles looked like they might break at any moment, and her fingers were long and knobby, like a skeleton's, with no nail polish. She noticed him looking at her, and looked up from her notebook. He hurried to say something, anything.

'What are you writing?'

She studied her notes.

'Questions. In just a few hours I'm going to interview Nizar Aziz.'

The way she said the name implied that he should know who that was, which he didn't.

'And what is he up to these days?'

She was startled by his ignorance, but she collected herself.

'He's still the leader of Hamas's military. There's been a rumour that he's dead, but now I'm going to meet him.'

'Well, that's fantastic. Congratulations.'

'Yes, it really is. Big thanks to you.'

She crossed something out in her notebook. He frowned.

'Why are you thanking me?'

'We got the interview thanks to you. We're smuggling over a famous Swedish ophthalmologist, and in return we get a half-hour interview with Nizar Aziz.'

Eric tried to make the connection. He knew that Samir Mustaf was part of the Lebanese Hezbollah. But where did Hamas fit in? Why would Hamas offer an interview in exchange for a Swedish professor? Or a Swedish doctor, if that was who they believed he was?

'How is the relationship between Hamas and Hezbollah?'

'It's so-so. There have been times when they've co-operated, but the relationship has always come crashing down. Each accuses the other of being too weak, too friendly to Israel, too populist, too right-wing, too left-wing.'

A distant rumble, which he first thought was thunder, quickly became more intense, and was on top of them with a boom so loud that the van vibrated. Then the roar faded and died out. The woman looked unconcerned.

'Israeli F-16s.'

She bent forward and stuck her notebook into an army-green bag on the floor. Then she looked out the window.

'This might take a long time. Normally, Erez is a crossing for pedestrians. Palestinians with visas used to be able to cross by car; but starting a few years ago, everyone had to walk. They leave their cars on the other side of the gate, knowing that they'll be bashed in or stolen. What choice do they have? People say Hamas wrecks the cars. They don't like it when citizens of Gaza enter Israel.'

'So what makes them go?'

'Many of them lived on this side until Israel was created. I'm sure you saw all the deserted brick houses on the way here — residences with overgrown gardens and broken windows. Those are the former homes of the Palestinians. Some of them still have relatives in Israel. Others work in construction, in the harbours, or on plantations. But that was before. Now they're no longer allowed out of their prison.'

'Prison?'

'Gaza is the world's largest open-air prison. One-and-a-half million prisoners live there. There are only two cities, but there are eight refugee camps. We're doing what we can to show the world what's going on, but the world would rather watch colourful game shows. It's a losing battle.'

'But you haven't given up?'

She smacked her thigh. 'Never. As Gino said, we're the Rai Uno action team. Always ready to go.'

One of the men put up his hand for a high five, and the woman leaned forward and hit it with a crack. Suddenly, the young soldier was back, this time along with an older officer. The officer stopped and spoke quietly with Gino through the window while the younger soldier went to the side of the van and pulled the door open.

'Out! Everyone out!'

The soldier's voice was aggressive. They tumbled out, grimacing in the bright sunlight, and stretched their stiff joints. The woman and Gino conversed in a subdued tone. The two men who had been sitting across from Eric seemed to be discussing their baggage. If he was reading their body language correctly, one wanted to take out the cases of equipment while the other preferred that they remain in the van. The officer left them and disappeared back toward the customs station. The soldier collected their passports and also received a bundle of papers from Gino. Just as he was about to leave, he stopped and turned to them, opened each passport, studied each photograph, and looked for its respective owner. Eric felt a lump in his throat. What if the Mossad hadn't informed them that he was under their protection? He would never be able to trick the Israeli border police. Was Rachel somewhere in the shadows, protecting him? It didn't seem very likely. Did he even want to get through? Was it better to be revealed? The soldier looked at him, at the passport, and back at him. Then he muttered something, and took the passport aside.

'Wait here.'

The soldier walked quickly across the concrete pavement. The woman placed a hand on Eric's shoulder.

'*Calma*. Relax. Your shoulders are up to your ears, and your face is as red as a tomato. Take it easy.'

'It's all gone to hell. Didn't you see what happened?'

'We'll have to wait and see. Maybe we'll get through anyway. Maybe you'll be left behind. Maybe we'll all be left behind. That would be a damn shame. I'm really looking forward to the meeting with Nizar Aziz. But let's not give up.'

Gino walked up to them with a wild look in his eyes. He had the earpiece of his glasses in his mouth, and seemed to be about to eat it up.

'*Cazzo!*'

The woman placed a hand on his shoulder. 'Ginito. You need to calm down, too. What can we do? We have to deal with shit as it happens.'

There was no shade where they stood, and the heat seemed

to come as much from inside his body as from outside, like in a microwave oven. Eric was insanely thirsty. He looked at the woman beseechingly.

'Do you have anything to drink?'

She nodded and climbed into the van, rooted around, and came back with a plastic bottle of Neviot.

He thankfully took the bottle, fumbled with the cap, and took a big gulp. The water tasted like old plastic, but it quenched his thirst. He held the bottle out to her, and she took a sip and handed it on to Gino, who was nervous and angry by turns. Eric studied the enormous gate again.

'Why is it so tall?'

She followed his gaze.

'To protect it from car bombs. It wasn't always like this. Before, it was just a kind of frame around the entrance. The gate was put up after the unrest during the past year, and the decision to close the border to civilian traffic.'

Eric's eyes moved along the concrete and barbed wire to the rows of empty, dusty cars, the trash blowing in the wind, and the gathering of people at the other end of the gate. He didn't see any children, but several of them seemed to be teenagers. They all shared the same empty, expressionless gazes as they sat together on the ground, among bags of plastic and cloth. Several of them weren't wearing shoes. Against the wall behind them was a sign in red Arabic script. He turned to the Italians.

'Do you have more water?'

The woman gestured at the bottle.

'Here. There's some left.'

'No, I mean for them.'

Gino shook his head.

'We only have one case, and we'll need it whether we get through or not.' He looked at his colleagues, adding, 'And if we

334

want to have any chance of getting through, we absolutely can't be seen with them.' Eric looked at him doubtfully.

'Them? Come on. You have a whole case of water; they have nothing.'

The man closest to the woman said something to her in Italian. She nodded and ducked into the car. When she came back, she had three bottles of Neviot in her arms. She gave them to Eric.

'You want to do it?'

He took them and was just about to go when the man placed his bag of sweets on the bottles. Gino shook his head and kept mumbling curses. Eric couldn't see any soldiers, but there were several security cameras on the gate. He walked purposefully over to the group of Palestinians. There were many more than he'd thought at first; there must have been at least thirty. And now he saw that there were children there, too, including at least one little boy. The boy was the first to react. He tugged at his mother's arm and pointed. She seemed to be sick, or maybe she was just detached. She kept looking down at the ground. One of the men stood up. He was a large man of about Eric's age.

'*Esh beddak?*'

His voice was threatening. Eric stopped and held out the bottles of water. The bag of sweets fell to the ground. The man made eye contact. Eric smiled, trying to show that the water was for them.

'Please.'

The man swallowed and nodded. He threw a hasty glance at the woman, and then took the bottles. Eric bent down, picked up the bag of sweets, and held it out to the little boy. The boy hesitated. The man shouted something, and the boy flew forward and snatched the sweets. The woman, who was thin and dark-skinned, with narrow, cracked lips and yellowed eyes, reached out to Eric.

'*Assalamu alaikum. Shukran. Shukran.*'

Without meaning to, he backed away. Something about her scared him. He wanted to get away. There was an odour about the group that made him feel ill. The man raised both his hands.

'*Shukran. Shukran.*'

Eric gave a forced smile, turned around, and started walking quickly back to the Italians. His pulse throbbed in his head, and he had to lean against the scorching metal of the van. Was this the most heroic and unselfish thing he'd ever done? He had risked the possibility of getting into Gaza — all to give those people a little warm water. He caught sight of a purple sweet on the ground. He bent down, picked it up, and unpeeled the rustling paper. It tasted like sugar with grape flavouring. He sneaked a look at the Palestinians. Was he sharing the experience of a sugary grape taste with the little boy right now? He was filled with a peculiar sense of satisfaction. He let the sun burn his face as he sucked on the juice from the sweet.

'Here they come again.'

Gino pointed at the customs station. The officer and the soldier were on their way toward them. The woman was whispering quietly.

'*Il momento della verità.*' — 'The moment of truth.'

Eric noticed that they hadn't brought the passports. The younger soldier got into the driver's seat of the van and stuck his hand out of the window expectantly.

'Keys.'

Gino rolled his eyes and looked at the others in desperation.

'What the fuck. Not the van.'

The officer held up his hands.

'Calm down. Everything is in order. You may come through. But Weizman is driving the car to our inspection garage. You have to walk through the customs station anyway. Follow me.'

Without further ado, he turned around and walked back the same way he'd come. Gino stood as if petrified, but when the guard honked the horn he quickly got out the keys. The woman thumped Eric on the back.

'There you go. The Madonna likes you. Now an endless number of security checks, long concrete corridors, and thousands of questions await us. If we're lucky, we'll be in Gaza in about an hour.'

Stockholm, Sweden

Paul Clinton had never been to Sweden before. He'd been to Norway, Finland, and Denmark, but never Sweden. The sun was shining, and the fields along the highway from the airport were fertile and green. He saw horses, and in one field something that looked like small deer. Michael Yates was dozing with his head against the car window. They had been supposed to land at the more centrally located Bromma airport, but it had been closed when the control tower's computers were infected with the virus. They had ended up at Arlanda, just over thirty kilometres north of Stockholm.

The taxi passed a nearly-empty golf course. He tried to remember the last time he'd played. It was before his heart attack — over five years ago. Damn. He looked away from the course, instead going through the inbox on his phone. There were eighty-four unread messages in it. The flight from Tel Aviv had only taken a bit more than five hours. How the hell could a person end up with eighty-four emails in just five hours? Just then, a short email from David Yassur caught his attention:

He looked out the window again; they were just passing a McDonald's drive-through. It looked like home. What was going on with Rachel? She seemed to be a hardy girl. And Ben Shavit? He was weak. He was about to give in to Hezbollah's demands. Shouldn't they inform Shavit that they had gotten a break? That they might be about to find the terrorists? That would totally change the playing field, and give him a shot in the arm. Speaking of which, how were things going for Eric Söderqvist? He scrolled through the emails and found a status report on Eric. He had arrived in Erez and was on his way into Gaza. That was probably a good thing. Gaza was a mess, but it was a mess they were relatively familiar with — except for all the damn rat tunnels, of course. It was definitely time to give Ben Shavit some good news. He finished an answer to David Yassur just as the taxi driver turned around.

'Do you want to go to the hotel first? The other way around would be better.'

Paul leaned forward and looked briefly at the driver's ID card. Andre Bajic. Must be of Serbian or Croatian origin.

'Excuse me?'

'You said you wanted to go to hotel first. Then to hospital. But hospital is now.'

He saw the sign up ahead and to the right. Karolinska Hospital. He thought quickly.

'Let me off here, and drive my colleague and the bags to the hotel. That will be better. Thanks.'

The driver nodded. His powerful forearms were full of tattoos, and an ugly scar ran across his right wrist. This part of the world had had its wars, too. The taxi turned in at the hospital's main entrance, and Paul hopped out with just his jacket under his arm. Michael wouldn't have a clue when he woke up, but what the hell. He was trained to expect the unexpected. On his way to the reception desk, he thought about what he should say — probably not that the FBI suspected Hanna Söderqvist of having been infected with a biological weapon. A flower delivery person would be a good disguise, except he didn't have any flowers. What were the rules for hospital visits in Sweden? Could he pass as a relative?

When the woman at the reception desk gave him a tired smile, he went with the family-member option. After she searched in the computer, he was directed toward the far elevators. He was a distant relative who had come all the way from the US to see how dear, sweet Hanna was doing. Ten minutes later, he was putting on shoe protectors, rubbing clear gel on his hands, and stepping into unit I62. According to the receptionist, Hanna had just been moved to a closed unit. Paul wanted to speak with the attending physician, but he was unavailable. A cute nurse with a blonde ponytail explained that Hanna Söderqvist was in a single room with an airlock, something that was only used for patients who might be carrying an airborne infection. The nurse also told him that Hanna's sister was usually there with her. And Jens, of course. Maybe he ought to have known who Jens was, since he was supposed to be a relative, but he asked anyway.

She laughed.

'Jens has become part of the unit. He's a close friend of Hanna's, and takes such good care of her, now that her husband is gone. He actually takes care of all of us up here — buys us treats and flowers. Unfortunately, we're not allowed to have flowers in this unit, but he keeps buying them anyway. And the other night he brought along wine and cheese. A fantastic guy. Big heart.'

While she was speaking, she made notes on a form that was hanging beside the door to the office. The unit was quiet. A red light was blinking at the far end of the corridor; otherwise, everything was still. It smelled like disinfectant and coffee. The nurse secured the pen beside the form, ran her hands down her jacket a few times, as though to brush off dirt, and then studied him up and down.

'It's not actually visiting hours right now, but since it's quiet and you've come so far, we can make an exception.'

She started down the corridor, and he followed her closely.

'Where is her husband?'

They stopped outside room 115.

'Apparently, he's out of the country. We hope he'll come home soon. That would probably be good for her.'

'How is she?'

She looked at him and bit her lip.

'You'll have to ask the doctor, but I think it's very serious. We're having trouble coming up with a diagnosis. It's possible she'll be moved to Huddinge's isolation clinic.'

She opened the door. Inside was a small space and another door — an airlock. There was a sink, and hangers for yellow protective gowns made of thin paper. The nurse put her hand into a silver container and took out facemasks with small, blue plastic filters, and thin rubber gloves. She handed them to him, and as he put them on she opened the other door and nodded toward the windows.

'You can sit on the chair over there. We ask that you avoid touching her. Like I said, there's a potential risk of infection. Don't take off your mask. When you've finished, wait for me in the anteroom. You may not move around the unit after you've been in here. I'll come in and help you with your decontamination.'

He nodded and went in, and the door slid shut behind him. He adjusted his mask and looked around. The room was large for just one patient. A lone bed stood by the window, surrounded by machines. A thin body was outlined under the sheet, the face hidden by the screens of the respirator and two oxygen tank, and the room was filled with the smell of freshly washed sheets. The rhythmic sound of the artificial lungs was far too familiar to him — he had visited many friends and enemies in a similar condition. A carafe of water and a glass stood beside the bed. At first, he stood by the foot of the bed and studied her. She was more beautiful in real life than in photographs, despite all of this. Someone had washed and brushed her hair, but it looked dull. Her skin was pale, and her cheeks were sunken. He walked cautiously around the bed and stood alongside it. Her thin arm was exposed, and there was an IV line in it. He leaned over her face. It was strange. It looked as if she might wake up at any moment — she just appeared to be dozing lightly. He stood still for a long time, studying her.

How would he get her to Oslo? How do you make off with a seriously ill Swedish citizen? Plan A was to take a chance that the Swedish authorities would be willing to co-operate, but he had the feeling that this crap would get tied up in the local bureaucracy. It was notorious, worse than in Russia. The bureau had had problems with the Swedes before. He contemplated coming back later the same evening with Michael and just taking her — putting her in a wheelchair and going right out the door. That was Plan B. He carefully ran his gloved fingertips along her face, from her forehead along the bridge of her nose, around her lips and her chin. He let his hand rest on her throat. Then he leaned even closer to her and whispered, hardly audible through the mask. 'I have greetings from Eric. He misses you.' Perhaps her eyelids twitched. Or perhaps it was just his imagination.

Gaza, Erez

The border facility at Erez had been built to handle twenty-five thousand people per day, but since no one was allowed to cross through anymore, the hallways were empty and the waiting rooms deserted. For the others on the TV team, each security check they made it through was a victory, another step toward their goal. But Eric's courage sank each time he got closer to Gaza.

After one hour and forty minutes, they were standing on the other side of the facility, waiting for a car they all hoped would show up. All but Eric — he hoped that it would be confiscated. There were no other people in sight.

Twenty minutes later, a siren sounded, and the iron gate opened with a faint clatter. The group cheered as the white van showed up. The soldier driving it hopped out and nodded curtly to them before he went back into the customs station. They climbed back into the bus. Eric placed the black bag on his lap and looked out the window. The engine was already running, and he heard the vehicle's characteristic bang as it was put into first gear. The van rolled down a narrow concrete ramp and out onto a deserted road. Cultivated fields rolled along the left side, and dry, cracked fields of mud spread as far as he could see on the other side. Gino looked at Eric in the rear-view mirror.

'Dr Söderqvist, we ought to see your friends soon. They were going to meet us around here somewhere. Keep your eyes peeled.'

Eric fought back the panic. The woman smiled at him.

'That was nice, what you did.'

He looked at her, bewildered.

'What did I do?'

'Back there — with the bottles of water.'

He smiled weakly.

'Thanks.'

Gino slowed down.

'Here you are. This is your last stop, *amico*.'

Eric searched along the grey road, and caught sight of a lone man about a hundred metres ahead, dressed completely in black. As the bus approached, he saw that the man's face was covered with fabric, too. He held an automatic weapon in his right hand. Gino chuckled.

'With friends like that, you don't need enemies.'

His bright tone echoed emptily in the van. Eric took his bag in one hand and got up just as the van stopped.

'And, doctor, don't forget the passport.'

He gave a short nod and handed the red document to the woman. She took it and looked into his eyes.

'Is everything okay?'

He forced a smile.

'Everything is okay. Good luck with your interview. I hope it's worth all the trouble.'

She didn't return his smile.

'Take care of yourself. *In bocca al lupo*.'

He didn't bother to ask what that meant. He opened the door and stepped out into the oppressive heat. A strong wind carried the scent of the sea, which he instantly wished he could see. As soon as he closed the door, he heard the bang of the gear stick, and the van sped off along the dusty road. After a minute or two, it was out of sight. He turned toward the man in black, and nodded. The man was shorter than he was, but his shoulders were broad. The barrel of the weapon was aimed at Eric's chest. The man pointed at the bag.

'*Iftah!* Open!' Eric nodded, sank to his knees, and opened the bag. The man waved Eric back with the weapon. He backed up slowly. The man dug through the bag without putting down the gun, then he stood up and gestured to Eric that he should put his hands on his head. He did as he was told, and the man patted him firmly across the back, chest, and thighs. There was a powerful smell of tobacco and spices that Eric couldn't identify on the man. Then he took a step back and nodded at the bag. Eric cautiously picked it up and stood there, waiting for his next order. The man looked around, apparently waiting for something or someone to appear on the deserted road. The wind tugged at his black clothes, and he gestured with his weapon toward the field on the side of the road. *Am I going to die here? In the middle of a dry mud flat in Gaza?* Eric didn't really feel fear — just resignation. He walked across the dry, cracked earth, away from the road. A plastic bag with a faded red logo was stuck in a spiny, brown bush, crinkling in the breeze. He considered just putting down the bag and sitting in the gravel. What did it matter? He might as well get it over with.

'*Waqef!*'

The word startled him. He was out of breath; his clothes were wet with sweat. He turned around and saw that the man was on his knees. At first, Eric thought he was praying; he had put down his weapon. But then he noticed that the man was searching through the low bushes with his hands. His body tensed, and as he got up he brought a large part of the bush with him. He'd revealed a hatch — a thick, steel hatch door that covered a half-metre-wide hole in the ground. The man backed away from the hatch, picked up his weapon, and pointed. There was no misinterpreting the order. The man looked around him all the while, as if he were worried that someone would see them. Eric approached the opening. A ladder led down into the darkness. He put one strap of the bag across his shoulder and climbed onto the first step, and then looked at the man one last time and started to climb down. He had read about these — the smuggling tunnels. The Gaza Strip was full of them.

Larry Lavon closed his eyes for a long time and tried to gather his strength. The signal was gone. He didn't understand how this was possible. Eric Söderqvist had three transmitters on him, and Gaza had hardly any mobile-phone traffic to interfere with the signal. The terrain was level, so there was nothing to act as a reflector or obstruction. Their mistake had been in not following them by car. It was his own decision; he couldn't pin it on someone else. But a tag-along car on the deserted roads of Gaza would have been too easy to discover, and it would have jeopardised the whole project and possibly scared away the target. He had been counting on a good signal and assuming that they would quickly pick it up out of thin air. He had kept the TV team in Erez until he'd gotten the helicopter there. As soon as it was in place, he had told border security to let Eric Söderqvist and the TV team pass. He had waited exactly fifteen minutes before he sent in the helicopter. Maybe that was his mistake — waiting too long. A lot could happen in fifteen minutes, in nine hundred seconds. And yet it was just flat land; there were no cities or villages that Söderqvist could have reached in that short amount of time. All he knew was that, when the helicopter found the van, the signal was no longer on board. The team on the ground that stopped the van seven minutes later learned that one of the passengers, Dr Eric Söderqvist, had been picked up by a lone man just a few kilometres from the border. The team had searched the entire area, from the ground and from the air. Nothing. Now Larry Lavon was leaning against the wall of the officers' room at Erez border control, smoking a cigarette and squinting at the Gaza side. How the hell could he report this to command in Tel Aviv? He spat in the gravel. He was truly fucked.

Near Khan Younis, Gaza

It was chilly in the tunnel. His clothes, which had been wet with sweat, felt icy now, and Eric was so cold he was shaking. It was hard to walk, and he kept tripping. The passage was uneven and narrow; the ground was mud and gravel. The only light came from the man's flashlight, and time and again it disappeared, causing Eric to bump into rocks and parts of the wall that jutted out. Not a word had been uttered in over forty minutes. His back and neck ached from stooping, and the bag was heavy and unwieldy. Twice he had stepped on something alive, or maybe previously alive — probably rats — and the air stank of decay.

Suddenly, he walked straight into an earthen wall. The collision was so unexpected that he gave a shout. Behind him, the man shone the light on the walls around them and found another ladder — this time, a regular painter's ladder that was leaning against the wall. The man knocked on the ladder with the flashlight and moved his head to indicate that they were going up it. With stiff joints and frozen fingers, Eric started to climb. When he came to the top of the ladder, he could feel that the ceiling consisted of a loose slab of wood. He pushed up. The slab fell away, letting in a burst of sunlight that blinded him. He closed his eyes instinctively and then opened them slowly, took a deep breath, and heaved himself up.

He was standing behind a low shed. Two of the walls were made of concrete, but the other two were made of plywood; the roof was made of hung fabric. The building occupied no more than perhaps twenty square metres. The air was still very warm, and he was grateful for the sun as it sucked the chill from his body. The building was at the edge of a large field, with a small gravel road alongside it. He could see grazing sheep, and green and purple thistles; further off, tall palm trees were swaying. The

346

wind was dry. The scent of the sea was gone.

The black-clad man boosted himself out of the hole with the automatic weapon on his back. This was the first time in almost an hour that Eric had seen his guide — or perhaps 'guard' was a better word. His dark clothes were soiled with mud and dirt, and the scarf that covered his face had come loose at one side, revealing thick, black hair. The man moved one of the pieces of plywood aside and went into the building. Eric waited outside. After about a minute, the man returned with a cloak made of black fabric. Eric struggled to pull it over his head, finding it too small and tight, and smelling of mud. The man gestured with his hand that they should go around the building. Eric took his bag and started walking. As they came around the corner, the man pointed at two green bikes that were leaning against the wall. Eric took one of the rickety bikes, secured his bag on the luggage carrier, and got on. The man did the same, and they rolled off down the gravel road. The sheep paid them no attention, even though they were riding very close to them. It was a strange feeling suddenly to be sitting on a bike amid tall palms and grazing sheep. Each time he rode over an uneven spot, the bell dinged — a familiar and friendly sound. There was too little air in the tyres, which made bicycling on the gravel slow going. The tight black cloak didn't help, but now they looked like two local farmers — at least from a distance. The disguise was simple but effective.

His watch indicated that it was quarter past four in the afternoon. It had been more than nine hours since he had left the library in Tel Aviv. After a while, the road split in two, and he threw a questioning glance at the man, who nodded toward the left. They continued across dry fields, and their surroundings become more and more undulating, with hills that rose like large blisters out of the dry ground. Eric was thirsty, but he chose to keep pedalling. His thigh muscles were sore; it had been many years since he'd biked. They passed a large tractor that was halfway down the ditch, its giant, useless tyres looking like empty eyes on the sides of a wrinkled and rusty head. Then they biked up such a steep hill that Eric had to stand up on the pedals to make it. When they got to the top, the man shouted '*Waqef!*' from behind him.

He stopped, put a foot on the ground, and leaned over the handlebars, out of breath. The man studied the road, which sloped down the hill and wound off across yet another dry field. Eric followed his gaze and tried to figure out what he was looking at. Far out on the field was an old ruin. Alongside the collapsed building, he could make out a few pieces of white plastic furniture — a table and three chairs. One of the chairs had tipped over, surely felled by the same strong wind that was causing the little bell on his bike to ding. They stood on top of the hill for a long time, and the man continued to stare across the field. Finally, he signalled that they should keep going. They rolled down the hill with crunching tyres and jingling bells, and went across the bumpy field in the direction of the ruin. From a distance, the wall looked like it was covered in brown freckles.

Another black-clad man moved out of the shadows by the house. He, too, was masked and carrying an automatic weapon. Eric pedalled toward the man, who stood waiting for them with a wide stance and a straight back. He was taller than the others. By now, Eric was so thirsty that he felt he would faint. He had tried to alternately collect saliva in his mouth and swallow it, to at least simulate some sort of liquid. Now, even that well was dry, and all his saliva was gone. They stopped at the ruin. The dotted pattern wasn't freckles; it was made up of large bullet holes. The whole wall was full of them — thousands of them, in different shapes and sizes.

The two men in black each lifted a bike over the shot-up stone wall and hid them in the shadows behind it. They were speaking Arabic in low voices. A car went by, far off on the horizon, on a road that Eric couldn't see. The men grew silent, and watched the car as it slowly crept across the landscape, followed closely by a large cloud of dust. After a while, the car disappeared from sight, and the sound died out. The taller man quickly walked a few metres out into the field, bent down, and lifted another hatch door from the ground. Unlike the last one, electric light flooded out of the small entrance. It was starting to get dark, which made the glow from the hole seem even stronger. They both turned to him. He nodded, went over to the hole, pulled his bag over his shoulder, and stepped onto the first rung of the ladder. The ladder was solid; it was made of bent rebar set into rough concrete.

Once he was down, he found himself in a surprisingly large room lit by bare light bulbs hanging from the ceiling. The room was empty, except for a pile of jackets and dirty boots, and he stepped onto the floor just as the door above him closed with a bang. He saw that the room wasn't really a room; it was more like a widened part of a long tunnel, large enough to drive a car in. The tunnel went in both directions, and was lit by more light bulbs at regular intervals. He thought he could hear music — maybe an Arabic song — somewhere far off. Should he keep standing here? Wait for someone? Had he reached his goal? He took a few steps in one direction, and strained to see in the darkness.

'The creator of Mind Surf. I'm honoured.'

The voice was so unexpected — and in American English, to boot, with no accent whatsoever — that Eric dropped his bag. He took a deep breath and turned around. The man was standing just a few metres behind him. He was barefoot on the bare concrete, and was wearing brown pants and a grey sweatshirt. His clothes were loose, and he seemed to be very thin. A pair of white earbud wires wound up out of his pants pocket and ended around his neck. Eric recognised him from the photograph. So this was the end of his journey — the goal he had given himself in the bathtub on Banérgatan. The man stood still, studying him with a neutral expression. Was it obvious that Eric was close to tears? He swallowed, and stuck out his hand; to his alarm, he realised it was trembling. The man took it and squeezed it gently.

'Welcome, Eric Söderqvist.'

'Salah ad-Din.'

The man smiled faintly.

'My name is Samir.'

They stood across from each other for a long time without saying anything. The air was loaded, as if they were two boxers studying each other before the first round. Eric looked around.

'Where are we?'

'In a transport tunnel. An important distribution channel, until the Israelis bombed it. Nowadays, it's not good for much. For us, it's a temporary home. Come on, let's sit down — you must be tired.'

He started toward the tunnel on the right-hand side, and Eric hurried after him. His steps echoed through the passage. Samir spoke without turning around: 'I was expecting you earlier. Was the journey long?'

'It took a while at Erez.'

Samir nodded thoughtfully.

'It's not easy to get into Gaza. Or out.' Eric thought of the fake passport.

'It's a miracle I got through.' Samir stopped and looked at him, searching for something in his gaze.

'A miracle? Yes, I suppose that's the right word. Truly a miracle.' Perhaps he was being sarcastic. He started walking again, and Eric followed him. The air smelled sweet, from some sort of incense.

'How many of you are there here?'

'Usually, five of us, if I count the two Palestinians out there. They're not really part of our group — they're brothers from Hamas who are helping us for the time being.'

'Usually?'

'One of us has gone for a few days. Our leader.'

'When will he be back?'

'Tonight, tomorrow, in a week. Only Allah knows.'

They arrived in another section where the tunnel widened into a chamber, this time with a row of openings that seemed to lead to smaller side rooms or storage areas. Blankets and cushions covered part of the floor. Two drinking glasses and a small grey teapot stood next to the pillows. Samir gestured with his hand.

'Sit down. As I'm sure you understand, I have many questions.'

Eric sank down onto the cushions. When he looked into the man's dark eyes, he was struck by a dizzying sense of unreality. He was sitting with Hezbollah in a smuggling tunnel under Gaza, across from Samir Mustaf, the most wanted man in the world — the creator of Mona.

To an untrained ear, the propeller sounded like any aeroplane at all. But the sound was brighter, at a higher frequency. The unmanned Heron 1 plane swept over the dark fields of Gaza at an altitude of three hundred metres and a speed of two hundred kilometres per hour. With a length of eight-and-a-half metres and a wingspan of just over sixteen metres, the Heron was one of the Israeli Air Force's largest drones. This model was equipped for scouting and searching, with infra-red video, synthetic aperture radar, MPR systems, satellite links, and UAV transmitters. The plane could work for fifty hours without stopping. This evening, all nineteen drones over Gaza had the same task: find Eric Söderqvist.

Jerusalem, Israel

Prime Minister Ben Shavit had cancelled dinner with the British ambassador, Matthew Gould. They knew each other well, so it wasn't a problem, and Meir Pardo had sounded very anxious on the phone. Now he was sitting at his desk, waiting for the director of the Mossad. He had spent most of the day discussing the gas deposits outside Haifa. The crashing financial markets were threatening to upset the whole exploitation project — the two foreign banks that had promised to put up loans had sent notice late the previous night that they were pulling out. The Mona virus had scared them away. He looked out the window. It was pitch black. Yet another victim from the mall — a young woman — had died. There was a knock at the door.

'*Ken!*'

Meir Pardo was wearing a bright-blue shirt and light-brown pants. He had been smoking his pipe; that was clear as soon as he entered the room. There was something soothing and secure about the fact that this particular man was a pipe smoker. Meir nodded curtly and sat down in one of the easy chairs across from Ben. They looked at one another without saying anything. Finally, Meir took off his glasses and straightened his back.

'How are things with you, Ben?'

'I'm screwed. You?'

'Somewhat better. I want you to become acquainted with a person from Sweden — Eric Söderqvist.'

Ben frowned.

'Sweden?'

Meir nodded, leaned forward, and placed a blue binder on the table in front of him. Ben opened it, coming across a black-and-white picture on the first page. The man in the picture was in his forties, and he looked kind; he had a smile on his lips, and a sheaf of papers under his arm.

'Who is he?'

'An IT professor from Stockholm. Married to a Jew.'

'And?'

'It's a long and improbable story. I've written it all down in the memo. The short version is that he's managed to make contact with the terrorist cell behind Mona.'

Ben raised his eyebrows and leaned over his desk. The chair creaked under his weight.

'Where is he?'

Meir smiled, pleased to finally be able to deliver some good news.

'He has been invited by Samir Mustaf himself to take part in the project. He's on his way to the group's base in Gaza. There's a transmitter on him, and we're following him, close on his heels.'

Ben sat with his elbows on the table and his eyes on the photograph. The director of the Mossad lowered his voice.

'Ben, this is what we were waiting for. If everything goes according to plan, we will soon have their exact co-ordinates.'

As Ben looked at the surly man on the other side of the table, he was filled with gratitude. How the hell had Meir managed to find this guy? He nodded in approval.

'It's really about time that you made yourselves useful.'

Meir blinked in surprise, but recovered quickly.

'This is what you pay us for. As soon as we've established his position, we can go in.'

He stood up and started toward the door.

'I apologise if I've disrupted your dinner plans, but I thought you'd want to know about this. Otherwise, there was the risk that you might give up.'

Ben didn't answer; he was looking at the photograph. Meir went on. 'It's all in the report. Only a small group knows about this. It's important to keep it that way.'

He closed the door silently. The prime minister was still sitting there with his hands on the binder.

Everyone in his family was sleeping soundly on the top floor, but he was standing on the large terrace, looking down at the lights of Jerusalem. He needed to breathe fresh air in order to calm down. If it hadn't been so dark he would have gone out on his bike. The short phone conversation with Ben Shavit had turned everything upside down. The prime minister had sounded relieved — and triumphant. Sure, he had promised not to pass on Meir Pardo's information, but he hadn't been able to help himself. And who was a better confidant than his best friend? Sinon had listened. He didn't usually lose his composure, but the conversation had knocked him off balance. He had mumbled something about how fantastic it was, and had hung up. Then he had stood on the terrace under the starry sky, serenely. He was breathing heavily, his eyes on the illuminated al-Aqsa cupola.

So Troy had its own Sinon. Meir had managed to infiltrate Ahmad Waizy's group. How was this possible? There were only five people left on the Gaza team: Ahmad Waizy, Mohammad Murid, Samir Mustaf, and the two Palestinians whom Ahmad had borrowed from Hamas. And then a Swedish IT engineer had made his way into the group. It sounded completely absurd. How could they be so stupid? How could Samir do something so insane? They had to be warned, but Ahmad was in Gaza City. Sinon had tried to call him, but couldn't get through. Gaza was a shithole — a shithole without a functioning mobile network. He couldn't reach Mohammad either. And he didn't dare call Samir; he didn't trust the wonder child from Qana. The Palestinians had no phones. What more could he do?

Ben Shavit had been so close to going along with their demands. In the past twenty-four hours, he had accepted the idea of new borders, and of freeing the prisoners as well as giving orders for a cease-fire. The US had finally found a Norwegian UN diplomat, and their first meeting was scheduled for the day after tomorrow. They had been so close to their goal, but now all their plans had been upended. As soon as the prime minister had learned about the Swede, he had cancelled the meeting. Now he wanted to wait for them to find the Swedish spy and the anti-virus. Meir was ready to go into Gaza; the attack could occur at any moment.

How had the Swede contacted Samir? What other mistakes had they made? The more he thought about it, the more questions he came up with. Ahmad had to get back to the tunnel immediately and clean up the evidence. If the Swede got his throat cut, Ben would have to go back to the bargaining table. But now it was a race against time — it was a matter of hours, maybe minutes. And he couldn't get hold of that fucking Ahmad. He tried dialling the number again. Nothing. This was the second piece of bad news in a matter of a few hours. The first was that that little Mossad slut had survived the bombing. It was unclear how — she was injured, but not dead. He would make sure it was taken care of, but that was a project for later. Right now, everything hinged upon quickly getting Ahmad into the tunnel to kill the spy. He dialled the number again. His eyes followed the well-lit wall that wound around the old city. This time, the call went through. Ahmad answered on the fourth ring.

Near Khan Younis, Gaza

They had sparred and jabbed, testing each other's techniques, strengths, and knowledge. After they had tossed Mona algorithms back and forth for an hour, Samir Mustaf had seemed to relax; maybe he was satisfied with the answers. If this was a job interview, the worst part was over. Samir had since left Eric alone, and he now sat quietly on the dusty blankets in a daze, trying to collect his thoughts. The air was stale and cold. Eric hadn't seen any other people.

Should he hate Samir? Mats Hagström was dead, and Hanna was gravely ill — maybe dying. But was it really Samir's fault? He had created a virus to destroy computers and digital networks, but he never could have dreamed that it would physically affect people. It wasn't Samir's creation that had made Mats and Hanna sick. It was his own — Mind Surf. He was the guilty one, or at least an accomplice. They were both to blame. In different ways. In different forms.

Samir returned with a tea tray and a plate of small cookies in different colours. After the break, their discussion became more theoretical. Eric took a sip of jasmine tea while using his free hand to rub out the mathematical formula he had written in the dust on the floor. Samir shook his head.

'There's still no one who has been able to implement Lov Grover's algorithm.'

Eric put his teacup down back on the small metal tray.

'That's true, but Matthew Hayward has proven that all the operations are quite possible.'

'Do you mean that Peter Shor's reasoning was relevant?'

Eric nodded.

'Absolutely. Discrete logarithms for prime factorisation. I've used a variation myself, in Mind Surf.'

Samir looked at him for a moment. He seemed sceptical.

'You talk a lot about quantum data. What's your opinion on singularity in relation to the quantum computer?'

'Are you thinking of science fiction? A scenario in which we create artificial quantum computers with higher intelligence than we have, which will then take over the world?'

Samir was silent. Eric took a neon-green cookie, swallowed it in one bite, and continued.

'Like I said, science fiction — an apocalyptic theory with no base in reality.'

Samir's voice took on a sharp tone. 'Even today we can do some pretty apocalyptic things with the help of technology.'

Eric met his gaze.

'You mean Mona?'

Samir answered with a question: 'How much have you worked with ANN?'

'Artificial neural networks? In Mind Surf, I work with genetic algorithms. Why?'

'Do you agree that the human nervous system and the most sophisticated ANN systems are quite similar?'

Eric nodded. 'Absolutely. They're self-healing, and the nodes are similar to our own nerve cells.'

'Do you also agree that biological viruses and computer viruses are the same in many respects?'

Eric sat as if petrified. He was excited, and suddenly uncertain.

Samir frowned.

'Did I say something wrong?'

Could it be a coincidence? He looked at the man across from him, trying to figure out if he was playing a cynical game. Did Samir know everything? He felt ill at ease, unsure. Samir's eyes were dark and lifeless, and impossible to read. Eric cleared his throat and struggled to smile, uncertain whether he had managed to.

'I agree. There are a lot of similarities. But there are also some differences.'

'There are. But in order for me to create the world's foremost computer virus, and for me there was no other option, I first had to learn everything I could about biological viruses — how they work, how they reproduce, how they protect themselves. And, not least, how they attack their host.'

Eric looked at the floor. Samir took a yellow cookie from the plate and went on in a lower voice.

'You could say that Mona is the world's first biological computer virus.'

Tel Aviv, Israel

The cup hit the wall beside the large map of Israel with a bang. Coffee and porcelain flew onto the piles of paper and folders that were piled on the floor. When David Yassur was younger he'd had a notoriously bad temper, but he had learned to keep himself under control — up to a point. They had just passed that point. It was quiet on the other end of the phone. He swallowed hard and tried to calm himself. It was late, and he was tired. He hissed into the small receiver.

'So when was the last time you had contact with Eric Söderqvist?'

Larry Lavon answered in a weak voice. 'In Erez. Six-and-a-half hours ago.'

'Why the hell did you wait three hundred and ninety minutes to call?'

Silence. He threw the phone down on the desk and did a lap around the room. He couldn't call Meir Pardo and say they'd lost the Swede. Ben Shavit had already been informed of their successes, and Meir was working on putting together a task force. He went back to the phone.

'Now listen up, Larry.'

'I'm listening.'

'Tear Gaza up. Do you hear me? Blow out every last fucking tunnel, empty all the houses and farms. If you don't find the signal within three hours, I'm going in with a full-scale ground invasion. And it will be at your expense.'

Near Khan Younis, Gaza

He should have seized the opportunity and put all his cards on the table. Samir's comment about the similarities between computer and biological viruses was an invitation — a chance to ask about the anti-virus. But Eric was too cowardly. Instead, he changed the subject, and he hated himself for it.

'What are you listening to?'

He nodded at the earbuds hanging around Samir's neck. At first, Samir didn't understand what he was referring to, but then he took a red iPod from his pocket and glanced at it.

'The latest was Johann Pachelbel, *Hexachordum Apollinis*.'

Eric nodded appreciatively.

'Apollo's six strings.'

Samir looked at him with the same expression he'd had when he mentioned Shor's theories — possibly sceptical, or just cautious.

'You listen to Pachelbel, too?'

'I have several of his works on my own iPod, but *Hexachordum* is probably my favourite.'

'Which of the arias do you like best?'

'The sixth one. *Sebaltina*. It's different from the others.'

Samir nodded, clearly excited.

Eric reached for his black bag and found his own iPod. He tossed it to Samir, who leaned against the wall and started scrolling through his music library. Without taking his eyes from the small screen, he said, 'Isn't it funny that two devoted IT experts like you and me are still using iPods?'

'They have great battery life. And the format is great, too.'

Samir nodded, his eyes still on the screen. 'It is without a doubt the most precious thing I own. At least now, after everything that has happened to me. Not so much the player itself, but the music. The memories.'

Eric was just about to ask him what he meant, even though he knew very well, when he was interrupted by steps in the tunnel. He looked up from his spot among cushions and blankets. A tall, thin man was just walking into the larger room. The man was wearing worn grey sweatpants, a brown linen shirt, and sandals. As he came closer, Eric saw that he had a large, ugly birthmark on one cheek. The man ignored him, and walked up to Samir and whispered something in his ear. Samir nodded. It seemed like he might be nervous.

'Eric, this is my colleague, Mohammad Murid. He is responsible for the administration of the group.'

The thin man gave a brief nod without looking at Eric. He remained standing near Samir for a moment. Eric happened to look at his toes. He had yellow nails — fungus. Mohammad seemed to make some decision and rushed off with flapping sandals. Samir picked up Eric's iPod again and continued to browse through the music, but Eric could tell he was no longer looking at the information. Mohammad's message had thrown him off balance. He didn't say anything for a long time, and when he finally looked up their eyes met.

'Mohammad told me that my boss, Ahmad Waizy, will be here soon. He's very eager to meet you.'

Something in his voice made Eric feel ill at ease. The room was cold, and the air felt thinner. He cleared his throat and said, 'Where has he been?' mostly just to say something, anything, and perhaps shake off the uneasy feeling that now filled the air between them.

Samir looked at him with his inscrutable eyes.

'Not very far away.'

Eric changed the subject.

'You said the iPod is your most precious belonging. You said "after everything that's happened to me." What happened?'

Samir's eyes narrowed. At first, Eric thought he'd gone too far, that he'd barged into a topic that was off limits. But then Samir answered in a faint voice.

'In the war against Hezbollah, southern Lebanon was bombed eighty times in one month. In almost all of the attacks they used cluster bombs.'

He stopped talking and lifted his teacup; at first, it looked as though he was going to drink from it, but then he changed his mind and put it back on the tray. He sat for a long time with his hand on the cup. Eric had to change position because one leg had gone to sleep. His movement seemed to rouse Samir.

'Mona, my daughter, loved animals. Not just pets or dolphins, like all kids do. To her, each little bug was a miracle — a living wonder that deserved all her attention and love.'

Eric thought of the little girl with the curly hair. He remembered that the photograph was in his pocket.

'It was my sister-in-law's birthday, and the party was at my mother-in-law's house in Qana. My wife, Nadim, and Mona went there early.'

He stopped to catch his breath.

'A grenade got into Elif's kitchen. I don't know how. Maybe it was Mona — maybe she found it when she was out playing. Someone said that's what happened. The grenade wiped everything out. Everything that was important. I ...'

His voice died out. Eric couldn't bear to look at his tortured face, and lowered his eyes. Samir's hands were clasped as if in prayer. The gap around his wedding ring spoke to the fact that his finger had been fatter when the ring was made. They sat in silence for a long while. Something creaked in the distance, making a chilling sound like nails on a chalkboard. The echo rolled off down the tunnel.

'The Mona virus is your revenge?'

Samir didn't answer. His head hung heavily, and his shoulders were slumped. After a moment, Eric tried again.

'I'm very sorry for your loss. And I understand even better why you fight.'

Samir looked at him. When he spoke, his voice took on a harsher tone.

'And you, Eric Söderqvist from Sweden. Why are you here?'

Eric stiffened. A deep hole opened in his stomach. It had all come down to this. Samir's dark eyes drilled into him, and he was about to be swallowed up by his own lies. Where should he start? How could he explain something so crazy without coming off as insane? He cleared his throat and tried to find the right tone of voice.

'You might not believe what I'm about to say, but give me a chance. My wife, Hanna Söderqvist ...'

A sudden crash from the right-hand tunnel made him stop. He could hear the quick steps of several people, and then one of the Palestinian guards came into the room. He worked the bolt action of his automatic rifle as he breathlessly placed himself between them on the cushions. One of his boots landed on the cookie plate and upset Samir's teacup. The barrel of the gun pointed at Eric's face, black and mute. The Palestinian yelled something he didn't understand, but he instinctively put his hands up over his head. The guard glanced at the mouth of the tunnel. A short, pale man stepped into the light from the bulb. He was wearing baggy brown pants, a long brown shirt, and a thin keffiyeh with a black pattern. The guard looked back and forth between him and Eric. He didn't dare even to breathe. The man smiled, but only with his mouth.

'Mr Söderqvist, welcome to Khan Younis. I hope you two have had a rewarding meeting.'

He spoke English perfectly, with a faint British accent. No one answered.

'I'm sorry to stomp in like this, but your conversation is over for the time being.'

He barked something at the Palestinian, who immediately took a step closer to Eric, raised his weapon, and hit him in the head. The sound of it was soft and dull, like being hit with a wet towel. The ground came toward him, and then he was lying at the man's boot. The sounds around him were distant and warped. His last conscious thought was of Rachel. How could she let this happen?

Tel Aviv, Israel

Reality was merciless, the opposite of the morphine buzz. In reality, her limbs were pulled out of joint, and the blisters and scales on her skin had burst. As her morphine dose was decreased, reality gradually became more present. The pain ran over her like boiling water. She wasn't dead; she wasn't alive. She had no concept of time or space. She could see Tara's face before her. Tara was keeping her there. It had been tempting to let go, to just let herself be carried along — so easy. But Tara wouldn't make it without her. Tara needed her. Beautiful, sweet Tara.

What had happened? She had just put on 'Careless Whispers'. A white wall had hit her, thrown her here, to a place between life and death. Rachel lay still, her body burning. All she wanted was to crawl out of it and escape. Eric was also there in her thoughts, but not like Tara. Not as clearly. She had to protect Tara. Rachel would overcome the pain. That's what she was trained to do. She slid back into a dreamless sleep.

Near Khan Younis, Gaza

It was very dark, but there were scents and sounds all around him. He was lying on a hard, rough surface — concrete with a layer of gravel. There was a stale odour in the air, like wet dirt or mud, or maybe urine. Eric cautiously felt his head where the butt of the automatic rifle had hit him. It didn't seem to be bleeding, but there was a large, painful swelling there. He felt sick; he knew he was concussed. He struggled to prop himself up on his side, and whimpered from the pain in his head.

'Shit.'

He sank back down, and lay still for a long time, breathing. He stretched out one arm and fumbled around, but nothing came to hand. He felt behind himself and immediately struck a cool wall. He was in some sort of cell or storage room. He remembered the thin man with the British accent. Was that Ahmad Waizy? The man Samir called his boss? Was he the same person who had written the chat entries under the signature 'A?' Probably — which meant he was the man who had planned and ordered the suicide bombings. And he knew that Eric was a fraud. But they hadn't shot him. Maybe they were awaiting orders, or else they wanted to interrogate him first.

He rolled onto his back again and closed his eyes. Not that it made a difference to have them closed, but it had a calming effect. He had failed. The Mossad had failed. Maybe they had never expected him to make it. He was probably just one of many lures they had cast, in the hope that one would work. And now he had been crossed off the list. Rachel had moved on to new tasks.

There was a metallic taste in his mouth. He thought of the little library at Herzl Street 44, of the woman and her fantastic story, of the paper brigade and the poet Abraham Sutzkever. Then Hanna popped up in his thoughts. They had never been apart for this long. After a while, he dozed off, his sleep uneasy. After an hour or so, he was awoken by a creaking sound that cut through his head like a sharp knife. He opened his eyes and stared into the darkness. Someone opened the door to the chamber, and a silhouette appeared against the light.

'Mister?'

The voice sounded uncertain. Eric lay still in the dark, not daring to move.

'Mister?'

It wasn't Samir or Ahmad. He cleared his throat.

'Yes.'

The silhouette waved its hand slightly.

'Come.'

He got up and immediately hit his head on the ceiling. The pain was so sharp that he fell to his knees, and his eyes instantly filled with tears. He breathed heavily, waited until he had regained his balance, and then stood up carefully and walked toward the light, stooping. The man in the doorway was Samir's assistant — the tall man with the birthmark. He indicated that Eric should follow him. They walked quickly through the partially lit tunnel, with Eric expecting to come eye-to-eye with Ahmad at any moment. Finally, they arrived at the large area at the entrance. The man nodded at the ladder. Eric hesitated. The man pointed.

'Up.'

He had no choice, so he grabbed the rebar and started climbing. What was about to happen? Was Ahmad waiting outside? The Palestinians? An execution patrol? The hatch door was open, and he saw the star-filled sky like a round, glittering eye at the top of the ladder. When he got to the last rung of rebar and boosted himself out, he saw a campfire some way off. A light breeze brought with it the scent of burning wood. The face with the birthmark popped out of the hatch, but its owner didn't climb out. Instead, he pointed at the campfire.

'There.'

Eric turned toward the flaming light. He hadn't noticed until now that someone was sitting over there — a figure hunched by the fire, which was sheltered from the wind by the wall of the ruin. As he came closer, he recognised the man. Samir didn't look at Eric as he approached. Instead, Samir kept staring blankly into the flames. Eric stood still, hesitant, barely a metre from the sitting man. When Samir spoke, it was in barely above a whisper.

'Shalom.'

The Hebrew greeting was unexpected. But there was nothing sarcastic in his tone; instead, he sounded resigned. Eric answered cautiously, warily.

'Shalom.'

From the crackling fire, pungent white smoke cast ghostly veils over the otherwise clear night.

'Sit with me.'

Eric sat down and dug his hands into the warm sand.

'I'm sorry. If you only knew what ...'

Samir interrupted him.

'I've never been to Scandinavia, so I know very little about your world. But I lived in France for many years.'

Eric didn't say anything, and Samir went on.

'Like Lebanon, it's a part of me. And I read in French, almost exclusively. No other country has such a rich literature. So many authors. Beautiful stories that come to me at all imaginable times. Like now, when I look at these stars, a book by Le Clézio — *Wandering Star*.'

'What is it about?'

'A young Jewish woman named Esther who flees the Nazis in southern France. Her journey leads her to Jerusalem. When Israel is declared a state, a Palestinian woman named Nejma has to flee to a camp where the situation is horrible. One girl goes to the place of her dreams; the other goes to an eternal nightmare. The sense of not belonging, of vulnerability — I see myself in it. It's not one of his best books, but the two women's stories, where the salvation of one is the ruin of the other, are very beautiful at times.'

Eric thought of the group of people waiting hopelessly at the large gate in Erez — especially of the little boy with the candy. Samir gestured toward the horizon.

'In the book, Le Clézio writes about Jerusalem very beautifully. He writes that it is a city where there cannot be war. Where those who have wandered around without a homeland can live in peace.'

Eric couldn't help himself.

'But you tried to detonate bombs in the city — to kill innocent people.'

Samir's cheeks were red with the heat.

'I was against it. I've seen enough death, but Ahmad was relentless.'

He met Eric's gaze.

'He is very dangerous. A fundamentalist.'

Eric sighed.

'Religion is a curse.'

'You talk like an atheist.'

'I *am* an atheist.'

Samir was quiet for a long time. When he finally spoke, his voice was lower, as if he were afraid someone might hear.

'How can you live without an anchor? Without a keel? How can you waste your existence?'

'I don't.'

'But you don't believe in anything.'

'I believe in science. If you're asking about a higher power, it has to be science.'

Samir shook his head.

'There's no opposing force there.'

'No? The church has always condemned science.'

'Maybe Christianity has. But science has always been important to Islam. The Quran urges us to seek understanding of the symbols of Allah in the world. Natural science is considered to promote our understanding of Allah.'

'I have complete respect for your beliefs, and for everyone's beliefs. I just haven't been able to find myself in all of that.'

'You are there, believe me. There are one-and-a-half billion Muslims in the world. There are just as many interpretations of Islam. Everyone has his own way.'

'Including madmen like Ahmad Waizy?'

'There are extreme examples everywhere. Fundamentalism isn't part of Islam; it's part of humanity. The very reason we need religion is to counteract these forces. Read the Quran. Let something spiritual in. Or read the Bible, the Torah, whatever works for you. But don't live without a keel.'

Eric let sand run through his fingers.

'I'm sorry I tricked you and lied to you.'

The fire snapped, and a few small, glowing slivers of wood flew up like wild fireflies. Samir nodded thoughtfully.

'I wanted to talk to you tonight because I have thought a lot about your coda.'

'My coda?'

'You can see our initial conversation as a symphony. We followed the rules of a sonata: a main theme that was varied in different forms — the Mona virus and program code. We could have stopped there, in harmony, but then you introduced a coda ... a completely new melody.'

Eric shook his head. He didn't understand. Samir held up his hand.

'I've always loved the coda in classical music, when the sonata takes on a new shape at the end, and the melody changes. The composer lets us get a glimpse of an alternate world just before he brings it to an end.'

'I still don't understand. What was my coda?'

'Just before Ahmad arrived, you said that you were going to tell me something I would never believe. Something about your wife. That was your coda.'

The wind hissed around them. Eric looked into the fire.

'And now you want to hear the rest of the piece?'

Samir nodded and then lowered his head, waiting for the truth.

'To start with, I'm no secret agent or Mossad spy. I really am a professor of IT from a college in Stockholm.'

There was no reaction.

'You know about Mind Surf, so I don't have to explain my research. A few weeks ago, I finally got the system to work. The experience was indescribable.'

Samir turned his head and looked at him.

'What does this have to do with your *Jewish* wife?' There was a bitter tone in his voice.

Eric clenched his hands in the sand.

'She got to try the system.'

He had gone through this monologue so many times. He had practised it, dreamed of it — the moment when he would tell the creator of Mona about Hanna. But you could never prepare yourself for reality.

'Using Mind Surf, she went to TBI's website. The computer was infected by the virus, and Hanna got sick.'

'You think that Mona was what made her sick.'

This direct statement took him by surprise. He had expected Samir to wave off such an absurd idea. Now he didn't know how he should continue. He looked down at his hands in the yellow sand.

Samir asked, 'So why did you come here? To avenge her?'

'To plead with you to give me hope. An opening. The doctors can't get the illness under control. I'm going to lose her. She's all I have. All I love.'

Samir sat motionlessly, staring blankly straight ahead. Then he chuckled.

'Here we sit, you and I, two men meeting in a desert. We find ourselves on two completely different journeys. I'm already in hell. You, at least, if hope wins out, are on the way to saving your beloved. Le Clézio's *Wandering Star*. The Muslim and the Jew. But neither of us is carrying a weapon.'

He laughed. It was a dry and empty sound.

'All we have is our iPods. I guess we should call ourselves iPod cowboys.'

The fire was about to go out, and the darkness was creeping closer. Eric knew now that he was not going to receive any miracle medicine from Samir. It had been a hopeless and desperate dream, a story he'd told himself in order to keep going, a reason to keep moving. He got to his knees so he could reach into his pocket, and he took out the small, creased colour photo of Mona.

'Here.'

Samir took the photo, and, in the faint light of the fire, Eric could see his eyes widen. He held it in both hands.

'She looks good in colour. She ...'

He stopped short. Then he closed his hand around the photograph and looked at Eric.

'Where did you get this?'

'The Mossad gave it to me. They interrogated me about you, and they gave me the picture.'

Samir looked past him, far off into the night.

'Do you know how Ahmad learned that you were a traitor?'

'No.'

'From the Mossad.'

'That's strange. I thought ...'

'Not from the Mossad itself. They told the prime minister, Ben Shavit. And he told one of his closest friends — a man in the Knesset. That man is our man. Or, rather, Ahmad's.'

'He has a man in the Israeli government?'

Samir nodded softly. Then he straightened up.

'You have to go back to being imprisoned. Mohammad is waiting for you by the tunnel.'

Eric lingered for a moment. He somehow felt degraded — degraded and betrayed. His hope was gone, and the hatch down into the tunnel felt like the gates of hell. He stood up. Samir held up the small photograph.

'May I keep the picture of my daughter? It would mean a lot.'

Eric nodded. 'It's yours.'

Then he turned around and started walking toward the tunnel opening.

At a quarter to three in the morning, Heron 158 registered a weak signal that matched the archived identification code. Seven hundred and twenty-two metres above ground, the drone stored the co-ordinates 31°20'39.55'N 34°18'11.13'E/31.3443194°N. Two minutes after the drone made contact, the communications centre in Ashdod sent a memo to military intelligence. At eight past three, Daniel Lewin, the captain of the elite force Sayeret Matkal, got the go-ahead and the target data. He had been waiting at the Bahad Zikim army training camp, along with a hand-picked task-force group. The camp was just a few kilometres from the Gaza border. As soon as Lewin hung up, he went to wake the helicopter pilots.

Near Khan Younis, Gaza

Eric was back in the dark cave. The stink of urine was more apparent than it had been earlier — maybe it served as the group's toilet when it wasn't being used as a cell. He was half-sitting, leaning against the rough wall. About half an hour before, he had heard a faint rustling on his left. It was some sort of animal or insect. A rat? Or a scorpion?

He had told Samir the truth. Was that wrong? If Samir told Ahmad Waizy, would that change anything? Hardly. Ahmad already knew everything. Would he ever see Samir again?

He shifted. He heard the rustling sound again.

Sweet, wonderful Hanna. How was she doing? Had she gotten worse? Had Jens tried to reach him? He could picture Hanna before him with her mass of hair, blonde and slightly curly. Nowadays there were white strands in it; he loved them.

He was startled by a scraping sound. There was another creak, and the door to the cell opened. He sat stock-still in the dark. A faint light found its way in behind the silhouette at the door.

'Eric?'

It was Samir's soft voice.

'I'm here,' Eric whispered.

'Watch your eyes — I'm turning on the light.'

There was a click, and the room was bathed in light. Eric looked around. The light was coming from a bulb that hung from the ceiling by a black cord. The room was smaller than he'd thought, and it was oblong. He saw large cracks in the wall; it wouldn't be hard for rats to come and go through those. The rough floor was full of paper, plastic bottles, and dirty scraps of fabric. Samir stooped and came through the door.

'How are you?'

'I'm alive.'

Samir shoved a greenish-brown rag aside with his foot and sat down softly next to him, tailor-style.

'Allah is testing you.'

Eric smiled weakly.

'I'm sure he is.'

373

Samir gazed at him with a sad look in his eyes.

'I've enjoyed our discussions.'

'I have, too. They've been very rewarding.'

'I'm glad you came here. I just wish things could have ended differently.'

'Me, too. But it's not over yet.'

'You're quite right. The night is long, and only Allah knows its secrets.'

Samir grew silent. Eric said nothing; he just looked at the man who was sitting less than fifty centimetres away from him. After all their discussions, they knew each other, at least on some level. Samir extended his hand and grasped Eric's wrist.

'Your fate is not in my hands. I'll try to talk to Ahmad — maybe I can convince him to hand you over to Hamas. It's not great, but it's the closest thing you can find to an authority here in Gaza. Better than a bullet.'

Eric felt infinitely alone. Samir gazed into his eyes for a long time. Then he turned Eric's wrist over, opened his hand, and placed a small, flat object in his palm. When Eric looked down, he saw that it was the iPod — his own iPod. Samir had held onto it when the guard had knocked him down.

'A cowboy needs his iPod.'

Samir lowered his voice.

'I put Tchaikovsky's seventh symphony on it for you. It's a perfect composition. I think you'll like it. Maybe it can even give you your love back. Remember my family … my story.'

Samir let go of his hand and stood up. Eric remained on the floor.

'I promise.'

Samir raised a hand to say goodbye.

'*Insha'Allah*.' He went back out the low door, and left the light on. Then came the creaking sound again as the bar was lowered on the other side. Eric looked at the small silver player in his hand. *Tchaikovsky. A fantastic composition.* But he had no headphones, so he couldn't listen to it. He pulled his legs up close to his body again and tried to remember some of Tchaikovsky's themes. Strangely, he had never heard of the seventh symphony. He thought of the fifth instead. It was reminiscent of Beethoven's fifth, but Tchaikovsky was not as rule-bound. He summoned up the primary theme first. It was in an unstable E-minor, and then D-minor, eluding the strong, leading tones, but finally overcoming the darkness. He hummed to himself, his voice sounding thin and hollow. The bass fell an octave or so. The second movement was more like classic Tchaikovsky, complicated and colourful, with prominent wind instruments. He heard a clatter outside the door, and then the creaking again as the bar was lifted. The door opened, and he smiled toward it.

'Unfortunately, I don't have any headphones, but I'm doing my best to remember Tchaikovsky.'

'Not much to remember — a homosexual mongrel ruined by cholera and vodka.'

Eric's stomach clenched as he made eye contact with Ahmad, who ducked into the cell.

'Who were you talking to? Samir Mustaf? I thought I saw him coming from this direction.'

Eric looked reflexively down at the iPod, for a second too long. Ahmad smiled.

'Did you get a present?'

Eric clenched the player. Ahmad leaned calmly against the wall and looked around.

'This place is pretty dirty, but unfortunately there was nothing better to offer. We hadn't counted on having to lock you up. The fact is, we had prepared a much nicer space for you. But things changed.'

Eric didn't answer.

'So Samir has been here looking after you? Did he give you a farewell gift? I don't get why everyone walks around with those things in their ears — it's idiotic. You miss everything that's going on around you. You don't take in the details. Details are everything.'

'What are you going to do with me?'

'I don't like talking to a man who won't look me in the eye.'

Eric raised his eyes.

'What am I going to do with you? First of all, I'm going to let you have this night. I don't believe in doing things in haste. Tomorrow morning, you and I will talk. I'm not going to hide the fact that it will be rough for you. You see, it's important to me that I learn all the facts. And I have to be sure you're telling the truth. In my world, there's only one way to make sure of that.'

Eric couldn't keep looking into those burning eyes. He looked down at his pale hands again. In the light, he could see that they were full of scrapes, and that two of the knuckles on his left hand were covered in dried blood. Ahmad moved, and something gave a click. It sounded like a weapon.

'Hold out your hand. No, not the one with the music thing. The other one. The empty one.'

Eric's heart was pounding in his chest as he slowly and shakily extended his arm after a moment's hesitation.

'Open your hand. Hold still.'

Something fell through the air and landed heavily in his palm. He looked at the small object — a matte grey top on shining copper. It was a bullet.

'I can give presents, too. It might feel like a threat right now, but after we've spoken for a few hours it will become your most precious possession. This little piece of lead will be worth more to you than pure gold. When it finally comes, you'll welcome it with open arms.'

Ahmad straightened up.

'You have a long night ahead of you. Be sure to make peace with your God.'

Turning out the light, he left without saying anything more. The door closed, and the bar was put back in place. The dense darkness had its own symbolism. The cool iPod lay in one hand; in the other was the bullet. Infinite music and infinite silence.

Ahmad Waizy walked briskly through the tunnel and looked at his watch; it was three-thirty in the morning. He knew where to look: Samir Mustaf often went out to get fresh air between shifts when he was working. Ahmad swung up onto the ladder and climbed quickly up the bent rebar rungs. The hatch door was open, and he boosted himself into the darkness. It was windy — a hard wind full of stinging sand. He made a face and turned his back to the wind. Then he caught sight of the solitary silhouette that was outlined against the campfire. It was Samir, standing still with his head bent. The old ruin was probably protecting him from the wind. In the faint light, Ahmad couldn't tell what he was doing; maybe he was crying. Ahmad hunched his shoulders and walked toward the glowing point of light. Samir was wearing only pants; his thin upper body was pale, and his skin was pulled tightly across his ribs. They stood still for a long time, side by side. The glow of the fire still gave off a faint warmth, a mild caress along his legs. Samir broke the silence.

'What's going to happen to him?'

'He's going to be interrogated.'

Samir poked at the charred logs with one sandal.

'What are you hoping to learn?'

'How he managed to get into our database, who he talked to.'

'And then?'

'Then? A shot to the right eye. Or maybe the left. It depends on the angle. What are you doing out here?'

'I'm thinking about my daughter. I'm trying to remember her voice. What she smelled like. Everything disappears so fast — the colours, the details. Everything fades.'

He pushed a piece of wood into the fire with his foot.

'And I'm thinking about what I've done — everything we've done. Does it really make a difference? The grenade that exploded in our kitchen will never go away. My family will never come back. I swore revenge, and I got it. But for what? Revenge hasn't filled the emptiness in my heart.'

Ahmad shook his head.

'You're wrong, my friend. *Qisas* gives you the right to retaliate. The Prophet, may peace be upon him, cannot be misinterpreted. The right to redress goes far back in time. The Babylonian laws established an eye for an eye, a tooth for a tooth.'

'According to the holy Quran, forgiveness is greater.'

Ahmad laughed scornfully.

'Do you claim to forgive those who took your daughter away from you? Your wife?'

Ahmad placed a hand on his shoulder.

'Look at me, Samir.'

Samir turned around. The contact and the voice made him tense involuntarily. Ahmad's face was just a few centimetres from his own.

'I believe in revenge. Retaliation has been a crucial force in many successful battles. You were the one who chose Salah ad-Din as your alias online. His vengeance was uncompromising. Yours must be as well.'

When Samir didn't answer, he went on. 'And, besides, that's how we were able to recruit you.'

There was a sudden chill between them, or maybe just inside Samir. It wasn't fear — at least not fear of physical harm. It was something considerably worse. Something he'd always suspected, but had never dared to put into words. He looked at Ahmad as though the devil himself were standing before him. His eyes begged him not to continue, begged him not to say what he was about to say — that inevitable thing. Ahmad raised his voice a bit and squeezed Samir's shoulder harder.

'Hate was the only thing that could make you see the fight from our perspective. To truly feel for those who had been affected, those who are vulnerable. Revenge was the only thing that could make you join us.'

Samir wanted to tear the man's tongue from his mouth — whatever would stop him from talking. But, instead, his numb lips opened and demanded that Ahmad utter the ultimate curse.

'What are you saying?'

Ahmad smiled, his hand still on Samir's shoulder.

'You know exactly what I'm talking about. You were crucial to our plan; we had to get you to go along with it. There was no other way.'

Samir's legs gave way and he sank down to the sand. The anguish that filled him was so overwhelming and unfathomable that he could no longer stand. He didn't cry. He stared with eyes wide open, past Ahmad, up into black space. Ahmad lowered his voice.

'They were a small sacrifice for a great thing. Paradise welcomed them with open arms. Those who die a martyr's death for Allah aren't dead; they are alive and have been born again.'

Samir sat crumpled at the edge of the fire. He tried to collect his thoughts, but they all pulled apart and disappeared. He picked up the creased picture of Mona and stared into her brown eyes.

Ahmad had been prepared for aggression, so Samir's collapse

disappointed him. He had been looking forward to telling him the truth about Qana. But now that he was revealing the truth, he was met only with degraded weakness and unmanly apathy. He pressed harder in a last attempt to provoke a reaction.

'We pretended that it was a little tiger cub. Apparently, little Mona loved animals.'

Samir didn't answer. He just sat there, staring at his pathetic photograph. Ahmad took out the Glock he was carrying in the lining of his pants. There was no reaction, even when he cocked it. The Lebanese bastard didn't even lift his head. Ahmad pressed the barrel just behind Samir's ear and fired. Everyone was the same when faced with death. One of the world's leading IT engineers, one minute; the next, just a pile of clothes in the sand. He shook his head and looked out into the night. There was still a strong wind. He listened to his intuition. There was something going on. Something was about to happen. He turned back toward the tunnel.

Tel Aviv, Israel

Two days after the attack, Rachel Papo was able to walk on her own. The doctors had forbidden it, but she did it anyway. She had been out wandering in the hallway, back and forth. It did not go quickly. The pain was unimaginable. Each step was a victory.

Most people would have died in such a violent explosion. Rachel was physically stronger than many people, but that wasn't the deciding factor. It was her mind.

When the drugs left her body, she could start to think again. A bomb had exploded in her bedroom. Her lover was dead. How had someone gotten hold of her address? It was a safe house that wasn't listed in any directories — at least not any official ones. That meant there was a leak in the Mossad — a leak at the highest security level. She struggled to open the door to the next unit. The floor was cold under her bare feet. This time, she was going to walk all the way to the cafeteria.

Near Khan Younis, Gaza

At first, Eric thought it was thunder. The first crash was dull and far off, a distant reminder of the world that still existed up there. He thought of the house on Dalarö, of how he and Hanna would stand at the large glass window and enjoy watching the lightning over Jungfrujärden. Then came the second explosion. It was deafening, and it caused the mortar in the wall to crack and fall on top of him in a shower of splinters. He screamed and curled up into a foetal position. His ears howled, and there was a sudden caustic smell in the air. He heard rattling. Tack-tack-tack — short bursts that sounded like the sound of a giant typewriter. He could hear someone shouting through the steel door, and maybe running feet. Dirt and mud ran over his hands and face. Another explosion shook the floor. He desperately pulled his legs to his body. He had never been so scared, so panicked. The typewriter kept up its clacking. Tack-tack-tack. A few words at a time. Tack-tack.

Despite the howling in his ears, he could make out the sound of the bar on the door. The door opened, and someone came in; he recognised the silhouette. It was Ahmad Waizy. He closed the door behind him, and someone replaced the bar on the outside. Was Ahmad coming to kill him? Eric lay perfectly still. The typewriter had stopped. He heard a shuffling noise, a quick intake of air, a sharp sound like fabric ripping, and then everything was quiet.

He could hear only the rapid breathing in the dark. He didn't dare move; he waited to be stabbed or kicked or shot. But nothing happened. The dirt had stopped running over him. The ceiling hadn't collapsed. The burned smell was still there, and maybe the smell of Ahmad, too. He smelled sweat, and sensed fear. Eric heard voices and movements outside the door. Ahmad's breathing changed rhythm, suddenly becoming calmer. Then came the creak of the bar. The door flew open and someone turned on the light. The small room was flooded with light, making him squint at the entrance. A soldier towered up in the glow like a god stepping right out of the sun. He was wearing a helmet, goggles, a headset, and a black jumpsuit. He held an automatic rifle in front of him, with the barrel aimed at the far corner of the cell. Eric slowly turned his head and saw Ahmad. He was in the corner, in torn clothes and with his hands taped in front of him. The soldier shouted something. He aimed the gun back and forth between Eric and Ahmad, who was mumbling.

The words caused the soldier to take a step closer and fix the weapon on the wiry Arab. Ahmad got to his knees and spoke louder. Eric recognised the language. It was Hebrew. *He's trying to pass himself off as a prisoner.* He wanted to warn the guard, but he didn't dare move, didn't dare make a sound. Ahmad repeated the sentence again and again. He nodded toward Eric and held his hands in the air. Sweat was running down his forehead and under his nose. Without lowering his weapon, the soldier turned his arm and studied something just above his wrist. Then he straightened up, and the room exploded in a brief inferno of deafening explosions, compressed and intensified by the close walls. Eric couldn't hold back his scream. Bullet casings clinked around him, their ring echoing. The soldier roared something.

When Eric opened his eyes, he found he was staring into a smoking gun. Out of the corner of his eye, he saw Ahmad's body, pressed up against the wall like a rag doll. Large red spots were blooming on his chest and stomach. The man repeated his order. Eric swallowed and answered weakly, 'I don't understand what you're saying.' The man turned his arm again and studied what was printed just above his wrist. Then he looked at Eric and lowered his weapon. He said something into his headset and nodded. Then he pointed at the door.

'Söderqvist — come with me.'

When the soldier bent down to help him, Eric saw what he'd been looking at. On his forearm, in a transparent plastic pocket sewn into the black fabric of the jumpsuit, was a colour picture of Eric. When they came out into the tunnel, they met several other soldiers in identical jumpsuits — black fabric, with no marks or badges. All of them had his picture on their left arms. At least two of the soldiers they passed were women. They arrived at the large chamber he'd climbed down into just over twenty-four hours before. A soldier was crouching beside a body. Eric recognised the dead man immediately: Mohammad Murid. The birthmark was impossible to miss. The soldier behind him pointed at the ladder.

'Up and out.'

He started climbing. The closer he got to the hatch door, the louder he heard a whining roar. The noise hit him hard as he opened the hatch, causing him to recoil. About twenty metres from the hatch, bathed in the pink light of dawn, were two large helicopters whose engines were roaring. He climbed out of the hatch. The air was chilly. A soldier with a night-vision visor on his helmet pointed at the closest helicopter. He hunched over in the wind from the spinning rotor blades, and fought his way toward the open side door. The ground was burned in several places, and he could glimpse bodies in the sand — the Palestinians. Just as he was about to step onto the foot rail, he caught sight of a lone body a few metres behind the second helicopter. He recognised the pants. A wave of nausea washed over him, causing him to lose his balance. He fell onto the hard-packed sand and threw up, in waves of powerful retches that made his stomach clench. The warm vomit splashed over his spread hands. He breathed heavily, crying. He rested on all fours, leaning over the yellowish-white puddle and still crying. Snot and tears ran down his cheeks. Someone took hold of his arms, pulling him up and into the cabin. The wind disappeared, and the roar of the engines became muffled. He sank onto one of the worn seats with teary eyes. The man who had helped him into the cabin crouched down and studied his face. He, too, was dressed in a black jumpsuit, but he had no combat pack, helmet, or headset.

'Mr Söderqvist, I'm Captain Lewin. We're going to move you to a temporary base for a medical examination. From there, we'll fly you to Tel Aviv. You can relax. It's all over.'

The man stood up, patted him gently on the shoulder, and climbed out of the helicopter. As soon as he had closed the door, the cabin swayed, and the ground sank away from the windows. With aching joints, Eric straightened up and looked out. They were already so high up that it was impossible to make out any of the camp. The earth below was just a grey patchwork quilt. Expanding above them was an endless pink morning sky. His body hurt all over. There was still a high-pitched ringing in his ears. He blinked and tried to shut out the chaos. Captain Lewin's last words lingered in the cabin. It's all over.

The wind stirred up the lovely flakes and filled the air with snow-like clouds. The white dust stung her throat and stuck to her face. She coughed. The sky over Hamngatan was a strange shade of red, as though it were reflecting a fire burning far away. Each step seemed to intrude upon the oppressive silence. Something in her tired memory was squirming and fighting to be heard. Something about a girl and an illness. About the future. She looked out over the wrecked cars. If everyone was dead, where were the bodies? Newspapers, posters, and plastic bags danced in circles above the footpaths and traffic islands, quickly gaining height, spinning faster and faster as the wind got stronger. It whistled and whined through the car wrecks around her. A car door slammed with a dull bang. She crossed Hamngatan. The broad stairs down to the subway platform were full of boxes, boards, and papers. She took the stairs in great steps, suddenly terrified of the street, the façades of the buildings, and the whirling trash. It took a moment for her eyes to adjust to the darkness. The entrance to the bottom floor of NK gaped darkly. The large sliding doors were wide open. The kitchen department was in there, in the dark. She shivered. Maybe the girl was still there. Maybe she was standing there, watching her. Guarding her, awaiting the faceless man.

They had stayed at the Bahad Zikim military base for three hours. He had taken an ice-cold shower, drunk a cup of coffee, and eaten a mealy apple. The base was nearly deserted, and only one of the long barracks was in use. Everyone he saw was from the same group as those who had attacked the tunnel. They all had the same quiet manner and looked at him with the same evasive glances, and they all wore black jumpsuits with no patches. An older female doctor had felt him all over and listened to his heart. Then a serious man with thick glasses had interrogated him. He hadn't called it an interrogation — 'debriefing' was the word he had used. They had sat on their respective folding chairs in an empty cafeteria. The man had asked hundreds of questions, and Eric's answers had been captured by a simple video camera on a tripod. The man had said that this was only a preliminary conversation and that he would have to submit to a number of similar sessions in the next few days. They wanted to know who was in charge of the camp, who he had met, what he had seen, what he hadn't seen, whether they'd had weapons, what kind of weapons, whether they'd had maps, and whether he'd heard any names. But Eric was too shaken up to answer coherently. He himself could tell that he was distracted and unclear. The man was patient, and did what he could to help him put his story together.

Now Eric was back in the helicopter, and flying with him was a young man in civilian clothes and dark glasses. The man was reading a dog-eared book, and only gave him a quick nod as he sat down in the cramped cabin. The silence was welcome — Eric had no desire to talk to anyone. Despite the vibrations, he leaned his head against the wall and tried to relax. Everything had happened so incredibly quickly. Just a few hours ago he had been talking to Samir. He still had his iPod in his pocket. But Samir was gone now — murdered. The helicopter banked and lost altitude, and pain shot through his stomach. He grabbed one of the handgrips and looked around. The man across from him was still reading calmly. Samir's death was a catastrophe. Without him, there was no anti-virus and no Nadim. Hanna would fade away, just as Mats had. The only thing he had accomplished with his journey was to waste what was left of their time together. He had let them all down: Jens, Judith, Mats, and Hanna.

The helicopter turned sharply and descended toward the ground. He pressed his face against the round window. They were on their way down to an asphalt landing pad among several low buildings. He recognised the area. It was the airport — Ben Gurion. The large machine landed gently. The man with the book stood up and walked to the door, crouching. He turned a grey handle, opened the door, and hopped out. The engine shut down and was replaced by a more distant hum from the airport. Eric remained seated, his body heavy and stiff. The door to the cockpit opened to reveal a young pilot in green military clothes with headphones around his neck. The pilot nodded at him.

'This is the final stop.'

'And where am I supposed to go?'

'Follow me. Come on.'

He climbed out through the half-open door, and Eric followed him. When he got down onto the asphalt, he remembered his bag. He turned to the pilot.

'I brought a bag with me to the camp in Gaza. A black Gucci bag.'

The man stared at him as though trying to figure out if he was serious. Then he shook his head.

'Come on. They're waiting for you.'

They walked toward a narrow, one-storey building of grey-painted concrete about fifty metres from the helicopter. Several smaller helicopters stood around the building, which bore no signs or markings whatsoever. They went in through a simple particleboard door, and came into a crowded room with brown-leather sofas and a large coffee machine. The pilot hung his headphones on a hook next to the machine, and pointed at the sofas.

'Wait here.'

Then he disappeared through a tinted-glass door. Eric sat on one of the worn sofas. The windows rattled as a plane took off and flew just above the roof. Again, he thought about his bag. It was idiotic to ask about it; the only thing he really missed was the Sutzkever book. The glass door opened, and two people came into the room. He recognised the first as the Mossad director who had interrogated him in Tel Aviv — David something-or-other. The other ... he gasped.

'Rachel?'

'Hello there, Professor.'

Her voice was weak. A light-brown compress, secured with tape, hid half of her left eye. Her face was full of cuts, and her lips were swollen. One arm was partially wrapped in some sort of cloth stocking. She walked slowly to the sofa, and gingerly sat down across from him. She was dressed simply, in blue sweatpants and a grey hoodie. He looked at her curiously.

'I slipped in the shower. How are you?' she asked.

He hesitated a second before answering.

'I'm okay.'

She tried to smile. Surely it was a warm smile, but her swollen lips made it look like a sarcastic grimace. The director of the Mossad stood behind her.

'Eric, good work. Unfortunately, we haven't got hold of any anti-virus. But we did secure two computers that we're in the process of analysing. Maybe we can find something there.'

'So what happens now?'

'Don't you want to go back to Sweden?'

Eric looked first at David Yassur and then at Rachel.

'Am I free to go?'

Both of them nodded. David smiled.

'We want to hear more about your time in the tunnel, but right now there's something more urgent.'

'I don't understand.'

'There's something you need to do.'

'What?'

'We're very worried about your wife.'

His stomach sank.

'Do you have any news about her?'

'She's very sick. The Swedish doctors don't seem able to do anything. Our American friends have offered to try to cure her.

But, as you know, in order to do so they have to move her to a military hospital in Norway. You would have to authorise this. The Swedish Ministry of Foreign Affairs is adamant on that point. So for your own sake, and for us all, help us help her.'

'And what do you want me to do?'

'We want you to fly to Stockholm — there's a plane leaving in less than two hours — and meet up with Paul Clinton from the FBI.'

He was startled.

'Clinton? The guy I ran away from?'

David nodded. 'He's in Sweden, and well aware of the situation. Don't worry about him bringing up past misdeeds. If you just go with him to the hospital and sign the papers, you'll be friends for life. Look at him as your last chance to save your wife.'

Eric looked at Rachel, who lowered her eyes. Something was wrong — David wasn't telling the whole truth. This all felt like a bad movie. Maybe they really did believe his story, that Hanna had a computer virus in her body. Could they cure her? Was that even their goal? There were too many warning signs; too many things felt wrong, just as they had the first time Rachel mentioned the hospital in Norway. He was still convinced that Hanna shouldn't leave Sweden, but he nodded anyway. He no longer had a better alternative. Without Nadim, his arsenal was empty.

'I'll sign the documents. Just take me home, and I'll get the authorisation in order.'

David looked pleased.

'Excellent. Good. That's the right decision. I think we'll manage to straighten out your woman. She's strong — like all Jewish women.'

Eric tried to look happy, too, but he wasn't sure he succeeded.

David leaned over the sofa and put out his hand.

'Then I'll say goodbye. You'll be called in for more debriefings in Sweden, which I'm guessing will take place at the Israeli embassy. But, hopefully, we won't see each other again.'

They shook hands.

'Someone will come to get you when it's time to board.'

David left them, and the glass door closed with a rattling bang. Another plane took off low above the building, filling the room with a deafening roar. Rachel looked at him, waiting for the noise to abate. Soon he would be on board a plane — on his way home, away from here. It was all there in her eyes. He swallowed. She shook her head gently.

'It would never work. I know.'

'Rachel … I …' Her eyes remained on him. She was waiting for him to continue, but he couldn't. Maybe he didn't want to. He changed the subject.

'Were you the ones who arranged things at the checkpoint at Erez?'

'What do you think? The border police had your fingerprints, your picture, your description, and your DNA. You would have needed more than a passport from an Italian sound technician to get through.' She shook her head. 'You didn't even look alike …'

'Strange. How could Samir, or Ahmad Waizy, or whoever it was, believe that a borrowed passport would work?'

'Maybe they didn't care if you made it or not. If you got through, great. If not, whatever. Or maybe it was a test. If you got through Erez, they knew you were a spy.'

Eric didn't say anything, shaken by the possibility that Samir already knew he was a spy when they met. What had he said? 'A miracle.' It was a miracle that he had got through.

'How did you find the camp? I never called.'

'You're so naïve. Do you really think we were relying on you to *call* us?'

He felt hurt, and stupid. Of course they had their own ways of keeping an eye on him.

'So how did you find me?'

'You had transmitters on you.'

'Where?'

'Here and there.'

'Why didn't you say anything?'

'It might have endangered the mission. If you'd become afraid, you might have destroyed the transmitters, or gotten rid of them. Or if you had been tortured … It was better for you not to know about them.'

'So the telephone was a joke that I was dumb enough to fall for.'

'Something like that.'

She leaned forward and put her hand on his knee.

'You did something huge. You accomplished something that none of the intelligence organisations in the world has managed to do. Something the whole world ought to thank you for.'

He let the words sink in. Was that true? It all just felt like one big failure to him. Then he suddenly remembered something important.

'Not all the terrorists are dead.'

She cocked her head — a habit he remembered from their dinner in Tel Aviv.

'What do you mean?'

'I don't really know. It was something Samir said to me. There's one more — an infiltrator.'

'An infiltrator of what?'

'The Knesset. One of them is in the Knesset, or maybe even in the government.'

She looked sceptical.

'I know it sounds crazy, but they have someone on the inside — someone close to Ben Shavit. That's how they knew that you were on their trail, that they had to switch targets in Tel Aviv.'

Rachel said nothing for a long time. He was well aware of her hand, which was still on his leg.

'Did you learn anything else? A name? What he does? Anything?'

He shook his head.

'I'm sorry. That's all I know.'

She looked up at the ceiling, and seemed to be gathering her strength. He ran his fingers over her hand. It was rough with scabs and cuts.

'That must have been a very odd shower you fell in.'

'Explosive.'

'Why did the soldiers kill him?'

'Who?'

'Samir Mustaf.'

She shook her head.

'You're not thinking clearly. Samir Mustaf was the creator of Mona. So our team's orders were clear: he was not to be harmed under any circumstances. With all due respect, he was the one who was supposed to be picked up at the camp. You were, too, of course, but Samir Mustaf was the highest priority. They were all trained to recognise him and to fire selectively during the operation. Unfortunately, he was already dead when they got there.'

Instantly, Eric realised what had happened. Ahmad had killed Samir for letting a spy into the camp. *No, not Ahmad. He was just a tool. I killed him. I kill everyone.*

She took his hand. They sat like that for a while, their fingers interlaced. When the front door was opened by a young police officer, Eric instinctively tried to take his hand back, but she held onto it.

'Eric?'

'Yes?'

'Don't let them move her.'

'What?'

'They're not interested in her survival. What they want is to limit the spread of the virus, and to carry out analyses — an autopsy.'

He shuddered. She squeezed his hand harder.

'Find a way, Eric. Don't let them move her.'

He nodded.

'I promise.'

She let go of him and stood up.

'Good luck, Professor. And remember that you were right when you saw the taxi driver at the hotel.'

'What do you mean?'

'There are good people around. Even in Tel Aviv.'

'I know.'

She gave a short nod and walked toward the glass door, limping on her left leg.

'Rachel.'

She stopped, but didn't turn around.

'Take care of yourself.'

She answered quietly, her back still to him.

'*Nesi'a tova.*'

'What?'

'Bon voyage.'

Then she disappeared through the glass door without closing it. He stood there, staring at the half-open door. The police officer behind him cleared his throat.

'Eric Söderqvist, I'm going to escort you to the Norwegian

Air flight to Stockholm.'

He nodded and followed the man. Just outside was a police car with flashing lights. The man opened the back door, and Eric sat down on the black-leather seat. On it was a white envelope with his name written sloppily on the front. As the car accelerated in the direction of the large terminal, he picked up the envelope and tore it open. There was only one thing in it — a small red booklet. It was ordinary and a bit worn. He had no money, no phone, and no house keys, but now he had his passport back. He had his identity back. He held the document tightly in his hand, and sank back against the seat.

Stockholm, Sweden

Martin Abrahamsson opened and closed his hand a few times to get his circulation going. He had mouse arm. Was that what it was called? Or maybe it was mouse hand. He had been working at the keyboard for six hours straight. His boss, Gabriella Malmborg, was finally on her way home from Brussels. She had made herself clear on the phone: they were to surrender Hanna Söderqvist. Not officially. Unofficially. But how could someone be unofficially surrendered? Gabriella had told him she'd gone through the Söderqvist case with the minister for foreign affairs. He had given the okay, but at the same time had stressed that he would deny all knowledge of this if it leaked. Martin understood what that implied. Despite the risks, Gabriella's orders were clear: Sweden would comply with the Americans' wishes, and Hanna Söderqvist would be quietly handed over to the FBI. Gabriella had asked about any precedents — any argument the Ministry of Foreign Affairs could lean on — so he had spent the last hour focusing on extradition laws and the Ministry of Justice's archives. The government certainly could give special permission for extradition, but only if a crime had been committed. Had a crime been committed? If what the FBI said was true, the husband had committed a crime. But Hanna Söderqvist hadn't. And therein lay the problem.

He closed his eyes. He hadn't slept more than three or four hours in two days, and given even a moment his body would jump at the chance. He sank down in the small desk chair, and was soon leaning alarmingly far to one side. Then the phone rang. He jolted upright and looked at the blinking handset on the table, still half asleep. It was an unknown number. He stiffly reached out and answered it.

'Mr. Abrahamsson! I have good news.'

It was Paul Clinton. He hated him already.

'What's that?'

'He's on his way home.'

'Who is?'

'Eric Söderqvist.'

Martin stood up.

'How do you know that?'

Paul laughed.

'Hey, you're forgetting who you're talking to. He's on his way here from Tel Aviv. I'm meeting him at the airport in a few hours. We're going straight to the hospital. I suggest you meet us there with the order and affidavit, and we'll get this taken care of right away. Then you can go home to your family and snuggle up with the wife.'

'Has he been informed that you want to move Hanna Söderqvist to Oslo?'

'He has been informed, and his attitude is positive.'

'Positive?'

'You bet. He's going to sign all the necessary documents, and he's promised to help in every way he can. He wants nothing more than for her to be healthy. It's that simple.'

'What about the suspicions against him?'

'It's a long story. Unfortunately, it's all top secret. But, in any case, he's no longer a suspect.'

Martin tried to catch his breath as his tired brain tried to absorb this information.

'If he's no longer a suspect, then what's the nature of the virus that you think is in Hanna Söderqvist? And how did it get there?'

Paul didn't speak for a moment.

'We don't know. The change in his status doesn't solve the problem with Hanna Söderqvist. She's still sick, and we still have every reason to fear that a biological weapon is involved. Do what you need to do, and we'll see each other at the hospital at four o'clock. You'll get to meet Eric Söderqvist then, too.'

The connection was broken. He looked at the clock — four hours left. There was an awful lot to do to obtain all the orders. He sat down and logged into the Ministry for Foreign Affairs's intranet. *Go home and snuggle up with the wife.* God, what an idiot.

Tel Aviv, Israel

Eric was allowed to board before the other passengers, and he sat at the very front of the cabin. The plane smelled like dusty fabric. The cockpit door was open; inside, he could see a pilot reading material in a binder. Two flight attendants were clattering around in the galley. Rachel's words rang in his ears: *autopsy.* Could it really be true? And how could he rescue Hanna from the FBI? As soon as he got to Sweden, Paul Clinton would be waiting for him in the arrivals hall, and they would go straight to the hospital. Could he refuse to sign the Ministry for Foreign Affairs's agreement? Hardly. The FBI and the ministry would find other ways to move her.

He was on his way home. It felt completely surreal. He was on his way to Hanna, but he was terrified of seeing her — terrified of being faced with her illness, terrified of real life in the white room at Karolinska, far from Gaza and Tel Aviv.

Passengers started streaming in; they were crowding and jostling around him. An older couple stopped, and the woman nodded at the seats near the window. He stood up and let them by. The woman sat by the window and the man, who was short and heavy with bushy white hair, sat down next to Eric with a grunt. Eric took his seat again and fastened his seatbelt. The woman poked the man and said in a broad southern-Swedish accent, 'Stig, don't forget to turn off your phone.'

The man groaned, picked up a backpack, and dug out a black Sony Ericsson. Then Eric had an idea.

'Excuse me. I forgot something very important, and I would be very grateful if I could borrow your phone for a minute. I'm just going to send a text.'

The man turned to his wife, who shook her head.

'We're about to take off. You have to turn it off.'

The man gave him the phone.

'You heard her. Be quick — no time to write a novel.'

Eric nodded gratefully, took the phone, and typed in Jens's number:

ON MY WAY HOME ON NORWEGIAN. GOING STRAIGHT TO THE
HOSPITAL. MFA TO SURRENDER HANNA TO FBI.
//ERIC

Once he'd made sure the text had been sent, he erased it and handed back the phone.

'Thanks so much. That was really nice of you.'

'No problem. Have you been in Israel for a long time?'

He shook his head. 'Just a few days.'

'Did you have time to see anything?'

'Quite a bit. And you?'

'We sure did. We're travelling with the Church of Sweden, and we visited Jerusalem and Bethlehem. It was fantastic. It should do us for a long time. Right, Monica?'

He looked at his wife, who was still irritated about the phone. She pointedly turned away. Eric returned to his chaotic thoughts. Samir Mustaf was dead, and the camp had been razed. Would the Israelis find anything useful in the confiscated computers? Maybe. But it might take weeks, or even longer. And, anyway, they wouldn't share what they found. Hanna wouldn't receive any magical medicine. That was a fact. What would happen? Would she be in a coma forever? Would her body eventually give up? Could she be cured without the anti-virus? Miracles could happen. Absolutely, they could. But the ache in his stomach, the pressure in his chest — these were painful proof that his subconscious knew better.

The airplane banked, and the engines revved loudly. He looked out of the small window next to the woman. Thousands of small houses passed below them, separated by winding lines of cars. He wished he could listen to some music — anything to loosen the knots in his stomach — and fished the little iPod out of his pocket. It was the only thing he still had from when he'd left home, apart from his passport and the clothes on his back. When he clicked on the round menu, the screen lit up, and he browsed through the composers, feeling a certain sense of calm just from seeing the familiar names. He straightened up in his seat and looked around. A stewardess was standing in the galley, packing boxed lunches on a red-and-white cart.

'Excuse me.'

She put two boxes down beside the cart and came up to him with a broad smile.

'What can I do for you?'

'I'm wondering if there are any headphones I could borrow.'

'I'll see what I can find.'

She disappeared toward the rear of the plane.

Eric spun the thin little iPod between his fingers and thought about when Samir had come into the cell with it. Music was something they shared — something that gave both of them comfort, maybe more than religion, revenge, or love. It was what they turned to when things were at their worst. Samir had wanted to do something for him before his difficult night. Music was the best thing — maybe the only thing — he had to offer.

'Here. They're not great, but they're better than nothing.'

The flight attendant handed him a pair of simple black headphones with a thin silver band and large black ear cushions.

'I think they'll work.'

'Thank you very much. They'll be fine.'

He plugged them in and returned to the playlist. Then he happened to think of Samir's last words. He'd said that he had loaded some music for him, by Tchaikovsky. A masterpiece, he'd called it — Tchaikovsky's seventh symphony. What else had he said? *Maybe it can give you your love back.* That sounded nice. It was the only memory, the only trace, of Samir he had left — one symphony. He found Tchaikovsky, and scrolled through his works. He found his old files: the second, fifth, and sixth symphonies; *Pathétique*; two of his ballets, *Swan Lake* and *The Nutcracker*; several piano and violin concertos, *Romeo and Juliet*; and chamber music — but no seventh symphony. He was convinced he'd never heard of Tchaikovsky's seventh symphony.

'What did you say?'

He looked up and met the eyes of the man with the bushy white hair.

'Me? Did I say something?'

The man nodded. 'You said "seven".'

'Sorry. I was talking to myself.'

'It's an interesting number — an important number with a lot of symbolic meaning.'

Eric felt irritated, and pointedly tried to indicate that he was listening to music. He left the headphones on and held up the iPod.

'The number seven is a universal symbol of consummation. Or completion. Perfection.'

He recalled that Samir had said it was a perfect symphony. He took off his headphones.

'Interesting.'

Inspired, the man went on. 'Just think of Jesus's seven words on the cross, the seven sacraments in the Catholic church, the seven cardinal sins. In the Bible, Jacob had to work seven years to earn Rachel, and the Book of Revelations talks about the scroll with the seven seals.'

'Did you write a dissertation on a number?'

The man laughed.

'No, no, but I'm interested in symbols. The number seven is also the fourth prime number.'

'I knew that.'

'Good. But maths isn't my subject; religion is. The Ottomans liked the number seven, too. For example, they built seven minarets in the city of Bitola in Macedonia just after they'd conquered it — in the mid-seventeenth century, if I'm not mistaken.'

Eric went rigid and stared ahead in silence. He nodded curtly at the man.

'Excuse me.'

He went back to the iPod. Was it a code? Had Samir meant something else? It was impossible that one of the world's foremost IT experts hadn't been able to transfer a music file to an iPod. So why wasn't there any seventh symphony by Tchaikovsky on the playlist? He returned to the main menu and scrolled through the options. At the very bottom, a totally new category popped up:

To Eric

He took a breath, opened the folder, and found one file. He stared at it as though bewitched.

Tchaikovsky nr. 7 // Concert for Nadim

The world around him disappeared. The trays of food arrived, but he ignored them. What had Samir said? *Maybe it can give you your love back.* Jesus Christ. Jesus fucking Christ. Tchaikovsky's seventh wasn't a music file. It was Nadim — the anti-virus. Samir had loaded the anti-virus on his iPod. He must have hoped that Eric would somehow survive — make it out of the camp, and get home. Samir himself had died a few hours later, but he'd managed to leave a legacy within this thin slab of steel. Eric squeezed it in his hand and looked out the window at the blue sky, and at the sunlight flashing on the metal wing.

The exhaustion was too tempting, too final. She couldn't fight anymore; she collapsed. She pressed her naked body against the bare wall. It was now almost completely dark in the passage outside the ground floor of

NK. She could still hear the storm at the top of the stairs. She pulled her legs up to her chin, and rested her head on her knees. She thought of the old alarm clock. Humanity was over. All life was gone. The world would either start over or just slowly give up. Nature would dry out, suffocated by the white ash. She shuddered. It didn't matter. Nothing mattered. She just wanted to sleep. Perhaps she could hear a girl's voice, sobbing and urging her to wake up, begging, shouting that she couldn't fall asleep. Maybe she felt small, as cold hands shook her. But she wanted to sleep. She wanted to sleep and never wake up.

Eric didn't have any luggage, so he went straight through the empty customs hall. When he came out into the arrivals hall, he stopped and looked around. Paul Clinton was supposed to be waiting for him. It felt unreal. The thought of seeing the FBI agent in the midst of this Swedish environment, among Pressbyrån kiosks and yellow Arlanda Express signs, was bizarre. He looked around but couldn't see him, and was just starting to hope that he wouldn't be there when he saw him sitting alone at the café near the exit. Their eyes met. He steeled himself against the desire to run in the other direction, and instead walked up to the American.

'On time — not bad. Nice to see you again. Was your flight okay?'

'It was fine.'

Paul took a blue folder from the table and stood up.

'We're going straight to the hospital. We can take care of the paperwork when we get there. The Ministry for Foreign Affairs will meet us there.'

They went toward the revolving doors and on toward the parking lot. The air was warm, and full of the Swedish summer. *The Ministry for Foreign Affairs will meet us there.* So it was all settled and arranged. There was no way out. He was angry. Could they really hand over a citizen just like that? He hated the chubby man ahead of him. How do you negotiate with the American government? How do you explain that they've got it all wrong? And how the hell could the Swedish authorities just swallow all the bullshit they were being fed? What would happen if he didn't sign the consent form, if he simply refused? All he wanted was to be alone with Hanna for a few minutes — long enough to transfer Nadim. He glanced at Paul. What if he knew that Eric had the anti-virus in his pocket? Should he tell him? Could he use the anti-virus as a bargaining chip to keep Hanna in Sweden?

It was too risky. Nadim was too desirable. They would just take the iPod away from him, and then he would have no chance to use the anti-virus on her. It would have to be his last resort. He decided not to tell anyone about Tchaikovsky's seventh symphony, but he did feel a bit better. Having Nadim was an advantage, whatever it was worth.

A black Volvo V70 started up as they approached the parking lot. He recognised the other FBI agent at the wheel. It was the arrogant one — the man he had tripped over when he was thrown out of the little booth in the security area. Paul opened the back door for him, but then he changed his mind and laughed.

'Sorry, my old police reflexes are showing. You take the front seat; I'll sit in back. You're no bad guy.'

Eric opened the door and sat down on the grey-fabric seat beside the driver. He didn't remember his name; he didn't even know if he'd ever learned it. The car smelled new, with a rental contract from Avis on the floor by his feet. The man gave a quick nod, and backed out of the parking spot. Paul leaned forward between the seats.

'I heard you did a good job in the sandpit the other night.'

'I survived.'

'So you did. But not the towelheads.'

'The towelheads?'

'The terrorists. Haven't you noticed they like to wear towels on their heads? In every fucking possible colour. But I'm not complaining. It makes it easier to see them.'

'I'm sure it does.'

'You bet. But you have to be careful. All of a sudden, one of those little bastards will take off the towel and put on a suit. Or a Yankees jersey and a baseball cap. Those are the really dangerous ones — the ones in camouflage.'

He thumped the back of the seat.

'But they can't trick me, dammit. You can tell that their suits fit like potato sacks. And they smell like kebabs.'

The car was speeding along as they passed the exit for Kista. Paul's tone changed, and he became more earnest.

'Do you understand that we're the only ones who can save your wife? No one else has the experience of CBRN.'

'CBRN?'

'Chemical, biological, radioactive, and nuclear threats. We believe she might be infected with some sort of biological weapon. Maybe a prototype for a terror virus.'

'So now you believe my story?'

'At first I was sure that you'd cooked something up on Hezbollah's orders. After your home run in Gaza, though, I don't know what to think. But it's not up to me to give a diagnosis — the experts in Oslo will have to do that. If everything goes well, we can move her as soon as tonight. We're all set. And do you know what the best thing is?'

'No.'

'It won't cost you a thing. Just thank Uncle Sam.'

Eric's mouth was dry. Hanna was to be tossed onto a butcher's table in an American military lab. Over his dead body.

Something woke her. She cautiously lifted her head. Farther down the passage toward the shopping centre, the darkness took over and swallowed up every colour and shape. The storm was over, and everything was quiet once again.

'Is anyone there?'

The words rolled along the black-and-white paving stones, and dissolved into the dark. The seconds plodded on. Nothing happened. She gathered her courage, took a deep breath, and stood up. She was on her way to the stairs when she heard the girl's voice.

'Hanna.' She sounded frightened. Hanna carefully approached the open door of NK.

'Un. Ge … ou … er.' The voice was distant and faint. All the nerves in her body resisted. Not into the darkness. Not in. She went in. 'Un. Ge … o … er.' The echo made it hard to understand what she was saying. Could the girl be in danger? She remembered that there was a wide staircase a bit farther in — a staircase that led down to the kitchen department. She was now far inside the department store, and the door behind her hung like a distant rectangle in black space. She felt the stairs with her feet. She swallowed and called out.

'I'm here. Where are you? As she reached the last stair, the girl's voice came back, this time loudly and clearly.

'Hanna! Run. Get out of here.'

Panic flooded her. A trap. She backed up, but ran into something and took a hard fall.

'Hanna, run! Please. Run!'

With her tailbone throbbing, she got up, fumbled in the darkness, and found the stairs. As she came to the top stair, she could see the glowing rectangle hovering far ahead. Freedom. The exit. She went faster, half-running toward the light, sure that the evil was catching up. She tripped over boxes and nearly fell, but regained her balance. A silhouette moved out of the blackness and stood in the middle of the bright rectangle. She gasped and stopped short. Death wasn't behind *her. It was ahead — an impenetrable wall between her and freedom. She knew that she would never be able to escape. She didn't even have the strength to try, and she sank to the floor, panting. The man got bigger and bigger, and his shape soon filled the whole rectangle. He was coming toward her. All three of them knew that it was over — the naked woman on the floor among shards of glass, ash, and stationery; the little girl in the darkness by the stairs; and the faceless man. This was the end. She was the last one.*

They turned off the road and stopped in one of the handicap spots outside Karolinska Hospital. As they walked toward the entrance, Eric suddenly realised that he was about to see Hanna — realised it emotionally, and not just intellectually. How would she look? Would he even be able to handle seeing her? Shame, anguish, and worry tumbled through him and made him stop. He realised that he was breathing too fast, and tried to pull himself together. Paul Clinton noticed him lagging behind, and threw up his hands.

'Come on. What are you doing?'

There was a hint of anxiety in his voice as well. For him, too, there was a lot at stake. They arrived at the large elevators, and Paul's taciturn colleague pressed the button. Eric tried to think clearly, but his nerves blocked out all of his thoughts. How could he keep Hanna in Sweden? He couldn't exactly throw himself on top of her and hold on tightly. Paul seemed to read his mind; he took out the blue folder, and from it he pulled a piece of paper full of writing. In the upper-right-hand corner was the yellow-and-blue three-crowns emblem of the government offices of Sweden.

'Before we get up there, you need to sign this. Don't bother reading all the fine print. It just gives us permission to move her into the care of specialists in Norway.'

He handed over the paper, along with a green pen from Grand Hôtel.

'The government guys are waiting for you upstairs, and all they need is your signature.'

The thought that Hanna was now only a few floors away helped push away his doubts. He took the paper and looked at it without seeing it. The elevator arrived, a nurse rolled a large bed out of it, and the three of them stepped in. The doors closed. Paul pressed the button for the sixth floor. Eric was still standing with the paper in one hand and the pen in the other. The sixth floor — she hadn't been there before. They must have moved her. Paul leaned toward him impatiently.

'Here. Sign on this line.'

'What if I refuse?'

The FBI agent slammed the emergency-stop button, and the elevator stopped with a jerk. Paul's colleague moved at lightning speed. He clamped Eric's shoulders as hard as a vice. Paul looked him in the eye.

'Listen here, you little shit. The only reason you're here is because I told the Mossad to let you go, on the condition that you'd co-operate. If you don't sign, we'll take the elevator right back down and take a walk in the woods.'

His face was so close that Eric could see each nose hair, and each red pore in his skin. He smelled like coffee.

'Don't think for a second that we can't do to you exactly what we did to the towelheads. If Michael is given free rein, you'll be begging to sign that fucking piece of paper. I guarantee you, it's better to do it now.'

He straightened up and tucked in his shirt, which had come loose from his waistband. Michael let go of Eric.

'And, besides, it will buy you time. Every second we lose could be disastrous for your wife.'

Eric no longer had the strength to resist. He had no better ideas or plans. He pressed the piece of paper against the elevator wall and signed it. Paul yanked the document back from him.

'That was a damn-smart choice.'

He pressed the elevator button.

'You can keep the pen.'

The elevator moved again. They arrived at the sixth floor, and the doors opened with a ding. As soon as they were out, Paul took out his phone, signalled to them to wait, and made a call. He turned away when he received an answer and spoke quietly. Eric looked around. There were frosted-glass doors in both directions. The one on the right had a green sign that said 'Unit I61. Observation.' The one on the left had a similar sign that said 'Unit I62. Isolation Unit.' Under the sign was a list of instructions about shoe covers, hair covers, and masks. On the glass was a red biohazard symbol on a white background. He recognised the symbol from movies: a circle in the middle with three half-open circles above it, like rings left by a coffee mug. Beside this threatening sign was a black-and-yellow triangle that warned of gas canisters inside. Paul hung up and turned to them in frustration.

'The idiot from the Ministry for Foreign Affairs went down to get a coffee. We'll wait here — there's no point in going in without him.'

Eric ran a hand through his hair.

'Is Dr Wethje here?'

Paul nodded.

'He should be. I assume the government guy has already talked to him.'

The elevators dinged, and one of them opened. A young man with thin blond hair and round glasses came out. He was obviously nervous. He walked up to the trio waiting between the glass doors, and put out his hand to Eric.

'Welcome home. My name is Martin Abrahamsson. I work for the Ministry for Foreign Affairs.'

Eric shook his hand.

'I'm really sorry about your wife's condition. Hopefully, the American doctors can help her.'

Eric didn't answer; he just looked at him blankly. The man looked uncertain, as if he wanted to say something more, but Paul took over.

'Mr Abrahamsson, here's your authorisation. Signed, sealed, and delivered.'

He handed over the document, and Abrahamsson took it and studied the signature closely, clearly still thinking. Paul seemed to sense his hesitation, and cleared his throat.

'Gentlemen, I suggest that we all go in and talk to the doctor to figure out arrangements for the transfer.'

He opened the glass door into the isolation unit. Abrahamsson let his gaze linger on Eric before he followed the Americans through the door. Eric remained outside for a long moment; he couldn't find the strength to go in. The others were standing just inside the door, pulling on shoe covers and washing their hands. Paul caught sight of him.

'Hey, come on. It's time to see the wife.'

Eric walked slowly into the long corridor, which was similar to the one he'd been in the last time he visited Hanna. He remembered the angry nurse and the large Securitas guard. The unit was quiet, and the lights were dim. He grabbed two blue shoe covers from a pile on the floor, and pulled them over his shoes. Paul seemed to have relaxed a bit, but Abrahamsson still looked stressed. Michael's face was expressionless; he still hadn't said a word since they'd met in the car at Arlanda. Paul gestured theatrically at the corridor.

'Shall we?'

They started walking, and Martin Abrahamsson flipped through his papers. Without turning around, Paul called out, 'If I remember correctly, it's room one-fifteen.'

One of the doors flew open with a bang, and several people came out into the corridor. At first, Eric recognised only Thomas Wethje. There was a flash, and a tumult broke out. Thomas said something, his voice shrill and agitated. Eric grimaced as a camera flashed in his eyes. Then someone shouted, over and over. He recognised the voice immediately. It was Jens! Eric took a step to the side and caught sight of his friend, with his green loafers, yellow pants, dark-blue shirt, and bushy blond hair. He was standing with his legs planted wide apart, in front of a pale Martin Abrahamsson, pushing his press card with its yellow-and-red *Aftonbladet* logo into Abrahamsson's face. He bellowed his questions with exaggerated aggression.

'Can the ministry confirm that the government of Sweden is selling out a sick Swedish citizen to the American FBI? Can the ministry confirm that they're trying to hush up a risk of infection by getting rid of the patient instead of treating her? Can the ministry confirm that the surrender of the patient has been pushed by anti-Semitic voices in the government?

Abrahamsson backed away and tried to protect himself from the flashing cameras. Behind Jens were two photographers — a black-haired woman in a leather jacket, and a young man with greasy hair, wearing a T-shirt. Their cameras were clattering like automatic weapons.

'What the fuck!'

Paul turned around and looked at Eric, his eyes glowing in fury.

'You did this! You fucking idiot!'

Martin Abrahamsson tore open a door at random to get away

410

from the commotion. The last thing Eric saw was him fumbling with the buttons on his mobile phone. Jens turned his attention to the Americans.

'Who do you report to? Does the American ambassador know that the FBI is trying to kidnap Swedish citizens?'

Paul shoved the camera away.

'Go to hell.'

He tried to shove past Jens to get to Hanna's room, but the reporter was too large and bulky. Thomas Wethje had moved around the photographers, and was now standing beside Eric. He placed a hand on his shoulder, and nodded toward the agents swearing under the flood of flashes.

'Don't worry, it will be okay. We're just waiting to see what instructions the ministry guy gets.'

They didn't have to wait long. The door opened, and Martin Abrahamsson looked out, waving Paul and Michael over. Jens and the photographers let them go while they stayed in the middle of the corridor. The Ministry for Foreign Affairs and the FBI closed the door on what one could only assume was an emergency meeting. Things had not gone at all as Paul had planned. Jens must have received the text message that Eric had sent just before the plane took off. And now *Aftonbladet's* involvement had changed the rules of the game. This was the Fourth Estate at its best.

Eric made eye contact with Jens for the first time. Jens gave him a short nod, and Eric smiled wanly and nodded back. Paul came out into the corridor. His hands were balled into fists, and his face was red. He walked past Eric without a word. Just behind him was Michael, who jostled Eric as he went by. They both disappeared through the glass door, slamming it behind them. Martin Abrahamsson also came out of the room, now looking much calmer. He walked up to Eric.

'I've spoken with my boss, and I'm sorry to have to tell you that we can no longer agree to the surrender of your wife. I hope this isn't too much of a disappointment to you. I'm sure that the Swedish health-care system will also be able to help her get better.'

Eric gave a weak smile.

'I think so, too. What's going on with our American friends?'

'They're going straight to Arlanda. They will be declared *persona non grata*. Tell your journalist over there that the ministry has no comment on what just happened. I would appreciate it if we were left out of it. Good luck.'

He walked briskly toward the exit and disappeared. Eric turned to Thomas Wethje.

'How is my wife?'

'I wish I had good news, but unfortunately I don't. She is not well at all.'

They started toward Jens.

'Which means?'

'She's still in a coma, and her heartbeat is irregular. Her body is worn out, her vital functions are under great stress, and we still haven't seen anything to indicate that her illness might take a different course than Mats Hagström's. You're aware that we lost him?'

Eric nodded.

'How come he died, but Hanna is still alive?'

'We're not really sure. The body is placed under great strain when the virus attacks the vital organs. Mats couldn't handle it. Hanna has been able to withstand it, so far.' They came up to Jens, who was just thanking his two colleagues.

'I was right, wasn't I? You didn't even need to have memory cards in your cameras. Thanks again. See you.'

The woman in the leather jacket hugged him. Then they walked down the corridor, with the woman humming something as she went. When the door closed again, the three men looked at each other in silence. Eric realised that they were standing outside room 115. He sought his friend's gaze.

'Hi, Jens.'

'Hey, you. How have things been?'

'Turbulent. How are you?'

'Worried.'

They became quiet again. Jens ran both hands over his face — a gesture that indicated how tired he was. Then he looked at Eric.

'Do you have it?'

'What?'

'The anti-virus?'

Eric was nonplussed. Was he being sarcastic? He collected himself and nodded.

'I have it.'

He dug in his pocket, found the iPod, and held it up.

'Here, embedded in symphonies and minuets.'

'What are you planning to do with it?'

'I'm planning to upload it to Mind Surf and transfer it to her.'

Jens nodded.

'Good. What can I do?' This was incredible. Jens must have been feeling desperate — ready to try anything, even a digital anti-virus. Eric turned triumphantly to Thomas. The doctor shook his head.

'We've just started trying the anti-retroviral drug Centric Novatrone. In a few days we'll know if it has any effect. It's a modified version; I have high hopes for it.'

He hesitated.

'I remember your theory about the computer virus. But it's impossible for a person to be affected by a computer virus. Thus the hypothesis that Hanna could be cured by an anti-virus is completely absurd — absurd and impossible.'

Jens placed a hand on the doctor's shoulder.

'Thomas, I know you have a hard time believing this story, so I'll ask you this instead: do you really think it might be dangerous for Hanna to be hooked up to Eric's computer? I mean, you've already got a whole ton of machines hooked up to her in there.' He nodded toward the closed room. 'Surely one more won't make any damn difference?'

'That's where you're wrong. Her neural activity is very fragile, and the tiniest disturbance could do her harm. Forget the science-fiction stories, and let's wait for the anti-retroviral.'

Eric couldn't restrain his rage.

'Don't you get it? We have no time to waste. You've been testing all kinds of shit for several weeks. One of your patients is already dead. What are the chances that this drug will work when everything else has failed?'

Thomas looked him straight in the eye.

'And why would your method be any better?'

'Because it's something totally different. Something new.'

He clenched his fists.

'Thomas, I truly believe we can save her. Honestly. It's unorthodox. It's totally crazy, without a doubt. But I've travelled around the world to get hold of this fucking program. I'm her husband. I love her. And what have we got to lose?'

The doctor looked up at the ceiling, standing stock-still with his neck bent back, apparently studying the grooves on the ceiling tiles. Then he lowered his head and looked at them, first at Jens and then at Eric.

'Do you two really believe that this is an actual possibility?'

Jens nodded.

'Eric is no idiot. And if we don't try everything, what hope do we have?'

Thomas threw up his hands.

'I'll try Centric Novatrone, but if it doesn't work I have no

414

more weapons in my arsenal. All that's left is magic spells and ...' He sighed in resignation. '... science fiction. Bring in your program and the equipment you need. But before you do anything clinical, you will explain to me in detail what you're planning to do. If there's anything that risks harming my patient or making her worse, I will refuse.'

Eric nodded.

'You won't regret it. Thank you for being willing to believe in something so far-fetched.'

The doctor shook his head.

'No, you've misunderstood. I don't believe for a second that a computer virus could have infected Hanna Söderqvist. But as long as I know that what you do won't harm her, I will let you have your way. I would have done the same thing if you'd wanted to hang a Star of David over her bed, put garlic under her pillow, or have a rabbi read over her. It's all for your sake, Eric. If, God forbid, we should lose her, you won't have to regret that you didn't get to try everything. But I would prefer not to inform the rest of the staff. And this isn't something I'm going to write about for a journal. If anybody claims later on that I agreed to this, I will deny it. Understood?'

Eric nodded and looked excitedly at Jens.

'I'll stay here and go through the plans with the doctor. You go to my house and get the Mind Surf equipment. I'll write down everything I need.'

He looked around for a piece of paper. Thomas handed him a notepad and a small green pen, which Eric used to fill a page before handing it to Jens.

'And you'll need my keys.'

Eric smacked his forehead.

'No ... Shit. I don't have any.'

For a few seconds, he was at a loss. Then Jens placed a hand on his shoulder.

'Brother, I still have your keys from when I watered your flowers at Christmas. Just have to go home and get them.'

'Brilliant! But I'm warning you, there are a lot of things to bring. Can you manage by yourself?'

Jens nodded, stuck the paper in his pocket, and left.

Eric turned to the doctor.

'Can we sit down somewhere? I'm going to try to explain what I'm planning to do.'

Thomas shook his head.

'No rush. Jens won't be back for at least an hour, will he?'

He reached out and held open the door to room 115.

'Before we talk about your computer program, I think you should sit with the lady in here for a while.'

Eric got a lump in his throat. He had purposefully put off seeing her again.

'You have to put on a gown, gloves, and an FFP3.'

'A what?' He stepped into the small room between the doors.

'A face mask. They're in that box. And don't take it off while you're in there with her.' Thomas let go of the door, which closed softly after him. Eric was alone in the little anteroom. He put on the protective gear, swallowed, and entered the room.

It was nearly dark. There was just a dim ceiling light, and a small reading lamp beside the single bed on the far side of the room, next to a window with drawn curtains. A rhythmic clicking and hissing sound came from the respirator, and blue lines ran gently across two black screens. The room smelled of disinfectant. He walked quietly, as though not to wake her, and held his breath all the way up to the bed. The face mask was pinching his nose. When he saw her, the dam broke and he started crying, sobbing violently in a release of weeping that had built up during the last day and had only trickled out here and there — until now. The tears streamed down his cheeks, and he grasped the silver rail at the end of the bed.

'Dear, dear love. I'm sorry. I'm sorry for all this crap. For everything I've done.'

The words streamed out of him as uncontrollably as the tears, and he mumbled and sniffled. She was so beautiful lying there, like a porcelain doll — a Sleeping Beauty. Her arms rested on top of the blanket; her thin hands were clasped as if in prayer. He swallowed and tried to compose himself. Then he sat down on the chair beside the bed. He smoothed the blanket and then carefully stroked her cheek with the back of his gloved hand. He whispered quietly, 'I'm here. And I'll never leave you again. Never.'

The room was enormous, like a giant hangar. Everything was blindingly white — walls, floor, ceiling. She was lying on a metal bed in the middle of the room. Like on an altar. She was lying on an altar like a holy goddess. A temple! That's what it was, she was in a temple. There were no windows, and no furniture except for the steel altar. She tried to lift her head, but something stopped her. She was tied down. White straps crossed her chest, her waist, her knees, and her ankles. Even though she was vulnerable and captive, there was something calming about the situation. Something fantastic was about to happen — something she'd dreamed of. She was meant to be here. Everything was in balance. Like a distant dream, there was NK and the silhouette that had come toward her. But the man she had seen no longer seemed frightening. Now she longed for him. Longed for the man without a face.

The door of the unit opened with a bang, and Jens shoved in a stretcher loaded with boxes and plastic bags. Thomas Wethje hurried to help him.

'Put it all into room 115.' When they arrived in Hanna's room, he nodded at Eric and panted through his mask.

'Hey, that was an awful lot of stuff you needed. I emptied your whole house. I opened the windows while I was there — it was pretty stuffy. And don't even ask about your flowers.'

Thomas popped up just behind him, and shot a doubtful look at the boxes. Maybe he had changed his mind. Eric was just about to say something when a nurse with short blonde hair opened the door behind him. She looked at them in bewilderment.

Thomas cast a quick glance at Eric and then gave a strained nod to the woman.

'Hi, Pia, everything is fine. Apparently, we're getting a new EKG. Finally.'

The short woman looked sceptically at the tense men standing around the stretcher full of cardboard boxes and ICA grocery bags. Then she turned to Thomas.

'Another EKG?'

Thomas's tone became sharper. 'That's right. I'd appreciate it if you dealt with Lannerstedt in 117. She's been complaining of a headache. Considering her hypertension and medication ...'

The woman stood still for a moment, her eyes on the stretcher, and then she shook her head and went back into the corridor. Thomas turned to Eric.

'Pia's a great gal. I might have to tell her what we ... what you're doing.'

'That's for you to decide. As long as all hell doesn't break loose and we aren't interrupted before we've finished.'

Thomas didn't answer. He still looked doubtful, but didn't say anything as they rolled the stretcher into the room. They aligned it with the bed, and Eric immediately started digging through the boxes and bags. He found the computer in the largest box. It took him about an hour to hook up the system, find the right cords, find extension cords to plug things in, and place all fifty wires from the sensor helmet into the converter. Nurse Pia hovered around the room, and finally Thomas took her into the office to explain. He had worked with her for many years, and assured them that they could trust her. Jens was restless.

'How's it going?'

'I'm almost ready. You brought the nanogel, right?'

Jens nodded and searched through the ICA bags.

'Here.'

He fished out a small tube of shimmering purple liquid. Thomas showed up with a clipboard in his hand.

'Like me, Pia didn't understand any of this science fiction, but she respects the fact that you believe in it. She won't cause any trouble.'

'Thanks.'

'No problem. Now I need to do some tests on my patient. As I said, several hours ago we started a trial of a modified version of the anti-retroviral Centric Novatrone. This new formula has just been approved for clinical use. We're the first ones in Europe to use it.'

Eric looked up at him from his spot on the floor where he was braiding wires together.

'The first? That sounds alarming.'

Thomas gave a small smile.

'Yes, unfortunately it wasn't manufactured in a cellar full of terrorists. It was developed by one of the world's largest pharmaceutical companies, so there is every reason to worry.'

'Touché. But you know what you're doing, right?'

'I know what I'm doing. I have a hypothesis about how the virus reproduces. If I'm right, Centric Novatrone might make a big difference.'

He went over to Hanna and started typing commands on a small keyboard just below the black screens. Eric pulled a chair over and sat at the stretcher, which was functioning as an improvised computer table. He pressed the start button on the keyboard, and heard the fans start up on the server that stood on the floor under the stretcher. The screen flickered into life and started listing drivers. He took the small tube of gel and went to Hanna. Thomas stood beside him, writing on the clipboard.

'No effect yet from the medicine, but it should start working very soon. And you?'

Eric opened the tube and pushed the hair out of Hanna's face with one hand.

'I'm going to apply the gel. It needs to be absorbed for half an hour before we start.'

'I understand. I'm still not satisfied with your explanation of what is in that gunk.'

'I know, but as I said, I'm not the one who made it. And I couldn't get hold of the professor at Kyoto University who's responsible for it — we're in different time zones. But I gave you the contents list for the previous version, and that should be 95 per cent accurate.'

'But, jellyfish?'

'Yes, jellyfish. Natural material from the sea. Can't do any harm.'

'I don't know — it's not exactly great.'

Thomas put the screens back over Hanna and squeezed past Eric.

'I have to take some data to the lab. You've got my pager number, and Pia's here on the floor. Good luck.'

'Thanks. We'll start in about fifteen minutes.'

'Okay, we'll see if I make it back. The most important thing for me is the Centric Novatrone test. Nothing against what you're doing, but I think you understand.' Eric smiled faintly.

'I understand.'

After the doctor had gone, Eric started rubbing the

shimmering gel into Hanna's hair. He remembered the first time he had put it on her. She had asked for a massage, laughing and smiling, wanting to cuddle. But instead of making love, he had hooked up the system and infected her with a deadly virus. Now he ran his fingers along her ears, over her forehead, and all the way around her scalp, and then replaced the cap on the empty tube and wiped his hands on a napkin. Back at the keyboard, he started Mind Surf. Jens was sitting silently on one of the visitors' chairs; perhaps he had dozed off. Ten minutes later, everything was ready to go. Now it was time for the most important thing of all — to see if Nadim really could conquer Mona. Eric knew that the Mind Surf computer was infected. If he loaded the anti-virus onto the server, the program ought to search out Mona and erase it. This was no easy task, considering that the virus was camouflaged, it mutated in real time, and it was sure to contain a number of defence mechanisms that were completely unknown to him. He took out the little iPod and hooked it up to the computer's USB port. It showed up as an external device on the screen, and with rising anxiety he found the invaluable file:

TCHAIKOVSKY NR. 7 // CONCERT FOR NADIM

He hesitated at the Enter key for a few seconds. If something went wrong, or if the file were corrupt, all hope would be gone. He was back holding a lottery ticket. As long as the file was there on the screen, the dream was alive. He looked at Hanna; the gel shimmered like a halo on her forehead. Soon he would put the sensor helmet on her and hook her up to Mind Surf, but it was all going to depend on Samir's anti-virus program working. The arrow trembled over Tchaikovsky Number Seven. It was time to listen to the master's final symphony, posthumously. He hit Enter.

They were dressed in white — the faceless man and the little girl. Her hair was no longer matted; it had been brushed and put up with a broad diadem. The man was wearing white gloves. In one hand he held the girl; in the other, he held a strange object — a cone-shaped wand, sharp at one end and softly rounded on the other. It was enchantingly beautiful, unlike anything she'd ever seen. The man was wearing a suit; the girl had a thin summer dress and pretty canvas shoes. She was taller than she'd first believed. Bigger. She smiled at him. As the smooth face leaned over her, she could feel her body tense. He was beautiful, purer and more honest than anyone else. Unspoiled. He straightened up and finally placed his palm between her breasts. She tried to heave herself up in an attempt to meet him, but the straps held her down. There was something dizzily erotic about their contact. Now it was just her and the faceless man. They were one. Then she remembered the little girl, and fought to turn her head. The pressure on her ribcage increased. The girl was standing a few metres from the bed, tears streaming down her cheeks. When their eyes met, it was like a hammer striking a wall of crystal. The insight and the panic hit her simultaneously. She tried to scream, but there was no air. She stared into the smooth face in terror. He was going to press his hand through her ribs, lungs, and heart. Her ribcage would soon give way. She had been right. This was a temple, and she was lying on an altar. But not as a goddess — as a sacrifice. Then there was suddenly air, and with it came the scream. High and piercing. But she wasn't the one screaming. It was the little girl.

It took less than five seconds for Nadim to trace the Mona virus in the computer. Eric stared at the screen. The only thing on it was a blinking clock with rotating hands. It was strange — the hands were moving counter-clockwise, in the wrong direction. Even though he couldn't follow what the anti-virus program was doing, he imagined that a digital war was taking place. It was a war of life and death between a mutated Mona

422

and a very powerful Nadim — a battle between mother and daughter.

It was completely silent in the dim room, except for Hanna's respirator. He was on pins and needles, and hardly dared to breathe. The anti-virus program had to conquer the infection in the computer. If it failed, it wouldn't be possible to save Hanna either. After seven long minutes, the clock disappeared, and for a few seconds the screen was black. Then the computer let out a bright 'ding', and a short message popped up on the screen:

MONA DELETED

He stared at the words in surprise. Was it really that simple? No symphonies or drumrolls? No colourful animations or graphic fireworks? The world's most dreaded computer virus had been destroyed in a few minutes, and all he got was a 'ding.'

'Un-fucking-believable!'

Jens stretched in his chair and blinked, half-asleep.

'What?'

'It works. The anti-virus works!'

Jens got up and stood behind him.

'But does it work on people? Will it work on Hanna?'

'I have no idea. Probably not. But it's high time to find out. If it doesn't work, we'll have to follow Thomas's advice and call for a rabbi.'

Jens placed his large hands on Eric's shoulders and rubbed them a few times.

'Brother, you're the rabbi today. Let's do it.'

Eric nodded resolutely and stood up.

'Help me.'

He carefully lifted the helmet, making sure not to get tangled in it. Jens gathered up the bundle of colourful wires, and gently laid them across Hanna's abdomen. Then Eric pressed the helmet onto her sticky head. For a moment, he considered not bothering to screw on the eye sensors, but decided in the end that it was a good idea to have as many contact points as possible. He lowered the black glasses and tightened the screws on either side. A drop of blood ran down Hanna's cheek and spotted the pillow. Jens looked at him, worried.

'Everything under control?'

'Pretty much.'

He went back to the keyboard. The system was establishing contact with Hanna's brain. Within a few seconds, a series of messages popped up on the screen:

CONTACT ESTABLISHED
RECEIVING NEURODATA
SIGNAL STRENGTH 87%

The contact wasn't as strong as it had been earlier, but it ought to be high enough. The crucial question was whether the connection was enough for Nadim to register that there was another infected entity for it to deal with: Hanna's brain. Hopefully, the anti-virus program had instructions to search additional hard drives and servers — and Eric assumed that Hanna's brain would be treated as an external hard drive.

Eric activated Nadim. The screen blinked, and the little clock popped up again. The hands spun backward. The anti-virus program was working on something, and it couldn't be the infection in the computer, because that had already been dealt with. Nadim must have found another infection, and it could only be from one place. Jens stood at the window like a statue, his eyes fixed on Hanna's face. Suddenly, an alarm started ringing out in the corridor, and it took Eric a few seconds to realise that it was coming from Hanna. The graphs on the two screens at the head of the bed had changed. The EEG was jumping wildly, far beyond normal levels. The EKG had also deviated from its gentle path, and was now jerky and uneven. Jens looked at him in panic.

'What the hell is going on? What have we done?'

The door flew open, and Pia stormed into the room.

'Don't touch anything! The doctor is on his way.'

She ran to the bed, felt Hanna's forehead, and then studied the graphs on the two monitors.

'Oh, God.'

She took a step back. Eric turned to her.

'What?'

'I've never seen anything like it. She's having an attack.'

She bent over and typed commands into the computer by the bed. Eric flung out his hands impatiently.

'What's going on? What can we do?' Pia answered without taking her eyes from the screens.

'Take her hand.'

He looked at her in bewilderment, but reached out and grasped Hanna's soft hand.

'What now?'

She didn't answer. He looked beseechingly at Jens.

'Take her other hand.'

Jens nodded. They stood there, holding Hanna's hands in theirs, staring at the ominous patterns of the lines. Jens whispered, mostly to himself, 'What have we done?'

There was nothing she could do. The straps held her firmly, and the man was pressing down so hard that her sternum would soon crack. She didn't want to die. She wanted to live and live and live. She caught sight of the cone-shaped wand; it was in his other hand, and he raised it above his head. She clenched her hands into fists, steeling herself against the pain. Then she was there, the little girl. She flew at the man in a reckless rage, shoving, biting, and clawing. He took an unsteady step to the side; his hand disappeared from her chest. The girl's arms clawed and windmilled. The man struck her, and she landed hard on the floor. He seemed dazed. But then he collected himself, shook his head, and stood before her once again. Was the girl dead? No, she was moving. She lay in a pile on the floor, but she lifted her head and looked at Hanna. Hanna tried to smile at her. The man placed his heavy hand on her shoulder and held her down. She didn't need to look at him to know what he was going to do. Instead, she fixed her gaze on the girl. It will all be okay. I'm ready. She could tell that the girl understood. She loved her. More than anything. Suddenly, something happened. The walls, ceiling, and floor of the temple turned to sand. It started behind the girl. At first, Hanna thought it was a hallucination, caused by panic and lack of oxygen. But it came closer, moving quickly, like a silent tidal wave. Everything turned into flowing white sand, surging out into the black nothingness. The girl looked at her with wide eyes. She raised her hand and tried to say something, but she dissolved. Disappeared. Hanna looked up at the man, and for a second she thought she could see a face in the smooth skin. Then everything turned into white sand — the room, the bed, the man. The world sank away, and she was in freefall, tumbling headlong through a starless space. Faster and faster.

They heard running steps in the corridor. Thomas Wethje burst through the door, dressed in dark grey jeans and a burgundy polo shirt. He wasn't wearing gloves, and had only a simple mask on. He ran up to the screens of graphs, and read them for a few breathless seconds before typing in commands and looking at the rows of digits in silence. Then he turned to Pia.

'When did it start?'

'The alarm went off eight minutes ago.'

Thomas looked at Eric.

'Did you do something?'

'It happened a short time after I hooked her up to Mind Surf.'

The doctor clenched his fists and turned back to Pia.

'We have to stop it. She's having an attack. It's just like what happened to Mats Hagström. This time we'll act fast. Give her more Centric Novatrone — and Phenobarbital, if she needs it. Hurry!'

Pia nodded and ran out of the room. Thomas spoke without taking his eyes from the numbers. His voice was bitter.

'You might want to take those things off her head.'

Eric realised that Hanna still had the sensor helmet on her head, with the colourful cables curling down along her shoulder to the floor. He turned to Mind Surf, and saw that the little clock was still blinking on the screen; the hands were still turning counter-clockwise. Nadim was still fighting the virus. He looked at Thomas.

'I want to leave the helmet on. It can't make any difference.'

This was a lie. He had no idea if Nadim was what had caused Hanna's crisis, so it might be a fatal decision to leave the computer attached. Thomas shook his head vehemently as Pia returned with an IV bag. She stopped at Hanna's bed, quickly unhooked the existing bag, and put the new one in place. Thomas pressed his lips together, crossed his arms, and stared at the screens. The lines were still jumpy.

'Come on.'

He leaned closer to the monitors; he seemed to be talking to them.

'Come on. Results — give me results.' Jens and Eric looked at each other.

Then the frantic line on the EEG calmed down and went back to tracing its zig-zag pattern within the normal parameters. Just after that, the EKG line calmed down as well. Eric fell heavily into the chair by the Mind Surf computer and let out the air he'd been holding in, possibly ever since the alarm had gone off. Jens still stood with Hanna's hand in his own. His face was white.

'Say something, doctor. Does she look better? What's going on?'

The doctor didn't answer for a long time. Then he nodded faintly.

'It looks better. Or, rather, it looks like it did before.'

He turned to Eric.

'We've managed to curtail the most acute struggle.'

Eric looked at the computer screen and shook his head.

'The struggle continues.' The little clock was still flickering on the screen.

She must have fainted. When she opened her eyes, she was lying face-down in a glittering gold desert. The sand was warm and as fine as powdered sugar. She sat up and looked around. The sky was dark red, and the desert stretched endlessly in all directions. She had been here before. She didn't remember when. There was no breeze here, no smells, no sounds. She gently stretched out her legs and lay on her back. The warm sand enveloped her and made her drowsy. She looked up at the red sky, which was covered in a fluffy, dense layer of clouds. It felt good to run her fingers through the fine sand. How had she gotten here? Where was this place? Her left hand nudged something hard. She propped herself up on one elbow. It was an old alarm clock with flaky black paint. It was rusty, and its glass was cracked. The thin hands stood still, and it must have been several years since they'd worked. This clock seemed familiar, too. She turned it over and looked at the flat winding mechanism. Could she get the clock to work? Just as she wrapped her fingers around the thin key, a blinding sun tore through the red layer of clouds. It was so unexpected, and the light was so bright, that she dropped the clock, threw her hands up over her face, and fell

428

back into the sand. The sun burned away the red clouds, and the world was filled with its white glow.

As Eric sat on one of the visitors' chairs beside the bed in the dim room, images came back to him: faces, places, events. It had all gone so fast, and he hadn't relaxed for a single moment. Not really. There was Mats Hagström, smiling and tossing his fateful apple. There was the thirteenth investor meeting. There was Promenade des Anglais in Nice, the library in Tel Aviv, and the flowering thistles in Gaza. Somehow, it felt like none of that had happened to him. They were like images from a movie, something he'd observed. He thought of Samir's body in the whirling sand. Would anyone give him a proper burial? Hardly. It could easily have been Eric's body, lying there in the morning haze. Or he might have fallen with a bullet in his back at the gate at Ben Gurion airport. It might have ended for him even earlier, if he had tried Mind Surf himself after Hanna had visited the TBI website. He looked at her. Three hours had passed since her vital signs had stabilised. He had unhooked Mind Surf. Everything was quiet in the room. In some way, it was as if the air had been discharged, like after a terrible storm.

Thomas Wethje came in, along with two other doctors. They stood beside the bed for a moment, whispering. Someone nodded and smiled. As they were about to leave, Thomas squeezed his shoulder.

'The Centric Novatrone seems to be working. It's surprising how much she has improved in just a few hours.'

'What does that mean?'

'It's too soon to say, but she's proved that she's strong. Now the anti-retroviral will help her fight the virus.'

'That sounds fantastic.'

'It is. But — and this is an important "but" — after so many

429

days in a coma, and after all the ups and downs she's gone through, there might be damage — heart, brain, or nerve damage. I'm not saying this to put a damper on things, but it's my job to be a bit of a pessimist. Or maybe "realist" is a better word.'

He could see that Eric was worried, and hurried to add, 'But, like I said, right now, things seem to be moving in the right direction.'

'So what do we do now?'

Thomas looked over at Hanna's silhouette against the window. Then he opened the door to the corridor.

'We wait.'

The door closed softly after him. Eric remained seated, his eyes on the floor. Hanna's condition was improving, and Thomas was convinced it was thanks to the antiretroviral drug. Maybe he was right. Or it might be due to Nadim. Whatever it was, it was moving things in the right direction. But she might have suffered damage. He stood up restlessly and went over to the computer table, where he disconnected the iPod. Needing a little music to calm his nerves, he returned to the chair and started scrolling through the music. He wished he'd had the real Tchaikovsky's seventh to listen to — if it even existed. He would have liked to know if it were melancholy or cheerful. Considering how Tchaikovsky felt toward the end, one could guess that it would be in a minor key. Eric exited the music section and went to the main menu to relive the fantastic feeling he'd gotten when he first discovered the anti-virus program. He scrolled down to the category 'To Eric' and opened it. It was empty. He looked more closely at the little screen. Nothing. Tchaikovsky's seventh was gone. Nadim was gone. How was this possible? He stood up and walked over to the computer and started the servers. While he waited for the system to warm up, he looked at the iPod again. Apparently, Nadim had erased itself after it had been used on the device. He hoped it was still in the computer. The program was invaluable to Israel, to the world. Nadim could revive the hundreds of thousands of infected computers all over the world that were currently useless. The desktop came up, and he searched in vain for Nadim. The computer searched for a few seconds and then returned the result — the result he had known he would get even before he started the search:

Nadim not found

He stood still with both hands on the keyboard and gathered his thoughts. Samir Mustaf had wanted to help him save Hanna. But he had also made sure that Eric couldn't spread the anti-virus or use it for anything else. The version of Nadim he'd received must have been instructed to erase itself after a certain amount of time, or after a certain series of events. The program had been transferable to his main computer, and transferable once more after that — in this case, to Hanna. Eric shuddered as he thought of what the consequences would have been if he had tried the anti-virus program on a second computer before he had hooked Hanna up. Or if he had let Paul Clinton have a copy.

He stared at the three words that flickered on the screen. The world would have to do without Nadim, and Tchaikovsky's seventh symphony. Without a working anti-virus, it would be a slow and difficult task to rebuild all the infected systems. Presumably, all the affected data and programs would have to be deleted, and rewritten all over again. The costs would be inconceivable. He shook his head in resignation, fetched the chair by the door, and sat down as close to the bed as he could. The anti-virus was gone. Now it only existed in Hanna's body. Perhaps they were both in there, Nadim and Mona. Or maybe one of them had already been obliterated, and only the victor remained. Who was stronger? Mother or daughter? He had never received confirmation that the virus was destroyed. The little clock had just disappeared, replaced by an empty screen. It was impossible to know if the operation had succeeded.

The room was quiet, and it was almost surreal how distant from the rest of the world it felt. It was as though he and Hanna were the only people left on earth, alone in a white cube. He ran his hand through his hair and looked at the black screens. The respirator had been removed; Hanna was breathing on her own. He listened to her calm breathing, which was was quiet and regular, like distant ocean waves. He had always dreamed of living by the sea. He thought of their little house on Dalarö. They hadn't been there a single time this summer. There was nothing he wanted more than to be there with her — lying on the dock, near her body, listening to the sea.

All night, Eric sat there on the chair, looking at her and dreaming that she would wake, imagining that he would finally see her open her eyes. How would it feel? What would he say? As it turned out, it ended up the other way around. He fell asleep around four-thirty, and slept deeply for an hour-and-a-half. When he returned, half-asleep, to his aching body in its uncomfortable position — crowded between the wall and the respirator — she was looking at him. He tried to focus, sure that he was still asleep. But then she smiled. Her head was sweaty, and it had sunk deep into the pillow; her hair ran along her shoulder and over her chest, flowing like a golden sea around her pale face. He sat stock-still, as if a sudden movement might scare her away. After a few long seconds, he softly whispered the only thing he could think of to say: 'I'm sorry.' Tears caught in his throat. 'I'm sorry about everything.'

She looked at him, following him as he stood up, pulled off his mask, leaned forward, and kissed her carefully — on her forehead, on her eyelids, on the bridge of her nose. It was all so familiar, so safe. Before he pressed his lips to hers, wrapped in her light breath, he whispered, 'Welcome back, my darling.'

Jerusalem, Israel

In the fall, Bianchi was coming out with a completely new frame. He had read about it in *Bicycling* — a frame that was lighter, but also more rigid than the one he had now. He had written to the company to try to order one, but they hadn't yet decided on the price and delivery date. He wasn't interested in the price. He had already spent over four hundred thousand shekels on his hobby. But then, it was the only extravagance he allowed himself; in everything else he was an ascetic.

As he pedalled along, he inhaled one scent after another. The humidity in the air intensified their nuances, as he cut through puddles that had formed in the holes of the asphalt. There was no traffic this early, so he could use the whole road to straighten the curves and keep up his tempo. His thigh muscles were working hard, and he stood more than he sat. The first half of his route was uphill and sometimes very steep. He did intense cardio first, pushing his body to the limit. Then the road went downhill, where concentration and technique were crucial.

Sinon thought about everything that had happened in the past few weeks. The Mossad had infiltrated the group and had guided in a task force. Now everyone was gone — Ahmad Waizy, Samir Mustaf, Mohammad Murid — and the Palestinians he had borrowed from Hamas, both specially trained in Iran. Ben Shavit was being praised as an international hero. This was an historic failure for Hezbollah. If only they'd had another day, Ben would have signed the agreement. But there was no point in dwelling on it. Allah had had other plans. He passed a lone jogger, panting and struggling his way up to the top of the Mount of Olives.

He thought of his own situation. No one had uncovered him yet. His true role was inconceivable to them. He couldn't believe it. Imagine — if the world only knew that the fêted Mossad had missed an enemy who'd been right before its eyes for so long. What was the best way for him to make use of his valuable position? He could still cause damage to the enemy. Sure, it was dangerous to be too confident; sooner or later, they'd expose him. He could leave the country tomorrow. With all he'd done, he'd already secured his place in heaven. But he was a soldier; he had to make use of this unique opportunity.

He glanced at his watch. It looked like he'd finish the first stage in a new record time. He pushed harder. Probably the best thing he could do would be to cut Ben's throat — in his own home, right in front of his family. What headlines that would create! What great revenge for the Gaza fiasco! He reached the crest of the hill and didn't bother to stop, not when his time was so good. The road turned downhill, becoming steeper and steeper. He bent over the handlebars so that he could rush forward like a projectile. He thought of Rachel Papo. She had survived. That had been improbably good luck. Now she would be more on guard, and they would increase security around her. But he still had one trump card left: the address of the home where her retarded sister lived. It would be easy to go there and get her. The idea excited him. He would videotape everything he did to her and then send the tape to Rachel.

He pressed himself closer to the frame. The wind whined in his ears and drew out tears that ran up and back across his cheeks. When he rode bent over at high speeds, he was one with the bike, and his head was clear of all thoughts. He managed to keep up this speed for nearly seven kilometres, and finally turned into the street that led up to his house. The street was deserted, and he changed gears and pedalled with his last stores of energy to guarantee what he already knew would be a new personal best. Two kilometres later, he skidded in behind the large house and looked at his watch, full of expectation. It was incredible: four minutes better than his previous record. He was weak but happy. This was a sign — a sign that he was stronger than ever, that he had Allah on his side and that everything was possible.

He leaned the bike against the wall, grabbed his helmet, stiffly stretched his sore joints, and started walking to the front of the house. He was thirsty and exhausted. None of the windows seemed to be open; his family was still sleeping. If he was lucky, he'd be able to cuddle up with his wife and sleep for half an hour before breakfast. Just then, as he rounded the corner of the house, he saw a girl sitting on the hood of his car. He blinked to see better in the bright sunlight. Was she one of his daughter's friends? Was she sitting there waiting for them to go to school? But would she be here this early? And on his car? She was wearing a tracksuit and black gym shoes. He became angry, and walked more quickly. But when he was just a few metres from the car and the girl turned her head, he realised his mistake. He stopped and let his helmet fall to the ground, too tired to come up with a single sensible thought. He knew there was nothing he could do — not in this situation, not with this person. Rachel Papo smiled at him.

'Good morning, Mr Katz,' she said.

Epilogue

Their simple cabin was squeezed between enormous New England-style designer homes and architect-designed glass palaces. Their cabin, in its Falu-red paint, was not winterised or modernised. Outhouses and hand pumps were scarce on Dalarö. Maybe they should spend the money and improve the standard; maybe not. They liked everything just as it was. They had fought, laughed, cried, and made love here throughout the summers. Even their boat was unusual for this island. While everyone else had big day-cruisers, jet-skis, and RIB boats, they had an old rowboat with a grey-green, two-stroke Husqvarna engine. Eric couldn't remember the last time it had started; right now, the boat was bobbing gently at its buoy. The wine he had drunk warmed his body. A light breeze was blowing off Jungfrufjärden. It had rained, and the air was fresh and humid. The boards under his bare back were slippery with seaweed and algae. He couldn't tell if it was early in the morning or late at night. It didn't matter.

She twined her fingers into his and whispered, hardly audibly, 'I want to have a baby.' He kissed her wet hair and hugged her hard. His happiness, at this very moment, in this very heartbeat, was greater than he had ever experienced before. It was a feeling of peace, security, and a wonderful future. She pressed her face to his chest. 'Her name will be Mona.'

He laughed. 'What if it's a boy?'

She turned her face toward the bay, hesitating to speak, as if she were listening inside herself. 'A boy?' The horizon was swept in haze, and it was still raining over Rögrund. She let go of him and rolled onto her back. 'It won't be.'

Dr Thomas Wethje blinked in irritation at the bright lights on the ceiling. He had a bad migraine, and he felt tired. In front of him were all the documents, transcriptions, notes, and case histories from Mats Hagström and Hanna Söderqvist. He had been working since very early that morning, and he ought to have gone home a long time ago. But he couldn't let go of the strange cases that had taken up practically all of his time recently. In his twenty years as a doctor, he had never seen anything like this. Sure, the human body was and remained a miracle, and just as humanity was still discovering new species of animals and plants, there was an infinite amount still to be discovered in the body. There were certain generic patterns, a biological logic that influenced and governed the systems in a somewhat similar direction — basic laws of medicine that helped decode new sequences of events. But the cases of Mats Hagström and Hanna Söderqvist were different. Every time he had thought he had found the logic of their illnesses, the conditions changed. Every time he was ready to give a diagnosis, even with a great deal of uncertainty, new symptoms showed up that blew his theories apart.

He had consulted a number of experts, within and outside Sweden, and had received hundreds of articles, suggestions, and recommendations in response. But nothing had helped him come to a satisfactory conclusion. After a great number of tests and analyses, he knew that he was dealing with a virus that was in many ways reminiscent of the coronavirus that caused SARS — the contagious, acute pneumonia that had caused epidemics in Asia, Canada, and the Middle East. It was spherical in shape, with a diameter of ninety nanometres. Like SARS, it had spikes that stuck out of the protective membrane and made it look like a crown under the electron microscope. The lab in Huddinge had managed to describe an inner capsule consisting of very complex virus proteins. Also, like HIV, the virus had the ability to trick the body's immune system. The new virus had been given the name NCoLV, Novel Corona-Like Virus.

After all their attempts, using conventional and unconventional methods of treatment, Centric Novatrone had finally beaten NCoLV in Hanna Söderqvist. It had worked improbably quickly and with no apparent side effects. What made the whole thing even more puzzling, though, was that the tests they had done just hours after Hanna left the hospital hadn't shown any reaction at all between NCoLV and Centric Novatrone. The medicine had worked only in her body, and it hadn't been possible to recreate the results in a laboratory. All the data conflicted. They had been able to identify certain similarities during a comparative analysis of Mats Hagström and Hanna Söderqvist, and there was no doubt that they had both been attacked by NCoLV, but at the same time the virus seemed to be unique in each host.

What worried Thomas was that they had discovered, mostly by chance, that there might be two more cases of the illness. One was a woman who had been admitted to Huddinge Hospital two days before with similar symptoms; it turned out that she had worked at the same bank as Hanna. The other was an ambulance driver who was exhibiting NCoLV-like symptoms. He had driven Mats Hagström to the hospital. They had tried Centric Novatrone on him at Söder Hospital, but so far to no effect.

Maybe it wasn't NCoLV. The tests wouldn't be finished before early afternoon tomorrow. And they still didn't know how the virus was transmitted. So what should he write in his report? How could he summarise it? Up to today, there had been *de facto* only two defined and established cases of the virus. The other two might turn out to have something completely different wrong with them. If they did, NCoLV was just a biological fluke — something that wouldn't be repeated. Thomas fervently hoped that this was the case. Otherwise, they had waited too long to move Hanna Söderqvist to an isolation unit. He hadn't succeeded in getting permission to move her until after Mats Hagström's death. By then, a great number of doctors and nurses had had contact with her.

He took a sip of water. Nurse Pia opened the door to the office and sat down on the chair next to him.

'How's it going?'

'Not well. I don't know what to write.'

She gave a small smile.

'Maybe it's better to wait until tomorrow, when you've gotten some rest.'

He leaned back and took off his glasses.

'And what about you? How long are you planning to stay?'

She shook her head.

'I'd been planning to stay until the morning shift at six, but actually think I won't make it. I didn't sleep very well.'

Thomas gathered the documents and put them in a green hanging file.

'Did you drink too much coffee?'

'It's not that. I …'

She stopped talking.

'What?'

'I've been having nightmares. Horrible nightmares that wake me up.'

He opened the filing cabinet and hung the file in it.

'What kind of nightmares?'

'I can't remember everything, but they were scary. They

were about the apocalypse — the end of the world. There was an alarm clock. For some reason, I remember that. There was a rusty old alarm clock, and a little girl — a dirty, dark-skinned girl with curly hair.'

Thomas looked into her eyes. She gave a laugh. It was a nervous laugh, as though she were ashamed that she'd told him about her dream. Then she cleared her throat.

'Well ... what does the doctor think of that?'

He didn't answer. He had no words. During the last few nights, he, too, had met the little girl with the curly hair.

Outside the window of Karolinska Hospital, the early-morning sun was turning the night's rain to steam. The drops were going back the same way they'd come. Garbage trucks rumbled along outside the doors, and there was a faint scent of baking bread around the hospital, perhaps from Kungsholmens Bakery. The breeze was blowing across the bed of an open truck at Norrtull carrying white construction dust that settled in a thin film on the windshields of parked cars at Haga Forum. Solnavägen was filling with people hurrying to work, day care, and school. Stockholm was waking to yet another warm late-summer day.

Nothing spreads like a computer virus.

'The flower is grey now and its petals are withered,
but tomorrow, in the dew, it will bloom again.'
Abraham Sutzkever